The Best Short Stories of J. G. Ballard

The Drowned World
The Voices of Time
The Terminal Beach
The Drought
The Crystal World
The Day of Forever
The Venus Hunters
The Disaster Area
The Atrocity Exhibition
Vermilion Sands
Concrete Island
Crash
High-Rise
Low-Flying Aircraft
The Unlimited Dream Company
Hello America
Myths of the Near Future
Empire of the Sun
The Day of Creation
Running Wild
War Fever
The Kindness of Women

The Best Short Stories

of

J. G. BALLARD

Introduction by Anthony Burgess

Picador
Henry Holt and Company
New York

Picador® is a U.S. registered trademark and is used by Henry Holt and Company under license from Pan Books Limited.

For information on Picador Reading Group Guides, as well as ordering, please contact the Trade Marketing department at St. Martin's Press.
Phone: 1-800-221-7945 extension 763
Fax: 212-677-7456
E-mail: trademarketing@stmartins.com

Designed by Amy Hill

The stories in this collection were first published in the following magazines:
New Worlds, Fantasy & Science Fiction, Amazing, Playboy, Ambit, and *International Times.*

Library of Congress Cataloging-in-Publication Data

Ballard, J. G.
[Short stories. Selections]
The best short stories of J. G. Ballard / introduction by Anthony Burgess.
p. cm.
ISBN 0-312-27844-6
1. Science fiction, English. I. Title.

PR6052.A46A6   1995
823'.914—dc20

94-42290
CIP

First published in the United States in 1978 by Holt, Rinehart and Winston

10 9

Contents

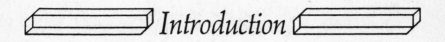 *Introduction*

by Anthony Burgess

The first thing to say about J. G. Ballard is not that he is among our finest writers of science fiction but that he is among our finest writers of fiction *tout court* period. Ballard himself might retort that, granted the first claim, the second is redundant, since the only important fiction being produced today is science fiction (or the fiction of the untrammeled imagination, or of hypothesis, or of the metaphysical pushing to the limit of a scientific datum: unsatisfactory as it is, we always end up with science fiction). I understand that the only living writers Ballard really admires are Isaac Asimov and William Burroughs. This can be interpreted negatively as a rejection of the kind of fiction that pretends there has been no revolution in thought and sensibility since, say, 1945. And this, alas, means the greater part of contemporary fiction, which remains thematically and stylistically torpid, limiting itself, as to subject matter, to what can be observed and inferred from observation and, as to language, what might be regarded by George Eliot as a little advanced but, on the whole, perfectly intelligible. Ballard considers that the kind of limitation that most contemporary fiction accepts is immoral, a shameful consequence of the rise of the bourgeois novel. Language exists less to record the actual than to liberate the imagination. To go forward, as Ballard does, is also to go back—scientific apocalypse and pre-scientific myth meet in the same creative region, where the great bourgeois novelists of tradition would not feel at home.

Ballard is a writer who accepts thematic limitations, but they are his own. His aesthetic instinct tells him that the task of the science fiction writer is not primarily to surprise or shock with bizarre inventions but, as with all fiction writers, to present human beings in credible, if extreme, situations and to imagine their reactions. Ballard's characters are creatures of the earth, not from outer space. Why devise fanciful new planets when we have our own planet, on which strange things are already happening, on which the ultimate strange happening is linked to present actualities or latencies by cause and effect? There is nothing in the evolutionary theory that denies living things the ability to develop leaden carapaces as a protection against nuclear fallout. In time, the demographic explosion will bring about not only fantastic living-space regulations but a habit of mind that sees a broom closet as a desirable residence. Man will suck up oxygen from the oceans to aerate habitats in orbit, the Atlantic will be diminished to a salt pool, and in the pool will be the final fish of the world, to be battered to death by vicious boys. A new kind of man evolves, enslaved by engines of subliminal persuasion to ever-increasing consumption. Our response to Ballard's visions is twofold: we reject this impossible world; we recognize that it is all too possible. The mediator between that world and this is a credible human being in a classic situation—tragical-stoical: he fights change on our behalf, but he cannot win. Faulkner, in "The Overloaded Man," comes closest to victory by devising an epistemological trick—reducing the objects of the detestable world to sense-data, turning the sense-data to ideas, then killing the ideas by killing himself.

It would be too easy to call Ballard a prophet of doom. It is not the fiction writer's job to moralize about Man the Overreacher, in the manner of the old Faust plays. He lays down a premise and pursues a syllogism. If we do this, then that inevitably follows: choice remains free. We associate prophecies of impending damnation, anyway, with the kind of mentality that rejects all technological progress: once admit the acoustic phonograph and the internal combustion engine and you are lost. Both H. G. Wells and Aldous Huxley built their utopias (eutopias, dystopias) on unassailable scientific knowledge. Ballard's own authority in various specialist fields seems, to this non-scientist, to be very considerable: I never see evidence of a false step in reasoning or a hypothesis untenable to an athletic enough imagination. The intellectual content of many of the stories is too stimulating for depression and so, one might add, is the unfailing grace and energy of the writing.

In my view, two of the most beautiful stories of the world canon of short fiction are to be found in this selection. They are not, in the strictest sense, science fiction stories: their premises are acceptable only in terms of storytelling as ancient as those of Homer. In "The Drowned Giant" the corpse of a colossus of classical perfection of form is washed up on the beach. Children climb into the ears and nostrils; scientists inspect it; eventually the big commercial scavengers cart it off in fragments. The idea, perhaps, is nothing, but the skill lies in the exactness of the observation and the total credibility of the imagined human response to the presence of a drowned giant. Swift, in *Gulliver*, evaded too many physical problems, concerned as he was with a politico-satirical intention. Ballard evades nothing except the easy moral: to say that his story means this or that is to diminish it. In "The Garden of Time" a doomed aristocrat, aptly named Axel, plucks crystalline flowers whose magic holds off for a while the advancing hordes that will destroy his castle and the civilized order it symbolizes. In an older kind of fairy story, the magic of the flowers would be potent but unspecified, vaguely apotropaic. In Ballard the flowers drug time into a brief trance—specific and, if one is a little off one's guard, almost rationally acceptable. The rhythms of poignancy which animate both stories are masterly: Ballard is a *moving* writer.

There are three short pieces at the end of this selection which show Ballard moving in a new direction. His novel *Crash* evinces a fascination with the erotic aspects of violent death, or the thanatotic elements in Eros. These little sketches, highly original in form as well as content (though Burroughs seems to be somewhere underneath) play grim love-death games with public, or pubic, figures. They will serve as a reminder that Ballard, master of traditional narrative styles, is restless to try new things. Through him only is science fiction likely to make a formal and stylistic breakthrough of the kind achieved by Joyce, for whom Vico's *La Scienza Nuova* was new science enough. That Ballard is already important literature this selection will leave you in no doubt.

Monaco 1978

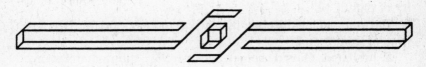

The Concentration City

Noon talk on Millionth Street:

"Sorry, these are the West millions. You want 9775335th East."

"Dollar five a cubic foot? Sell!"

"Take a westbound express to 495th Avenue, cross over to a Red-line elevator and go up a thousand levels to Plaza Terminal. Carry on south from there and you'll find it between 568th Avenue and 422nd Street."

"There's a cave-in down at KEN county! Fifty blocks by twenty by thirty levels."

"Listen to this—'PYROS STAGE MASS BREAKOUT! FIRE POLICE CORDON BAY COUNTY!' "

"It's a beautiful counter. Detects up to .005 percent monoxide. Cost me three hundred dollars."

"Have you seen those new intercity sleepers? Takes only ten minutes to go up three thousand levels!"

"Ninety cents a foot? Buy!"

"You say the idea came to you in a dream?" the voice jabbed out. "You're sure no one else gave it to you?"

"No," M. said flatly. A couple of feet away from him a spot lamp threw a cone of dirty yellow light into his face. He dropped his eyes from the glare and waited as the sergeant paced over to his desk, tapped his fingers on the edge, and swung around on him again.

"You talked it over with your friends?"

"Only the first theory," M. explained quietly. "About the possibility of flight."

"But you told me the other theory was more important. Why keep it quiet from them?"

M. hesitated. Outside somewhere a trolley shunted and clanged along the elevated. "I was afraid they wouldn't understand what I meant."

The sergeant laughed sourly. "You mean they would have thought you really were crazy?"

M. shifted uncomfortably on the stool. Its seat was only six inches off the floor and his thighs and lumbar muscles felt like slabs of inflamed rubber. After three hours of cross-questioning, logic had faded and he groped helplessly. "The concept was a little abstract. There weren't any words for it."

The sergeant snorted. "I'm glad to hear you say it." He sat down on the desk, watched M. for a moment and then went over to him.

"Now look," he said confidentially. "It's getting late. Do you still think both theories are reasonable?"

M. looked up. "Aren't they?"

The sergeant turned angrily to the man watching in the shadows by the window.

"We're wasting our time," he snapped. "I'll hand him over to Psycho. You've seen enough, haven't you, Doc?"

The surgeon stared thoughtfully at his hands. He was a tall heavy-shouldered man, built like a wrestler, with thick coarsely-lined features.

He ambled forward, knocking back one of the chairs with his knee.

"There's something I want to check," he said curtly. "Leave me alone with him for half an hour."

The sergeant shrugged. "All right," he said, going over to the door. "But be careful with him."

When the sergeant had gone the surgeon sat down behind the desk and stared vacantly out of the window, listening to the dull hum of air through the huge ninety-foot ventilator shaft which rose out of the street below the station. A few roof-lights were still burning and two hundred yards away a single policeman slowly patrolled the iron catwalk running above the street, his boots ringing across the darkness.

M. sat on the stool, elbows between his knees, trying to edge a little life back into his legs.

Eventually the surgeon glanced down at the charge sheet.

> *Name:* Franz M.
> *Age:* 20.
> *Occupation:* Student.
> *Address:* 3599719 West 783rd Str.,
>   Level 549-7705-45 KNI (Local).
> *Charge:* Vagrancy.

"Tell me about this dream," he said slowly, idly flexing a steel rule between his hands as he looked across at M.

"I think you've heard everything, sir," M. said.

"In detail."

M. shifted uneasily. "There wasn't much to it, and what I do remember isn't too clear now."

The surgeon yawned. M. waited and then started to recite what he had already repeated twenty times.

"I was suspended in the air above a flat stretch of open ground, something like the floor of an enormous arena. My arms were out at my sides, and I was looking down, floating—"

"Hold on," the surgeon interrupted. "Are you sure you weren't swimming?"

"No," M. said. "I'm certain I wasn't. All around me there was free space. That was the most important part about it. There were no walls. Nothing but emptiness. That's all I remember."

The surgeon ran his finger along the edge of the rule.

"Go on."

"Well, the dream gave me the idea of building a flying machine. One of my friends helped me construct it."

The surgeon nodded. Almost absently he picked up the charge sheet, crushed it with a single motion of his hand, and flicked it into the wastebasket.

"Don't be crazy, Franz!" Gregson remonstrated. They took their places in the chemistry cafeteria queue. "It's against the laws of hydrodynamics. Where would you get your buoyancy?"

"Suppose you had a rigid fabric vane," Franz explained as they shuffled past the hatchways. "Say ten feet across, like one of those composition wall sections, with handgrips on the ventral surface. And then you jump down from the gallery at the Coliseum Stadium. What would happen?"

"You'd make a hole in the floor. Why?"

"No, seriously."

"If it was large enough and held together you'd swoop down like a paper dart."

"Glide," Franz said. "Right." Thirty levels above them one of the intercity expresses roared over, rattling the tables and cutlery in the cafeteria. Franz waited until they reached a table and sat forward, his food forgotten.

"And say you attached a propulsive unit, such as a battery-driven ventilator fan, or one of those rockets they use on the Sleepers. With enough thrust to overcome your weight. What then?"

Gregson shrugged. "If you could control the thing, you'd..." He frowned at Franz. "What's the word? You're always using it."

"Fly."

"Basically, Mattheson, the machine is simple," Sanger, the physics lector, commented as they entered the Science Library. "An elementary application of the Venturi Principle. But what's the point of it? A trapeze would serve its purpose equally well, and be far less dangerous. In the first place consider the enormous clearances it would require. I hardly think the traffic authorities will look upon it with any favor."

"I know it wouldn't be practicable here," Franz admitted. "But in a large open area it should be."

"Allowed. I suggest you immediately negotiate with the Arena Garden on Level 347-25," the lector said whimsically. "I'm sure they'll be glad to hear about your scheme."

Franz smiled politely. "That wouldn't be large enough. I was really thinking of an area of totally free space. In three dimensions, as it were."

Sanger looked at Franz curiously. "Free space? Isn't that a contradiction in terms? Space is a dollar a cubic foot." He scratched his nose. "Have you begun to construct this machine yet?"

"No," Franz said.

"In that event I should try to forget all about it. Remember, Mattheson, the task of science is to consolidate existing knowledge, to systematize and reinterpret the discoveries of the past, not to chase wild dreams into the future."

He nodded and disappeared among the dusty shelves.

Gregson was waiting on the steps.

"Well?" he asked.

"Let's try it out this afternoon," Franz said. "We'll cut Text Five Pharmacology. I know those Fleming readings backward. I'll ask Dr. McGhee for a couple of passes."

They left the library and walked down the narrow, dimly lit alley which ran behind the huge new Civil Engineering laboratories. Over 75 percent of the student enrollment was in the architectural and engineering faculties, a meager 2 percent in pure sciences. Consequently the physics and chemistry libraries were housed in the oldest quarter of the University, in two virtually condemned galvanized hutments which once contained the now closed Philosophy School.

At the end of the alley they entered the university plaza and started to climb the iron stairway leading to the next level a hundred feet above. Halfway up a white-helmeted FP checked them cursorily with his detector and waved them past.

"What did Sanger think?" Gregson asked as they stepped up into 637th Street and walked across to the Suburban Elevator station.

"He's no use at all," Franz said. "He didn't even begin to understand what I was talking about."

Gregson laughed ruefully. "I don't know whether I do."

Franz took a ticket from the automat and mounted the Down platform. An elevator dropped slowly toward him, its bell jangling.

"Wait until this afternoon," he called back. "You're really going to see something."

The floor manager at the Coliseum initialed the two passes.

"Students, eh? All right." He jerked a thumb at the long package Franz and Gregson were carrying. "What have you got there?"

"It's a device for measuring air velocities," Franz told him.

The manager grunted and released the stile.

Out in the center of the empty arena Franz undid the package and they assembled the model. It had a broad fanlike wing of wire and paper, a narrow strutted fusilage and a high curving tail.

Franz picked it up and launched it into the air. The model glided for twenty feet and then slithered to a stop across the sawdust.

"Seems to be stable," Franz said. "We'll tow it first."

He pulled a reel of twine from his pocket and tied one end to the nose.

As they ran forward the model lifted gracefully into the air and followed them around the stadium, ten feet off the floor.

"Let's try the rockets now," Franz said.

He adjusted the wing and tail settings and fitted three firework display rockets into a wire bracket mounted above the wing.

The stadium was four hundred feet in diameter and had a roof two hundred and fifty high. They carried the model over to one side and Franz lit the tapers.

There was a burst of flame and the model accelerated off across the floor, two feet in the air, a bright trail of colored smoke spitting out behind it. Its wings rocked gently from side to side. Suddenly the tail burst into flames. The model lifted steeply and looped up toward the roof, stalled just before it hit one of the pilot lights, and dived down into the sawdust.

They ran across to it and stamped out the glowing cinders.

"Franz!" Gregson shouted. "It's incredible! It actually works."

Franz kicked the shattered fuselage.

"Of course it works," he said impatiently, walking away. "But as Sanger said, what's the point of it?"

"The point? It flies! Isn't that enough?"

"No. I want one big enough to hold me."

"Franz, slow down. Be reasonable. Where could you fly it?"

"I don't know," Franz said fiercely. "But there must be somewhere. Somewhere!"

The floor manager and two assistants, carrying fire extinguishers, ran across the stadium to them.

"Did you hide that match?" Franz asked quickly. "They'll lynch us if they think we're pyros."

Three afternoons later Franz took the elevator up 150 levels to 677-98, where the Precinct Estate Office had its bureau.

"There's a big development between 493 and 554 in the next sector," one of the clerks told him. "I don't know whether that's any good to you. Sixty blocks by twenty by fifteen levels."

"Nothing bigger?" Franz queried.

The clerk looked up. "Bigger? No. What are you looking for? A slight case of agoraphobia?"

Franz straightened the maps spread across the counter.

"I wanted to find an area of more or less continuous development. Two or three hundred blocks long."

The clerk shook his head and went back to his ledger. "Didn't you go to Engineering School?" he asked scornfully. "The City won't take it. One hundred blocks is the maximum."

Franz thanked him and left.

A southbound express took him to the development in two hours. He left the car at the detour point and walked the three hundred yards to the end of the level.

The street, a seedy but busy thoroughfare of garment shops and small business premises running through the huge ten-mile-thick BIR Industrial Cube, ended abruptly in a tangle of ripped girders and concrete. A steel rail had been erected along the edge and Franz looked down over it into the cavity, three miles long, a mile wide, and twelve hundred feet deep, which thousands of engineers and demolition workers were tearing out of the matrix of the City.

Eight hundred feet below him unending lines of trucks and rail cars carried away the rubble and debris, and clouds of dust swirled up into the arc lights blazing down from the roof.

As he watched a chain of explosions ripped along the wall on his left and the whole face suddenly slipped and fell slowly toward the floor, revealing a perfect cross-section through fifteen levels of the City.

Franz had seen big developments before, and his own parents had died in the historic QUA County cave-in ten years earlier, when three master pillars had sheared and two hundred levels of the City had abruptly sunk ten thousand feet, squashing half a million people like flies in a concertina, but the enormous gulf of emptiness still made his imagination gape.

All around him, standing and sitting on the jutting terraces of girders, a silent throng stared down.

"They say they're going to build gardens and parks for us," an elderly man at Franz's elbow remarked in a slow patient voice. "I even heard they might be able to get a tree. It'll be the only tree in the whole county."

A man in a frayed sweat shirt spat over the rail. "That's what they always say. At a dollar a foot promises are all they can waste space on."

Below them a woman who had been looking out into the air started to simper nervously. Two bystanders took her by the arms and tried to lead her away. The woman began to thresh about and an FP came over and dragged her away roughly.

"Poor fool," the man in the sweat shirt commented. "She probably lived out there somewhere. They gave her ninety cents a foot when they took it away from her. She doesn't know yet she'll have to pay a dollar ten to get it back. Now they're going to start charging five cents an hour just to sit up here and watch."

Franz looked out over the railing for a couple of hours and then bought a postcard from one of the vendors and walked back thoughtfully to the elevator.

He called in to see Gregson before returning to the student dormitory.

The Gregsons lived up in the West millions on 985th Avenue, in a top three-room flat right under the roof. Franz had known them since his parents' death, but Gregson's mother still regarded him with a mixture of sympathy and suspicion, and as she let him in with her customary smile of welcome he noticed her glancing quickly at the detector mounted in the hall.

Gregson was in his room, happily cutting out frames of paper and pasting them onto a great rickety construction that vaguely resembled Franz's model.

"Hullo, Franz. What was it like?"

Franz shrugged. "Just a development. Worth seeing."

Gregson pointed to his construction. "Do you think we can try it out there?"

"We could do." Franz sat down on the bed, picked up a paper dart lying beside him, and tossed it out of the window. It swam out into the street, lazed down in a wide spiral and vanished into the open mouth of a ventilator shaft.

"When are you going to build another model?" Gregson asked.

"I'm not."

Gregson swung round. "Why? You've proved your theory."

"That's not what I'm after."

"I don't get you, Franz. What are you after?"

"Free space."

"Free?" Gregson repeated.

Franz nodded. "In both senses."

Gregson shook his head sadly and snipped out another paper panel. "Franz, you're crazy."

Franz stood up. "Take this room," he said. "It's twenty feet by fifteen by ten. Extend its dimensions infinitely. What do you find?"

"A development."

"*Infinitely!*"

"Nonfunctional space."

"Well?" Franz asked patiently.

"The concept's absurd."

"Why?"

"Because it couldn't exist."

Franz pounded his forehead in despair. "*Why* couldn't it?"

Gregson gestured with the scissors. "It's self-contradictory. Like the statement 'I am lying.' Just a verbal freak. Interesting theoretically, but it's pointless to press it for meaning." He tossed the scissors onto the table. "And anyway, do you know how much free space would cost?"

Franz went over to the bookshelf and pulled out one of the volumes. "Let's have a look at your street atlas."

He turned to the index. "This gives a thousand levels. KNI County, one hundred thousand cubic miles, population thirty million."

Gregson nodded.

Franz closed the atlas. "Two hundred fifty counties, including KNI, together form the 493rd Sector, and an association of fifteen hundred adjacent sectors comprise the 298th Local Union."

He broke off and looked at Gregson. "As a matter of interest, ever heard of it?"

Gregson shook his head. "No. How did—"

Franz slapped the atlas onto the table. "Roughly 4×10^{15} cubic Great-Miles." He leaned on the window ledge. "Now tell me: what lies beyond the 298th Local Union?"

"Other Unions, I suppose," Gregson said. "I don't see your difficulty."

"And beyond those?"

"Further ones. Why not?"

"Forever?" Franz pressed.

"Well, as far as forever is."

"The great street directory in the old Treasury Library on 247th Street is the largest in the County," Franz said. "I went down there this morning. It occupies three complete levels. Millions of volumes. But it doesn't extend beyond the 598th Local Union. No one there had any idea what lay further out. Why not?"

"Why should they?" Gregson asked. "Franz, what are you driving at?"

Franz walked across to the door. "Come down to the Bio-History Museum. I'll show you."

The birds perched on humps of rock or waddled about the sandy paths between the water pools.

"ARCHAEOPTERYX," Franz read off one of the cage indicators. The bird, lean and mildewed, uttered a painful croak when he fed a handful of beans to it.

"Some of these birds have the remnants of a pectoral girdle," Franz said. "Minute fragments of bone embedded in the tissues around their rib cages."

"Wings?"

"Dr. McGhee thinks so."

They walked out between the lines of cages.

"When does he think they were flying?"

"Before the Foundation," Franz said. "Three hundred billion years ago."

When they got outside the Museum they started down 859th Avenue. Halfway down the street a dense crowd had gathered and people were packed into the windows and balconies above the Elevated, watching a squad of Fire Police break their way into a house.

The bulkheads at either end of the block had been closed and heavy steel traps sealed off the stairways from the levels above and below. The ventilator and exhaust shafts were silent and already the air was stale and soupy.

"Pyros," Gregson murmured. "We should have brought our masks."

"It's only a scare," Franz said. He pointed to the monoxide detectors which were out everywhere, their long snouts sucking at the air. The dial needles stood safely at zero.

"Let's wait in the restaurant opposite."

They edged their way over to the restaurant, sat down in the window, and ordered coffee. This, like everything else on the menu, was cold. All cooking appliances were thermostated to a maximum 95°F., and only in the more expensive restaurants and hotels was it possible to obtain food that was at most tepid.

Below them in the street a lot of shouting went up. The FP's seemed unable to penetrate beyond the ground floor of the house and had started to baton back the crowd. An electric winch was wheeled up and bolted to the girders running below the curb, and half a dozen heavy steel grabs were carried into the house and hooked around the walls.

Gregson laughed. "The owners are going to be surprised when they get home."

Franz was watching the house. It was a narrow shabby dwelling sandwiched between a large wholesale furniture store and a new supermarket. An old sign running across the front had been painted over and evidently the ownership had recently changed. The present tenants had made a halfhearted attempt to convert the ground floor room into a cheap stand-up diner.

The FP's appeared to be doing their best to wreck everything and pies and smashed crockery were strewn all over the pavement.

"Crowd's pretty ugly," Franz said. "Do you want to move?"

"Hold on."

The noise died away and everyone waited as the winch began to revolve. Slowly the hawsers wound in and tautened, and the front wall of the house bulged and staggered outward in rigid jerky movements.

Suddenly there was a yell from the crowd.

Franz raised his arm.

"Up there! Look!"

On the fourth floor a man and woman had come to the window and were looking down frantically. The man helped the woman out onto the ledge and she crawled out and clung to one of the waste pipes.

The crowd roared, "Pyros! You bloody pyros!"

Bottles were lobbed up at them and bounced down among the police. A wide crack split the house from top to bottom and the floor on which the man was standing dropped and catapulted him backward out of sight.

Then one of the lintels in the first floor snapped and the entire house tipped over and collapsed.

Franz and Gregson stood up involuntarily, almost knocking over the table.

The crowd surged forward through the cordon. When the dust had settled there was nothing left but a heap of masonry and twisted beams. Embedded in this was the battered figure of the man. Almost smothered by the dust he moved slowly, painfully trying to free himself with one hand, and the crowd started roaring again as one of the grabs wound in and dragged him down under the rubble.

The manager of the restaurant pushed past Franz and leaned out of the window, his eyes fixed on the dial of a portable detector.

Its needle, like all the others, pointed to zero.

A dozen hoses were playing on the remains of the house and after a couple of minutes the crowd shifted and began to thin out.

The manager switched off the detector and left the window, nodding to Franz.

"Damn pyros. You can relax now, boys."

Franz pointed at the detector.

"Your dial was dead. There wasn't a trace of monoxide anywhere here. How do you know they were pyros?"

"Don't worry, we knew." He smiled obliquely. "We don't want that sort of element in this neighborhood."

Franz shrugged and sat down. "I suppose that's one way of getting rid of them."

The manager eyed Franz unpleasantly. "That's right, boy. This is a good five-dollar neighborhood." He smirked to himself. "Maybe a six-dollar now everybody knows about our safety record."

"Careful, Franz," Gregson warned him when the manager had gone. "He may be right. Pyros do take over small cafés and food bars."

Franz stirred his coffee. "Dr. McGhee estimates that at least fifteen percent of the City's population are submerged pyros. He's convinced the number's growing and that eventually the whole City will flame out."

He pushed away his coffee. "How much money have you got?"

"On me?"

"Altogether."

"About thirty dollars."

"I've saved up fifteen," Franz said thoughtfully. "Forty-five dollars; that should be enough for three or four weeks."

"Where?" Gregson asked.

"On a Supersleeper."

"Super—!" Gregson broke off, alarmed. "Three or four weeks! What do you mean?"

"There's only one way to find out," Franz explained calmly. "I can't just sit here thinking. Somewhere there's free space and I'll ride the Sleeper until I find it. Will you lend me your thirty dollars?"

"But Franz—"

"If I don't find anything within a couple of weeks I'll change tracks and come back."

"But the ticket will cost..." Gregson searched "... billions. Forty-five dollars won't even get you out of the Sector."

"That's just for coffee and sandwiches," Franz said. "The ticket will be free." He looked up from the table. "You know..."

Gregson shook his head doubtfully. "Can you try that on the Supersleepers?"

"Why not? If they query it I'll say I'm going back the long way around. Greg, will you?"

"I don't know if I should." Gregson played helplessly with his coffee. "Franz, how can there be free space? How?"

"That's what I'm going to find out," Franz said. "Think of it as my first physics practical."

Passenger distances on the transport system were measured point to point by the application of $a = \sqrt{b^2 + c^2 + d^2}$. The actual itinerary taken was the passenger's responsibility, and as long as he remained within the system he could choose any route he liked.

Tickets were checked only at the station exits, where necessary surcharges were collected by an inspector. If the passenger was unable to pay the surcharge—ten cents a mile—he was sent back to his original destination.

Franz and Gregson entered the station on 984th Street and went over to the large console where tickets were automatically dispensed.

Franz put in a penny and pressed the destination button marked 984. The machine rumbled, coughed out a ticket, and the change slot gave him back his coin.

"Well, Greg, good-bye," Franz said as they moved toward the barrier. "I'll see you in about two weeks. They're covering me down at the dormitory. Tell Sanger I'm on Fire Duty."

"What if you don't get back, Franz?" Gregson asked. "Suppose they take you off the Sleeper?"

"How can they? I've got my ticket."

"And if you do find free space? Will you come back then?"

"If I can."

Franz patted Gregson on the shoulder reassuringly, waved and disappeared among the commuters.

He took the local Suburban Green to the district junction in the next county. The Greenline train traveled at an interrupted 70 mph and the ride took two and a half hours.

At the Junction he changed to an express elevator which got him up out of the Sector in ninety minutes, at 400 mph.

Another fifty minutes in a Through-sector Special brought him to the Mainline Terminus which served the Union.

There he bought a coffee and gathered his determination together. Supersleepers ran east and west, halting at this and every tenth station. The next arrived in seventy-two hours' time, westbound.

The Mainline Terminus was the largest station Franz had seen, a vast mile-long cavern tiered up through thirty levels. Hundreds of elevator shafts sank into the station and the maze of platforms, escalators, restaurants, hotels, and theaters seemed like an exaggerated replica of the City itself.

Getting his bearings from one of the information booths Franz made his way up an escalator to Tier 15, where the Supersleepers berthed. Running the length of the station were two gigantic steel vacuum tunnels, each two hundred feet in diameter, supported at thirty-foot intervals by massive concrete buttresses.

Franz walked slowly along the platform and stopped by the telescopic gangway that plunged into one of the airlocks.

Two hundred and seventy degrees true, he thought, all the way, gazing up at the curving underbelly of the tunnel. It must come out somewhere. He had forty-five dollars in his pocket, sufficient coffee and sandwich money to last him three weeks, six if he needed it, time anyway to find the City's end.

He passed the next three days nursing coffees in any of the thirty cafeterias in the station, reading discarded newspapers and sleeping in the local Red trains, which ran four-hour journeys around the nearest sector.

When at last the Supersleeper came in he joined the small group of Fire Police and municipal officials waiting by the gangway, and followed them into the train. There were two cars: a sleeper which no one used, and a day coach.

Franz took an inconspicuous corner seat near one of the indicator panels in the day coach, pulled out his notebook and got ready to make his first entry.

1st Day: West 270°. Union 4,350.

"Coming out for a drink?" a Fire Captain across the aisle asked. "We have a ten-minute break here."

"No thanks," Franz said. "I'll hold your seat for you."

Dollar five a cubic foot. Free space, he knew, would bring the price down. There was no need to leave the train or make too many inquiries. All he had to do was borrow a paper and watch the market averages.

2nd Day: West 270°. Union 7,550.

"They're slowly cutting down on these Sleepers," someone told him. "Everyone sits in the day coach. Look at this one. Seats sixty, and only four people in it. There's no need to move around. People are staying where they are. In a few years there'll be nothing left but the suburban services."

Ninety-seven cents.

At an average of a dollar a cubic foot, Franz calculated idly, it's so far worth about 4×10^{27}.

"Going on to the next stop, are you? Well, good-bye, young fellow."

Few of the passengers stayed on the Sleeper for more than three or four hours. By the end of the second day Franz's back and neck ached from the constant acceleration. He got a little exercise walking up and down the narrow corridor in the deserted sleeping coach, but had to spend most of his time strapped to his seat as the train began its long braking runs into the next station.

3rd Day: West 270°. Federation 657.

"Interesting, but how could you demonstrate it?"

"It's just an odd idea of mine," Franz said, screwing up the sketch and dropping it in the disposal chute. "Hasn't any real application."

"Curious, but it rings a bell somewhere."

Franz sat up. "Do you mean you've seen machines like this? In a newspaper or a book?"

"No, no. In a dream."

Every half-day's run the pilot signed the log, the crew handed it over to their opposites on an eastbound sleeper, crossed the platform, and started back for home.

One hundred twenty-five cents.

8×10^{33}.

4th Day: West 270°. Federation 1,255.

"Dollar a cubic foot. You in the estate business?"

"Starting up," Franz said easily. "I'm hoping to open a new office of my own."

He played cards, bought coffee and rolls from the dispenser in the washroom, watched the indicator panel and listened to the talk around him.

"Believe me, a time will come when each union, each sector, almost I might say, each street and avenue will have achieved complete local independence. Equipped with its own power services, aerators, reservoirs, farm laboratories..."

The car bore.

6×10^{75}.

5th Day: West 270°. 17th Greater Federation.

At a kiosk on the station Franz bought a clip of razor blades and glanced at the brochure put out by the local chamber of commerce.

"Twelve thousand levels, ninety-eight cents a foot, unique Elm Drive, fire safety records unequaled..."

He went back to the train, shaved and counted the thirty dollars left. He was now ninety-five million Great-Miles from the suburban station on 984th Street and he knew he couldn't delay his return

much longer. Next time he'd save up a couple of thousand.
7×10^{127}.

7th Day: West 270°. 212th Metropolitan Empire.

Franz peered at the indicator.

"Aren't we stopping here?" he asked a man three seats away. "I wanted to find out the market average."

"Varies. Anything from fifty cents a—"

"Fifty!" Franz shot back, jumping up. "When's the next stop? I've got to get off!"

"Not here, son." He put out a restraining hand. "This is Night Town. You in real estate?"

Franz nodded, holding himself back. "I thought..."

"Relax." He came and sat opposite Franz. "It's just one big slum. Dead areas. In places it goes as low as five cents. There are no services, no power."

It took them two days to pass through.

"City Authority are starting to seal it off," the man told him. "Huge blocks. It's the only thing they can do. What happens to the people inside I hate to think."

He chewed on a sandwich. "Strange, but there are a lot of these black areas. You don't hear about them, but they're growing. Starts in a back street in some ordinary dollar neighborhood; a bottleneck in the sewage disposal system, not enough ash cans, and before you know it—a million cubic miles have gone back to jungle. They try a relief scheme, pump in a little cyanide, and then—brick it up. Once they do that they're closed for good."

Franz nodded, listening to the dull humming air.

"Eventually there'll be nothing left but these black areas. The City will be one huge cemetery. What a thought!"

10th Day: East 90°. 755th Greater Metropolitan—

"Wait!" Franz leaped out of his seat and stared at the indicator panel.

"What's the matter?" someone opposite asked.

"East!" Franz shouted. He banged the panel sharply with his hand but the lights held. "Has the train changed direction?"

"No, it's eastbound," another of the passengers told him. "Are you on the wrong train?"

"It should be heading west," Franz insisted. "It has been for the last ten days."

"Ten days!" the man exclaimed. "Have you been on this Sleeper for ten days? Where the hell are you going?"

Franz went forward and grabbed the car attendant.

"Which way is this train going? West?"

The attendant shook his head. "East, sir. It's always been going east."

"You're crazy," Franz snapped. "I want to see the pilot's log."

"I'm afraid that isn't possible. May I see your ticket, sir?"

"Listen," Franz said weakly, all the accumulated frustration of the last twenty years mounting inside him. "I've been on this..."

He stopped and went back to his seat.

The five other passengers watched him carefully.

"Ten days," one of them was still repeating in an awed voice.

Two minutes later someone came and asked Franz for his ticket.

"And of course it was completely in order," the police surgeon commented.

He walked over to M. and swung the spot out of his eyes. "Strangely enough there's no regulation to prevent anyone else doing the same thing. I used to go for free rides myself when I was younger, though I never tried anything like your journey."

He went back to the desk.

"We'll drop the charge," he said. "You're not a vagrant in any indictable sense, and the Transport authorities can do nothing against you. How this curvature was built into the system they can't explain. Now about yourself. Are you going to continue this search?"

"I want to build a flying machine," M. said carefully. "There must be free space somewhere. I don't know... perhaps on the lower levels."

The surgeon stood up. "I'll see the sergeant and get him to hand you over to one of our psychiatrists. He'll be able to help you with that dream."

The surgeon hesitated before opening the door. "Look," he began to explain sympathetically, "you can't get out of time, can you? Subjectively it's a plastic dimension, but whatever you do to yourself you'll never be able to stop that clock"—he pointed to the one on the desk "—or make it run backward. In exactly the same way you can't get out of the City."

"The analogy doesn't hold," M. said. He gestured at the walls around them and the lights in the street outside. "All this was built by us. The question nobody can answer is: what was here before we built it?"

"It's always been here," the surgeon said. "Not these particular bricks and girders, but others before them. You accept that time has no beginning and no end. The City is as old as time and continuous with it."

"The first bricks were laid by someone," M. insisted. "There was the Foundation."

"A myth. Only the scientists believe in that, and even they don't try to make too much of it. Most of them privately admit that the Foundation Stone is nothing more than a superstition. We pay it lip service out of convenience, and because it gives us a sense of tradition. Obviously there can't have been a first brick. If there was, how can you explain who laid it, and even more difficult, where they came from?"

"There must be free space somewhere," M. said doggedly. "The City must have bounds."

"Why?" the surgeon asked. "It can't be floating in the middle of nowhere. Or is that what you're trying to believe?"

M. sank back limply. "No."

The surgeon watched M. silently for a few minutes and paced back to the desk. "This peculiar fixation of yours puzzles me. You're caught between what the psychiatrists call paradoxical faces. I suppose you haven't misinterpreted something you've heard about the Wall?"

M. looked up. "Which wall?"

The surgeon nodded to himself. "Some advanced opinion maintains that there's a wall around the City, through which it's impossible to penetrate. I don't pretend to understand the theory myself. It's far too abstract and sophisticated. Anyway I suspect they've confused this Wall with the bricked-up black areas you passed through on the Sleeper. I prefer the accepted view that the City stretches out in all directions without limits."

He went over to the door. "Wait here, and I'll see about getting you a probationary release. Don't worry, the psychiatrists will straighten everything out for you."

When the surgeon had left, M. stared emptily at the floor, too exhausted to feel relieved. He stood up and stretched himself, walking unsteadily around the room.

Outside the last pilot lights were going out and the patrolman on the catwalk under the roof was using his torch. A police car roared down one of the avenues crossing the street, its rails screaming. Three lights snapped on along the street and then one by one went off again.

M. wondered why Gregson hadn't come down to the station. Then the calendar on the desk riveted his attention. The date exposed on the flyleaf was the twelfth of August. That was the day he had started off on his journey.

Exactly three weeks ago.

Today!

Take a westbound Green to 298th Street, cross over at the intersection and get a Red elevator up to Level 237. Walk down to the station on Route 175, change to a 438 suburban and go down to 795th Street. Take a Blueline to the Plaza, get off at 4th and 275th, turn left at the roundabout and...

You're back where you started from. $\$HELL \times 10^n$.

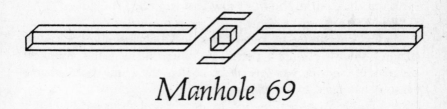

Manhole 69

For the first few days all went well.

"Keep away from windows and don't think about it," Dr. Neill told them. "As far as you're concerned it was just another compulsion. At eleven thirty or twelve go down to the gym and throw a ball around, play some table tennis. At two they're running a film for you in the neurology theater. Read the papers for a couple of hours, put on some records. I'll be down at six. By seven you'll be in a manic swing."

"Any chance of a sudden blackout, Doctor?" Avery asked.

"Absolutely none," Neill said. "If you get tired, rest, of course. That's the one thing you'll probably have a little difficulty getting used to. Remember, you're still using only thirty-five hundred calories, so your kinetic level—and you'll notice this most by day—will be about a third lower. You'll have to take things easier, make allowances. Most of these have been programmed in for you, but start learning to play chess, focus that inner eye."

Gorrell leaned forward. "Doctor," he asked, "if we want to, can we look out of the windows?"

Dr. Neill smiled. "Don't worry," he said. "The wires are cut. You couldn't go to sleep now if you tried."

Neill waited until the three men had left the lecture room on their way back to the Recreation Wing and then stepped down from the dais and shut the door. He was a short, broad-shouldered man in his fifties, with a sharp, impatient mouth and small features. He swung a chair out of the front row and straddled it deftly.

"Well?" he asked.

Morley was sitting on one of the desks against the back wall, playing aimlessly with a pencil. At thirty he was the youngest member of the team working under Neill at the Clinic, but for some reason Neill liked to talk to him.

He saw Neill was waiting for an answer and shrugged.

"Everything seems to be all right," he said. "Surgical convalescence is over. Cardiac rhythms and EEG are normal. I saw the X rays this morning and everything has sealed beautifully."

Neill watched him quizzically. "You don't sound as if you approve."

Morley laughed and stood up. "Of course I do." He walked down the aisle between the desks, white coat unbuttoned, hands sunk deep in his pockets. "No, so far you've vindicated yourself on every point. The party's only just beginning, but the guests are in damn good shape. No doubt about it. I thought three weeks was a little early to bring them out of hypnosis, but you'll probably be right there as well. Tonight is the first one they take on their own. Let's see how they are tomorrow morning."

"What are you secretly expecting?" Neill asked wryly. "Massive feedback from the medulla?"

"No," Morley said. "There again the psychometric tests have shown absolutely nothing coming up at all. Not a single trauma." He stared at the blackboard and then looked round at Neill. "Yes, as a cautious estimate I'd say you've succeeded."

Neill leaned forward on his elbows. He flexed his jaw muscles. "I think I've more than succeeded. Blocking the medullary synapses has eliminated a lot of material I thought would still be there—the minor quirks and complexes, the petty aggressive phobias, the bad change in the psychic bank. Most of them have gone, or at least they don't show in the tests. However, they're the side targets, and thanks to you, John, and to everyone else in the team, we've hit a bull's-eye on the main one."

Morley murmured something, but Neill ran on in his clipped

voice. "None of you realize it yet, but this is as big an advance as the step the first ichthyoid took out of the protozoic sea three-hundred million years ago. At last we've freed the mind, raised it out of that archaic sump called sleep, its nightly retreat into the medulla. With virtually one cut of the scalpel we've added twenty years to those men's lives."

"I only hope they know what to do with them," Morley commented.

"Come, John," Neill snapped back. "That's not an argument. What they do with the time is their responsibility anyway. They'll make the most of it, just as we've always made the most, eventually, of any opportunity given us. It's too early to think about it yet, but visualize the universal application of our technique. For the first time Man will be living a full twenty-four-hour day, not spending a third of it as an invalid, snoring his way through an eight-hour peep show of infantile erotica."

Tired, Neill broke off and rubbed his eyes. "What's worrying you?"

Morley made a small, helpless gesture with one hand. "I'm not sure, it's just that I . . ." He played with the plastic brain mounted on a stand next to the blackboard. Reflected in one of the frontal whorls was a distorted image of Neill, with a twisted chinless face and vast domed cranium. Sitting alone among the desks in the empty lecture room he looked like an insane genius patiently waiting to take an examination no one could set him.

Morley turned the model with his finger, watched the image blur and dissolve. Whatever his doubts, Neill was probably the last person to understand them.

"I know all you've done is close off a few of the loops in the hypothalamus, and I realize the results are going to be spectacular. You'll probably precipitate the greatest social and economic revolution since the Fall. But for some reason I can't get that story of Chekhov's out of my mind—the one about the man who accepts a million-ruble bet that he can't shut himself up alone for ten years. He tries to, nothing goes wrong, but one minute before the time is up he deliberately steps out of his room. Of course, he's insane."

"So?"

"I don't know. I've been thinking about it all week."

Neill let out a light snort. "I suppose you're trying to say that sleep is some sort of communal activity and that these three men are now isolated, exiled from the group unconscious, the dark oceanic dream. Is that it?"

"Maybe."

"Nonsense, John. The further we hold back the unconscious the better. We're reclaiming some of the marshland. Physiologically sleep is nothing more than an inconvenient symptom of cerebral anoxemia. It's not *that* you're afraid of missing, it's the dream. You want to hold on to your front-row seat at the peep show."

"No," Morley said mildly. Sometimes Neill's aggressiveness surprised him; it was almost as if he regarded sleep itself as secretly discreditable, a concealed vice. "What I really mean is that for better or worse Lang, Gorrell, and Avery are now stuck with themselves. They're never going to be able to get away, not even for a couple of minutes, let alone eight hours. How much of yourself can you stand? Maybe you need eight hours off a day just to get over the shock of being yourself. Remember, you and I aren't always going to be around, feeding them with tests and films. What will happen if they get fed up with themselves?"

"They won't," Neill said. He stood up, suddenly bored by Morley's questions. "The total tempo of their lives will be lower than ours, these stresses and tensions won't begin to crystallize. We'll soon seem like a lot of manic-depressives to them, running round like dervishes half the day, then collapsing into a stupor the other half."

He moved toward the door and reached out to the light switch. "Well, I'll see you at six o'clock."

They left the lecture room and started down the corridor together.

"What are you doing now?" Morley asked.

Neill laughed. "What do you think?" he said. "I'm going to get a good night's sleep."

A little after midnight Avery and Gorrell were playing table tennis in the floodlit gymnasium. They were competent players, and passed the ball backward and forward with a minimum of effort. Both felt strong and alert; Avery was sweating slightly, but this was due to the arc lights blazing down from the roof—maintaining, for safety's sake, an illusion of continuous day—rather than to any excessive exertion of his own. The oldest of the three volunteers, a tall and somewhat detached figure, with a lean, closed face, he made no attempt to talk to Gorrell and concentrated on adjusting himself to the period ahead. He knew he would find no trace of fatigue, but as he played he carefully checked his respiratory rhythms and muscle tonus, and kept one eye on the clock.

Gorrell, a jaunty, self-composed man, was also subdued. Between strokes he glanced cautiously around the gymnasium, noting the hangarlike walls, the broad, polished floor, the shuttered skylights in the roof. Now and then, without realizing it, he fingered the circular trepan scar at the back of his head.

Out in the center of the gymnasium a couple of armchairs and a sofa had been drawn up around a Gramophone, and here Lang was playing chess with Morley, doing his section of night duty. Lang hunched forward over the chessboard. Wiry-haired and aggressive, with a sharp nose and mouth, he watched the pieces closely. He had played regularly against Morley since he arrived at the Clinic four months earlier, and the two were almost equally matched, with perhaps a slight edge to Morley. But tonight Lang had opened with a new attack and after ten moves had completed his development and begun to split Morley's defense. His mind felt clear and precise, focused sharply on the game in front of him, though only that morning had he finally left the cloudy limbo of posthypnosis through which he and the two others had drifted for three weeks like lobotomized phantoms.

Behind him, along one wall of the gymnasium, were the offices housing the control unit. Over his shoulder he saw a face peering at him through the circular observation window in one of the doors. Here, at constant alert, a group of orderlies and interns sat around waiting by their emergency trolleys. (The end door, into a small ward containing three cots, was kept carefully locked.) After a few moments the face withdrew. Lang smiled at the elaborate machinery watching over him. His transference onto Neill had been positive and he had absolute faith in the success of the experiment. Neill had assured him that, at worst, the sudden accumulation of metabolites in his bloodstream might induce a mild torpor, but his brain would be unimpaired.

"Nerve fiber, Robert," Neill had told him time and again, "never fatigues. The brain cannot tire."

While he waited for Morley to move he checked the time from the clock mounted against the wall. Twelve-twenty. Morley yawned, his face drawn under the gray skin. He looked tired and drab. He slumped down into the armchair, face in one hand. Lang reflected how frail and primitive those who slept would soon seem, their minds sinking off each evening under the load of accumulating toxins, the edge of their awareness worn and frayed. Suddenly he realized that at that very moment Neill himself was asleep. A curiously disconcerting vision of Neill, huddled in a rumpled bed two floors above, his blood sugar low, his mind drifting, rose before him.

Lang laughed at his own conceit, and Morley retrieved the rook he had just moved.

"I must be going blind. What am I doing?"

"No," Lang said. He started to laugh again. "I've just discovered I'm awake."

Morley smiled. "We'll have to put that down as one of the sayings of the week." He replaced the rook, sat up, and looked across at the table tennis pair. Gorrell had hit a fast backhand low over the net and Avery was running after the ball.

"They seem to be OK. How about you?"

"Right on top of myself," Lang said. His eyes flicked up and down the board and he moved before Morley caught his breath back.

Usually they went right through into the end game, but tonight Morley had to concede on the twentieth move.

"Good," he said encouragingly. "You'll be able to take on Neill soon. Like another?"

"No. Actually the game bores me. I can see that's going to be a problem."

"You'll face it. Give yourself time to find your legs."

Lang pulled one of the Bach albums out of its rack in the record cabinet. He put a Brandenburg Concerto on the turntable and lowered the sapphire. As the rich, contrapuntal patterns chimed out he sat back, listening intently to the music.

Morley thought: Absurd. How fast can you run? Three weeks ago you were strictly a hepcat.

The next few hours passed rapidly.

At 1:30 they went up to the surgery, where Morley and one of the interns gave them a quick physical, checking their renal clearances, heart rate, and reflexes.

Dressed again, they went into the empty cafeteria for a snack and sat on the stools, arguing what to call this new fifth meal. Avery suggested "Midfood," Morley, "Munch."

At 2:00 they took their places in the neurology theater, and spent a couple of hours watching films of the hypno-drills of the past three weeks.

When the program ended they started down for the gymnasium, the night almost over. They were still relaxed and cheerful; Gorrell led the way, playfully teasing Lang over some of the episodes in the films, mimicking his trancelike walk.

"Eyes shut, mouth open," he demonstrated, swerving into Lang, who jumped nimbly out of his way. "Look at you; you're doing it even now. Believe me, Lang, you're not awake, you're somnambulating." He called back to Morley, "Agreed, Doctor?"

Morley swallowed a yawn. "Well, if he is, that makes two of us." He followed them along the corridor, doing his best to stay awake, feeling as if he, and not the three men in front of him, had been without sleep for the last three weeks.

Though the Clinic was quiet, at Neill's orders all lights along the corridors and down the stairway had been left on. Ahead of them two orderlies checked that windows they passed were safely screened and doors were shut. Nowhere was there a single darkened alcove or shadow trap.

Neill had insisted on this, reluctantly acknowledging a possible reflex association between darkness and sleep: "Let's admit it. In all but a few organisms the association *is* strong enough to be a reflex. The higher mammals depend for their survival on a highly acute sensory apparatus, combined with a varying ability to store and classify information. Plunge them into darkness, cut off the flow of visual data to the cortex, and they're paralyzed. Sleep is a defense reflex. It lowers the metabolic rate, conserves energy, increases the organism's survival potential by merging it into its habitat..."

On the landing halfway down the staircase was a wide, shuttered window that by day opened out onto the parkscape behind the Clinic. As he passed it Gorrell stopped. He went over, released the blind, then unlatched the shutter.

Still holding it closed, he turned to Morley, watching from the flight above.

"Taboo, Doctor?" he asked.

Morley looked at each of the three men in turn. Gorrell was calm and unperturbed, apparently satisfying nothing more sinister than an idle whim. Lang sat on the rail, watching curiously with an expression of clinical disinterest. Only Avery seemed slightly anxious, his thin face wan and pinched. Morley had an irrelevant thought: 4:00 A.M. shadow—they'll need to shave twice a day. Then: why isn't Neill here? He knew they'd make for a window as soon as they got the chance.

He noticed Lang giving him an amused smile and shrugged, trying to disguise his uneasiness.

"Go ahead, if you want to. As Neill said, the wires are cut."

Gorrell threw back the shutter, and they clustered around the window and stared out into the night. Below, pewter-gray lawns stretched toward the pines and low hills in the distance. A couple of miles away on their left a neon sign winked and beckoned.

Neither Gorrell nor Lang noticed any reaction, and their interest began to flag within a few moments. Avery felt a sudden lift under the heart, then controlled himself. His eyes began to sift the darkness; the sky was clear and cloudless, and through the stars he picked out the narrow, milky traverse of the galactic rim. He watched it silently, letting the wind cool the sweat on his face and neck.

Morley stepped over to the window and leaned his elbows on the sill next to Avery. Out of the corner of his eye he carefully waited for any motor tremor—a fluttering eyelid, accelerated breathing—that would signal a reflex discharging. He remembered Neill's warning: "In Man sleep is largely volitional, and the reflex is conditioned by habit. But just because we've cut out the hypothalamic loops regulating the flow of consciousness doesn't mean the reflex won't discharge down some other pathway. However, sooner or later we'll have to take the risk and give them a glimpse of the dark side of the sun."

Morley was musing on this when something nudged his shoulder.

"Doctor," he heard Lang say. "Doctor Morley."

He pulled himself together with a start. He was alone at the window. Gorrell and Avery were halfway down the next flight of stairs.

"What's up?" Morley asked quickly.

"Nothing," Lang assured him. "We're just going back to the gym." He looked closely at Morley. "Are you all right?"

Morley rubbed his face. "God, I must have been asleep." He glanced at his watch. Four-twenty. They had been at the window for over fifteen minutes. All he could remember was leaning on the sill. "And I was worried about *you*."

Everybody was amused, Gorrell particularly. "Doctor," he drawled, "if you're interested I can recommend you to a good narcotomist."

After 5:00 they felt a gradual ebb of tonus from their arm and leg muscles. Renal clearances were falling and breakdown products were slowly clogging their tissues. Their palms felt damp and numb, the soles of their feet like pads of sponge rubber. The sensation was vaguely unsettling, allied to no feelings of mental fatigue.

The numbness spread. Avery noticed it stretching the skin over his cheekbones, pulling at his temples, and giving him a slight frontal migraine. He doggedly turned the pages of a magazine, his hands like lumps of putty.

Then Neill came down, and they began to revive. Neill looked fresh and spruce, bouncing on the tips of his toes.

"How's the night shift going?" he asked briskly, walking round each one of them in turn, smiling as he sized them up. "Feel all right?"

"Not too bad, Doctor," Gorrell told him. "A slight case of insomnia."

Neill roared, slapped him on the shoulder and led the way up to the surgery laboratory.

At 9:00, shaved and in fresh clothes, they assembled in the lecture room. They felt cool and alert again. The peripheral numbness and slight head torpor had gone as soon as the detoxication drips had been plugged in, and Neill told them that within a week their kidneys would have enlarged sufficiently to cope on their own.

All morning and most of the afternoon they worked on a series of IQ, associative, and performance tests. Neill kept them hard at it, steering swerving blips of light around a cathode screen, juggling with intricate numerical and geometric sequences, elaborating word chains.

He seemed more than satisfied with the results.

"Shorter access times, deeper memory traces," he pointed out to Morley when the three men had gone off at 5:00 for the rest period. "Barrels of prime psychic marrow." He gestured at the test cards spread out across the desk in his office. "And you were worried about the Unconscious. Look at those Rorschachs of Lang's. Believe me, John, I'll soon have him reminiscing about his fetal experiences."

Morley nodded, his first doubts fading.

Over the next two weeks either he or Neill was with the men continuously, sitting out under the floodlights in the center of the gymnasium, assessing their assimilation of the eight extra hours, carefully watching for any symptoms of withdrawal. Neill carried everyone along, from one program phase to the next, through the test periods, across the long hours of the interminable nights, his powerful ego injecting enthusiasm into every member of the unit.

Privately, Morley worried about the increasing emotional overlay apparent in the relationship between Neill and the three men. He was afraid they were becoming conditioned to identify Neill with the experiment. (Ring the meal bell and the subject salivates; but suddenly stop ringing the bell after a long period of conditioning and it temporarily loses the ability to feed itself. The hiatus barely harms a dog, but it might trigger disaster in an already oversensitized psyche.)

Neill was fully alert to this. At the end of the first two weeks, when he caught a bad head cold after sitting up all night and decided to spend the next day in bed, he called Morley into his office.

"The transference is getting much too positive. It needs to be eased off a little."

"I agree," Morley said. "But how?"

"Tell them I'll be asleep for forty-eight hours," Neill said. He picked up a stack of reports, plates, and test cards and bundled them under one arm. "I've deliberately overdosed myself with sedatives to get some rest. I'm worn to a shadow, full fatigue syndrome, load cells screaming. Lay it on."

"Couldn't that be rather drastic?" Morley asked. "They'll hate you for it."

But Neill only smiled and went off to requisition an office near his bedroom.

That night Morley was on duty in the gymnasium from 10:00 P.M. to 6:00 A.M. As usual he first checked that the orderlies were ready with their emergency trolleys, read through the log left by the previous supervisor, one of the senior interns, and then went over to the circle of chairs. He sat back on the sofa next to Lang and leafed through a magazine, watching the three men carefully. In the glare of the arc lights their lean faces had a sallow, cyanosed look. The senior intern had warned him that Avery and Gorrell might overtire themselves at table tennis, but by 11:00 P.M. they stopped playing and settled down in the armchairs. They read desultorily and made two trips up to the cafeteria, escorted each time by one of the orderlies. Morley told them about Neill, but surprisingly none of them made any comment.

Midnight came slowly. Avery read, his long body hunched up in an armchair. Gorrell played chess against himself.

Morley dozed.

Lang felt restless. The gymnasium's silence and absence of movement oppressed him. He switched on the Gramophone and played through a Brandenburg, analyzing its theme trains. Then he ran a word-association test on himself, turning the pages of a book and using the top right-hand corner words as the control list.

Morley leaned over. "Anything come up?" he asked.

"A few interesting responses." Lang found a notepad and jotted something down. "I'll show them to Neill in the morning—or whenever he wakes up." He gazed up pensively at the arc lights. "I was just speculating. What do you think the next step forward will be?"

"Forward where?" Morley asked.

Lang gestured expansively. "I mean up the evolutionary slope. Three hundred million years ago we became air-breathers and left the seas behind. Now we've taken the next logical step forward and eliminated sleep. What's next?"

Morley shook his head. "The two steps aren't analogous. Anyway, in point of fact you haven't left the primeval sea behind. You're still carrying a private replica of it around as your bloodstream. All you did was encapsulate a necessary piece of the physical environment in order to escape it."

Lang nodded. "I was thinking of something else. Tell me, has it ever occurred to you how completely death-orientated the psyche is?"

Morley smiled. "Now and then," he said, wondering where this led.

"It's curious," Lang went on reflectively. "The pleasure-pain principle, the whole survival-compulsion apparatus of sex, the superego's obsession with tomorrow—most of the time the psyche can't see farther than its own tombstone. Now why has it got this strange fixation? For one very obvious reason." He tapped the air with his forefinger. "Because every night it's given a pretty convincing reminder of the fate in store for it."

"You mean the black hole," Morley suggested wryly. "Sleep?"

"Exactly. It's simply a pseudodeath. Of course, you're not aware of it, but it must be terrifying." He frowned. "I don't think even Neill realizes that, far from being restful, sleep is a genuinely traumatic experience."

So that's it, Morley thought. The great father analyst has been caught napping on his own couch. He tried to decide which were worse—patients who knew a lot of psychiatry, or those who only knew a little.

"Eliminate sleep," Lang was saying, "and you also eliminate all the fear and defense mechanisms erected around it. Then, at last, the psyche has a chance to orientate toward something more valid."

"Such as...?" Morley asked.

"I don't know. Perhaps... Self?"

"Interesting," Morley commented. It was 3:10 A.M. He decided to spend the next hour going through Lang's latest test cards.

He waited a discretionary five minutes, then stood up and walked over to the surgery office.

Lang hooked an arm across the back of the sofa and watched the orderly room door.

"What's Morley playing at?" he asked. "Have either of you seen him anywhere?"

Avery lowered his magazine. "Didn't he go off into the orderly room?"

"Ten minutes ago," Lang said. "He hasn't looked in since. There's supposed to be someone on duty with us continuously. Where is he?"

Gorrell, playing solitaire chess, looked up from his board. "Perhaps these late nights are getting him down. You'd better wake him before Neill finds out. He's probably fallen asleep over a batch of your test cards."

Lang laughed and settled down on the sofa. Gorrell reached out to the Gramophone, took a record out of the rack and slid it on to the turntable.

As the Gramophone began to hum Lang noticed how silent and deserted the gymnasium seemed. The Clinic was always quiet, but even at night a residual ebb and flow of sound—a chair dragging in the orderly room, a generator charging under one of the theaters—eddied through and kept it alive.

Now the air was flat and motionless. Lang listened carefully. The whole place had the dead, echoless feel of an abandoned building.

He stood up and strolled over to the orderly room. He knew Neill discouraged casual conversation with the control crew, but Morley's absence puzzled him.

He reached the door and peered through the window to see if Morley was inside.

The room was empty.

The light was on. Two emergency trolleys stood in their usual place against the wall near the door, a third was in the middle of the floor, a pack of playing cards strewn across its deck, but the group of three or four interns had gone.

Lang hesitated, reached down to open the door, and found it had been locked.

He tried the handle again, then called out over his shoulder: "Avery. There's nobody in here."

"Try next door. They're probably being briefed for tomorrow."

Lang stepped over to the surgery office. The light was off but he could see the white enameled desk and the big program charts around the wall. There was no one inside.

Avery and Gorrell were watching him.

"Are they in there?" Avery asked.

"No." Lang turned the handle. "The door's locked."

Gorrell switched off the Gramophone and he and Avery came over. They tried the two doors again.

"They're here somewhere," Avery said. "There must be at least one person on duty." He pointed to the end door. "What about that one?"

"Locked," Lang said, "Sixty-nine always has been. I think it leads down to the basement."

"Let's try Neill's office," Gorrell suggested. "If they aren't in there we'll stroll through to Reception and try to leave. This must be some trick of Neill's."

There was no window in the door to Neill's office. Gorrell knocked, waited, knocked again more loudly.

Lang tried the handle, then knelt down. "The light's off," he reported.

Avery turned and looked around at the two remaining doors out of the gymnasium, both in the far wall, one leading up to the cafeteria and the neurology wing, the other into the car park at the rear of the Clinic.

"Didn't Neill hint that he might try something like this on us?" he asked. "To see whether we can go through a night on our own."

"But Neill's asleep," Lang objected. "He'll be in bed for a couple of days. Unless..."

Gorrell jerked his head in the direction of the chairs. "Come on. He and Morley are probably watching us now."

They went back to their seats.

Gorrell dragged the chess stool over to the sofa and set up the pieces. Avery and Lang stretched out in armchairs and opened magazines, turning the pages deliberately. Above them the banks of arc lights threw their wide cones of light down into the silence.

The only noise was the slow left-right, left-right motion of the clock.

Three fifteen A.M.

The shift was imperceptible. At first a slight change of perspective, a fading and regrouping of outlines. Somewhere a focus slipped, a shadow swung slowly across a wall, its angles breaking and lengthening. The motion was fluid, a procession of infinitesimals, but gradually its total direction emerged.

The gymnasium was shrinking. Inch by inch, the walls were moving inward, encroaching across the periphery of the floor. As they shrank toward each other their features altered: the rows of skylights below the ceiling blurred and faded, the power cable running along the base of the wall merged into the skirting board, the square baffles of the air vents vanished into the gray distemper.

Above, like the undersurface of an enormous lift, the ceiling sank toward the floor...

Gorrell leaned his elbows on the chessboard, face sunk in his hands. He had locked himself in a perpetual check, but he continued to shuttle the pieces in and out of one of the corner squares, now and then gazing into the air for inspiration, while his eyes roved up and down the walls around him.

Somewhere, he knew, Neill was watching him.

He moved, looked up, and followed the wall opposite him down to the far corner, alert for the telltale signs of a retractable panel. For some while he had been trying to discover Neill's spy hole, but without any success. The walls were blank and featureless; he had twice covered every square foot of the two facing him, and apart from the three doors there appeared to be no fault or aperture of even the most minute size anywhere on their surface.

After a while his left eye began to throb painfully, and he pushed away the chessboard and lay back. Above him a line of fluorescent tubes hung down from the ceiling, mounted in checkered plastic brackets that diffused the light. He was about to comment on his search for the spy hole to Avery and Lang when he realized that any one of them could conceal a microphone.

He decided to stretch his legs, stood up, and sauntered off across the floor. After sitting over the chessboard for half an hour he felt cramped and restless, and would have enjoyed tossing a ball up and down, or flexing his muscles on a rowing machine. But annoyingly no recreational facilities, apart from the three armchairs and the Gramophone, had been provided.

He reached the end wall and wandered around, listening for any sound from the adjacent rooms. He was beginning to resent Neill spying on him and the entire keyhole conspiracy, and he noted with relief that it was a quarter past three: in under three hours it would all be over.

The gymnasium closed in. Now less than half its original size, its walls bare and windowless, it was a vast, shrinking box. The sides slid into each other, merging along an abstract hairline, like planes severing in a multidimensional flux. Only the clock and a single door remained...

Lang had discovered where the microphone was hidden.

He sat forward in his chair, cracking his knuckles until Gorrell returned, then rose and offered him his seat. Avery was in the other armchair, feet up on the Gramophone.

"Sit down for a bit," Lang said. "I feel like a stroll."

Gorrell lowered himself into the chair. "I'll ask Neill if we can have a Ping-Pong table in here. It should help pass the time and give us some exercise."

"A good idea," Lang agreed. "If we can get the table through the door. I doubt if there's enough room in here, even if we moved the chairs right up against the wall."

He walked off across the floor, surreptitiously peering through the orderly room window. The light was on, but there was still no one inside.

He ambled over to the Gramophone and paced up and down near it for a few moments. Suddenly he swung around and caught his foot under the flex leading to the wall socket.

The plug fell out onto the floor. Lang left it where it lay, went over, and sat down on the arm of Gorrell's chair.

"I've just disconnected the microphone," he confided.

Gorrell looked around carefully. "Where was it?"

Lang pointed. "Inside the Gramophone." He laughed softly. "I thought I'd pull Neill's leg. He'll be wild when he realizes he can't hear us."

"Why do you think it was in the Gramophone?" Gorrell asked.

"What better place? Besides, it couldn't be anywhere else. Apart from in there." He gestured at the light bowl suspended from the center of the ceiling. "It's empty except for the two bulbs. The Gramophone is the obvious place. I had a feeling it was there, but I wasn't sure until I noticed we had a Gramophone, but no records."

Gorrell nodded sagely.

Lang moved away, chuckling to himself.

Above the door of Room 69 the clock ticked on at 3:15.

> The motion was accelerating. What had once been the gymnasium was now a small room, seven feet wide, a tight, almost perfect cube. The walls plunged inward, along colliding diagonals, only a few feet from their final focus...

Avery noticed Gorrell and Lang pacing around his chair. "Either of you want to sit down yet?" he asked.

They shook their heads. Avery rested for a few minutes and then climbed out of the chair and stretched himself.

"Quarter past three," he remarked, pressing his hands against the ceiling. "This is getting to be a long night."

He leaned back to let Gorrell pass him, and then started to follow the others around the narrow space between the armchair and the walls.

"I don't know how Neill expects us to stay awake in this hole for twenty-four hours a day," he went on. "Why haven't we got a television set in here? Even a radio would be something."

They sidled around the chair together, Gorrell, followed by Avery, with Lang completing the circle, their shoulders beginning to hunch, their heads down as they watched the floor, their feet falling into the slow, leaden rhythm of the clock.

This, then, was the manhole: a narrow, vertical cubicle, a few feet wide, six deep. Above, a solitary, dusty bulb gleamed down from a steel grille. As if crumbling under the impetus of their own momentum, the surface of the walls had coarsened, the texture was that of stone, streaked and pitted...

Gorrell bent down to loosen one of his shoelaces and Avery bumped into him sharply, knocking his shoulder against the wall.

"All right?" he asked, taking Gorrell's arm. "This place is a little overcrowded. I can't understand why Neill ever put us in here."

He leaned against the wall, head bowed to prevent it from touching the ceiling, and gazed about thoughtfully.

Lang stood squeezed into the corner next to him, shifting his weight from one foot to the other.

Gorrell squatted down on his heels below them.

"What's the time?" he asked.

"I'd say about three fifteen," Lang offered. "More or less."

"Lang," Avery asked, "where's the ventilator here?"

Lang peered up and down the walls and across the small square of ceiling. "There must be one somewhere." Gorrell stood up and they shuffled about, examining the floor between their feet.

"There may be a vent in the light grille," Gorrell suggested. He reached up and slipped his fingers through the cage, running them behind the bulb.

"Nothing there. Odd. I should have thought we'd use the air in here within half an hour."

"Easily," Avery said. "You know, there's something—"

Just then Lang broke in. He gripped Avery's elbow.

"Avery," he asked. "Tell me. How did we get here?"

"What do you mean, get here? We're on Neill's team."

Lang cut him off. "I know that." He pointed at the floor. "I mean, in here."

Gorrell shook his head. "Lang, relax. How do you think? Through the door."

Lang looked squarely at Gorrell, then at Avery.

"What door?" he asked calmly.

Gorrell and Avery hesitated, then swung around to look at each wall in turn, scanning it from floor to ceiling. Avery ran his hands over the heavy masonry, then knelt down and felt the floor, digging his fingers at the rough stone slabs. Gorrell crouched beside him, scrabbling at the thin seams of dirt.

Lang backed out of their way into a corner, and watched them impassively. His face was calm and motionless, but in his left temple a single vein fluttered insanely.

When they finally stood up, staring at each other unsteadily, he flung himself between them at the opposite wall.

"Neill! Neill!" he shouted. He pounded angrily on the wall with his fists. "Neill! Neill!"

Above him the light began to fade.

Morley closed the door of the surgery office behind him and went over to the desk. Though it was 3:15 A.M., Neill was probably awake, working on the latest material in the office next to his bedroom. Fortunately that afternoon's test cards, freshly marked by one of the interns, had only just reached his in-tray.

Morley picked out Lang's folder and started to sort through the cards. He suspected that Lang's responses to some of the key words and suggestion triggers lying disguised in the question forms might throw illuminating sidelights onto the real motives behind his equation of sleep and death.

The communicating door to the orderly room opened and an intern looked in.

"Do you want me to take over in the gym, Doctor?"

Morley waved him away. "Don't bother. I'm going back in a moment."

He selected the cards he wanted and began to initial his withdrawals. Glad to get away from the glare of the arc lights, he delayed his return as long as he could, and it was 3:25 A.M. when he finally left the office and stepped back into the gymnasium.

The men were sitting where he had left them. Lang watched him approach, head propped comfortably on a cushion. Avery was slouched down in his armchair, nose in a magazine, while Gorrell hunched over the chessboard, hidden behind the sofa.

"Anybody feel like coffee?" Morley called out, deciding they needed some exercise.

None of them looked up or answered. Morley felt a flicker of annoyance, particularly at Lang, who was staring past him at the clock.

Then he saw something that made him stop.

Lying on the polished floor ten feet from the sofa was a chess piece. He went over and picked it up. The piece was the black king. He wondered how Gorrell could be playing chess with one of the two essential pieces of the game missing when he noticed three more pieces lying on the floor nearby.

His eyes moved to where Gorrell was sitting.

Scattered over the floor below the chair and sofa was the rest of the set. Gorrell was slumped over the stool. One of his elbows had slipped and the arm dangled between his knees, knuckles resting on the floor. The other hand supported his face. Dead eyes peered down at his feet.

Morley ran over to him, shouting: "Lang! Avery! Get the orderlies!"

He reached Gorrell and pulled him back off the stool.

"Lang!" he called again.

Lang was still staring at the clock, his body in the stiff, unreal posture of a waxworks dummy.

Morley let Gorrell loll back onto the sofa, leaned over and glanced at Lang's face.

He crossed to Avery, stretched out behind the magazine, and jerked his shoulder. Avery's head bobbed stiffly. The magazine slipped and fell from his hands, leaving his fingers curled in front of his face.

Morley stepped over Avery's legs to the Gramophone. He switched it on, gripped the volume control, and swung it round to full amplitude.

Above the orderly room door an alarm bell shrilled out through the silence.

"Weren't you with them?" Neill asked sharply.

"No," Morley admitted. They were standing by the door of the emergency ward. Two orderlies had just dismantled the electrotherapy unit and were wheeling the console away on a trolley. Outside in the gymnasium a quiet, urgent traffic of nurses and interns moved past. All but a single bank of arc lights had been switched off, and the gymnasium seemed like a deserted stage at the end of a performance.

"I slipped into the office to pick up a few test cards," he explained. "I wasn't gone more than ten minutes."

"You were supposed to watch them continuously," Neill snapped. "Not wander off by yourself whenever you felt like it. What do you think we had the gym and this entire circus set up for?"

It was a little after 5:30 A.M. After working hopelessly on the three men for a couple of hours, he was close to exhaustion. He looked down at them, lying inertly in their cots, canvas sheets buckled up to their chins. They had barely changed, but their eyes were open and unblinking, and their faces had the empty, reflexless look of psychic zero.

An intern bent over Lang, thumbing a hypodermic. Morley stared at the floor. "I think they would have gone anyway."

"How can you say that?" Neill clamped his lips together. He felt frustrated and impotent. He knew Morley was probably right—the three men were in terminal withdrawal, unresponsive to either insulin or electrotherapy, and a vise-tight catatonic seizure didn't close in out of nowhere—but as always refused to admit anything without absolute proof.

He led the way into his office and shut the door.

"Sit down." He pulled a chair out for Morley and prowled off around the room, slamming a fist into his palm.

"All right, John. What is it?"

Morley picked up one of the test cards lying on the desk, balanced it on a corner and spun it between his fingers. Phrases swam through his mind, tentative and uncertain, like blind fish.

"What do you want me to say?" he asked. "Reactivation of the infantile imago? A regression into the great, slumbering womb? Or to put it more simply still—just a fit of pique?"

"Go on."

Morley shrugged. "Continual consciousness is more than the brain can stand. Any signal repeated often enough eventually loses its meaning. Try saying the word *sleep* fifty times. After a point the brain's self-awareness dulls. It's no longer able to grasp who or why it is, and it rides adrift."

"What do we do then?"

"Nothing. Short of rescoring all the way down to Lumbar One. The central nervous system can't stand narcotomy."

Neill shook his head. "You're lost," he said curtly. "Juggling with generalities isn't going to bring those men back. First, we've got to find out what happened to them, what they actually felt and saw."

Morley frowned dubiously. "That jungle is marked *private*. Even if you do, is a psychotic's withdrawal drama going to make any sense?"

"Of course it will. However insane it seems to us, it was real enough to them. If we know the ceiling fell in or the whole gym filled with ice cream or turned into a maze, we've got something to work on." He sat down on the desk. "Do you remember that story of Chekhov's you told me about?"

"'The Bet'? Yes."

"I read it last night. Curious. It's a lot nearer what you're really trying to say than you know." He gazed around the office. "This room in which the man is penned for ten years symbolizes the mind driven to the furthest limits of self-awareness... Something very similar happened to Avery, Gorrell, and Lang. They must have reached a stage beyond which they could no longer contain the idea of their own identity. But far from being unable to grasp the idea, I'd say that they were conscious of nothing else. Like the man in the spherical mirror, who can only see a single gigantic eye staring back at him."

"So you think their withdrawal is a straightforward escape from the eye, the overwhelming ego?"

"Not escape," Neill corrected. "The psychotic never escapes from anything. He's much more sensible. He merely readjusts reality to suit himself. Quite a trick to learn, too. The room in Chekhov's story gives me an idea as to how they might have readjusted. Their particular equivalent of this room was the gym. I'm beginning to realize it was a mistake to put them in there—all those lights blazing down, the huge floor, high walls. They merely exaggerate the sensation of overload. In fact the gym might easily have become an external projection of their own egos."

Neill drummed his fingers on the desk. "My guess is that at this moment they're either striding around in there the size of hundred-foot giants, or else they've cut it down to their own dimensions. More probably that. They've just pulled the gym in on themselves."

Morley grinned bleakly. "So all we've got to do now is pump them full of honey and apomorphine and coax them out. Suppose they refuse?"

"They won't," Neill said. "You'll see."

There was a rap on the door. An intern stuck his head through. "Lang's coming out of it, Doctor. He's calling for you."

Neill bounded out.

Morley followed him into the ward.

Lang was lying in his cot, body motionless under the canvas sheet. His lips were parted slightly. No sound came from them, but Morley, bending over next to Neill, could see his hyoid bone vibrating in spasms.

"He's very faint," the intern warned.

Neill pulled up a chair and sat down next to the cot. He made a visible effort of concentration, flexing his shoulders. He bent his head close to Lang's and listened.

Five minutes later it came through again.

Lang's lips quivered. His body arched under the sheet, straining at the buckles, and then subsided.

"Neill... Neill," he whispered. The sounds, thin and strangled, seemed to be coming from the bottom of a well. "Neill... Neill... Neill..."

Neill stroked his forehead with a small, neat hand.

"Yes, Bobby," he said gently. His voice was feather-soft, caressing. "I'm here, Bobby. You can come out now."

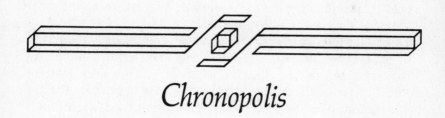

Chronopolis

His trial had been fixed for the next day. Exactly when, of course, neither Newman nor anyone else knew. Probably it would be during the afternoon, when the principals concerned—judge, jury, and prosecutor—managed to converge on the same courtroom at the same time. With luck his defense attorney might also appear at the right moment, though the case was such an open and shut one that Newman hardly expected him to bother—besides, transport to and from the old penal complex was notoriously difficult, involved endless waiting in the grimy depot below the prison walls.

Newman had passed the time usefully. Luckily, his cell faced south and sunlight traversed it for most of the day. He divided its arc into ten equal segments, the effective daylight hours, marking the intervals with a wedge of mortar prized from the window ledge. Each segment he further subdivided into twelve smaller units.

Immediately he had a working timepiece, accurate to within virtually a minute (the final subdivision into fifths he made mentally). The sweep of white notches, curving down one wall, across the floor and metal bedstead, and up the other wall, would have been recognizable to anyone who stood with his back to the window, but no one ever did. Anyway, the guards were too stupid to understand, and the sundial had given Newman a tremendous advantage over them. Most of the time, when he wasn't recalibrating the dial, he would press against the grille, keeping an eye on the orderly room.

"Brocken!" he would shout at 7:15 as the shadow line hit the first interval. "Morning inspection! On your feet, man!" The sergeant would come stumbling out of his bunk in a sweat, rising the other warders as the reveille bell split the air.

Later, Newman sang out the other events on the daily roster: roll call, cell fatigues, breakfast, exercise, and so on around to the evening roll just before dusk. Brocken regularly won the block merit for the best-run cell deck and he relied on Newman to program the day for him, anticipate the next item on the roster, and warn him if anything went on for too long—in some of the other blocks fatigues were usually over in three minutes while breakfast or exercise could go on for hours, none of the warders knowing when to stop, the prisoners insisting that they had only just begun.

Brocken never inquired how Newman organized everything so exactly; once or twice a week, when it rained or was overcast, Newman would be strangely silent, and the resulting confusion reminded the sergeant forcefully of the merits of cooperation. Newman was kept in cell privileges and all the cigarettes he needed. It was a shame that a date for the trial had finally been named.

Newman, too, was sorry. Most of his research so far had been inconclusive. Primarily his problem was that, given a northward-facing cell for the bulk of his sentence, the task of estimating the time might become impossible. The inclination of the shadows in the exercise yards or across the towers and walls provided too blunt a reading. Calibration would have to be visual; an optical instrument would soon be discovered.

What he needed was an internal timepiece, an unconsciously operating psychic mechanism regulated, say, by his pulse or respiratory rhythms. He had tried to train his time sense, running an elaborate series of tests to estimate its minimum in-built error, and this had been disappointingly large. The chances of conditioning an accurate reflex seemed slim.

However, unless he could tell the exact time at any given moment, he knew he would go mad.

His obsession, which now faced him with a charge of murder, had revealed itself innocently enough.

As a child, like all children, he had noticed the occasional ancient clock tower, bearing the same white circle with its twelve intervals. In the seedier areas of the city the round characteristic dials often hung over cheap jewelry stores, rusting and derelict.

"Just signs," his mother explained. "They don't mean anything, like stars or rings."

Pointless embellishment, he had thought.

Once, in an old furniture shop, they had seen a clock with hands, upside down in a box full of fire irons and miscellaneous rubbish.

"Eleven and twelve," he had pointed out. "What does it mean?"

His mother had hurried him away, reminding herself never to visit that street again. "Nothing," she told him sharply. "It's all finished." To herself she added experimentally: Five and twelve. Five *to* twelve. Yes.

Time unfolded at its usual sluggish, half-confused pace. They lived in a ramshackle house in one of the amorphous suburbs, a zone of endless afternoons. Sometimes he went to school, until he was ten spent most of his time with his mother queuing outside the closed food stores. In the evenings he would play with the neighborhood gang around the abandoned railway station, punting a homemade flatcar along the overgrown tracks, or break into one of the unoccupied houses and set up a temporary command post.

He was in no hurry to grow up; the adult world was unsynchronized and ambitionless. After his mother died he spent long days in the attic, going through her trunks and old clothes, playing with the bric-a-brac of hats and beads, trying to recover something of her personality.

In the bottom compartment of her jewelry case he came across a flat gold-cased object, equipped with a wrist strap. The dial had no hands but the twelve-numbered face intrigued him and he fastened it to his wrist.

His father choked over his soup when he saw it that evening.

"Conrad, my God! Where in heaven did you get that?"

"In Mamma's bead box. Can't I keep it?"

"No. Conrad, give it to me! Sorry, son." Thoughtfully: "Let's see, you're fourteen. Look, Conrad, I'll explain it all in a couple of years."

With the impetus provided by this new taboo there was no need to wait for his father's revelations. Full knowledge came soon. The older boys knew the whole story, but strangely enough it was disappointingly dull.

"Is that all?" he kept saying. "I don't get it. Why worry so much about clocks? We have calendars, don't we?"

Suspecting more, he scoured the streets, carefully inspecting every derelict clock for a clue to the real secret. Most of the faces had been mutilated, hands and numerals torn off, the circle of minute intervals stripped away, leaving a shadow of fading rust. Distributed apparently at random all over the city, above stores, banks, and public buildings, their real purpose was hard to discover. Sure enough, they measured the progress of time through twelve arbitrary intervals, but this seemed barely adequate grounds for outlawing them. After all, a whole variety of timers were in general use: in kitchens, factories, hospitals, wherever a fixed period of time was needed. His father had one by his bed at night. Sealed into the standard small black box, and driven by miniature batteries, it emitted a high penetrating whistle shortly before breakfast the next morning, woke him if he overslept. A clock was no more than a calibrated timer, in many ways less useful, as it provided you with a steady stream of irrelevant information. What if it was half past three, as the old reckoning put it, if you weren't planning to start or finish anything then?

Making his questions sound as naive as possible, he conducted a long, careful poll. Under fifty no one appeared to know anything at all about the historical background, and even the older people were beginning to forget. He also noticed that the less educated they were the more they were willing to talk, indicating that manual and lower-class workers had played no part in the revolution and consequently had no guilt-charged memories to repress. Old Mr. Crichton, the plumber who lived in the basement apartment, reminisced without any prompting, but nothing he said threw any light on the problem.

"Sure, there were thousands of clocks then, millions of them, everybody had one. Watches we called them, strapped to the wrist, you had to screw them up every day."

"But what did you *do* with them, Mr. Crichton?" Conrad pressed.

"Well, you just—looked at them, and you knew what time it was. One o'clock, or two, or half past seven—that was when I'd go off to work."

"But you go off to work now when you've had breakfast. And if you're late the timer rings."

Crichton shook his head. "I can't explain it to you, lad. You ask your father."

But Mr. Newman was hardly more helpful. The explanation promised for Conrad's sixteenth birthday never materialized. When his questions persisted Mr. Newman, tired of sidestepping, shut him up with an abrupt: "Just stop thinking about it, do you understand? You'll get yourself and the rest of us into a lot of trouble."

Stacey, the young English teacher, had a wry sense of humor, liked to shock the boys by taking up unorthodox positions on marriage or economics. Conrad wrote an essay describing an imaginary society completely preoccupied with elaborate rituals revolving around a minute-by-minute observance of the passage of time.

Stacey refused to play, however, and gave him a noncommittal beta plus. After class he quietly asked Conrad what had prompted the fantasy. At first Conrad tried to back away, then finally came out with the question that contained the central riddle.

"Why is it against the law to have a clock?"

Stacey tossed a piece of chalk from one hand to the other.

"Is it against the law?"

Conrad nodded. "There's an old notice in the police station offering a bounty of one hundred pounds for every clock or wristwatch brought in. I saw it yesterday. The sergeant said it was still in force."

Stacey raised his eyebrows mockingly. "You'll make a million. Thinking of going into business?"

Conrad ignored this. "It's against the law to have a gun because you might shoot someone. But how can you hurt anybody with a clock?"

"Isn't it obvious? You can time him, know exactly how long it takes him to do something."

"Well?"

"Then you can make him do it faster."

At seventeen, on a sudden impulse, he built his first clock. Already his preoccupation with time was giving him a marked lead over his classmates. One or two were more intelligent, others more conscientious, but Conrad's ability to organize his leisure and homework periods allowed him to make the most of his talents. When the others were lounging around the railway yard on their way home Conrad had already completed half his prep, allocating his time according to its various demands.

As soon as he finished he would go up to the attic playroom, now his workshop. Here, in the old wardrobes and trunks, he made his first experimental constructions: calibrated candles, crude sundials, sandglasses, an elaborate clockwork contraption developing about half a horsepower that drove its hands progressively faster and faster in an unintentional parody of Conrad's obsession.

His first serious clock was water-powered, a slowly leaking tank holding a wooden float that drove the hands as it sank downward. Simple but accurate, it satisfied Conrad for several months while he carried out his ever-widening search for a real clock mechanism. He soon discovered that although there were innumerable table clocks, gold pocket watches, and timepieces of every variety rusting in junk shops and in the back drawers of most homes, none of them contained their mechanisms. These, together with the hands, and sometimes the digits, had always been removed. His own attempts to build an escapement that would regulate the motion of the ordinary clockwork motor met with no success; everything he had heard about clock movements confirmed that they were precision instruments of exact design and construction. To satisfy his secret ambition—a portable timepiece, if possible an actual wristwatch—he would have to find one, somewhere, in working order.

Finally, from an unexpected source, a watch came to him. One afternoon in a cinema, an elderly man sitting next to Conrad had a sudden heart attack. Conrad and two members of the audience carried him out to the manager's office. Holding one of his arms, Conrad noticed in the dim aisle light a glint of metal inside the sleeve. Quickly he felt the wrist with his fingers, identified the unmistakable lens-shaped disk of a wristwatch.

As he carried it home its tick seemed as loud as a death knell. He clamped his hand around it, expecting everyone in the street to point accusingly at him, the Time Police to swoop down and seize him.

In the attic he took it out and examined it breathlessly, smothering it in a cushion whenever he heard his father shift about in the bedroom below. Later he realized that its noise was almost inaudible. The watch was of the same pattern as his mother's, though with a yellow and not a red face. The gold case was scratched and peeling, but the movement seemed to be in perfect condition. He prized off the rear plate, watched the frenzied flickering world of miniature cogs and wheels for hours, spellbound. Frightened of breaking the mainspring, he kept the watch only half wound, packed away carefully in cotton wool.

In taking the watch from its owner he had not, in fact, been motivated by theft; his first impulse had been to hide the watch before the doctor discovered it feeling for the man's pulse. But once the watch was in his possession he abandoned any thought of tracing the owner and returning it.

That others were still wearing watches hardly surprised him. The water clock had demonstrated that a calibrated timepiece added another dimension to life, organized its energies, gave the countless activities of everyday existence a yardstick of significance. Conrad spent hours in the attic gazing at the small yellow dial, watching its minute hand revolve slowly, its hour hand press on imperceptibly, a compass charting his passage through the future. Without it he felt rudderless, adrift in a gray purposeless limbo of timeless events. His father began to seem idle and stupid, sitting around vacantly with no idea when anything was going to happen.

Soon he was wearing the watch all day. He stitched together a slim cotton sleeve, fitted with a narrow flap below which he could see the face. He timed everything—the length of classes, football games, meal breaks, the hours of daylight and darkness, sleep and waking. He amused himself endlessly by baffling his friends with demonstrations of this private sixth sense, anticipating the frequency of their heartbeats, the hourly newscasts on the radio, boiling a series of identically consistent eggs without the aid of a timer.

Then he gave himself away.

Stacey, shrewder than any of the others, discovered that he was wearing a watch. Conrad had noticed that Stacey's English classes lasted exactly forty-five minutes; he let himself slide into the habit of tidying his desk a minute before Stacey's timer pipped up. Once or twice he noticed Stacey looking at him curiously, but he could not resist the temptation to impress Stacey by always being the first one to make for the door.

One day he had stacked his books and clipped away his pen when

Stacey pointedly asked him to read out a précis he had done. Conrad knew the timer would pip out in less than ten seconds, and decided to sit tight and wait for the usual stampede to save him the trouble.

Stacey stepped down from the dais, waiting patiently. One or two boys turned around and frowned at Conrad, who was counting away the closing seconds.

Then, amazed, he realized that the timer had failed to sound! Panicking, he first thought his watch had broken, just restrained himself in time from looking at it.

"In a hurry, Newman?" Stacey asked dryly. He sauntered down the aisle to Conrad. Baffled, his face reddening with embarrassment, Conrad fumbled open his exercise book, read out the précis. A few minutes later, without waiting for the timer, Stacey dismissed the class.

"Newman," he called out. "Here a moment."

He rummaged behind the rostrum as Conrad approached. "What happened then?" he asked. "Forget to wind up your watch this morning?"

Conrad said nothing. Stacey took out the timer, switched off the silencer and listened to the pip that buzzed out.

"Where did you get it from? Your parents? Don't worry, the Time Police were disbanded years ago."

Conrad examined Stacey's face. "It was my mother's," he lied. "I found it among her things." Stacey held out his hand and Conrad nervously unstrapped the watch and handed it to him.

Stacey slipped it half out of its sleeve, glanced briefly at the yellow face. "Your mother, you say? Hmm."

"Are you going to report me?" Conrad asked.

"What, and waste some overworked psychiatrist's time even further?"

"Isn't it breaking the law to wear a watch?"

"Well, you're not exactly the greatest living menace to public security." Stacey started for the door, gesturing Conrad with him. He handed the watch back. "Cancel whatever you're doing on Saturday afternoon. You and I are taking a trip."

"Where?" Conrad asked.

"Back into the past," Stacey said lightly. "To Chronopolis, the Time City."

Stacey had hired a car, a huge battered mastodon of chromium and fins. He waved jauntily to Conrad as he picked him up outside the Public Library.

"Climb into the turret." He pointed to the bulging briefcase Conrad slung onto the seat between them. "Have you had a look at those yet?"

Conrad nodded. As they moved off around the deserted square he opened the briefcase and pulled out a thick bundle of road maps. "I've just worked out that the city covers over five hundred square miles. I'd never realized it was so big. Where is everybody?"

Stacey laughed. They crossed the main street, cut down into a long tree-lined avenue of semidetached houses. Half of them were empty, windows wrecked and roofs sagging. Even the inhabited houses had a makeshift appearance, crude water towers on homemade scaffolding lashed to their chimneys, piles of logs dumped in overgrown front gardens.

"Thirty million people once lived in this city," Stacey remarked. "Now the population is little more than two, and still declining. Those of us left hang on in what were once the distal suburbs, so that the city today is effectively an enormous ring, five miles in width, encircling a vast dead center forty or fifty miles in diameter."

They wove in and out of various back roads, past a small factory still running although work was supposed to end at noon, finally picked up a long, straight boulevard that carried them steadily westward. Conrad traced their progress across successive maps. They were nearing the edge of the annulus Stacey had described. On the map it was overprinted in green so that the central interior appeared a flat, uncharted gray, a massive *terra incognita*.

They passed the last of the small shopping thoroughfares he remembered, a frontier post of mean terraced houses, dismal streets spanned by massive steel viaducts. Stacey pointed up at one as they drove below it. "Part of the elaborate railway system that once existed, an enormous network of stations and junctions that carried fifteen million people into a dozen great terminals every day."

For half an hour they drove on, Conrad hunched against the window, Stacey watching him in the driving mirror. Gradually, the landscape began to change. The houses were taller, with colored roofs, the sidewalks were railed off and fitted with pedestrian lights and turnstiles. They had entered the inner suburbs, completely deserted streets with multilevel supermarkets, towering cinemas, and department stores.

Chin in one hand, Conrad stared out silently. Lacking any means of transport he had never ventured into the uninhabited interior of the city, like the other children always headed in the opposite direction for the open country. Here the streets had died twenty or thirty years earlier; plate-glass shopfronts had slipped and smashed into the roadway, old neon signs, window frames and overhead wires hung down from every cornice, trailing a ragged webwork of disintegrating metal across the pavements. Stacey drove slowly, avoiding the occasional bus or truck abandoned in the middle of the road, its tires peeling off their rims.

Conrad craned up at the empty windows, into the narrow alleys and side streets, but nowhere felt any sensation of fear or anticipation. These streets were merely derelict, as unhaunted as a half-empty dustbin.

One suburban center gave way to another, to long intervening stretches of congested ribbon developments. Mile by mile, the architecture altered its character; buildings were larger, ten- or fifteen-story blocks, clad in facing materials of green and blue tiles, glass or copper sheathing. They were moving forward in time rather than, as Conrad had expected, back into the past of a fossil city.

Stacey worked the car through a nexus of side streets toward a six-lane expressway that rose on concrete buttresses above the rooftops. They found a side road that circled up to it, leveled out, and then picked up speed sharply, spinning along one of the clear center lanes.

Conrad craned forward. In the distance, two or three miles away, the rectilinear outlines of enormous apartment blocks reared thirty or forty stories high, hundreds of them lined shoulder to shoulder in apparently endless ranks, like giant dominoes.

"We're entering the central dormitories here," Stacey told him. On either side buildings overtopped the motorway, the congestion mounting so that some of them had been built right up against the concrete palisades.

In a few minutes they passed between the first of the apartment batteries, the thousands of identical living units with their slanting balconies shearing up into the sky, the glass in-falls of the aluminum curtain walling speckling in the sunlight. The smaller houses and shops of the outer suburbs had vanished. There was no room on the ground level. In the narrow intervals between the blocks there were small concrete gardens, shopping complexes, ramps banking down into huge underground car parks.

And on all sides there were the clocks. Conrad noticed them immediately, at every street corner, over every archway, three quarters of the way up the sides of buildings, covering every conceivable angle of approach. Most of them were too high off the ground to be reached by anything less than a fireman's ladder and still retained their hands. All registered the same time: 12:01.

Conrad looked at his wristwatch, noted that it was just 2:45.

"They were driven by a master clock," Stacey told him. "When that stopped, they all ceased at the same moment. One minute after midnight, thirty-seven years ago."

The afternoon had darkened, as the high cliffs cut off the sunlight, the sky a succession of narrow vertical intervals opening and closing around them. Down on the canyon floor it was dismal and oppressive, a wilderness of concrete and frosted glass. The expressway divided and pressed on westward. After a few more miles the apartment blocks gave way to the first office buildings in the central zone. These were even taller, sixty or seventy stories high, linked by spiraling ramps and causeways. The expressway was fifty feet off the ground yet the first floors of the office blocks were level with it, mounted on massive stilts that straddled the glass-enclosed entrance bays of lifts and escalators. The streets were wide but featureless. The sidewalks of parallel roadways merged below the buildings, forming a continuous concrete apron. Here and there were the remains of cigarette kiosks, rusting stairways up to restaurants and arcades built on platforms thirty feet in the air.

Conrad, however, was looking only at the clocks. Never had he visualized so many, in places so dense that they obscured each other. Their faces were multicolored: red, blue, yellow, green. Most of them carried four or five hands. Although the master hands had stopped at a minute past twelve, the subsidiary hands had halted at varying positions, apparently dictated by their color.

"What were the extra hands for?" he asked Stacey. "And the different colors?"

"Time zones. Depending on your professional category and the consumer-shifts allowed. Hold on, though, we're almost there."

They left the expressway and swung off down a ramp that fed them into the northeast corner of a wide open plaza, eight hundred yards long and half as wide, down the center of which had once been laid a continuous strip of lawn, now rank and overgrown. The plaza was empty, a sudden block of free space bounded by tall glass-faced cliffs that seemed to carry the sky.

Stacey parked, and he and Conrad climbed out and stretched themselves. Together they strolled across the wide pavement toward the strip of waist-high vegetation. Looking down the vistas receding from the plaza Conrad grasped fully for the first time the vast perspectives of the city, the massive geometric jungle of buildings.

Stacey put one foot up on the balustrade running around the lawn bed, pointed to the far end of the plaza, where Conrad saw a low-lying huddle of buildings of unusual architectural style, nineteenth-century perpendicular, stained by the atmosphere and badly holed by a number of explosions. Again, however, his attention was held by the clock face built into a tall concrete tower just behind the older buildings. This was the largest clock dial he had ever seen, at least a hundred feet across, huge black hands halted at a minute past twelve. The dial was white, the first they had seen, but on wide semicircular shoulders built below the main face were a dozen smaller faces, no more than twenty feet in diameter, running the full spectrum of colors. Each had five hands, the inferior three halted at random.

"Fifty years ago," Stacey explained, gesturing at the ruins below the tower, "that collection of ancient buildings was one of the world's greatest legislative assemblies." He gazed at it quietly for a few moments, then turned to Conrad. "Enjoy the ride?"

Conrad nodded fervently. "It's impressive, all right. The people who lived here must have been giants. What's really remarkable is that it looks as if they left only yesterday. Why don't we go back?"

"Well, apart from the fact that there aren't enough of us now, even if there were we couldn't control it. In its heyday this city was a fantastically complex social organism. The communications problems are difficult to imagine merely by looking at these blank facades. It's the tragedy of this city that there appeared to be only one way to solve them."

"Did they solve them?"

"Oh, yes, certainly. But they left themselves out of the equation.

Think of the problems, though. Transporting fifteen million office workers to and from the center every day; routing in an endless stream of cars, buses, trains, helicopters; linking every office, almost every desk, with a videophone, every apartment with television, radio, power, water; feeding and entertaining this enormous number of people; guarding them with ancillary services, police, fire squads, medical units—it all hinged on one factor."

Stacey threw a fist out at the great tower clock. "Time! Only by synchronizing every activity, every footstep forward or backward, every meal, bus halt, and telephone call, could the organism support itself. Like the cells in your body, which proliferate into mortal cancers if allowed to grow in freedom, every individual here had to serve the overriding needs of the city or fatal bottlenecks threw it into total chaos. You and I can turn on the tap any hour of the day or night, because we have our own private water cisterns, but what would happen here if everybody washed the breakfast dishes within the same ten minutes?"

They began to walk slowly down the plaza toward the clock tower. "Fifty years ago, when the population was only ten million, they could just provide for a potential peak capacity, but even then a strike in one essential service paralyzed most of the others; it took workers two or three hours to reach their offices, as long again to queue for lunch and get home. As the population climbed the first serious attempts were made to stagger hours; workers in certain areas started the day an hour earlier or later than those in others. Their railway passes and car number plates were colored accordingly, and if they tried to travel outside the permitted periods they were turned back. Soon the practice spread; you could only switch on your washing machine at a given hour, post a letter, or take a bath at a specific period."

"Sounds feasible," Conrad commented, his interest mounting. "But how did they enforce all this?"

"By a system of colored passes, colored money, an elaborate set of schedules published every day like TV or radio programs. And, of course, by all the thousands of clocks you can see around you here. The subsidiary hands marked out the number of minutes remaining in any activity period for people in the clock's color category."

Stacey stopped, pointed to a blue-faced clock mounted on one of the buildings overlooking the plaza. "Let's say, for example, that a lower-grade executive leaving his office at the allotted time, twelve o'clock, wants to have lunch, change a library book, buy some aspirin, and telephone his wife. Like all executives, his identity zone is blue. He takes out his schedule for the week, or looks down the blue-time columns in the newspaper, and notes that his lunch period for that day is twelve-fifteen to twelve-thirty. He has fifteen minutes to kill. Right, he then checks the library. Time code for today is given as three, that's the third hand on the clock. He looks at the nearest blue clock, the third hand says thirty-seven minutes past—he has twenty-three minutes, ample time, to reach the library. He starts down the street, but finds at the first intersection that the pedestrian lights are only shining red and green and he can't get across. The area's been temporarily zoned off for lower-grade women office workers—red, and manuals—green."

"What would happen if he ignored the lights?" Conrad asked.

"Nothing immediately, but all blue clocks in the zoned area would have returned to zero, and no shops or the library would serve him, unless he happened to have red or green currency and a forged set of library tickets. Anyway, the penalties were too high to make the risk worthwhile, and the whole system was evolved for his convenience, no one else's. So, unable to reach the library, he decides on the chemist. The time code for the chemist is five, the fifth, smallest hand. It reads fifty-four minutes past: he has six minutes to find a chemist and make his purchase. This done, he still has five minutes before lunch, decides to phone his wife. Checking the phone code he sees that no period has been provided for private calls that day—or the next. He'll just have to wait until he sees her that evening."

"What if he did phone?"

"He wouldn't be able to get his money in the coin box, and even then, his wife, assuming she is a secretary, would be in a red time zone and no longer in her office for that day—hence the prohibition on phone calls. It all meshed perfectly. Your time program told you when you could switch on your TV set and when to switch off. All electric appliances were fused, and if you strayed outside the programmed periods you'd have a hefty fine and repair bill to meet. The viewer's economic status obviously determined the choice of program, and vice versa, so there was no question of coercion. Each day's program listed your permitted activities: you could go to the hairdresser's, cinema, bank, cocktail bar, at stated times, and if you went then you were sure of being served quickly and efficiently."

They had almost reached the far end of the plaza. Facing them on its tower was the enormous clock face, dominating its constellation of twelve motionless attendants.

"There were a dozen socioeconomic categories: blue for executives, gold for professional classes, yellow for military and government officials—incidentally, it's odd your parents ever got hold of that wristwatch, none of your family ever worked for the government—green for manual workers and so on. Naturally, subtle subdivisions were possible. The lower-grade executive I mentioned left his office at twelve, but a senior executive, with exactly the same time codes, would leave at eleven forty-five and have an extra fifteen minutes, would find the streets clear before the lunch-hour rush of clerical workers."

Stacey pointed up at the tower: "This was the Big Clock, the master from which all others were regulated. Central Time Control, a sort of Ministry of Time, gradually took over the old parliamentary buildings as their legislative functions diminished. The programmers were, effectively, the city's absolute rulers."

As Stacey continued Conrad gazed up at the battery of timepieces, poised helplessly at 12:01. Somehow time itself seemed to have been suspended, around him the great office buildings hung in a neutral interval between yesterday and tomorrow. If one could only start the master clock the entire city would probably slide into gear and come to life, in an instant be repeopled with its dynamic jostling millions.

They began to walk back toward the car. Conrad looked over his shoulder at the clock face, its gigantic arms upright on the silent hour.

"Why did it stop?" he asked.

Stacey looked at him curiously. "Haven't I made it fairly plain?"

"What do you mean?" Conrad pulled his eyes off the scores of clocks lining the plaza, frowned at Stacey.

"Can you imagine what life was like for all but a few of the thirty million people here?"

Conrad shrugged. Blue and yellow clocks, he noticed, outnumbered all others; obviously the major governmental agencies had operated from the plaza area. "Highly organized but better than the sort of life we lead," he replied finally, more interested in the sights around him. "I'd rather have the telephone for one hour a day than not at all. Scarcities are always rationed, aren't they?"

"But this was a way of life in which everything was scarce. Don't you think there's a point beyond which human dignity is surrendered?"

Conrad snorted. "There seems to be plenty of dignity here. Look at these buildings, they'll stand for a thousand years. Try comparing them with my father. Anyway, think of the beauty of the system, engineered as precisely as a watch."

"That's all it was," Stacey commented dourly. "The old metaphor of the cog in the wheel was never more true than here. The full sum of your existence was printed for you in the newspaper columns, mailed to you once a month from the Ministry of Time."

Conrad was looking off in some other direction and Stacey pressed on in a slightly louder voice. "Eventually, of course, revolt came. It's interesting that in any industrial society there is usually one social revolution each century, and that successive revolutions receive their impetus from progressively higher social levels. In the eighteenth century it was the urban proletariat, in the nineteenth the artisan classes, in this revolt the white-collar office worker, living in his tiny so-called modern flat, supporting through credit pyramids an economic system that denied him all freedom of will or personality, chained him to a thousand clocks..." He broke off. "What's the matter?"

Conrad was staring down one of the side streets. He hesitated, then asked in a casual voice: "How were these clocks driven? Electrically?"

"Most of them. A few mechanically. Why?"

"I just wondered... how they kept them all going." He dawdled at Stacey's heels, checking the time from his wristwatch and glancing to his left. There were twenty or thirty clocks hanging from the buildings along the side street, indistinguishable from those he had seen all afternoon.

Except for the fact that one of them was working!

It was mounted in the center of a black glass portico over an entranceway fifty yards down the right-hand side, about eighteen inches in diameter, with a faded blue face. Unlike the others its hands registered 3:15, the correct time. Conrad had nearly mentioned this apparent coincidence to Stacey when he had suddenly seen the minute hand move on an interval. Without doubt someone had restarted the clock; even if it had been running off an inexhaustible battery, after thirty-seven years it could never have displayed such accuracy.

He hung behind Stacey, who was saying: "Every revolution has its symbol of oppression..."

The clock was almost out of view. Conrad was about to bend down and tie his shoelace when he saw the minute hand jerk downward, tilt slightly from the horizontal.

He followed Stacey toward the car, no longer bothering to listen to him. Ten yards from it he turned and broke away, ran swiftly across the roadway toward the nearest building.

"Newman!" he heard Stacey shout. "Come back!" He reached the pavement, ran between the great concrete pillars carrying the building. He paused for a moment behind an elevator shaft, saw Stacey climbing hurriedly into the car. The engine coughed and roared out, and Conrad sprinted on below the building into a rear alley that led back to the side street. Behind him he heard the car accelerating, a door slam as it picked up speed.

When he entered the side street the car came swinging off the plaza thirty yards behind him. Stacey swerved off the roadway, bumped up onto the pavement and gunned the car toward Conrad, throwing on the brakes in savage lurches, blasting the horn in an attempt to frighten him. Conrad sidestepped out of its way, almost falling over the bonnet, hurled himself up a narrow stairway leading to the first floor, and raced up the steps to a short landing that ended in tall glass doors. Through them he could see a wide balcony that ringed the building. A fire escape crisscrossed upward to the roof, giving way on the fifth floor to a cafeteria that spanned the street to the office building opposite.

Below he heard Stacey's feet running across the pavement. The glass doors were locked. He pulled a fire extinguisher from its bracket, tossed the heavy cylinder against the center of the plate. The glass slipped and crashed to the tiled floor in a sudden cascade, splashing down the steps. Conrad stepped through onto the balcony, began to climb the stairway. He had reached the third floor when he saw Stacey below, craning upward. Hand over hand, Conrad pulled himself up the next two flights, swung over a bolted metal turnstile into the open court of the cafeteria. Tables and chairs lay about on their sides, mixed up with the splintered remains of desks thrown down from the upper floors.

The doors into the covered restaurant were open, a large pool of water lying across the floor. Conrad splashed through it, went over to a window, and peered down past an old plastic plant into the street. Stacey seemed to have given up. Conrad crossed the rear of the restaurant, straddled the counter, and climbed through a window onto the open terrace running across the street. Beyond the rail he could see into the plaza, the double line of tire marks curving into the street below.

He had almost crossed to the opposite balcony when a shot roared out into the air. There was a sharp tinkle of falling glass and the sound of the explosion boomed away among the empty canyons.

For a few seconds he panicked. He flinched back from the exposed rail, his eardrums numbed, looking up at the great rectangular masses towering above him on either side, the endless tiers of windows like the faceted eyes of gigantic insects. So Stacey had been armed, almost certainly he was a member of the Time Police!

On his hands and knees Conrad scurried along the terrace, slid through the turnstiles and headed for a half-open window on the balcony.

Climbing through, he quickly lost himself in the building.

He finally took up a position in a corner office on the sixth floor, the cafeteria just below him to the right, the stairway up which he had escaped directly opposite.

All afternoon Stacey drove up and down the adjacent streets, sometimes freewheeling silently with the engine off, at others blazing through at speed. Twice he fired into the air, stopping the car afterward to call out, his words lost among the echoes rolling from one street to the next. Often he drove along the pavements, swerved about below the buildings as if he expected to flush Conrad from behind one of the banks of escalators.

Finally he appeared to drive off for good, and Conrad turned his attention to the clock in the portico. It had moved on to 6:45, almost exactly the time given by his own watch. Conrad reset this to what he assumed was the correct time, then sat back and waited for whoever had wound it to appear. Around him the thirty or forty other clocks he could see remained stationary at 12:01.

For five minutes he left his vigil, scooped some water off the pool in the cafeteria, suppressed his hunger, and shortly after midnight fell asleep in a corner behind the desk.

He woke the next morning to bright sunlight flooding into the office. Standing up, he dusted his clothes, turned around to find a small gray-haired man in a patched tweed suit surveying him with sharp eyes. Slung in the crook of his arm was a large black-barreled weapon, its hammers menacingly cocked.

The man put down a steel ruler he had evidently tapped against a cabinet, waited for Conrad to collect himself.

"What are you doing here?" he asked in a testy voice. Conrad noticed his pockets were bulging with angular objects that weighed down the sides of his jacket.

"I ... er ..." Conrad searched for something to say. Something about the old man convinced him that this was the clock winder. Suddenly he decided he had nothing to lose by being frank, and blurted out, "I saw the clock working. Down there on the left. I want to help wind them all up again."

The old man watched him shrewdly. He had an alert birdlike face, twin folds under his chin like a cockerel's.

"How do you propose to do that?" he asked.

Stuck by this one, Conrad said lamely, "I'd find a key somewhere."

The old man frowned. "One key? That wouldn't do much good." He seemed to be relaxing, and shook his pockets with a dull chink.

For a few moments neither of them said anything. Then Conrad had an inspiration, bared his wrist. "I have a watch," he said. "It's seven forty-five."

"Let me see." The old man stepped forward, briskly took Conrad's wrist and examined the yellow dial. "Movado Supermatic," he said to himself. "CTC issue." He stepped back, lowering the shotgun, and seemed to be summing Conrad up. "Good," he remarked at last. "Let's see. You probably need some breakfast."

They made their way out of the building, and began to walk quickly down the street.

"People sometimes come here," the old man said. "Sightseers and police. I watched your escape yesterday, you were lucky not to be killed." They swerved left and right across the empty streets, the old man darting between the stairways and buttresses. As he walked he held his hands stiffly to his sides, preventing his pockets from swinging. Glancing into them, Conrad saw that they were full of keys, large and rusty, of every design and combination.

"I presume that was your father's watch," the old man remarked.

"Grandfather's," Conrad corrected. He remembered Stacey's lecture, and added, "He was killed in the plaza."

The old man frowned sympathetically, for a moment held Conrad's arm.

They stopped below a building, indistinguishable from the others nearby, at one time a bank. The old man looked carefully around him, eyeing the high cliff walls on all sides, then led the way up a stationary escalator.

His quarters were on the second floor, beyond a maze of steel grilles and strong doors, a stove and a hammock slung in the center of a large workshop. Lying about on thirty or forty desks in what had once been a typing pool was an enormous collection of clocks, all being simultaneously repaired. Tall cabinets surrounded them, loaded with thousands of spare parts in neatly labeled correspondence trays—escapements, ratchets, cogwheels, barely recognizable through the rust.

The old man led Conrad over to a wall chart, pointed to the total listed against a column of dates. "Look at this. There are now two hundred seventy-eight running continuously. Believe me, I'm glad you've come. It takes me half my time to keep them wound."

He made breakfast for Conrad and told him something about himself. His name was Marshall. Once he had worked in Central Time Control as a programmer. He had survived the revolt and the Time Police, and ten years later returned to the city. At the beginning of each month he cycled out to one of the perimeter towns to cash his pension and collect supplies. The rest of the time he spent winding the steadily increasing number of functioning clocks and searching for others he could dismantle and repair.

"All these years in the rain hasn't done them any good," he explained, "and there's nothing I can do with the electrical ones."

Conrad wandered off among the desks, gingerly feeling the dismembered timepieces that lay around like the nerve cells of some vast unimaginable robot. He felt exhilarated and yet at the same time curiously calm, like a man who has staked his whole life on the turn of a wheel and is waiting for it to spin.

"How can you make sure that they all tell the same time?" he asked Marshall, wondering why the question seemed so important.

Marshall gestured irritably. "I can't, but what does it matter? There is no such thing as a perfectly accurate clock. The nearest you can get is one that has stopped. Although you never know when, it *is* absolutely accurate twice a day."

Conrad went over to the window, pointed to the great clock visible in an interval between the rooftops. "If only we could start that, and run all the others off it."

"Impossible. The entire mechanism was dynamited. Only the chimer is intact. Anyway, the wiring of the electrically driven clocks perished years ago. It would take an army of engineers to recondition them."

Conrad looked at the scoreboard again. He noticed that Marshall appeared to have lost his way through the years—the completion dates he listed were seven and a half years out. Idly, Conrad reflected on the significance of this irony, but decided not to mention it to Marshall.

For three months Conrad lived with the old man, following him on foot as he cycled about on his rounds, carrying the ladder and the satchel full of keys with which Marshall wound up the clocks, helping him to dismantle recoverable ones and carry them back to the workshop. All day, and often through half the night, they worked together, repairing the movements, restarting the clocks, and returning them to their original positions.

All the while, however, Conrad's mind was fixed upon the great clock in its tower dominating the plaza. Once a day he managed to sneak off and make his way into the ruined Time buildings. As Marshall had said, neither the clock nor its twelve satellites would ever run again. The movement house looked like the engine room of a sunken ship, a rusting tangle of rotors and drive wheels exploded into contorted shapes. Every week he would climb the long stairway up to the topmost platform two hundred feet above, look out through the bell tower at the flat roofs of the office blocks stretching away to the horizon. The hammers rested against their trips in long ranks just below him. Once he kicked one of the treble trips playfully, sent a dull chime out across the plaza.

The sound drove strange echoes into his mind.

Slowly he began to repair the chimer mechanism, rewiring the hammers and the pulley systems, trailing fresh wire up the great height of the tower, dismantling the winches in the movement room below and renovating their clutches.

He and Marshall never discussed their self-appointed tasks. Like animals obeying an instinct they worked tirelessly, barely aware of their own motives. When Conrad told him one day that he intended to leave and continue the work in another sector of the city, Marshall agreed immediately, gave Conrad as many tools as he could spare, and bade him good-bye.

Six months later, almost to the day, the sounds of the great clock chimed out across the rooftops of the city, marking the hours, the half hours, and the quarter hours, steadily tolling the progress of the day. Thirty miles away, in the towns forming the perimeter of the city, people stopped in the streets and in doorways, listening to the dim haunted echoes reflected through the long aisles of apartment blocks on the far horizon, involuntarily counting the slow final sequences that told the hour. Older people whispered to each other: "Four o'clock, or was it five? They have started the clock again. It seems strange after these years."

And all through the day they would pause as the quarter and half hours reached across the miles to them, a voice from their childhoods reminding them of the ordered world of the past. They began to reset their timers by the chimes, at night before they slept they would listen to the long count of midnight, wake to hear them again in the thin clear air of the morning.

Some went down to the police station and asked if they could have their watches and clocks back again.

After sentence, twenty years for the murder of Stacey, five for fourteen offenses under the Time Laws, to run concurrently, Newman was led away to the holding cells in the basement of the court. He had expected the sentence and made no comment when invited by the judge. After waiting trial for a year the afternoon in the courtroom was nothing more than a momentary intermission.

He made no attempt to defend himself against the charge of killing Stacey, partly to shield Marshall, who would be able to continue their work unmolested, and partly because he felt indirectly responsible for the policeman's death. Stacey's body, skull fractured by a twenty- or thirty-story fall, had been discovered in the back seat of his car in a basement garage not far from the plaza. Presumably Marshall had discovered him prowling around. Newman recalled that one day Marshall had disappeared altogether and had been curiously irritable for the rest of the week.

The last time he had seen the old man had been during the three days before the police arrived. Each morning as the chimes boomed out across the plaza Newman had seen his tiny figure striding briskly down the plaza toward him, waving up energetically at the tower, bareheaded and unafraid.

Now Newman was faced with the problem of how to devise a clock that would chart his way through the coming twenty years. His fears increased when he was taken the next day to the cellblock which housed the long-term prisoners—passing his cell on the way to meet the superintendent he noticed that his window looked out onto a small shaft. He pumped his brains desperately as he stood at attention during the superintendent's homilies, wondering how he could retain his sanity. Short of counting the seconds, each one of the 86,400 in every day, he saw no possible means of assessing the time.

Locked into his cell, he sat limply on the narrow bed, too tired to unpack his small bundle of possessions. A moment's inspection confirmed the uselessness of the shaft. A powerful light mounted halfway up masked the sunlight that slipped through a steel grille fifty feet above.

He stretched himself out on the bed and examined the ceiling. A lamp was recessed into its center, but a second, surprisingly, appeared to have been fitted to the cell. This was on the wall, a few feet above his head. He could see the curving bowl of the protective case, some ten inches in diameter.

He was wondering whether this could be a reading light when he realized that there was no switch.

Swinging around, he sat up and examined it, then leaped to his feet in astonishment.

It was a clock! He pressed his hands against the bowl, reading the circle of numerals, noting the inclination of the hands. Four fifty-three, near enough the present time. Not simply a clock, but one in running order! Was this some sort of macabre joke, or a misguided attempt at rehabilitation?

His pounding on the door brought a warder.

"What's all the noise about? The clock? What's the matter with it?" He unlocked the door and barged in, pushing Newman back.

"Nothing. But why is it here? They're against the law."

"Is that what's worrying you?" The warder shrugged. "Well, you see, the rules are a little different in here. You lads have got a lot of time ahead of you, it'd be cruel not to let you know where you stood. You know how to work it, do you? Good." He slammed the door and bolted it fast, then smiled at Newman through the cage. "It's a long day here, son, as you'll be finding out. That'll help you get through it."

Gleefully, Newman lay on the bed, his head on a rolled blanket at its foot, staring up at the clock. It appeared to be in perfect order, electrically driven, moving in rigid half-minute jerks. For an hour after the warder left he watched it without a break, then began to tidy up his cell, glancing over his shoulder every few minutes to reassure himself that it was still there, still running efficiently. The irony of the situation, the total inversion of justice, delighted him, even though it would cost him twenty years of his life.

He was still chuckling over the absurdity of it all two weeks later when for the first time he noticed the clock's insanely irritating tick...

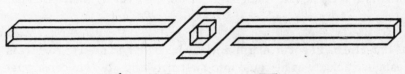

The Voices of Time

One

Later Powers often thought of Whitby, and the strange grooves the biologist had cut, apparently at random, all over the floor of the empty swimming pool. An inch deep and twenty feet long, interlocking to form an elaborate ideogram like a Chinese character, they had taken him all summer to complete, and he had obviously thought about little else, working away tirelessly through the long desert afternoons. Powers had watched him from his office window at the far end of the neurology wing, carefully marking out his pegs and string, carrying away the cement chips in a small canvas bucket. After Whitby's suicide no one had bothered about the grooves, but Powers often borrowed the supervisor's key and let himself into the disused pool, and would look down at the labyrinth of moldering gullies, half-filled with water leaking in from the chlorinator, an enigma now past any solution.

Initially, however, Powers was too preoccupied with completing his work at the Clinic and planning his own final withdrawal. After the first frantic weeks of panic he had managed to accept an uneasy compromise that allowed him to view his predicament with the detached fatalism he had previously reserved for his patients. Fortunately he was moving down the physical and mental gradients

67

simultaneously—lethargy and inertia blunted his anxieties, a slackening metabolism made it necessary to concentrate to produce a connected thought-train. In fact, the lengthening intervals of dreamless sleep were almost restful. He found himself beginning to look forward to them, and made no effort to wake earlier than essential.

At first he had kept an alarm clock by his bed, and tried to compress as much activity as he could into the narrowing hours of consciousness, sorting out his library, driving over to Whitby's laboratory every morning to examine the latest batch of X-ray plates, every minute and hour rationed like the last drops of water in a canteen.

Anderson, fortunately, had unwittingly made him realize the pointlessness of this course.

After Powers had resigned from the Clinic he still continued to drive in once a week for his check-up, now little more than a formality. On what turned out to be the last occasion Anderson had perfunctorily taken his blood count, noting Powers's slacker facial muscles, fading pupil reflexes, the unshaven cheeks.

He smiled sympathetically at Powers across the desk, wondering what to say to him. Once he had put on a show of encouragement with the more intelligent patients, even tried to provide some sort of explanation. But Powers was too difficult to reach—neurosurgeon extraordinary, a man always out on the periphery, only at ease working with unfamiliar materials. To himself he thought: *I'm sorry, Robert. What can I say—"Even the sun is growing cooler—"*? He watched Powers drum his fingers restlessly on the enamel desk top, his eyes glancing at the spinal level charts hung around the office. Despite his unkempt appearance—he had been wearing the same unironed shirt and dirty white sneakers a week ago—Powers looked composed and self-possessed, like a Conrad beachcomber more or less reconciled to his own weaknesses.

"What are you doing with yourself, Robert?" he asked. "Are you still going over to Whitby's lab?"

"As much as I can. It takes me half an hour to cross the lake, and I keep on sleeping through the alarm clock. I may leave my place and move in there permanently."

Anderson frowned. "Is there much point? As far as I could make out Whitby's work was pretty speculative—" He broke off, realizing the implied criticism of Powers's own disastrous work at the Clinic, but Powers seemed to ignore this, was examining the pattern of shadows on the ceiling. "Anyway, wouldn't it be better to stay where you are, among your own things, read through Toynbee and Spengler again?"

Powers laughed shortly. "That's the last thing I want to do. I want to *forget* Toynbee and Spengler, not try to remember them. In fact, Paul, I'd like to forget everything. I don't know whether I've got enough time, though. How much can you forget in three months?"

"Everything, I suppose, if you want to. But don't try to race the clock."

Powers nodded quietly, repeating this last remark to himself. Racing the clock was exactly what he had been doing. As he stood up and said good-bye to Anderson he suddenly decided to throw away his alarm clock, escape from his futile obsession with time. To remind himself he unfastened his wristwatch and scrambled the setting, then slipped it into his pocket. Making his way out to the car park he reflected on the freedom this simple act gave him. He would explore the lateral byways now, the side doors, as it were, in the corridors of time. Three months could be an eternity.

He picked his car out of the line and strolled over to it, shielding his eyes from the heavy sunlight beating down across the parabolic sweep of the lecture theater roof. He was about to climb in when he saw that someone had traced with a finger across the dust caked over the windshield:

96,688,365,498,721

Looking over his shoulder, he recognized the white Packard parked next to him, peered inside and saw a lean-faced young man with blond sun-bleached hair and a high cerebrotonic forehead watching him behind dark glasses. Sitting beside him at the wheel was a raven-haired girl whom he had often seen around the psychology department. She had intelligent but somehow rather oblique eyes, and Powers remembered that the younger doctors called her "the girl from Mars."

"Hello, Kaldren," Powers said to the young man. "Still following me around?"

Kaldren nodded. "Most of the time, Doctor." He sized Powers up shrewdly. "We haven't seen very much of you recently, as a matter of fact. Anderson said you'd resigned, and we noticed your laboratory was closed."

Powers shrugged. "I felt I needed a rest. As you'll understand, there's a good deal that needs rethinking."

Kaldren frowned half-mockingly. "Sorry to hear that, Doctor. But don't let these temporary setbacks depress you." He noticed the girl watching Powers with interest. "Coma's a fan of yours. I gave her your papers from *American Journal of Psychiatry*, and she's read through the whole file."

The girl smiled pleasantly at Powers, for a moment dispelling the hostility between the two men. When Powers nodded to her she leaned across Kaldren and said: "Actually I've just finished Noguchi's autobiography—the great Japanese doctor who discovered the spirochete. Somehow you remind me of him—there's so much of yourself in all the patients you worked on."

Powers smiled wanly at her, then his eyes turned and locked involuntarily on Kaldren's. They stared at each other somberly for a moment, and a small tic in Kaldren's right cheek began to flicker irritatingly. He flexed his facial muscles, after a few seconds mastered it with an effort, obviously annoyed that Powers should have witnessed this brief embarrassment.

"How did the clinic go today?" Powers asked. "Have you had any more... headaches?"

Kaldren's mouth snapped shut; he looked suddenly irritable. "Whose care am I in, Doctor? Yours or Anderson's? Is that the sort of question you should be asking now?"

Powers gestured deprecatingly. "Perhaps not." He cleared his throat; the heat was ebbing the blood from his head and he felt tired and eager to get away from them. He turned toward his car, then realized that Kaldren would probably follow, either try to crowd him into the ditch or block the road and make Powers sit in his dust all the way back to the lake. Kaldren was capable of any madness.

"Well, I've got to go and collect something," he said, adding in a firmer voice, "Get in touch with me, though, if you can't reach Anderson."

He waved and walked off behind the line of cars. Reflected in the windows he could see Kaldren looking back and watching him closely.

He entered the neurology wing and paused thankfully in the cool foyer, nodding to the two nurses and the armed guard at the reception desk. For some reason the terminals sleeping in the adjacent dormitory block attracted hordes of would-be sightseers, most of them cranks with some magical antinarcoma remedy, or merely the idly curious, but a good number of quite normal people, many of whom had traveled thousands of miles, impelled toward the clinic by some strange instinct, like animals migrating to a preview of their racial graveyards.

He walked along the corridor to the supervisor's office overlooking the recreation deck, borrowed the key and made his way out through the tennis courts and calisthenics rigs to the enclosed swimming pool at the far end. It had been disused for months, and only Powers's visits kept the lock free. Stepping through, he closed it behind him and walked past the peeling wooden stands to the deep end.

Putting a foot up on the diving board, he looked down at Whitby's ideogram. Damp leaves and bits of paper obscured it, but the outlines were just distinguishable. It covered almost the entire floor of the pool and at first glance appeared to represent a huge solar disk, with four radiating diamond-shaped arms, a crude Jungian mandala.

Wondering what had prompted Whitby to carve the device before his death, Powers noticed something moving through the debris in the center of the disk. A black, horny-shelled animal about a foot long was nosing about in the slush, heaving itself on tired legs. Its shell was articulated, and vaguely resembled an armadillo's. Reaching the edge of the disk, it stopped and hesitated, then slowly backed away into the center again, apparently unwilling or unable to cross the narrow groove.

Powers looked around, then stepped into one of the changing booths and pulled a small wooden clothes locker off its rusty wall bracket. Carrying it under one arm, he climbed down the chromium ladder into the pool and walked carefully across the slithery floor toward the animal. As he approached, it sidled away from him, but he trapped it easily, using the lid to lever it into the box.

The animal was heavy, at least the weight of a brick. Powers tapped its massive olive-black carapace with his knuckle, noting the triangular warty head jutting out below its rim like a turtle's, the thickened pads beneath the first digits of the pentadactyl forelimbs.

He watched the three-lidded eyes blinking at him anxiously from the bottom of the box.

"Expecting some really hot weather?" he murmured. "That lead umbrella you're carrying around should keep you cool."

He closed the lid, climbed out of the pool and made his way back to the supervisor's office, then carried the box out to his car.

> ... Kaldren continues to reproach me [*Powers wrote in his diary*]. For some reason he seems unwilling to accept his isolation, is elaborating a series of private rituals to replace the missing hours of sleep. Perhaps I should tell him of my own approaching zero, but he'd probably regard this as the final unbearable insult, that I should have in excess what he so desperately yearns for. God knows what might happen. Fortunately the nightmarish visions appear to have receded for the time being...

Pushing the diary away, Powers leaned forward across the desk and stared out through the window at the white floor of the lake bed stretching toward the hills along the horizon. Three miles away, on the far shore, he could see the circular bowl of the radio telescope revolving slowly in the clear afternoon air, as Kaldren tirelessly trapped the sky, sluicing in millions of cubic parsecs of sterile ether, like the nomads who trapped the sea along the shores of the Persian Gulf.

Behind him the air conditioner murmured quietly, cooling the pale blue walls half-hidden in the dim light. Outside the air was bright and oppressive, the heat was rippling up from the clumps of gold-tinted cacti below the Clinic, blurring the sharp terraces of the twenty-story neurology block. There, in the silent dormitories behind the sealed shutters, the terminals slept their long dreamless sleep. There were now over five hundred of them in the Clinic, the vanguard of a vast somnambulist army massing for its last march. Only five years had elapsed since the first narcoma syndrome had been recognized, but already huge government hospitals in the east were being readied for intakes in the thousands, as more and more cases came to light.

Powers felt suddenly tired, and glanced at his wrist, wondering how long he had till eight o'clock, his bedtime for the next week or so. Already he missed the dusk, and he knew he would soon wake to his last dawn.

His watch was in his hip pocket. He remembered his decision not to use his timepieces, and sat back and stared at the bookshelves beside the desk. There were rows of green-covered AEC publications he had removed from Whitby's library, papers in which the biologist described his work out in the Pacific after the H-tests. Many of them Powers knew almost by heart; he had read them a hundred times in an effort to grasp Whitby's last conclusions. Toynbee would certainly be easier to forget.

His eyes dimmed momentarily, as the tall black wall in the rear of his mind cast its great shadow over his brain. He reached for the diary, thinking of the girl in Kaldren's car—Coma, he had called her, another of his insane jokes—and her reference to Noguchi. Actually the comparison should have been made with Whitby, not himself; the monsters in the lab were nothing more than fragmented mirrors of Whitby's mind, like the grotesque radio-shielded frog he had found that morning in the swimming pool.

Thinking of the girl Coma, and the heartening smile she had given him, he wrote:

> Woke 6:33 A.M. Last session with Anderson. He made it plain he's seen enough of me, and from now on I'm better alone. To sleep 8:00? (These countdowns terrify me.)

He paused, then added:

> Good-bye, Eniwetok.

Two

He saw the girl again the next day at Whitby's laboratory. He had driven over after breakfast with the new specimen, eager to get it into a vivarium before it died. The only previous armored mutant he had come across had nearly broken his neck. Speeding along the lake road a month or so earlier he had struck it with the offside front wheel, expecting the small creature to flatten instantly. Instead its hard lead-packed shell had remained rigid, even though the organism within it had been pulped, and the impact had flung the car heavily into the ditch. He had gone back for the shell, later weighed it at the laboratory, found it contained over six hundred grams of lead.

Quite a number of plants and animals were building up heavy metals as radiological shields. In the hills behind the beach house a couple of old-time prospectors were renovating the derelict gold-panning equipment abandoned over eighty years ago. They had noticed the bright yellow tints of the cacti, run an analysis, and found that the plants were assimilating gold in extractable quantities, although the soil concentrations were unworkable. Oak Ridge was at last paying a dividend!

Waking that morning just after 6:45—ten minutes later than the previous day (he had switched on the radio, heard one of the regular morning programs as he climbed out of bed)—he had eaten a light unwanted breakfast, then spent an hour packing away some of the books in his library, crating them up and taping on address labels to his brother.

He reached Whitby's laboratory half an hour later. This was housed in a hundred-foot-wide geodesic dome built beside his chalet on the west shore of the lake about a mile from Kaldren's summerhouse. The chalet had been closed after Whitby's suicide, and many of the experimental plants and animals had died before Powers had managed to receive permission to use the laboratory.

As he turned into the driveway he saw the girl standing on the apex of the yellow-ribbed dome, her slim figure silhouetted against the sky. She waved to him, then began to step down across the glass polyhedrons and jumped nimbly into the driveway beside the car.

"Hello," she said, giving him a welcoming smile. "I came over to see your zoo. Kaldren said you wouldn't let me in if he came so I made him stay behind."

She waited for Powers to say something while he searched for his keys, then volunteered, "If you like, I can wash your shirt."

Powers grinned at her, peered down ruefully at his dust-stained sleeves. "Not a bad idea. I thought I was beginning to look a little uncared-for." He unlocked the door, took Coma's arm. "I don't know why Kaldren told you that—he's welcome here any time he likes."

"What have you got in there?" Coma asked, pointing at the

wooden box he was carrying as they walked between the gear-laden benches.

"A distant cousin of ours whom I found. Interesting little chap. I'll introduce you in a moment."

Sliding partitions divided the dome into four chambers. Two of them were storerooms, filled with spare tanks, apparatus, cartons of animal food and test rigs. They crossed the third section, almost filled by a powerful X-ray projector, a giant 250-amp G.E. Maxitron, angled onto a revolving table, concrete shielding blocks lying around ready for use like huge building bricks.

The fourth chamber contained Powers's zoo, the vivaria jammed together along the benches and in the sinks, with big colored cardboard charts and memos pinned onto the ventilator hoods above them. A tangle of rubber tubing and power leads trailed across the floor from the tanks. As they walked past the lines of tanks dim forms shifted behind the frosted glass, and at the far end of the aisle there was a sudden scurrying in a large-scale cage by Powers's desk.

Putting the box down on his chair, he picked a packet of peanuts off the desk and went over to the cage. A small black-haired chimpanzee wearing a dented jet pilot's helmet swarmed deftly up the bars to him, chirped happily, and then jumped down to a miniature control panel against the rear wall of the cage. Rapidly it flicked a series of buttons and toggles, and a succession of colored lights lit up like a jukebox and jangled out a two-second blast of music.

"Good boy," Powers said encouragingly, patting the chimp's back and shoveling the peanuts into its hands. "You're getting much too clever for that one, aren't you?"

The chimp tossed the peanuts into the back of its throat with the smooth easy motions of a conjurer, jabbering at Powers in a singsong voice.

Coma laughed and took some of the nuts from Powers. "He's sweet. I think he's talking to you."

Powers nodded. "Quite right, he is. Actually he's got a two-hundred-word vocabulary, but his voice box scrambles it all up." He opened a small refrigerator by the desk, took out half a packet of sliced bread and passed a couple of pieces to the chimp. It picked an electric toaster off the floor and placed it in the middle of a low wobbling table in the center of the cage, whipped the pieces into the slots. Powers pressed a tab on the switchboard beside the cage and the toaster began to crackle softly.

"He's one of the brightest we've had here, about as intelligent as a five-year-old child, though much more self-sufficient in a lot of ways." The two pieces of toast jumped out of their slots and the chimp caught them neatly, nonchalantly patting its helmet each time, then ambled off into a small ramshackle kennel and relaxed back with one arm out of a window, sliding the toast into its mouth.

"He built that house himself," Powers went on, switching off the toaster. "Not a bad effort, really." He pointed to a yellow polythene bucket by the front door of the kennel, from which a battered looking geranium protruded. "Tends that plant, cleans up the cage, pours out an endless stream of wisecracks. Pleasant fellow all around."

Coma was smiling broadly to herself. "Why the space helmet, though?"

Powers hesitated. "Oh, it—er—it's for his own protection. Sometimes he gets rather bad headaches. His predecessors all—" He broke off and turned away. "Let's have a look at some of the other inmates."

He moved down the line of tanks, beckoning Coma with him. "We'll start at the beginning." He lifted the glass lid off one of the tanks, and Coma peered down into a shallow bath of water, where a small round organism with slender tendrils was nestling in a rockery of shells and pebbles.

"Sea anemone. Or was. Simple coelenterate with an open-ended body cavity." He pointed down to a thickened ridge of tissue around the base. "It's sealed up the cavity, converted the channel into a rudimentary notochord. It's the first plant ever to develop a nervous system. Later the tendrils will knot themselves into a ganglion, but already they're sensitive to color. Look." He borrowed the violet handkerchief in Coma's breast pocket and spread it across the tank. The tendrils flexed and stiffened and then began to weave slowly, as if they were trying to focus.

"The strange thing is that they're completely insensitive to white light. Normally the tendrils register shifting pressure gradients, like the tympanic diaphragms in your ears. Now it's almost as if they can *hear* primary colors. That suggests it's readapting itself for a nonaquatic existence in a static world of violent color contrasts."

Coma shook her head, puzzled. "Why, though?"

"Hold on a moment. Let me put you in the picture first." They moved along the bench to a series of drum-shaped cages made of wire mosquito netting. Above the first was a large white cardboard screen bearing a blown-up microphoto of a tall pagodalike chain, topped by the legend: DROSOPHILA: 15 ROENTGENS/MIN.

Powers tapped a small perspex window in the drum. "Fruit fly. Its huge chromosomes make it a useful test vehicle." He bent down, pointed to a gray V-shaped honeycomb suspended from the roof. A few flies emerged from entrances, moving about busily. "Usually it's solitary, a nomadic scavenger. Now it forms itself into well-knit social groups, has begun to secrete a thin sweet lymph something like honey."

"What's this?" Coma asked, touching the screen.

"Diagram of a key gene in the operation." He traced a spray of arrows leading from a link in the chain. The arrows were labeled: LYMPH GLAND and subdivided SPHINCTER MUSCLES, EPITHELIUM, TEMPLATES.

"It's rather like the perforated sheet music of a player piano," Powers commented, "or a computer punch tape. Knock out one link with an X-ray beam, lose a characteristic, change the score."

Coma was peering through the window of the next cage and pulling an unpleasant face. Over her shoulder Powers saw she was watching an enormous spiderlike insect, as big as a hand, its dark hairy legs as thick as fingers. The compound eyes had been built up so that they resembled giant rubies.

"He looks unfriendly," she said. "What's that sort of rope ladder he's spinning?" As she moved a finger to her mouth the spider came to life, retreated into the cage, and began spewing out a complex skein of interlinked gray thread which it slung in long loops from the roof of the cage.

"A web," Powers told her. "Except that it consists of nervous tissue. The ladders form an external neural plexus; an inflatable brain as it were, that he can pump up to whatever size the situation calls for. A sensible arrangement, really, far better than our own."

Coma backed away. "Gruesome. I wouldn't like to go into his parlor."

"Oh, he's not as frightening as he looks. Those huge eyes staring at you are blind. Or, rather, their optical sensitivity has shifted down the band; the retinas will only register gamma radiation. Your wristwatch has luminous hands. When you moved it across the window he started thinking. World War IV should really bring him into his element."

They strolled back to Powers's desk. He put a coffee pan over a Bunsen and pushed a chair across to Coma. Then he opened the box, lifted out the armored frog, and put it down on a sheet of blotting paper.

"Recognize him? Your old childhood friend, the common frog. He's built himself quite a solid little air raid shelter." He carried the animal across to a sink, turned on the tap, and let the water play softly over its shell. Wiping his hands on his shirt, he came back to the desk.

Coma brushed her long hair off her forehead, watched him curiously.

"Well, what's the secret?"

Powers lit a cigarette. "There's no secret. Teratologists have been breeding monsters for years. Have you ever heard of the 'silent pair'?"

She shook her head.

Powers stared moodily at the cigarette for a moment, riding the kick the first one of the day always gave him. "The so-called 'silent pair' is one of modern genetics' oldest problems, the apparently baffling mystery of the two inactive genes which occur in a small percentage of all living organisms, and appear to have no intelligible role in their structure or development. For a long while now biologists have been trying to activate them, but the difficulty is partly in identifying the silent genes in the fertilized germ cells of parents known to contain them, and partly in focusing a narrow enough X-ray beam which will do no damage to the remainder of the chromosome. However, after about ten years' work Dr. Whitby successfully developed a whole-body irradiation technique based on his observation of radiobiological damage at Eniwetok."

Powers paused for a moment. "He had noticed that there appeared to be more biological damage after the tests—that is, a greater transport of energy—than could be accounted for by direct radiation. What was happening was that the protein lattices in the genes were building up energy in the way that any vibrating membrane accumulates energy when it resonates—you remember the analogy of the bridge collapsing under the soldiers marching in step—and it occurred to him that if he could first identify the critical resonance frequency of the lattices in any particular silent gene he could then radiate the entire living organism, and not simply its germ cells, with a low field that would act selectively on the silent gene and cause no damage to the remainder of the chromosomes, whose lattices would resonate critically only at other specific frequencies."

Powers gestured around the laboratory with his cigarette. "You see some of the fruits of this 'resonance transfer' technique around you."

Coma nodded. "They've had their silent genes activated?"

"Yes, all of them. These are only a few of the thousands of specimens who have passed through here, and as you've seen, the results are pretty dramatic."

He reached up and pulled across a section of the sun curtain. They were sitting just under the lip of the dome, and the mounting sunlight had begun to irritate him.

In the comparative darkness Coma noticed a stroboscope winking slowly in one of the tanks at the end of the bench behind her. She stood up and went over to it, examining a tall sunflower with a thickened stem and greatly enlarged receptacle. Packed around the flower, so that only its head protruded, was a chimney of gray-white stones, neatly cemented together and labeled:

CRETACEOUS CHALK: 60,000,000 YEARS

Beside it on the bench were three other chimneys, these labeled DEVONIAN SANDSTONE: 290,000,000 YEARS, ASPHALT: 20 YEARS, POLYVINYLCHLORIDE: 6 MONTHS.

"Can you see those moist white disks on the sepals?" Powers pointed out. "In some way they regulate the plant's metabolism. It literally *sees* time. The older the surrounding environment, the more sluggish its metabolism. With the asphalt chimney it will complete its annual cycle in a week, with the PVC one in a couple of hours."

"Sees time," Coma repeated, wonderingly. She looked up at Powers, chewing her lower lip reflectively. "It's fantastic. Are these the creatures of the future, Doctor?"

"I don't know," Powers admitted. "But if they are their world must be a monstrous and surrealist one."

Three

He went back to the desk, pulled two cups from a drawer, and poured out the coffee, switching off the Bunsen. "Some people have speculated that organisms possessing the silent pair of genes are the forerunners of a massive move up the evolutionary slope, that the silent genes are a sort of code, a divine message that we inferior organisms are carrying for our more highly developed descendants. It may well be true—perhaps we've broken the code too soon."

"Why do you say that?"

"Well, as Whitby's death indicates, the experiments in this laboratory have all come to a rather unhappy conclusion. Without exception the organisms we've irradiated have entered a final phase of totally disorganized growth, producing dozens of specialized sensory organs whose function we can't even guess. The results are catastrophic—the anemone will literally explode, the Drosophila cannibalize themselves, and so on. Whether the future implicit in these plants and animals is ever intended to take place, or whether we're merely extrapolating—I don't know. Sometimes I think, though, that the new sensory organs developed are parodies of their real intentions. The specimens you've seen today are all in an early stage of their secondary growth cycles. Later on they begin to look distinctly bizarre."

Coma nodded. "A zoo isn't complete without its keeper," she commented. "What about Man?"

Powers shrugged. "About one in every hundred thousand—the usual average—contains the silent pair. You might have them—or I. No one has volunteered yet to undergo whole-body irradiation. Apart from the fact that it would be classified as suicide, if the experiments here are any guide the experience would be savage and violent."

He sipped at the thin coffee, feeling tired and somehow bored. Recapitulating the laboratory's work had exhausted him.

The girl leaned forward. "You look awfully pale," she said solicitously. "Don't you sleep well?"

Powers managed a brief smile. "Too well," he admitted. "It's no longer a problem with me."

"I wish I could say that about Kaldren. I don't think he sleeps anywhere near enough. I hear him pacing around all night." She added: "Still, I suppose it's better than being a terminal. Tell me, Doctor, wouldn't it be worth trying this radiation technique on the sleepers at the Clinic? It might wake them up before the end. A few of them must possess the silent genes."

"They *all* do," Powers told her. "The two phenomena are very closely linked, as a matter of fact." He stopped, fatigue dulling his brain, and wondered whether to ask the girl to leave. Then he climbed off the desk and reached behind it, picked up a tape recorder.

Switching it on, he zeroed the tape and adjusted the speaker volume.

"Whitby and I often talked this over. Toward the end I took it all down. He was a great biologist, so let's hear it in his own words. It's absolutely the heart of the matter."

He flipped the tape on, adding: "I've played it over to myself a thousand times, so I'm afraid the quality is poor."

An older man's voice, sharp and slightly irritable, sounded out above a low buzz of distortion, but Coma could hear it clearly.

WHITBY: ... for heaven's sake, Robert, look at those FAO statistics. Despite an annual increase of five percent in acreage sown over the past fifteen years, world wheat crops have continued to decline by a factor of about two percent. The same story repeats itself ad nauseam. Cereals and root crops, dairy yields, ruminant fertility—are all down. Couple these with a mass of parallel symptoms, anything you care to pick from altered migratory routes to longer hibernation periods, and the overall pattern is incontrovertible.

POWERS: Population figures for Europe and North America show no decline, though.

WHITBY: Of course not, as I keep pointing out. It will take a century for such a fractional drop in fertility to have any effect in areas where extensive birth control provides an artificial reservoir. One must look at the countries of the Far East, and particularly at those where infant mortality has remained at a steady level. The population of Sumatra, for example, has declined by over fifteen percent in the last twenty years. A fabulous decline! Do you realize that only two or three decades ago the neo-Malthusians were talking

81

about a "world population explosion?" In fact, it's an implosion. Another factor is—

Here the tape had been cut and edited, and Whitby's voice, less querulous this time, picked up again.

... just as a matter of interest, tell me something: how long do you sleep each night?

POWERS: I don't know exactly; about eight hours, I suppose.

WHITBY: The proverbial eight hours. Ask anyone and they say automatically "eight hours." As a matter of fact you sleep about ten and a half hours, like the majority of people. I've timed you on a number of occasions. I myself sleep eleven. Yet thirty years ago people did indeed sleep eight hours, and a century before that they slept six or seven. In Vasari's *Lives* one reads of Michelangelo sleeping for only four or five hours, painting all day at the age of eighty and then working through the night over his anatomy table with a candle strapped to his forehead. Now he's regarded as a prodigy, but it was unremarkable then. How do you think the ancients, from Plato to Shakespeare, Aristotle to Aquinas, were able to cram so much work into their lives? Simply because they had an extra six or seven hours every day. Of course, a second disadvantage under which we labor is a lowered basal metabolic rate—another factor no one will explain.

POWERS: I suppose you could take the view that the lengthened sleep interval is a compensation device, a sort of mass neurotic attempt to escape from the terrifying pressures of urban life in the late twentieth century.

WHITBY: You could, but you'd be wrong. It's simply a matter of biochemistry. The ribonucleic acid templates which unravel the protein chains in all living organisms are wearing out, the dies enscribing the protoplasmic signature have become blunted. After all, they've been running now for over a thousand million years. It's time to retool. Just as an individual organism's life span is finite, or the life of a yeast colony or a given species, so the life of an entire biological kingdom is of fixed duration. It's always been assumed that the evolutionary slope reaches forever upward, but in fact the peak has already been reached, and the pathway now leads downward to the common biological grave. It's a despairing and at present unacceptable vision of the future, but it's the only one. Five thousand centuries from now our descendants, instead of being multibrained starmen, will probably be naked prognathous idiots with hair on their foreheads, grunting their way through the remains of this Clinic like neolithic men caught in a macabre inversion of time. Believe me, I pity them, as I pity myself. My total failure, my absolute lack of any moral or biological right to existence, is implicit in every cell of my body . . .

The tape ended, the spool ran free and stopped. Powers closed the machine, then massaged his face. Coma sat quietly, watching him and listening to the chimp playing with a box of puzzle dice.

"As far as Whitby could tell," Powers said, "the silent genes represent a last desperate effort of the biological kingdom to keep its head above the rising waters. Its total life period is determined by the amount of radiation emitted by the sun, and once this reaches a certain point the sure-death line has been passed and extinction is inevitable. To compensate for this, alarms have been built in which alter the form of the organism and adapt it to living in a hotter radiological climate. Soft-skinned organisms develop hard shells, these contain heavy metals as radiation screens. New organs of perception are developed too. According to Whitby, though, it's all wasted effort in the long run—but sometimes I wonder."

He smiled at Coma and shrugged. "Well, let's talk about something else. How long have you known Kaldren?"

"About three weeks. Feels like ten thousand years."

"How do you find him now? We've been rather out of touch lately."

Coma grinned. "I don't seem to see very much of him either. He makes me sleep all the time. Kaldren has many strange talents, but he lives just for himself. You mean a lot to him, Doctor. In fact, you're my one serious rival."

"I thought he couldn't stand the sight of me."

"Oh, that's nothing but a surface symptom. He really thinks of you continuously. That's why we spend all our time following you around." She eyed Powers shrewdly. "I think he feels guilty about something."

"Guilty?" Powers exclaimed. *"He* does? I thought I was supposed to be the guilty one."

"Why?" she pressed. She hesitated, then said, "You carried out some experimental surgical technique on him, didn't you?"

"Yes," Powers admitted. "It wasn't altogether a success, like so much of what I seem to be involved with. If Kaldren feels guilty, I suppose it's because he feels he must take some of the responsibility."

He looked down at the girl, her intelligent eyes watching him closely. "For one or two reasons it may be necessary for you to know. You said Kaldren paced around all night and didn't get enough sleep. Actually he doesn't get any sleep at all."

The girl nodded. "You..." She made a snapping gesture with her fingers.

"... narcotomized him," Powers completed. "Surgically speaking, it was a great success. One might well share a Nobel for it. Normally the hypothalamus regulates the period of sleep, raising the threshold of consciousness in order to relax the venous capillaries in the brain and drain them of accumulating toxins. However, by sealing off some of the control loops the subject is unable to receive the sleep cue, and the capillaries drain while he remains conscious. All he feels is a temporary lethargy, but this passes within three or four hours. Physically speaking, Kaldren has had another twenty years added to his life. But the psyche seems to need sleep for its own private reasons, and consequently Kaldren has periodic storms that tear him apart. The whole thing was a tragic blunder."

Coma frowned pensively. "I guessed as much. Your papers in the neurosurgery journals referred to the patient as K. A touch of pure Kafka that came all too true."

"I may leave here for good, Coma," Powers said. "Make sure that Kaldren goes to his clinics. Some of the deep scar tissue will need to be cleaned away."

"I'll try. Sometimes I feel I'm just another of his insane terminal documents."

"What are those?"

"Haven't you heard? Kaldren's collection of final statements about *Homo sapiens.* The complete works of Freud, Beethoven's silent quartets, transcripts of the Nuremberg trials, an automatic novel, and so on." She broke off. "What's that you're drawing?"

"Where?"

She pointed to the desk blotter, and Powers looked down and realized he had been unconsciously sketching an elaborate doodle, Whitby's four-armed sun. "It's nothing," he said. Somehow, though, it had a strangely compelling force.

Coma stood up to leave. "You must come and see us, Doctor. Kaldren has so much he wants to show you. He's just got hold of an old copy of the last signals sent back by the Apollo Seven twenty years ago when they reached the moon, and can't think about anything else. You remember the strange messages they recorded before they died, full of poetic ramblings about the white gardens. Now that I think about it they behaved rather like the plants in your zoo here."

She put her hands in her pockets, then pulled something out. "By the way, Kaldren asked me to give you this."

It was an old index card from the observatory library. In the center had been typed the number:

$$96,688,365,498,720$$

"It's going to take a long time to reach zero at this rate," Powers remarked dryly. "I'll have quite a collection when we're finished."

After she had left he chucked the card into the waste bin and sat down at the desk, staring for an hour at the ideogram on the blotter.

Halfway back to his beach house the lake road forked to the left through a narrow saddle that ran between the hills to an abandoned air force weapons range on one of the remoter salt lakes. At the nearer end were a number of small bunkers and camera towers, one or two metal shacks, and a low-roofed storage hangar. The white hills encircled the whole area, shutting it off from the world outside, and Powers liked to wander on foot down the gunnery aisles that had been marked down the two-mile length of the lake toward the concrete sight-screens at the far end. The abstract patterns made him feel like an ant on a bone-white chessboard, the rectangular screens at one end and the towers and bunkers at the other like opposing pieces.

His session with Coma had made Powers feel suddenly dissatisfied with the way he was spending his last months. *Good-bye, Eniwetok*, he had written, but in fact systematically forgetting everything was exactly the same as remembering it, a cataloging in reverse, sorting out all the books in the mental library and putting them back in their right places upside down.

Powers climbed one of the camera towers, leaned on the rail, and looked out along the aisles toward the sight-screens. Ricocheting shells and rockets had chipped away large pieces of the circular concrete bands that ringed the target bulls, but the outlines of the huge hundred-yard-wide disks, alternately painted blue and red, were still visible.

For half an hour he stared quietly at them, formless ideas shifting through his mind. Then without thinking, he abruptly left the rail and climbed down the companionway. The storage hangar was fifty yards away. He walked quickly across to it, stepped into the cool shadows and peered around the rusting electric trolleys and empty flare drums. At the far end, behind a pile of lumber and bales of wire, were a stack of unopened cement bags, a mound of dirty sand, and an old mixer.

Half an hour later he had backed the Buick into the hangar and hooked the cement mixer, charged with sand, cement, and water scavenged from the drums lying around outside, onto the rear bumper, then loaded a dozen more bags into the car's trunk and rear seat. Finally he selected a few straight lengths of timber, jammed them through the window, and set off across the lake toward the central target bull.

For the next two hours he worked away steadily in the center of the great blue disk, mixing up cement by hand, carrying it across to the crude wooden forms he had lashed together from the timber, smoothing it down so that it formed a six-inch-high wall around the perimeter of the bull. He worked without pause, stirring the cement with a tire lever, scooping it out with a hubcap prized off one of the wheels.

By the time he finished and drove off, leaving his equipment where it stood, he had completed a thirty-foot-long section of wall.

Four

June 7: Conscious, for the first time, of the brevity of each day. As long as I was awake for over twelve hours I still orientated my time around the meridian, morning and afternoon set their old rhythms. Now, with just over eleven hours of consciousness left, they form a continuous interval, like a length of tape measure. I can see exactly how much is left on the spool and can do little to affect the rate at which it unwinds. Spend the time slowly packing away the library; the crates are too heavy to move and lie where they are filled.

Cell count down to 400,000.

Woke 8:10. To sleep 7:15. (Appear to have lost my watch without realizing it, had to drive into town to buy another.)

June 14: 9 1/2 hours. Time races, flashing past like an expressway. However, the last week of a holiday always goes faster than the first. At the present rate there should be about 4–5 weeks left. This morning I tried to visualize what the last week or so—the final, 3, 2, 1, out—would be like, had a sudden chilling attack of pure fear, unlike anything I've ever felt before. Took me half an hour to steady myself enough for an intravenous.

Kaldren pursues me like luminescent shadow. He has chalked up on the gateway "96,688,365,498,702." Should confuse the mailman.

Woke 9:05. To sleep 6:36.

June 19: 8 3/4 hours. Anderson rang up this morning. I nearly put the phone down on him, but managed to go through the pretense of making the final arrangements. He congratulated me on my stoicism, even used the word *heroic*. Don't feel it. Despair erodes everything—courage, hope, self-discipline, all the better qualities. It's so damned difficult to sustain that impersonal attitude of passive acceptance implicit in the scientific tradition. I try to think of Galileo before the Inquisition, Freud surmounting the endless pain of his jaw cancer surgery.

Met Kaldren downtown, had a long discussion about the Apollo Seven. He's convinced that they refused to leave the moon deliberately, after the "reception party" waiting for them had put them in the cosmic picture. They were told by the mysterious emissaries from Orion that the exploration of deep space was pointless, that they were too late as the life of the universe is now virtually over! According to K. there are air force generals who take this nonsense seriously, but I suspect it's simply an obscure attempt on K.'s part to console me.

Must have the phone disconnected. Some contractor keeps calling me up about payment for fifty bags of cement he claims I collected ten days ago. Says he helped me load them onto a truck himself. I did drive Whitby's pickup into town but only to get some lead screening. What does he think I'd do with all that cement? Just the sort of irritating thing you don't expect to hang over your final exit. (Moral: don't try too hard to forget Eniwetok.)
Woke 9:40. To sleep 4:15.

June 25: 7 1/2 hours. Kaldren was snooping around the lab again today. Phoned me there. When I answered, a recorded voice he'd rigged up rambled out a long string of numbers, like an insane super-Tim. These practical jokes of his get rather wearing. Fairly soon I'll have to go over and come to terms with him, much as I hate the prospect. Anyway, Miss Mars is a pleasure to look at. One meal is enough now, topped up with a glucose shot. Sleep is still "black," completely unrefreshing. Last night I took a 16 mm. film of the first three hours, screened it this morning at the lab. The first true horror movie. I looked like a half-animated corpse.
Woke 10:25. To sleep 3:45.

July 3: 5 3/4 hours. Little done today. Deepening lethargy, dragged myself over to the lab, nearly left the road twice. Concentrated enough to feed the zoo and get the log up to date. Read through the operating manuals Whitby left for the last time, decided on a delivery rate of 40 roentgens/min., target distance of 530 cm. Everything is ready now.
Woke 11:05. To sleep 3:15.

Powers stretched, shifted his head slowly across the pillow, focusing on the shadows cast onto the ceiling by the blind. Then he looked down at his feet, saw Kaldren sitting on the end of the bed, watching him quietly.

"Hello, Doctor," he said, putting out his cigarette. "Late night? You look tired."

Powers heaved himself onto one elbow, glanced at his watch. It was just after eleven. For a moment his brain blurred, and he swung his legs around and sat on the edge of the bed, elbows on his knees, massaging some life into his face.

He noticed that the room was full of smoke. "What are you doing here?" he asked Kaldren.

"I came over to invite you to lunch." He indicated the bedside phone. "Your line was dead so I drove around. Hope you don't mind me climbing in. Rang the bell for about half an hour. I'm surprised you didn't hear it."

Powers nodded, then stood up and tried to smooth the creases out of his cotton slacks. He had gone to sleep without changing for over a week, and they were damp and stale.

As he started for the bathroom door Kaldren pointed to the camera tripod on the other side of the bed. "What's this? Going into the blue movie business, Doctor?"

Powers surveyed him dimly for a moment, glanced at the tripod without replying and then noticed his open diary on the bedside table. Wondering whether Kaldren had read the last entries, he went back and picked it up, then stepped into the bathroom and closed the door behind him.

From the mirror cabinet he took out a syringe and an ampule. After the shot he leaned against the door waiting for the stimulant to pick up.

Kaldren was in the lounge when he returned to him, reading the labels on the crates lying about in the center of the floor.

"O.K., then," Powers told him, "I'll join you for lunch." He examined Kaldren carefully. He looked more subdued than usual; there was an air almost of deference about him.

"Good," Kaldren said. "By the way, are you leaving?"

"Does it matter?" Powers asked curtly. "I thought you were in Anderson's care."

Kaldren shrugged. "Please yourself. Come around at about twelve," he suggested, adding pointedly, "That'll give you time to clean up and change. What's that all over your shirt? Looks like lime."

Powers peered down, brushed at the white streaks. After Kaldren had left he threw the clothes away, took a shower and unpacked a clean suit from one of the trunks.

Until the liaison with Coma, Kaldren had lived alone in the old abstract summerhouse on the north shore of the lake. This was a seven-story folly originally built by an eccentric millionaire mathematician in the form of a spiraling concrete ribbon that wound around itself like an insane serpent, serving walls, floors, and ceilings. Only Kaldren had solved the building, a geometric model of $\sqrt{-1}$, and consequently he had been able to take it off the agents' hands at a comparatively low rent. In the evenings Powers had often watched him from the laboratory, striding restlessly from one level to the next, swinging through the labyrinth of inclines and terraces to the rooftop, where his lean angular figure stood out like a gallows against the sky, his lonely eyes sifting out radio lanes for the next day's trapping.

Powers noticed him there when he drove up at noon, poised on a ledge 150 feet above, head raised theatrically to the sky.

"Kaldren!" he shouted up suddenly into the silent air, half-hoping he might be jolted into losing his footing.

Kaldren broke out of his reverie and glanced down into the court. Grinning obliquely, he waved his right arm in a slow semicircle.

"Come up," he called, then turned back to the sky.

Powers leaned against the car. Once, a few months previously, he had accepted the same invitation, stepped through the entrance and within three minutes lost himself helplessly in a second-floor cul-de-sac. Kaldren had taken half an hour to find him.

Powers waited while Kaldren swung down from his aerie, vaulting through the wells and stairways, then rode up in the elevator with him to the penthouse suite.

They carried their cocktails through into a wide glass-roofed studio, the huge white ribbon of concrete uncoiling around them like toothpaste squeezed from an enormous tube. On the staged levels running parallel and across them rested pieces of gray abstract furniture, giant photographs on angled screens, carefully labeled exhibits laid out on low tables, all dominated by twenty-foot-high black letters on the rear wall which spelled out the single vast word:

YOU

Kaldren pointed to it. "What you might call the supraliminal approach." He gestured Powers in conspiratorially, finishing his drink in a gulp. "This is *my* laboratory, Doctor," he said with a note of pride. "Much more significant than yours, believe me."

Powers smiled wryly to himself and examined the first exhibit, an old EEG tape traversed by a series of faded inky wriggles. It was labeled: EINSTEIN, A.; ALPHA WAVES, 1922.

He followed Kaldren around, sipping slowly at his drink, enjoying the brief feeling of alertness the amphetamine provided. Within two hours it would fade, leave his brain feeling like a block of blotting paper.

Kaldren chattered away, explaining the significance of the so-called Terminal Documents. "They're end-prints, Powers, final statements, the products of total fragmentation. When I've got enough together I'll build a new world for myself out of them." He picked a thick paperbound volume off one of the tables, riffled through its pages. "Association tests of the Nuremberg Twelve. I have to include these..."

Powers strolled on absently without listening. Over in the corner were what appeared to be three ticker-tape machines, lengths of tape hanging from their mouths. He wondered whether Kaldren was misguided enough to be playing the stock market, which had been declining slowly for twenty years.

"Powers," he heard Kaldren say. "I was telling you about the Apollo Seven." He pointed to a collection of typewritten sheets tacked to a screen. "These are transcripts of their final signals radioed back from the recording monitors."

Powers examined the sheets cursorily, read a line at random.

"... BLUE ... PEOPLE ... RECYCLE ... ORION ... TELEMETERS ..."

Powers nodded noncommittally. "Interesting. What are the ticker tapes for over there?"

Kaldren grinned. "I've been waiting for months for you to ask me that. Have a look."

Powers went over and picked up one of the tapes. The machine was labeled: AURIGA 225-G. INTERVAL: 69 HOURS.

The tape read:

$$96,688,365,498,695$$
$$96,688,365,498,694$$
$$96,688,365,498,693$$
$$96,688,365,498,692$$

Powers dropped the tape. "Looks rather familiar. What does the sequence represent?"

Kaldren shrugged. "No one knows."

"What do you mean? It must replicate something."

"Yes, it does. A diminishing mathematical progression. A countdown, if you like."

Powers picked up the tape on the right, tabbed: ARIES 44R951. INTERVAL: 49 DAYS.

Here the sequence ran:

876,567,988,347,779,877,654,434
876,567,988,347,779,877,654,433
876,567,988,347,779,877,654,432

Powers looked round. "How long does it take each signal to come through?"

"Only a few seconds. They're tremendously compressed laterally, of course. A computer at the observatory breaks them down. They were first picked up at Jodrell Bank about twenty years ago. Nobody bothers to listen to them now."

Powers turned to the last tape.

6,554
6,553
6,552
6,551

"Nearing the end of its run," he commented. He glanced at the label on the hood, which read: UNIDENTIFIED RADIO SOURCE, CANES VENATICI. INTERVAL: 97 WEEKS.

He showed the tape to Kaldren. "Soon be over."

Kaldren shook his head. He lifted a heavy directory-sized volume off a table, cradled it in his hands. His face had suddenly become somber and pallid. "I doubt it," he said. "Those are only the last four digits. The whole number contains over fifty million."

He handed the volume to Powers, who turned to the title page. "Master Sequence of Serial Signal received by Jodrell Bank Radio-Observatory, University of Manchester, England, 0012-59 hours, 21-5-72. Source: NGC 9743, Canes Venatici." He thumbed the thick stack of closely printed pages, millions of numerals, as Kaldren had said, running up and down across a thousand consecutive pages.

Powers shook his head, picked up the tape again, and stared at it thoughtfully.

"The computer only breaks down the last four digits," Kaldren explained. "The whole series comes over in each fifteen-second-long package, but it took IBM more than two years to unscramble one of them."

"Amazing," Powers commented. "But what is it?"

"A countdown, as you can see. NGC 9743, somewhere in Canes Venatici. The big spirals there are breaking up, and they're saying good-bye. God knows who they think we are but they're letting us know all the same, beaming it out on the hydrogen line for everyone in the universe to hear." He paused. "Some people have put other interpretations on them, but there's one piece of evidence that rules out everything else."

"Which is?"

Kaldren pointed to the last tape from Canes Venatici. "Simply that it's been estimated that by the time this series reaches zero the universe will have just ended."

Powers fingered the tape reflectively. "Thoughtful of them to let us know what the real time is," he remarked.

"I agree, it is," Kaldren said quietly. "Applying the inverse square law, that signal source is broadcasting at a strength of about three million megawatts raised to the hundredth power. About the size of the entire Local Group. Thoughtful is the word."

Suddenly he gripped Powers's arm, held it tightly, and peered into his eyes closely, his throat working with emotion.

"You're not alone, Powers, don't think you are. These are the voices of time, and they're all saying good-bye to you. Think of yourself in a wider context. Every particle in your body, every grain of sand, every galaxy carries the same signature. As you've just said, you know what the time is now, so what does the rest matter? There's no need to go on looking at the clock."

Powers took his hand, squeezed it firmly. "Thanks, Kaldren. I'm glad you understand." He walked over to the window, looked down across the white lake. The tension between himself and Kaldren had dissipated; he felt that all his obligations to him had at last been met. Now he wanted to leave as quickly as possible, forget him as he had forgotten the faces of the countless other patients whose exposed brains had passed between his fingers.

He went back to the ticker machines, tore the tapes from their slots, and stuffed them into his pockets. "I'll take these along to remind myself. Say good-bye to Coma for me, will you?"

He moved toward the door. When he reached it he looked back to see Kaldren standing in the shadow of the three giant letters on the far wall, his eyes staring listlessly at his feet.

As Powers drove away he noticed that Kaldren had gone up onto the roof, watched him in the driving mirror waving slowly until the car disappeared around a bend.

Five

The outer circle was now almost complete. A narrow segment, an arc about ten feet long, was missing, but otherwise the low perimeter wall ran continuously six inches off the concrete floor around the outer lane of the target bull, enclosing the huge rebus within it. Three concentric circles, the largest a hundred yards in diameter, separated from each other by ten-foot intervals, formed the rim of the device, divided into four segments by the arms of an enormous cross radiating from its center, where a small round platform had been built a foot above the ground.

Powers worked swiftly, pouring sand and cement into the mixer, tipping in water until a rough paste formed, then carrying it across to the wooden forms and tamping the mixture down into the narrow channel.

Within ten minutes he had finished. He quickly dismantled the forms, before the cement had set, and slung the timbers into the back seat of the car. Dusting his hands on his trousers, he went over to the mixer and pushed it fifty yards away into the long shadow of the surrounding hills.

Without pausing to survey the gigantic cipher on which he had labored patiently for so many afternoons, he climbed into the car and drove off in a wake of bone-white dust, splitting the pools of indigo shadow.

He reached the laboratory at three o'clock, and jumped from the car as it lurched back on its brakes. Inside the entrance he first switched on the lights, then hurried around, pulling the sun curtains down and shackling them to the floor slots, effectively turning the dome into a steel tent.

In their tanks behind him the plants and animals stirred quietly, responding to the sudden flood of cold fluorescent light. Only the chimpanzee ignored him. It sat on the floor of its cage, neurotically jamming the puzzle dice into the polythene bucket, exploding in bursts of sudden rage when the pieces refused to fit.

Powers went over to it, noticing the shattered glass fiber reinforcing panels bursting from the dented helmet. Already the chimp's face and forehead were bleeding from self-inflicted blows. Powers picked up the remains of the geranium that had been hurled through the bars, attracted the chimp's attention with it, then tossed a black pellet he had taken from a capsule in the desk drawer. The chimp caught it with a quick flick of the wrist, for a few seconds juggled the pellet with a couple of dice as it concentrated on the puzzle, then pulled it out of the air and swallowed it in a gulp.

Without waiting, Powers slipped off his jacket and stepped toward the X-ray theater. He pulled back the high sliding doors to reveal the long glassy metallic snout of the Maxitron, then started to stack the lead screening shields against the rear wall.

A few minutes later the generator hummed into life.

The anemone stirred. Basking in the warm subliminal sea of radiation rising around it, prompted by countless pelagic memories, it reached tentatively across the tank, groping blindly toward the dim uterine sun. Its tendrils flexed, the thousands of dormant neural cells in their tips regrouping and multiplying, each harnessing the unlocked energies of its nucleus. Chains forged themselves, lattices tiered upward into multifaceted lenses, focused slowly on the vivid spectral outlines of the sounds dancing like phosphorescent waves around the darkened chamber of the dome.

Gradually an image formed, revealing an enormous black fountain that poured an endless stream of brilliant light over the circle of benches and tanks. Beside it a figure moved, adjusting the flow through its mouth. As it stepped across the floor its feet threw off vivid bursts of color, its hands racing along the benches conjured up a dazzling chiaroscuro, balls of blue and violet light that exploded fleetingly in the darkness like miniature star-shells.

Photons murmured. Steadily, as it watched the glimmering screen of sounds around it, the anemone continued to expand. Its ganglia linked, heeding a new source of stimuli from the delicate diaphragms in the crown of its notochord. The silent outlines of the laboratory began to echo softly, waves of muted sound fell from the arc lights and echoed off the benches and furniture below. Etched in sound, their angular forms resonated with sharp persistent overtones.

The plastic-ribbed chairs were a buzz of staccato discords, the square-sided desk a continuous double-featured tone.

Ignoring these sounds once they had been perceived, the anemone turned to the ceiling, which reverberated like a shield in the sounds pouring steadily from the fluorescent tubes. Streaming through a narrow skylight, its voice clear and strong, interwoven by numberless overtones, the sun sang...

It was a few minutes before dawn when Powers left the laboratory and stepped into his car. Behind him the great dome lay silently in the darkness, the thin shadows of the white moonlit hills falling across its surface. Powers freewheeled the car down the long curving drive to the lake road below, listening to the tires cutting across the blue gravel, then let out the clutch and accelerated the engine.

As he drove along, the limestone hills half hidden in the darkness on his left, he gradually became aware that, although no longer looking at the hills, he was still in some oblique way conscious of their forms and outlines in the back of his mind. The sensation was undefined but nonetheless certain, a strange almost visual impression that emanated most strongly from the deep clefts and ravines dividing one cliff face from the next. For a few minutes Powers let it play upon him, without trying to identify it, a dozen strange images moving across his brain.

The road swung up around a group of chalets built onto the lake shore, taking the car right under the lee of the hills, and Powers suddenly felt the massive weight of the escarpment rising up into the dark sky like a cliff of luminous chalk, and realized the identity of the impression now registering powerfully within his mind. Not only could he see the escarpment, but he was aware of its enormous age, felt distinctly the countless millions of years since it had first reared out of the magma of the earth's crust. The ragged crests three hundred feet above him, the dark gullies and fissures, the smooth boulders by the roadside at the foot of the cliff, all carried a distinct image of themselves across to him, a thousand voices that together told of the total time that had elapsed in the life of the escarpment, a psychic picture as defined and clear as the visual image brought to him by his eyes.

Involuntarily, Powers had slowed the car, and turning his eyes away from the hill face he felt a second wave of time sweep across the first. The image was broader but of shorter perspectives, radiating from the wide disk of the salt lake, breaking over the ancient limestone cliffs like shallow rollers dashing against a towering headland.

Closing his eyes, Powers lay back and steered the car along the interval between the two time fronts, feeling the images deepen and strengthen within his mind. The vast age of the landscape, the inaudible chorus of voices resonating from the lake and from the white hills, seemed to carry him back through time, down endless corridors to the first thresholds of the world.

He turned the car off the road along the track leading toward the target range. On either side of the culvert the cliff faces boomed and echoed with vast impenetrable time fields, like enormous opposed magnets. As he finally emerged between them onto the flat surface of the lake it seemed to Powers that he could feel the separate identity of each sand grain and salt crystal calling to him from the surrounding ring of hills.

He parked the car beside the mandala and walked slowly toward the outer concrete rim curving away into the shadows. Above him he could hear the stars, a million cosmic voices that crowded the sky from one horizon to the next, a true canopy of time. Like jostling radio beacons, their long aisles interlocking at countless angles, they plunged into the sky from the narrowest recesses of space. He saw the dim red disk of Sirius, heard its ancient voice, untold millions of years old, dwarfed by the huge spiral nebulae in Andromeda, a gigantic carousel of vanished universes, their voices almost as old as the cosmos itself. To Powers the sky seemed an endless babel, the time-song of a thousand galaxies overlaying each other in his mind. As he moved slowly toward the center of the mandala he craned up at the glittering traverse of the Milky Way, searching the confusion of clamoring nebulae and constellations.

Stepping into the inner circle of the mandala, a few yards from the platform at its center, he realized that the tumult was beginning to fade, and that a single stronger voice had emerged and was dominating the others. He climbed onto the platform and raised his eyes to the darkened sky, moving through the constellations to the island galaxies beyond them, hearing the thin archaic voices reaching to him across the millennia. In his pockets he felt the paper tapes, and turned to find the distant diadem of Canes Venatici, heard its great voice mounting in his mind.

Like an endless river, so broad that its banks were below the horizons, it flowed steadily toward him, a vast course of time that spread outward to fill the sky and the universe, enveloping everything within them. Moving slowly, the forward direction of its majestic current was imperceptible, and Powers knew that its source was the source of the cosmos itself. As it passed him, he felt its massive magnetic pull, let himself be drawn into it, borne gently on its powerful back. Quietly it carried him away, and he rotated slowly, facing the direction of the tide. Around him the outlines of the hills and the lake had faded, but the image of the mandala, like a cosmic clock, remained fixed before his eyes, illuminating the broad surface of the stream. Watching it constantly, he felt his body gradually dissolving, its physical dimensions melting into the vast continuum of the current, which bore him out into the center of the great channel, sweeping him onward, beyond hope now but at last at rest, down the broadening reaches of the river of eternity.

As the shadows faded, retreating into the hill slopes, Kaldren stepped out of his car, walked hesitantly toward the concrete rim of the outer circle. Fifty yards away, at the center, Coma knelt beside Powers's body, her small hands pressed to his dead face. A gust of wind stirred the sand, dislodging a strip of tape that drifted toward Kaldren's feet. He bent down and picked it up, then rolled it carefully in his hands and slipped it into his pocket. The dawn air was cold, and he turned up the collar of his jacket, watching Coma impassively.

"It's six o'clock," he told her after a few minutes. "I'll go and get the police. You stay with him." He paused and then added, "Don't let them break the clock."

Coma turned and looked at him. "Aren't you coming back?"

"I don't know." Nodding to her, Kaldren swung on his heel and went over to the car.

He reached the lake road, five minutes later parked the car in the drive outside Whitby's laboratory.

The dome was in darkness, all its windows shuttered, but the generator still hummed in the X-ray theater. Kaldren stepped through the entrance and switched on the lights. In the theater he touched the grilles of the generator, felt the warm cylinder of the beryllium end-window. The circular target table was revolving slowly, its setting at 1 rpm, a steel restraining chair shackled to it hastily. Grouped in a semicircle a few feet away were most of the tanks and cages, piled on top of each other haphazardly. In one of them an enormous squidlike plant had almost managed to climb from its vivarium. Its long translucent tendrils clung to the edges of the tank, but its body had burst into a jellified pool of globular mucilage. In another an enormous spider had trapped itself in its own web and hung helplessly in the center of a huge three-dimensional maze of phosphorescing thread twitching spasmodically.

All the experimental plants and animals had died. The chimp lay on its back among the remains of the hutch, the helmet forward over its eyes. Kaldren watched it for a moment, then sat down on the desk and picked up the phone.

While he dialed the number he noticed a film reel lying on the blotter. For a moment he stared at the label, then slid the reel into his pocket beside the tape.

After he had spoken to the police he turned off the lights, went out to the car, and drove off slowly down the drive.

When he reached the summerhouse the early sunlight was breaking across the ribbonlike balconies and terraces. He took the lift to the penthouse, made his way through into the museum. One by one he opened the shutters and let the sunlight play over the exhibits. Then he pulled a chair over to a side window, sat back, and stared up at the light pouring through into the room.

Two or three hours later he heard Coma outside, calling up to him. After half an hour she went away, but a little later a second voice appeared and shouted up at Kaldren. He left his chair and closed all the shutters overlooking the front courtyard, and eventually he was left undisturbed.

Kaldren returned to his seat and lay back quietly, his eyes gazing across the lines of exhibits. Half-asleep, periodically he leaned up and adjusted the flow of light through the shutter, thinking to himself, as he would do through the coming months, of Powers and his strange mandala, and of the Seven and their journey to the white gardens of the moon, and the blue people who had come from Orion and spoken in poetry to them of ancient beautiful worlds beneath golden suns in the island galaxies, vanished forever now in the myriad deaths of the cosmos.

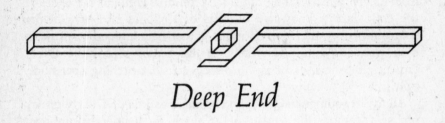

Deep End

They always slept during the day. By dawn the last of the townsfolk had gone indoors and the houses would be silent, heat curtains locked across the windows, as the sun rose over the deliquescing salt banks, filling the streets with opaque fire. Most of them were old people and fell asleep quickly in their darkened chalets, but Granger, with his restless mind and his one lung, often lay awake through the afternoons, while the metal outer walls of the cabin creaked and hummed, trying pointlessly to read through the old logbooks Holliday had salvaged for him from the crashed space platforms.

By six o'clock the thermal fronts would begin to recede southward across the kelp flats, and one by one the air conditioners in the bedrooms switched themselves off. While the town slowly came to life, its windows opening to the cool dusk air, Granger strode down to breakfast at the Neptune Bar, gallantly doffing his sunglasses to left and right at the elderly couples settling themselves out on their porches, staring at each other across the shadow-filled streets.

Five miles to the north, in the empty hotel at Idle End, Holliday usually rested quietly for another hour, and listened to the coral towers, gleaming in the distance like white pagodas, sing and whistle as the temperature gradients cut through them. Twenty miles away he could see the symmetrical peak of Hamilton, nearest of the Bermuda Islands, rising off the dry ocean floor like a flat-topped mountain, the narrow ring of white beach still visible in the sunset, a scum line left by sinking ocean.

That evening he felt even more reluctant than usual to drive down into the town. Not only would Granger be in his private booth at the Neptune, dispensing the same mixture of humor and homily—he was virtually the only person Holliday could talk to, and inevitably he had come to resent his dependence on the older man—but Holliday would have his final interview with the migration officer and make the decision which would determine his entire future.

In a sense the decision had already been made, as Bullen, the migration officer, had realized on his trip a month earlier. He did not bother to press Holliday, who had no special skills to offer, no qualities of character or leadership which would be of use on the new worlds. However, Bullen pointed out one small but relevant fact, which Holliday duly noted and thought over in the intervening month.

"Remember, Holliday," he warned him at the end of the interview in the requisitioned office at the rear of the sheriff's cabin, "the average age of the settlement is over sixty. In ten years' time you and Granger may well be the only two left here, and if that lung of his goes you'll be on your own."

He paused to let this prospect sink in, then added quietly, "All the kids are leaving on the next trip—the Merryweathers's two boys, Tom Juranda (*That lout! Good riddance,* Holliday thought to himself. *Look out, Mars*)—do you realize you'll literally be the only one here under the age of fifty?"

"Katy Summers is staying," Holliday pointed out quickly, the sudden vision of a white organdy dress and long straw hair giving him courage.

The migration officer had glanced at his application list and nodded obligingly. "Yes, but she's just looking after her grandmother. As soon as the old girl dies Katy will be off like a flash. After all, there's nothing to keep her here, is there?"

"No," Holliday had agreed automatically.

There wasn't now. For a long while he had mistakenly believed there was. Katy was his own age, twenty-two, the only person, apart from Granger, who seemed to understand his determination to stay behind and keep watch over a forgotten Earth. But the grandmother died three days after the migration officer left, and the next day Katy had begun to pack. In some insane way Holliday had assumed that she would stay behind, and what worried him was that all his assumptions about himself might be based on equally false premises.

Climbing off the hammock, he went onto the terrace and looked out at the phosphorescent glitter of the trace minerals in the salt banks stretching away from the hotel. His quarters were in the penthouse suite on the tenth floor, the only heat-sealed unit in the building, but its steady settlement into the ocean bed had opened in the load walls wide cracks which would soon reach up to the roof. The ground floor had already disappeared. By the time the next floor went—six months at the outside—he would have been forced to leave the old pleasure resort and return to the town. Inevitably, that would mean sharing a chalet with Granger.

A mile away, an engine droned. Through the dusk Holliday saw the migration officer's helicopter whirling along toward the hotel, the only local landmark, then veer off once Bullen identified the town and brake slowly toward the landing strip.

Eight o'clock, Holliday noted. His interview was at 8:30 the next morning. Bullen would rest the night with the sheriff, carry out his other duties as graves commissioner and justice of the peace, and then set off after seeing Holliday on the next leg of his journey. For twelve hours Holliday was free, still able to make absolute decisions (or, more accurately, not to make them) but after that he would have committed himself. This was the migration officer's last trip, his final circuit from the deserted cities near St. Helena up through the Azores and Bermudas around to the main Atlantic ferry site at the Canaries. Only two of the big launching platforms were still in navigable orbit—hundreds of others were continuously falling out of the sky—and once they came down Earth was, to all intents, abandoned. From then on the only people likely to be picked up would be a few military communications personnel.

Twice on his way into the town Holliday had to lower the salt plow fastened to the front bumper of the jeep and ram back the drifts which had melted across the wire roadway during the afternoon.

Mutating kelp, their gene shifts accelerated by the radiophosphorus, reared up into the air on either side of the road like enormous cacti, turning the dark salt banks into a white lunar garden. But this evidence of the encroaching wilderness only served to strengthen Holliday's need to stay behind on Earth. Most of the nights, when he wasn't arguing with Granger at the Neptune, trying to explain his philosophy to him, he would drive around the ocean floor, climbing over the crashed launching platforms, or wander with Katy Summers through the kelp forests. Sometimes he would persuade Granger to come with them, hoping that the older man's expertise—he had originally been a marine biologist—would help to sharpen his own awareness of the bathypelagic flora, but the original seabed was buried under the endless salt hills and they might as well have been driving about the Sahara.

As he entered the Neptune—a low cream and chromium saloon which abutted the landing strip and had formerly served as a passenger lounge when thousands of migrants from the Southern Hemisphere were being shipped up to the Canaries—Granger called out to him and rattled his cane against the window, pointing to the dark outline of the migration officer's helicopter parked on the apron fifty yards away.

"I know," Holliday said in a bored voice as he went over with his drink. "Relax, I saw him coming."

Granger grinned at him. Holliday, with his intent serious face under an unruly thatch of blond hair and his absolute sense of personal responsibility, always amused him.

"*You* relax," Granger said, adjusting the shoulder pad under his Hawaiian shirt which disguised his sunken lung. (He had lost it skindiving thirty years earlier.) "*I'm* not going to fly to Mars next week."

Holliday stared somberly into his glass. "I'm not either." He looked up at Granger's wry saturnine face, then added sardonically, "Or didn't you know?"

Granger roared, tapping the window with his cane as if to dismiss the helicopter. "Seriously, you're not going? You've made up your mind?"

"Wrong. And right. I haven't made up my mind yet—but at the same time I'm not going. You appreciate the distinction?"

"Perfectly, Dr. Schopenhauer." Granger began to grin again. He pushed away his glass. "You know, Holliday, your whole trouble is that you take yourself too seriously. You don't realize how ludicrous you are."

"Ludicrous? Why?" Holliday asked guardedly.

"What does it matter whether you've made up your mind or not? The only thing that counts now is to get together enough courage to head straight for the Canaries and take off into the wide blue yonder. For heaven's sake, what are you staying for? Earth is dead and buried. Past, present, and future no longer exist here. Don't you feel any responsibility to your own biological destiny?"

"Spare me that." Holliday pulled a ration card from his shirt pocket and passed it across to Granger, who was responsible for the store's allocations. "I need a new pump on the lounge refrigerator, thirty-watt Frigidaire. Any left?"

Granger groaned, took the card with a snort of exasperation. "Good God, man, you're just a Robinson Crusoe in reverse, tinkering about with all these bits of old junk, trying to fit them together. You're the last man on the beach who decides to stay behind after everyone else has left. Maybe you are a poet and dreamer, but don't you realize that those two species are extinct now?"

Holliday stared out at the helicopter on the apron, at the lights of the settlement reflected against the salt hills that encircled the town. Each day they moved in a little further. Already it was difficult to get together a weekly squad to push them back. In ten years' time his position might well be that of a Crusoe. Luckily the big water and kerosene tanks—giant cylinders, the size of gasometers—held enough for fifty years. Without them, of course, he would have had no choice.

"Let's give me a rest," he said to Granger. "You're merely trying to find in me a justification for your own enforced stay. Perhaps I am extinct, but I'd rather cling to life here than vanish completely. Anyway, I have a hunch that one day they'll be coming back. Someone's got to stay behind and keep alive a sense of what life here has meant. This isn't an old husk we can throw away when we've finished with it. We were born here. It's the only place we really remember."

Granger nodded slowly. He was about to speak when a brilliant white arc crossed the darkened window, then soared out of sight, its point of impact with the ground lost behind one of the storage tanks.

Holliday stood up and craned out of the window.

"Must be a launching platform. Looked like a big one, probably one of the Russians'." A long rolling crump reverberated through the night air, echoing away among the coral towers. Flashes of light flared up briefly. There was a series of smaller explosions, and then a wide diffuse pall of steam fanned out across the northwest.

"Lake Atlantic," Granger commented. "Let's drive out there and have a look. It may have uncovered something interesting."

Half an hour later, with a set of Granger's old sample beakers, slides, and mounting equipment in the back seat, they set off in the jeep toward the southern tip of Lake Atlantic ten miles away.

It was here that Holliday discovered the fish.

Lake Atlantic, a narrow ribbon of stagnant brine ten miles in length by a mile wide, to the north of the Bermuda Islands, was all that remained of the former Atlantic Ocean, and was, in fact, the sole remnant of the oceans which had once covered two-thirds of the Earth's surface. The frantic mining of the oceans in the previous century to provide oxygen for the atmospheres of the new planets had made their decline swift and irreversible, and with their death had come climatic and other geophysical changes which ensured the extinction of Earth itself. As the oxygen extracted electrolytically from seawater was compressed and shipped away, the hydrogen released was discharged into the atmosphere. Eventually only a narrow layer of denser, oxygen-containing air was left, little more than a mile in depth, and those people remaining on Earth were forced to retreat into the ocean beds, abandoning the poisoned continental tables.

At the hotel at Idle End, Holliday spent uncounted hours going through the library he had accumulated of magazines and books about the cities of the old Earth, and Granger often described to him his own youth when the seas had been half full and he had worked as a marine biologist at the University of Miami, a fabulous laboratory unfolding itself for him on the lengthening beaches.

"The seas are our corporate memory," he often said to Holliday. "In draining them we deliberately obliterated our own pasts, to a large extent our own self-identities. That's another reason why you should leave. Without the sea, life is unsupportable. We become nothing more than the ghosts of memories, blind and homeless, flitting through the dry chambers of a gutted skull."

They reached the lake within half an hour, and worked their way through the swamps which formed its banks. In the dim light the gray salt dunes ran on for miles, their hollows cracked into hexagonal plates, a dense cloud of vapor obscuring the surface of the water. They parked on a low promontory by the edge of the lake and looked up at the great circular shell of the launching platform. This was one of the larger vehicles, almost three hundred yards in diameter, lying upside down in the shallow water, its hull dented and burned, riven by huge punctures where the power plants had torn themselves loose on impact and exploded off across the lake. A quarter of a mile away, hidden by the blur, they could just see a cluster of rotors pointing up into the sky.

Walking along the bank, the main body of the lake on their right, they moved nearer the platform, tracing out its riveted CCCP markings along the rim. The giant vehicle had cut enormous grooves through the nexus of pools just beyond the tip of the lake, and Granger waded through the warm water, searching for specimens. Here and there were small anemones and starfish, stunted bodies twisted by cancers. Weblike algae draped themselves over his rubber boots, their nuclei beading like jewels in the phosphorescent light. They paused by one of the largest pools, a circular basin three hundred feet across, draining slowly as the water poured out through a breach in its side. Granger moved carefully down the deepening bank, forking specimens into the rack of beakers, while Holliday stood on the narrow causeway between the pool and the lake, looking up at the dark overhang of the space platform as it loomed into the darkness above him like the stern of a ship.

He was examining the shattered airlock of one of the crew domes when he saw something suddenly move across the surface of the deck. For a moment he imagined that he had seen a passenger who had somehow survived the vehicle's crash, then realized that it was merely the reflection in the aluminized skin of a ripple in the pool behind him.

He turned around to see Granger, ten feet below him, up to his knees in the water, staring out carefully across the pool.

"Did you throw something?" Granger asked quietly.

Holliday shook his head. "No." Without thinking, he added, "Must have been a fish jumping."

"Fish? There isn't a single fish alive on the entire planet. The whole zoological class died out ten years ago. Funny, though."

Just then the fish jumped again.

For a few moments, standing motionless in the half-light, they watched it together, as its slim silver body leaped frantically out of the tepid shallow water, its short glistening arcs carrying it to and fro across the pool.

"Dogfish," Granger muttered. "Shark family. Highly adaptable. It would need to be, to have survived here. Damn it, it may well be the only fish still living."

Holliday moved down the bank, his feet sinking in the oozing mud. "Isn't the water too salty?"

Granger bent down and scooped up some of the water, sipped it tentatively. "Saline, but comparatively dilute." He glanced over his shoulder at the lake. "Perhaps there's continuous evaporation off the lake surface and local condensation here. A freak distillation couple." He slapped Holliday on the shoulder. "Holliday, this should be interesting."

The dogfish was leaping frantically toward them, its two-foot body twisting and flicking. Low mudbanks were emerging all over the surface of the pool; in only a few places toward the center was the water more than a foot deep.

Holliday pointed to the breach in the bank fifty yards away, gestured Granger after him and began to run toward it.

Five minutes later they had effectively dammed up the breach. Then Holliday returned for the jeep and drove it carefully through the winding saddles between the pools. He lowered the ramp and began to force the sides of the fish pool in toward each other. After two or three hours he had narrowed the diameter from a hundred yards to under sixty, and the depth of the water had increased to over two feet. The dogfish had ceased to jump and swam smoothly just below the surface, snapping at the countless small plants which had been tumbled into the water by the jeep's ramp. Its slim white body seemed white and unmarked, the small fins trim and powerful.

Granger sat on the hood of the jeep, his back against the windshield, watching Holliday with admiration.

"You obviously have hidden reserves," he said ungrudgingly. "I didn't think you had it in you."

Holliday washed his hands in the water, then stepped over the churned mud which formed the boundary of the pool. A few feet behind him the dogfish veered and lunged.

"I want to keep it alive," Holliday said matter-of-factly. "Don't you see, Granger, the fish stayed behind when the first amphibians emerged from the seas two hundred million years ago, just as you and I, in turn, are staying behind now. In a sense all fish are images of ourselves seen in the sea's mirror."

He slumped down on the running board. His clothes were soaked and streaked with salt, and he gasped at the damp air. To the east, just above the long bulk of the Florida coastline, rising from the ocean floor like an enormous aircraft carrier, were the first dawn thermal fronts. "Will it be all right to leave it until this evening?"

Granger climbed into the driving seat. "Don't worry. Come on, you need a rest." He pointed up at the overhanging rim of the launching platform. "That should shade it for a few hours, help to keep the temperature down."

As they neared the town Granger slowed to wave to the old people retreating from their porches, fixing the shutters on the steel cabins.

"What about your interview with Bullen?" he asked Holliday soberly. "He'll be waiting for you."

"Leave here? After last night? It's out of the question."

Granger shook his head as he parked the car outside the Neptune. "Aren't you rather overestimating the importance of one dogfish? There were millions of them once; they were the vermin of the sea."

"You're missing the point," Holliday said, sinking back into the seat, trying to wipe the salt out of his eyes. "That fish means that there's still something to be done here. Earth isn't dead and exhausted after all. We can breed new forms of life, a completely new biological kingdom."

Eyes fixed on this private vision, Holliday sat holding the steering wheel while Granger went into the bar to collect a crate of beer. On his return the migration officer was with him.

Bullen put a foot on the running board, looked into the car. "Well, how about it, Holliday? I'd like to make an early start. If you're not interested I'll be off. There's a rich new life out there; it's the first step to the stars. Tom Juranda and the Merryweather boys are leaving next week. Do you want to be with them?"

"Sorry," Holliday said curtly. He pulled the crate of beer into the car and let out the clutch, then gunned the jeep away down the empty street in a roar of dust.

Half an hour later, as he stepped out onto the terrace at Idle End, cool and refreshed after his shower, he watched the helicopter roar overhead, its black propeller scudding, then disappear over the kelp flats toward the hull of the wrecked space platform.

"Come on, let's go! What's the matter?"

"Hold it," Granger said. "You're getting overeager. Don't interfere too much, you'll kill the damn thing with kindness. What have you got there?" He pointed to the can Holliday had placed in the dashboard compartment.

"Bread crumbs."

Granger sighed, then gently closed the door. "I'm impressed. I really am. I wish you'd look after me this way. I'm gasping for air too."

They were five miles from the lake when Holliday leaned forward over the wheel and pointed to the crisp tire prints in the soft salt flowing over the road ahead.

"Someone's there already."

Granger shrugged. "What of it? They've probably gone to look at the platform." He chuckled quietly. "Don't you want to share the New Eden with anyone else? Or just you alone, and a consultant biologist?"

Holliday laughed. "Those platforms annoy me, the way they're hurled down as if Earth were a garbage dump. Still, if it wasn't for this one I wouldn't have found the fish."

They reached the lake and made their way toward the pool, the erratic track of the car ahead winding in and out of the pools. Two hundred yards from the platform it had been parked, blocking the route for Holliday and Granger, its passengers having gone ahead on foot.

"That's the Merryweathers's car," Holliday said as they walked around the big stripped-down Buick, slashed with yellow paint and fitted with sirens and pennants. "The two boys must have come out here."

Granger pointed. "One of them's up on the platform."

The younger brother had scaled onto the rim and was shouting down like an umpire at the antics of two other boys, one his brother, the other Tom Juranda, a tall broad-shouldered youth in a space cadet's jerkin. They were standing at the edge of the fish pool, stones and salt blocks in their hands, hurling them into the pool.

Leaving Granger, Holliday sprinted on ahead, shouting at the top of his voice. Too preoccupied to hear him, the boys continued to throw their missiles into the pool, while the younger Merryweather egged them on from the platform above. Just before Holliday reached them Tom Juranda ran a few yards along the bank and began to kick the mud wall into the air, then resumed his target throwing.

"Juranda! Get away from there!" Holliday bellowed. "Put those stones down!"

He reached Juranda as the youth was about to hurl a brick-sized lump of salt into the pool, seized him by the shoulder and flung him round, knocking the salt out of his hand into a shower of damp crystals, then lunged at the elder Merryweather boy, kicking him away.

The pool had been drained. A deep breach had been cut through the bank and the water had poured out into the surrounding gullies and pools. Down in the center of the basin, in a litter of stones and spattered salt, was the crushed but still wriggling body of the dog-fish, twisting itself helplessly in the bare inch of water that remained. Dark red blood poured from wounds in its body, staining the salt.

Holliday hurled himself at Juranda, shook the youth savagely by the shoulders.

"Juranda! Do you realize what you've done, you—" Exhausted, Holliday released him and staggered down into the center of the pool, kicked away the stones, and stood looking at the fish twitching spasmodically at his feet.

"Sorry, Holliday," the older Merryweather boy said tentatively behind him. "We didn't know it was your fish."

Holliday waved him away, then let his arms fall limply to his sides. He felt numbed and baffled, unable to resolve his anger and frustration.

Tom Juranda suddenly began to laugh, and shouted something derisively. Their tension broken, the boys turned and ran off together across the dunes toward their car, yelling and playing catch with each other, mimicking Holliday's outrage.

Granger let them go by, then walked across to the pool, wincing when he saw the empty basin.

"Holliday," he called. "Come on, man."

Holliday shook his head, his eyes staring at the beaten body of the fish.

Granger stepped down the bank to him. Sirens hooted in the distance as the Buick roared off. "Those damn children." He took Holliday gently by the arm. "I'm sorry," he said quietly. "But it's not the end of the world."

Bending down, Holliday reached toward the fish, lying still now, the mud around it slick with blood. His hands hesitated, then retreated.

"Nothing we can do, is there?" he said impersonally.

Granger examined the fish. Apart from the large wound in its side and the flattened skull the skin was intact. "Why not have it stuffed?" he suggested seriously.

Holliday stared at him incredulously, his face contorting. For a moment he said nothing. Then, almost berserk, he shouted, "Have it stuffed? Are you crazy? Do you think I want to make a dummy of myself, fill my own head with straw?"

Turning on his heel, he shouldered past Granger and swung himself roughly out of the pool.

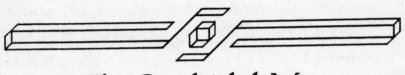

The Overloaded Man

Faulkner was slowly going insane.

After breakfast he waited impatiently in the lounge while his wife tidied up in the kitchen. She would be gone within two or three minutes, but for some reason he always found the short wait each morning almost unbearable. As he drew the Venetian blinds and readied the reclining chair on the veranda he listened to Julia moving about efficiently. In the same strict sequence she stacked the cups and plates in the dishwasher, slid the pot roast for that evening's dinner into the auto-cooker and selected the alarm, lowered the air conditioner–refrigerator and immersion heater settings, switched open the oil storage manifolds for the delivery tanker that afternoon, and retracted her section of the garage door.

Faulkner followed the sequence with admiration, counting off each successive step as the dials clicked and snapped.

You ought to be in B-52's, he thought, or in the control house of a petrochemicals plant. In fact Julia worked in the personnel section at the Clinic, and no doubt spent all day in the same whirl of efficiency, stabbing buttons marked JONES, SMITH, and BROWN, shunting paraplegics to the left, paranoids to the right.

She stepped into the lounge and came over to him, the standard executive product in brisk black suit and white blouse.

"Aren't you going to the school today?" she asked.

Faulkner shook his head, played with some papers on the desk. "No, I'm still on creative reflection. Just for this week. Professor Harman thought I'd been taking too many classes and getting stale."

She nodded, looking at him doubtfully. For three weeks now he had been lying around at home, dozing on the veranda, and she was beginning to get suspicious. Sooner or later, Faulkner realized, she would find out, but by then he hoped to be out of reach. He longed to tell her the truth, that two months ago he had resigned from his job as a lecturer at the Business School and had no intention of ever going back. She'd get a damn big surprise when she discovered they had almost expended his last pay check, might even have to put up with only one car. Let her work, he thought, she earns more than I did anyway.

With an effort Faulkner smiled at her. *Get out!* his mind screamed, but she still hovered around him indecisively.

"What about your lunch? There's no—"

"Don't worry about me," Faulkner cut in quickly, watching the clock. "I gave up eating six months ago. You have lunch at the Clinic."

Even talking to her had become an effort. He wished they could communicate by means of notes; had even bought two scribble pads for this purpose. However, he had never quite been able to suggest that she use hers, although he did leave messages around for her, on the pretext that his mind was so intellectually engaged that talking would break up his thought trains.

Oddly enough, the idea of leaving her never seriously occurred to him. Such an escape would prove nothing. Besides, he had an alternative plan.

"You'll be all right?" she asked, still watching him warily.

"Absolutely," Faulkner told her, maintaining the smile. It felt like a full day's work.

Her kiss was quick and functional, like the automatic peck of some huge bottle-topping machine. The smile was still on his face as she reached the door. When she had gone he let it fade slowly, then found himself breathing again and gradually relaxed, letting the tension drain down through his arms and legs. For a few minutes he wandered blankly around the empty house, then made his way into the lounge again, ready to begin his serious work.

His program usually followed the same course. First, from the center drawer of his desk he took a small alarm clock, fitted with a battery and wrist strap. Sitting down on the veranda, he fastened the strap to his wrist, wound and set the clock, and placed it on the table next to him, binding his arm to the chair so that there was no danger of dragging the clock onto the floor.

Ready now, he lay back and surveyed the scene in front of him.

Menninger Village, or the "Bin" as it was known locally, had been built about ten years earlier as a self-contained housing unit for the graduate staff of the Clinic and their families. In all there were some sixty houses in the development, each designed to fit into a particular architectonic niche, preserving its own identity from within and at the same time merging into the organic unity of the whole development. The object of the architects, faced with the task of compressing a great number of small houses into a four-acre site, had been, firstly, to avoid producing a collection of identical hutches, as in most housing estates, and secondly, to provide a showpiece for a major psychiatric foundation which would serve as a model for the corporate living units of the future.

However, as everyone there had found out, living in the Bin was hell on earth. The architects had employed the so-called psycho-modular system—a basic L-design—and this meant that everything under- or overlapped everything else. The whole development was a sprawl of interlocking frosted glass, white rectangles and curves, at first glance exciting and abstract (*Life* magazine had done several glossy photographic treatments of the new "living trends" suggested by the Village) but to the people within formless and visually exhausting. Most of the Clinic's senior staff had soon taken off, and the Village was now rented to anyone who could be persuaded to live there.

Faulkner gazed out across the veranda, separating from the clutter of white geometric shapes the eight other houses he could see without moving his head. On his left, immediately adjacent, were the Penzils, with the McPhersons on the right; the other six houses were directly ahead, on the far side of a muddle of interlocking garden areas, abstract rat-runs divided by waist-high white paneling, glass angle-pieces, and slatted screens.

In the Penzils' garden was a collection of huge alphabet blocks, each three high, which their two children played with. Often they left messages out on the grass for Faulkner to read, sometimes obscene, at others merely gnomic and obscure. This morning's came into the latter category. The blocks spelled out:

STOP AND GO

Speculating on the total significance of this statement, Faulkner let his mind relax, his eyes staring blankly at the houses. Gradually their already obscured outlines began to merge and fade, and the long balconies and ramps partly hidden by the intervening trees became disembodied forms, like gigantic geometric units.

Breathing slowly, Faulkner steadily closed his mind, then without any effort erased his awareness of the identity of the houses opposite.

He was now looking at a cubist landscape, a collection of random white forms below a blue backdrop, across which several powdery green blurs moved slowly backward and forward. Idly, he wondered what these geometric forms really represented—he knew that only a few seconds earlier they had constituted an immediately familiar part of his everyday existence—but however he rearranged them spatially in his mind, or sought their associations, they still remained a random assembly of geometric forms.

He had discovered this talent only about three weeks ago. Balefully eyeing the silent television set in the lounge one Sunday morning, he had suddenly realized that he had so completely accepted and assimilated the physical form of the plastic cabinet that he could no longer remember its function. It had required a considerable mental effort to recover himself and re-identify it. Out of interest he had tried out the new talent on other objects, found that it was particularly successful with overassociated ones such as washing machines, cars, and other consumer goods. Stripped of their accretions of sales slogans and status imperatives, their real claim to reality was so tenuous that it needed little mental effort to obliterate them altogether.

The effect was similar to that of mescaline and other hallucinogens, under whose influence the dents in a cushion became as vivid as the craters of the moon, the folds in a curtain, the ripples in the waves of eternity.

During the following weeks Faulkner had experimented carefully, training his ability to operate the cut-out switches. The process was slow, but gradually he found himself able to eliminate larger and larger groups of objects, the mass-produced furniture in the lounge, the overenameled gadgets in the kitchen, his car in the garage—de-identified, it sat in the half-light like an enormous vegetable marrow, flaccid and gleaming; trying to identify it had driven him almost out of his mind. "What on earth could it *possibly* be?" he had asked himself helplessly, splitting his sides with laughter—and as the facility developed he had dimly perceived that here was an escape route from the intolerable world in which he found himself at the Village.

He had described the facility to Ross Hendricks, who lived a few houses away, also a lecturer at the Business School and Faulkner's only close friend.

"It may actually be stepping out of time," Faulkner speculated. "Without a time sense consciousness is difficult to visualize. That is, eliminating the vector of time from the de-identified object frees it from all its everyday cognitive associations. Alternatively, I may have stumbled on a means of repressing the photo-associative centers that normally identify visual objects, in the same way that you can so listen to someone speaking your own language that none of the sounds has any meaning. Everyone's tried this at some time."

Hendricks had nodded. "But don't make a career out of it, though." He eyed Faulkner carefully. "You can't simply turn a blind eye to the world. The subject-object relationship is not as polar as Descartes's *'Cogito ergo sum'* suggests. By any degree to which you devalue the external world so you devalue yourself. It seems to me that your real problem is to reverse the process."

But Hendricks, however sympathetic, was beyond helping Faulkner. Besides, it was pleasant to see the world afresh again, to wallow in an endless panorama of brilliantly colored images. What did it matter if there was form but no content?

A sharp click woke him abruptly. He sat up with a jolt, fumbling with the alarm clock, which had been set to wake him at 11:00. Looking at it, he saw that it was only 10:55. The alarm had not rung, nor had he received a shock from the battery. Yet the click had been distinct. However, there were so many servos and robots around the house that it could have been anything.

A dark shape moved across the frosted glass panel which formed the side wall of the lounge. Through it, into the narrow drive separating his house from the Penzils', he saw a car draw to a halt and park, a young woman in a blue smock climb out and walk across the gravel. This was Penzil's sister-in-law, a girl of about twenty who had been staying with them for a couple of months. As she disappeared into the house Faulkner quickly unstrapped his wrist and stood up. Opening the veranda doors, he sauntered down into the garden, glancing back over his shoulder.

The girl, Louise (he had never spoken to her), went to sculpture classes in the morning, and on her return regularly took a leisurely shower before going out onto the roof to sunbathe.

Faulkner hung around the bottom of the garden, flipping stones into the pond and pretending to straighten some of the pergola slats, then noticed that the McPhersons' fifteen-year-old son Harvey was approaching along the other garden.

"Why aren't you at school?" he asked Harvey, a gangling youth with an intelligent ferretlike face under a mop of brown hair.

"I should be," Harvey told him easily. "But I convinced Mother I was overtense, and Morrison"—his father—"said I was ratiocinating too much." He shrugged. "Patients here are overpermissive."

"For once you're right," Faulkner agreed, watching the shower stall over his shoulder. A pink form moved about, adjusting taps, and there was the sound of water jetting.

"Tell me, Mr. Faulkner," Harvey asked. "Do you realize that since the death of Einstein in 1955 there hasn't been a single living genius? From Michelangelo, through Shakespeare, Newton, Beethoven, Goethe, Darwin, Freud, and Einstein there's always been a living genius. Now for the first time in five hundred years we're on our own."

Faulkner nodded, his eyes engaged. "I know," he said. "I feel damned lonely about it too."

When the shower was over he grunted to Harvey, wandered back to the veranda, and took up his position again in the chair, the battery lead strapped to his wrist.

Steadily, object by object, he began to switch off the world around him. The houses opposite went first. The white masses of the roofs and balconies he resolved quickly into flat rectangles, the lines of windows into small squares of color like the grids in a Mondrian abstract. The sky was a blank field of blue. In the distance an aircraft moved across it, engines hammering. Carefully Faulkner repressed the identity of the image, then watched the slim silver dart move slowly away like a vanishing fragment from a cartoon dream.

As he waited for the engines to fade he was conscious of the sourceless click he had heard earlier that morning. It sounded only a few feet away, near the French window on his right, but he was too immersed in the unfolding kaleidoscope to rouse himself.

When the plane had gone he turned his attention to the garden, quickly blotted out the white fencing, the fake pergola, the elliptical disk of the ornamental pool. The pathway reached out to encircle the pool, and when he blanked out his memories of the countless times he had wandered up and down its length it reared up into the air like a terra-cotta arm holding an enormous silver jewel.

Satisfied that he had obliterated the Village and the garden, Faulkner then began to demolish the house. Here the objects around him were more familiar, highly personalized extensions of himself. He began with the veranda furniture, transforming the tubular chairs and glass-topped table into a trio of involuted green coils, then swung his head slightly and selected the TV set inside the lounge on his right. It clung limply to its identity. Easily he unfocused his mind and reduced the brown plastic box, with its fake wooden veining, to an amorphous blur.

One by one he cleared the bookcase and desk of all associations, the standard lamps and picture frames. Like lumber in some psychological warehouse, they were suspended behind him *in vacuo*, the white armchairs and sofas like blunted rectangular clouds.

Anchored to reality only by the alarm mechanism clamped to his wrist, Faulkner craned his head from left to right, systematically obliterating all traces of meaning from the world around him, reducing everything to its formal visual values.

Gradually these too began to lose their meaning, the abstract masses of color dissolving, drawing Faulkner after them into a world of pure psychic sensation, where blocks of ideation hung like magnetic fields in a cloud chamber . . .

With a shattering blast, the alarm rang out, the battery driving sharp spurs of pain into Faulkner's forearm. Scalp tingling, he pulled himself back into reality and clawed away the wrist strap, massaging his arm rapidly, then slapped off the alarm.

For a few minutes he sat kneading his wrist, re-identifying all the objects around him, the houses opposite, the gardens, his home, aware that a glass wall had been inserted between them and his own psyche. However carefully he focused his mind on the world outside, a screen still separated them, its opacity thickening imperceptibly.

On other levels as well, bulkheads were shifting into place.

His wife reached home at 6:00, tired out after a busy intake day, annoyed to find Faulkner ambling about in a semistupor, the veranda littered with dirty glasses.

"Well, clean it up!" she snapped when Faulkner vacated his chair for her and prepared to take off upstairs. "Don't leave the place like this. What's the matter with you? Come on, *connect!*"

Cramming a handful of glasses together, Faulkner mumbled to himself and started for the kitchen, found Julia blocking the way out when he tried to leave. Something was on her mind. She sipped quickly at her martini, then began to throw out probes about the school. He assumed she had rung there on some pretext and had found her suspicions reinforced when she referred in passing to himself.

"Liaison is terrible," Faulkner told her. "Take two days off and no one remembers you work there." By a massive effort of concentration he had managed to avoid looking his wife in the face since she arrived. In fact, they had not exchanged a direct glance for over a week. Hopefully he wondered if this might be getting her down.

Supper was slow agony. The smells of the auto-cooked pot roast had permeated the house all afternoon. Unable to eat more than a few mouthfuls, he had nothing on which to focus his attention. Luckily Julia had a brisk appetite and he could stare at the top of her head as she ate, let his eyes wander around the room when she looked up.

After supper, thankfully, there was television. Dusk blanked out the other houses in the Village, and they sat in the darkness around the set, Julia grumbling at the programs.

"Why do we watch *every* night?" she asked. "It's a total time waster."

Faulkner gestured airily. "It's an interesting social document." Slumped down into the wing chair, hands apparently behind his neck, he could press his fingers into his ears, at will blot out the sounds of the program. "Don't pay any attention to what they're saying," he told his wife. "It makes more sense." He watched the characters mouthing silently like demented fish. The close-ups in melodramas were particularly hilarious; the more intense the situation the broader was the farce.

Something kicked his knee sharply. He looked up to see his wife bending over him, eyebrows knotted together, mouth working furiously. Fingers still pressed to his ears, Faulkner examined her face with detachment, for a moment speculated whether to complete the process and switch her off as he had switched off the rest of the world earlier that day. When he did he wouldn't bother to set the alarm...

"Harry!" he heard his wife bellow.

He sat up with a start, the row from the set backing up his wife's voice.

"What's the matter? I was asleep."

"You were in a trance, you mean. For God's sake answer when I talk to you. I was saying that I saw Harriet Tizzard this afternoon." Faulkner groaned and his wife swerved on him. "I know you can't stand the Tizzards but I've decided we ought to see more of them..."

As his wife rattled on, Faulkner eased himself down behind the wings. When she was settled back in her chair he moved his hands up behind his neck. After a few discretionary grunts, he slid his fingers into his ears and blotted out her voice, then lay quietly watching the silent screen.

By 10:00 the next morning he was out on the veranda again, alarm strapped to his wrist. For the next hour he lay back enjoying the disembodied forms suspended around him, his mind free of its anxieties. When the alarm woke him at 11:00 he felt refreshed and relaxed. For a few moments he was able to survey the nearby houses with the visual curiosity their architects had intended. Gradually, however, everything began to secrete its poison again, its overlay of nagging associations, and within ten minutes he was looking fretfully at his wristwatch.

When Louise Penzil's car pulled into the drive he disconnected the alarm and sauntered out into the garden, head down to shut out as many of the surrounding houses as possible. As he was idling around the pergola, replacing the slats torn loose by the roses, Harvey McPherson suddenly popped his head over the fence.

"Harvey, are you still around? Don't you ever go to school?"

"Well, I'm on this relaxation course of Mother's," Harvey explained. "I find the competitive context of the classroom is—"

"I'm trying to relax too," Faulkner cut in. "Let's leave it at that. Why don't you beat it?"

Unruffled, Harvey pressed on. "Mr. Faulkner, I've got a sort of problem in metaphysics that's been bothering me. Maybe you could help. The only absolute in space-time is supposed to be the speed of light. But as a matter of fact any estimate of the speed of light involves the component of time, which is subjectively variable—so, bam, what's left?"

"Girls," Faulkner said. He glanced over his shoulder at the Penzil house and then turned back moodily to Harvey.

Harvey frowned, trying to straighten his hair. "What are you talking about?"

"Girls," Faulkner repeated. "You know, the weaker sex, the distaff side."

"Oh, for Pete's sake." Shaking his head, Harvey walked back to his house, muttering to himself.

That'll shut you up, Faulkner thought. He started to scan the Penzils' house through the slats of the pergola, then suddenly spotted Harry Penzil standing in the center of his veranda window, frowning out at him.

Quickly Faulkner turned his back and pretended to trim the roses. By the time he managed to work his way indoors he was sweating heavily. Harry Penzil was the sort of man liable to straddle fences and come out leading with a right swing.

Mixing himself a drink in the kitchen, Faulkner brought it out onto the veranda and sat down waiting for his embarrassment to subside before setting the alarm mechanism.

He was listening carefully for any sounds from the Penzils's when he heard a familiar soft metallic click from the house on his right.

Faulkner sat forward, examining the veranda wall. This was a slab of heavy frosted glass, completely opaque, carrying white roof timbers, clipped onto which were slabs of corrugated polythene sheeting. Just beyond the veranda, screening the proximal portions of the adjacent gardens, was a ten-foot-high metal lattice extending about twenty feet down the garden fence and strung with japonica.

Inspecting the lattice carefully, Faulkner suddenly noticed the outline of a square black object on a slender tripod propped up behind the first vertical support just three feet from the open veranda window, the disk of a small glass eye staring at him unblinkingly through one of the horizontal slots.

A camera! Faulkner leaped out of his chair, gaping incredulously at the instrument. For days it had been clicking away at him. God alone knew what glimpses into his private life Harvey had recorded for his own amusement.

Anger boiling, Faulkner strode across to the lattice, prized one of the metal members off the support beam, and seized the camera. As he dragged it through the space the tripod fell away with a clatter and he heard someone on the McPhersons' veranda start up out of a chair.

Faulkner wrestled the camera through, snapping off the remote control cord attached to the shutter lever. Opening the camera, he ripped out the film, then put it down on the floor and stamped its face in with the heel of his shoe. Then, ramming the pieces together, he stepped forward and hurled them over the fence toward the far end of the McPhersons' garden.

As he returned to finish his drink the phone rang in the hall.

"Yes, what is it?" he snapped into the receiver.

"Is that you, Harry? Julia here."

"Who?" Faulkner said, not thinking. "Oh, yes. Well, how are things?"

"Not too good, by the sound of it." His wife's voice had become harder. "I've just had a long talk with Professor Harman. He told me that you resigned from the school two months ago. Harry, what are you playing at? I can hardly believe it."

"I can hardly believe it either," Faulkner retorted jocularly. "It's the best news I've had for years. Thanks for confirming it."

"Harry!" His wife was shouting now. "Pull yourself together! If you think I'm going to support you you're very much mistaken. Professor Harman said—"

"That idiot Harman!" Faulkner interrupted. "Don't you realize he was trying to drive me insane?" As his wife's voice rose to an hysterical squawk he held the receiver away from him, then quietly replaced it in the cradle. After a pause he took it off again and laid it down on the stack of directories.

Outside, the spring morning hung over the Village like a curtain of silence. Here and there a tree stirred in the warm air, or a window opened and caught the sunlight, but otherwise the quiet and stillness were unbroken.

Lying on the veranda, the alarm mechanism discarded on the floor below his chair, Faulkner sank deeper and deeper into his private reverie, into the demolished world of form and color which hung motionlessly around him. The houses opposite had vanished, their places taken by long white rectangular bands. The garden was a green ramp at the end of which poised the silver ellipse of the pond. The veranda was a transparent cube, in the center of which he felt himself suspended like an image floating on a sea of ideation. He had obliterated not only the world around him, but his own body, and his limbs and trunk seemed an extension of his mind, disembodied forms whose physical dimensions pressed upon it like a dream's awareness of its own identity.

Some hours later, as he rotated slowly through his reverie, he was aware of a sudden intrusion into his field of vision. Focusing his eyes, with surprise he saw the dark-suited figure of his wife standing in front of him, shouting angrily and gesturing with her handbag.

For a few minutes Faulkner examined the discrete entity she familiarly presented, the proportions of her legs and arms, the planes of her face. Then, without moving, he began to dismantle her mentally, obliterating her literally limb by limb. First he forgot her hands, forever snapping and twisting like frenzied birds, then her arms and shoulders, erasing all his memories of their energy and motion. Finally, as it pressed closer to him, mouth working wildly, he forgot her face, so that it presented nothing more than a blunted wedge of pink-gray dough, deformed by various ridges and grooves, split by apertures that opened and closed like the vents of some curious bellows.

Turning back to the silent dreamscape, he was aware of her jostling insistently behind him. Her presence seemed ugly and formless, a bundle of obtrusive angles.

Then at last they came into brief physical contact. Gesturing her away, he felt her fasten like a dog upon his arm. He tried to shake her off but she clung to him, jerking about in an outpouring of anger.

Her rhythms were sharp and ungainly. To begin with he tried to ignore them; then he began to restrain and smooth her, molding her angular form into a softer and rounder one.

As he worked away, kneading her like a sculptor shaping clay, he noticed a series of crackling noises, over which a persistent scream was just barely audible. When he finished he let her fall to the floor, a softly squeaking lump of spongy rubber.

Faulkner returned to his reverie, re-assimilating the unaltered landscape. His brush with his wife had reminded him of the one encumbrance that still remained—his own body. Although he had forgotten its identity it nonetheless felt heavy and warm, vaguely uncomfortable, like a badly made bed to a restless sleeper. What he sought was pure ideation, the undisturbed sensation of psychic being untransmuted by any physical medium. Only thus could he escape the nausea of the external world.

Somewhere in his mind an idea suggested itself. Rising from his chair, he walked out across the veranda, unaware of the physical movements involved, but propelling himself toward the far end of the garden.

Hidden by the rose pergola, he stood for five minutes at the edge of the pond, then stepped into the water. Trousers billowing around his knees, he waded out slowly. When he reached the center he sat down, pushing the weeds apart, and lay back in the shallow water.

Slowly he felt the puttylike mass of his body dissolving, its temperature growing cooler and less oppressive. Looking out through the surface of the water six inches above his face, he watched the blue disk of the sky, cloudless and undisturbed, expanding to fill his consciousness. At last he had found the perfect background, the only possible field of ideation, an absolute continuum of existence uncontaminated by material excrescences.

Steadily watching it, he waited for the world to dissolve and set him free.

Billennium

All day long, and often into the early hours of the morning, the tramp of feet sounded up and down the stairs outside Ward's cubicle. Built into a narrow alcove in a bend of the staircase between the fourth and fifth floors, its plywood walls flexed and creaked with every footstep like the timbers of a rotting windmill. Over a hundred people lived in the top three floors of the old rooming house, and sometimes Ward would lie awake on his narrow bunk until 2:00 or 3:00 A.M. mechanically counting the last residents returning from the all-night movies in the stadium half a mile away. Through the window he could hear giant fragments of the amplified dialogue booming among the rooftops. The stadium was never empty. During the day the huge four-sided screen was raised on its davit and athletics meetings or football matches ran continuously. For the people in the houses abutting the stadium the noise must have been unbearable.

Ward, at least, had a certain degree of privacy. Two months earlier, before he came to live on the staircase, he had shared a room with seven others on the ground floor of a house on 755th Street, and the ceaseless press of people jostling past the window had reduced him to a state of chronic exhaustion. The street was always full, an endless clamor of voices and shuffling feet. By six-thirty, when he woke, hurrying to take his place in the bathroom queue, the crowds already jammed it from sidewalk to sidewalk, the din punctuated every half minute by the roar of the elevated trains running over the shops on the opposite side of the road. As soon as he saw the advertisement describing the staircase cubicle (like everyone else, he spent most of his spare time scanning the classifieds in the newspapers, moving his lodgings an average of once every two months) he had left despite the higher rental. A cubicle on a staircase would almost certainly be on its own.

However, this had its drawbacks. Most evenings his friends from the library would call in, eager to rest their elbows after the bruising crush of the public reading room. The cubicle was slightly more than four and a half square meters in floor area, half a square meter over the statutory maximum for a single person, the carpenters having taken advantage, illegally, of a recess beside a nearby chimney breast. Consequently Ward had been able to fit a small straight-backed chair into the interval between the bed and the door, so that only one person at a time need sit on the bed—in most single cubicles host and guest had to sit side by side on the bed, conversing over their shoulders and changing places periodically to avoid neck strain.

"You were lucky to find this place," Rossiter, the most regular visitor, never tired of telling him. He reclined back on the bed, gesturing at the cubicle. "It's enormous, the perspectives really zoom. I'd be surprised if you hadn't got at least five meters here, perhaps even six."

Ward shook his head categorically. Rossiter was his closest friend, but the quest for living space had forged powerful reflexes. "Just over four and a half, I've measured it carefully. There's no doubt about it."

Rossiter lifted one eyebrow. "I'm amazed. It must be the ceiling then."

Manipulating the ceiling was a favorite trick of unscrupulous landlords—most assessments of area were made upon the ceiling, out of convenience, and by tilting back the plywood partitions the rated area of a cubicle could be either increased, for the benefit of a prospective tenant (many married couples were thus bamboozled into taking a single cubicle), or decreased temporarily on the visit of the housing inspectors. Ceilings were crisscrossed with pencil marks staking out the rival claims of tenants on opposite sides of a party wall. Someone timid of his rights could be literally squeezed out of existence—in fact, the advertisement "quiet clientele" was usually a tacit invitation to this sort of piracy.

"The wall does tilt a little," Ward admitted. "Actually, it's about four degrees out—I used a plumb line. But there's still plenty of room on the stairs for people to get by."

Rossiter grinned. "Of course, John. I'm just envious, that's all. My room's driving me crazy." Like everyone, he used the term "room" to describe his tiny cubicle, a hangover from the days fifty years earlier when people had indeed lived one to a room, sometimes, unbelievably, one to an apartment or house. The microfilms in the architecture catalogs at the library showed scenes of museums, concert halls, and other public buildings in what appeared to be everyday settings, often virtually empty, two or three people wandering down an enormous gallery or staircase. Traffic moved freely along the center of streets, and in the quieter districts sections of sidewalk would be deserted for fifty yards or more.

Now, of course, the older buildings had been torn down and replaced by housing batteries, or converted into apartment blocks. The great banqueting room in the former City Hall had been split horizontally into four decks, each of these cut up into hundreds of cubicles.

As for the streets, traffic had long since ceased to move about them. Apart from a few hours before dawn when only the sidewalks were crowded, every thoroughfare was always packed with a shuffling mob of pedestrians, perforce ignoring the countless KEEP LEFT signs suspended over their heads, wrestling past each other on their way to home and office, their clothes dusty and shapeless. Often "locks" would occur when a huge crowd at a street junction became immovably jammed. Sometimes these locks would last for days. Two years earlier Ward had been caught in one outside the stadium; for over forty-eight hours he was trapped in a gigantic pedestrian jam containing over seventy thousand people, fed by the crowds leaving the stadium on one side and those approaching it on the other. An entire square mile of the local neighborhood had been paralyzed, and he vividly remembered the nightmare of swaying helplessly on his feet as the jam shifted and heaved, terrified of losing his balance and being trampled underfoot. When the police had finally sealed off the stadium and dispersed the jam he had gone back to his cubicle and slept for a week, his body blue with bruises.

"I hear they may reduce the allocation to three and a half meters," Rossiter remarked.

Ward paused to allow a party of tenants from the sixth floor to pass down the staircase, holding the door to prevent it jumping off its latch. "So they're always saying," he commented. "I can remember that rumor ten years ago."

"It's no rumor," Rossiter warned him. "It may well be necessary soon. Thirty million people packed into this city now, a million increase in just one year. There's been some pretty serious talk at the Housing Department."

Ward shook his head. "A drastic revaluation like that is almost impossible to carry out. Every single partition would have to be dismantled and nailed up again; the administrative job alone is so vast it's difficult to visualize. Millions of cubicles to be redesigned and certified, licenses to be issued, plus the complete resettlement of every tenant. Most of the buildings put up since the last revaluation are designed around a four-meter module—you can't simply take half a meter off the end of each cubicle and then say that makes so many new cubicles. They may be only six inches wide." He laughed. "Besides, how can you live in just three and a half meters?"

Rossiter smiled. "That's the ultimate argument, isn't it? They used it twenty-five years ago at the last revaluation, when the minimum was cut from five to four. It couldn't be done, they all said, no one could stand living in only four square meters; it was enough room for a bed and suitcase, but you couldn't open the door to get in." Rossiter chuckled softly. "They were all wrong. It was merely decided that from then on all doors would open outward. Four square meters was here to stay."

Ward looked at his watch. It was seven-thirty. "Time to eat. Let's see if we can get into the food bar across the road."

Grumbling at the prospect, Rossiter pulled himself off the bed. They left the cubicle and made their way down the staircase. This was crammed with luggage and packing cases so that only a narrow interval remained around the bannister. On the floors below the congestion was worse. Corridors were wide enough to be chopped up into single cubicles, and the air was stale and dead, cardboard walls hung with damp laundry and makeshift larders. Each of the five rooms on the floors contained a dozen tenants, their voices reverberating through the partitions.

People were sitting on the steps above the second floor, using the staircase as an informal lounge, although this was against the fire regulations, women chatting with the men queuing in their shirtsleeves outside the washroom, children diving around them. By the time they reached the entrance Ward and Rossiter were having to force their way through the tenants packed together on every landing, loitering around the notice boards or pushing in from the street below.

Taking a breath at the top of the steps, Ward pointed to the food bar on the other side of the road. It was only thirty yards away, but the throng moving down the street swept past like a river at full tide, crossing them from right to left. The first picture show at the stadium started at nine o'clock, and people were setting off already to make sure of getting in.

"Can't we go somewhere else?" Rossiter asked, screwing his face up at the prospect of the food bar. Not only would it be packed and take them half an hour to be served, but the food was flat and unappetizing. The journey from the library four blocks away had given him an appetite.

Ward shrugged. "There's a place on the corner, but I doubt if we can make it." This was two hundred yards upstream; they would be fighting the crowd all the way.

"Maybe you're right." Rossiter put his hand on Ward's shoulder. "You know, John, your trouble is that you never go anywhere, you're too disengaged, you just don't realize how bad everything is getting."

Ward nodded. Rossiter was right. In the morning, when he set off for the library, the pedestrian traffic was moving with him toward the downtown offices; in the evening, when he came back, it was flowing in the opposite direction. By and large he never altered his routine. Brought up from the age of ten in a municipal hostel, he had gradually lost touch with his father and mother, who lived on the east side of the city and had been unable, or unwilling, to make the journey to see him. Having surrendered his initiative to the dynamics of the city he was reluctant to try to win it back merely for a better cup of coffee. Fortunately his job at the library brought him into contact with a wide range of young people of similar interests. Sooner or later he would marry, find a double cubicle near the library, and settle down. If they had enough children (three was the required minimum) they might even one day own a small room of their own.

They stepped out into the pedestrian stream, carried along by it for ten or twenty yards, then quickened their pace and sidestepped through the crowd, slowly tacking across to the other side of the road. There they found the shelter of the shop fronts, slowly worked their way back to the food bar, shoulders braced against the countless minor collisions.

"What are the latest population estimates?" Ward asked as they circled a cigarette kiosk, stepping forward whenever a gap presented itself.

Rossiter smiled. "Sorry, John, I'd like to tell you but you might start a stampede. Besides, you wouldn't believe me."

Rossiter worked in the Insurance Department at the City Hall, had informal access to the census statistics. For the last ten years these had been classified information, partly because they were felt to be inaccurate, but chiefly because it was feared they might set off a mass attack of claustrophobia. Minor outbreaks had taken place already, and the official line was that world population had reached a plateau, leveling off at twenty thousand million. No one believed this for a moment, and Ward assumed that the 3 percent annual increase maintained since the 1960s was continuing.

How long it could continue was impossible to estimate. Despite the gloomiest prophecies of the neo-Malthusians, world agriculture had managed to keep pace with the population growth, although intensive cultivation meant that 95 percent of the population was permanently trapped in vast urban conurbations. The outward growth of cities had at last been checked; in fact, all over the world former suburban areas were being reclaimed for agriculture and population additions were confined within the existing urban ghettos. The countryside, as such, no longer existed. Every single square foot of ground sprouted a crop of one type or other. The onetime fields and meadows of the world were now, in effect, factory floors, as highly mechanized and closed to the public as any industrial area. Economic and ideological rivalries had long since faded before one overriding quest—the internal colonization of the city.

Reaching the food bar, they pushed themselves into the entrance and joined the scrum of customers pressing six deep against the counter.

"What is really wrong with the population problem," Ward confided to Rossiter, "is that no one has ever tried to tackle it. Fifty years ago shortsighted nationalism and industrial expansion put a premium on a rising population curve, and even now the hidden incentive is to have a large family so that you can gain a little privacy. Single people are penalized simply because there are more of them and they don't fit conveniently into double or triple cubicles. But it's the large family with its compact, space-saving logistic that is the real villain."

Rossiter nodded, edging nearer the counter, ready to shout his order. "Too true. We all look forward to getting married just so that we can have our six meters."

Directly in front of them, two girls turned around and smiled. "Six square meters," one of them, a dark-haired girl with a pretty oval face, repeated. "You sound like the sort of young man I ought to get to know. Going into the real estate business, Henry?"

Rossiter grinned and squeezed her arm. "Hello, Judith. I'm thinking about it actively. Like to join me in a private venture?"

The girl leaned against him as they reached the counter. "Well, I might. It would have to be legal, though."

The other girl, Helen Waring, an assistant at the library, pulled Ward's sleeve. "Have you heard the latest, John? Judith and I have been kicked out of our room. We're on the street right at this minute."

"What?" Rossiter cried. They collected their soups and coffee and edged back to the rear of the bar. "What on earth happened?"

Helen explained. "You know that little broom cupboard outside our cubicle? Judith and I have been using it as a sort of study hole, going in there to read. It's quiet and restful, if you can get used to not breathing. Well, the old girl found out and kicked up a big fuss, said we were breaking the law and so on. In short, out." Helen paused. "Now we've heard she's going to let it as a single."

Rossiter pounded the counter ledge. "A broom cupboard? Someone's going to live there? But she'll never get a license."

Judith shook her head. "She's got it already. Her brother works in the Housing Department."

Ward laughed into his soup. "But how can she let it? No one will live in a broom cupboard."

Judith stared at him somberly. "You really believe that, John?"

Ward dropped his spoon. "No, I guess you're right. People will live anywhere. God, I don't know who I feel more sorry for—you two, or the poor devil who'll be living in that cupboard. What are you going to do?"

"A couple in a place two blocks west are subletting half their cubicle to us. They've hung a sheet down the middle and Helen and I'll take turns sleeping on a camp bed. I'm not joking, our room's about two feet wide. I said to Helen that we ought to split up again and sublet one half at twice our rent."

They had a good laugh over all this and Ward said good-night to the others and went back to his rooming house.

There he found himself with similar problems.

The manager leaned against the flimsy door, a damp cigar butt revolving around his mouth, an expression of morose boredom on his unshaven face.

"You got four point seven two meters," he told Ward, who was standing out on the staircase, unable to get into his room. Other tenants stepped past onto the landing, where two women in curlers and dressing gowns were arguing with each other, tugging angrily at the wall of trunks and cases. Occasionally the manager glanced at them irritably. "Four seven two. I worked it out twice." He said this as if it ended all possibility of argument.

"Ceiling or floor?" Ward asked.

"Ceiling, whaddya think? How can I measure the floor with all this junk?" He kicked at a crate of books protruding from under the bed.

Ward let this pass. "There's quite a tilt on the wall," he pointed out. "As much as three or four degrees."

The manager nodded vaguely. "You're definitely over the four. Way over." He turned to Ward, who had moved down several steps to allow a man and woman to get past. "I can rent this as a double."

"What, only four and a half?" Ward said incredulously. "How?"

The man who had just passed him leaned over the manager's shoulder and sniffed at the room, taking in every detail in a one-second glance. "You renting a double here, Louie?"

The manager waved him away and then beckoned Ward into the room, closing the door after him.

"It's a nominal five," he told Ward. "New regulation, just came out. Anything over four five is a double now." He eyed Ward shrewdly. "Well, whaddya want? It's a good room, there's a lot of space here, feels more like a triple. You got access to the staircase, window slit—" He broke off as Ward slumped down on the bed and started to laugh. "Whatsa matter? Look, if you want a big room like this you gotta pay for it. I want an extra half rental or you get out."

Ward wiped his eyes, then stood up wearily and reached for the shelves. "Relax, I'm on my way. I'm going to live in a broom cupboard. 'Access to the staircase'—that's really rich. Tell me, Louie, is there life on Uranus?"

Temporarily, he and Rossiter teamed up to rent a double cubicle in a semiderelict house a hundred yards from the library. The neighborhood was seedy and faded, the rooming houses crammed with tenants. Most of them were owned by absentee landlords or by the city corporation, and the managers employed were of the lowest type, mere rent collectors who cared nothing about the way their tenants divided up the living space, and never ventured beyond the first floors. Bottles and empty cans littered the corridors, and the washrooms looked like sumps. Many of the tenants were old and infirm, sitting about listlessly in their narrow cubicles, wheedling at each other back to back through the thin partitions.

Their double cubicle was on the third floor, at the end of a corridor that ringed the building. Its architecture was impossible to follow, rooms letting off at all angles, and luckily the corridor was a cul-de-sac. The mounds of cases ended four feet from the end wall and a partition divided off the cubicle, just wide enough for two beds. A high window overlooked the areaways of the building opposite.

Possessions loaded onto the shelf above his head, Ward lay back on his bed and moodily surveyed the roof of the library through the afternoon haze.

"It's not bad here," Rossiter told him, unpacking his case. "I know there's no real privacy and we'll drive each other insane within a week, but at least we haven't got six other people breathing into our ears two feet away."

The nearest cubicle, a single, was built into the banks of cases half a dozen steps along the corridor, but the occupant, a man of seventy, was deaf and bedridden.

"It's not bad," Ward echoed reluctantly. "Now tell me what the latest growth figures are. They might console me."

Rossiter paused, lowering his voice. "Four percent. *Eight hundred million extra people in one year*—just less than half the Earth's total population in 1950."

Ward whistled slowly. "So they will revalue. What to? Three and a half?"

"Three. From the first of next year."

"Three square meters!" Ward sat up and looked around him. "It's unbelievable! The world's going insane, Rossiter. For God's sake, when are they going to do something about it? Do you realize there soon won't be room enough to sit down, let alone lie down?"

Exasperated, he punched the wall beside him, on the second blow knocked in one of the small wooden panels that had been lightly papered over.

"Hey!" Rossiter yelled. "You're breaking the place down." He dived across the bed to retrieve the panel, which hung downward supported by a strip of paper. Ward slipped his hand into the dark interval, carefully drew the panel back onto the bed.

"Who's on the other side?" Rossiter whispered. "Did they hear?"

Ward peered through the interval, eyes searching the dim light. Suddenly he dropped the panel and seized Rossiter's shoulder, pulled him down onto the bed.

"Henry! Look!"

Rossiter freed himself and pressed his face to the opening, focused slowly, and then gasped.

Directly in front of them, faintly illuminated by a grimy skylight, was a medium-sized room, some fifteen feet square, empty except for the dust silted up against the skirting boards. The floor was bare, a few strips of frayed linoleum running across it, the walls covered with a drab floral design. Here and there patches of the paper had peeled off and segments of the picture rail had rotted away, but otherwise the room was in habitable condition.

Breathing slowly, Ward closed the open door of the cubicle with his foot, then turned to Rossiter.

"Henry, do you realize what we've found? Do you realize it, man?"

"Shut up. For Pete's sake keep your voice down." Rossiter examined the room carefully. "It's fantastic. I'm trying to see whether anyone's used it recently."

"Of course they haven't," Ward pointed out. "It's obvious. There's no door into the room. We're looking through it now. They must have paneled over this door years ago and forgotten about it. Look at that filth everywhere."

Rossiter was staring into the room, his mind staggered by its vastness.

"You're right," he murmured. "Now, when do we move in?"

Panel by panel, they pried away the lower half of the door, nailed it onto a wooden frame so that the dummy section could be replaced instantly.

Then, picking an afternoon when the house was half empty and the manager asleep in his basement office, they made their first foray into the room, Ward going in alone while Rossiter kept guard in the cubicle.

For an hour they exchanged places, wandering silently around the dusty room, stretching their arms out to feel its unconfined emptiness, grasping at the sensation of absolute spatial freedom. Although smaller than many of the subdivided rooms in which they had lived, this room seemed infinitely larger, its walls huge cliffs that soared upward to the skylight.

Finally, two or three days later, they moved in.

For the first week Rossiter slept alone in the room, Ward in the cubicle outside, both there together during the day. Gradually they smuggled in a few items of furniture: two armchairs, a table, a lamp fed from the socket in the cubicle. The furniture was heavy and Victorian; the cheapest available, its size emphasized the emptiness of the room. Pride of place was taken by an enormous mahogany wardrobe, fitted with carved angels and castellated mirrors, which they were forced to dismantle and carry into the house in their suitcases. Towering over them, it reminded Ward of the microfilms of Gothic cathedrals, with their massive organ lofts crossing vast naves.

After three weeks they both slept in the room, finding the cubicle unbearably cramped. An imitation Japanese screen divided the room adequately and did nothing to diminish its size. Sitting there in the evenings, surrounded by his books and albums, Ward steadily forgot the city outside. Luckily he reached the library by a back alley and avoided the crowded streets. Rossiter and himself began to seem the only real inhabitants of the world, everyone else a meaningless by-product of their own existence, a random replication of identity which had run out of control.

It was Rossiter who suggested they ask the two girls to share the room with them.

"They've been kicked out again and may have to split up," he told Ward, obviously worried that Judith might fall into bad company. "There's always a rent freeze after revaluation, but all the landlords know about it so they're not reletting. It's getting damned difficult to find a room anywhere."

Ward nodded, relaxing back around the circular redwood table. He played with a tassel of the arsenic-green lampshade, for a moment felt like a Victorian man of letters, leading a spacious, leisurely life among overstuffed furnishings.

"I'm all for it," he agreed, indicating the empty corners. "There's plenty of room here. But we'll have to make damn sure they don't gossip about it."

After due precautions, they let the two girls into the secret, enjoying their astonishment at finding this private universe.

"We'll put a partition across the middle," Rossiter explained, "then take it down each morning. You'll be able to move in within a couple of days. How do you feel?"

"Wonderful!" They goggled at the wardrobe, squinting at the endless reflections in the mirrors.

There was no difficulty getting them in and out of the house. The turnover of tenants was continuous and bills were placed in the mail rack. No one cared who the girls were or noticed their regular calls at the cubicle.

However, half an hour after they arrived neither of them had unpacked her suitcase.

"What's up, Judith?" Ward asked, edging past the girls' beds into the narrow interval between the table and wardrobe.

Judith hesitated, looking from Ward to Rossiter, who sat on his bed, finishing off the plywood partition. "John, it's just that..."

Helen Waring, more matter of fact, took over, her fingers straightening the bedspread. "What Judith's trying to say is that our position here is a little embarrassing. The partition is—"

Rossiter stood up. "For heaven's sake, don't worry, Helen," he assured her, speaking in the loud whisper they had all involuntarily cultivated. "No funny business, you can trust us. This partition is as solid as a rock."

The two girls nodded. "It's not that," Helen explained, "but it isn't up all the time. We thought that if an older person were here, say Judith's aunt—she wouldn't take up much room and be no trouble, she's really awfully sweet—we wouldn't need to bother about the partition—except at night," she added quickly.

Ward glanced at Rossiter, who shrugged and began to scan the floor.

"Well, it's an idea," Rossiter said. "John and I know how you feel. Why not?"

"Sure," Ward agreed. He pointed to the space between the girls' beds and the table. "One more won't make any difference."

The girls broke into whoops. Judith went over to Rossiter and kissed him on the cheek. "Sorry to be a nuisance, Henry." She smiled at him. "That's a wonderful partition you've made. You couldn't do another one for Auntie—just a little one? She's very sweet but she is getting on."

"Of course," Rossiter said. "I understand. I've got plenty of wood left over."

Ward looked at his watch. "It's seven-thirty, Judith. You'd better get in touch with your aunt. She may not be able to make it to-night."

Judith buttoned her coat. "Oh, she will," she assured Ward. "I'll be back in a jiffy."

The aunt arrived within five minutes, three heavy suitcases soundly packed.

"It's amazing," Ward remarked to Rossiter three months later. "The size of this room still staggers me. It almost gets larger every day."

Rossiter agreed readily, averting his eyes from one of the girls changing behind the central partition. This they now left in place as dismantling it daily had become tiresome. Besides, the aunt's sub-sidiary partition was attached to it and she resented the continuous upsets. Ensuring she followed the entrance and exit drills through the camouflaged door and cubicle was difficult enough.

Despite this, detection seemed unlikely. The room had obviously been built as an afterthought into the central well of the house and any noise was masked by the luggage stacked in the surrounding corridor. Directly below was a small dormitory occupied by several elderly women, and Judith's aunt, who visited them socially, swore that no sounds came through the heavy ceiling. Above, the fanlight let out through a dormer window, its lights indistinguishable from the hundred other bulbs burning in the windows of the house.

Rossiter finished off the new partition he was building and held it upright, fitting it into the slots nailed to the wall between his bed and Ward's. They had agreed that this would provide a little extra privacy.

"No doubt I'll have to do one for Judith and Helen," he confided to Ward.

Ward adjusted his pillow. They had smuggled the two armchairs back to the furniture shop as they took up too much space. The bed, anyway, was more comfortable. He had never got completely used to the soft upholstery.

"Not a bad idea. What about some shelving around the wall? I've got nowhere to put anything."

The shelving tidied the room considerably, freeing large areas of the floor. Divided by their partitions, the five beds were in line along the rear wall, facing the mahogany wardrobe. In between was an open space of three or four feet, a further six feet on either side of the wardrobe.

The sight of so much space fascinated Ward. When Rossiter mentioned that Helen's mother was ill and badly needed personal care he immediately knew where her cubicle could be placed—at the foot of his bed, between the wardrobe and the side wall.

Helen was overjoyed. "It's awfully good of you, John," she told him, "but would you mind if Mother slept beside me? There's enough space to fit an extra bed in."

So Rossiter dismantled the partitions and moved them closer together, six beds now in line along the wall. This gave each of them an interval of two and a half feet wide, just enough room to squeeze down the side of their beds. Lying back on the extreme right, the shelves two feet above his head, Ward could barely see the wardrobe, but the space in front of him, a clear six feet to the wall ahead, was uninterrupted.

Then Helen's father arrived.

Knocking on the door of the cubicle, Ward smiled at Judith's aunt as she let him in. He helped her swing out the made-up bed which guarded the entrance, then rapped on the wooden panel. A moment later Helen's father, a small gray-haired man in an undershirt, braces tied to his trousers with string, pulled back the panel.

Ward nodded to him and stepped over the luggage piled around the floor at the foot of the beds. Helen was in her mother's cubicle, helping the old woman to drink her evening broth. Rossiter, perspiring heavily, was on his knees by the mahogany wardrobe, wrenching apart the frame of the central mirror with a jimmy. Pieces of the wardrobe lay on his bed and across the floor.

"We'll have to start taking these out tomorrow," Rossiter told him. Ward waited for Helen's father to shuffle past and enter his cubicle. He had rigged up a small cardboard door, and locked it behind him with a crude hook of bent wire.

Rossiter watched him, frowning irritably. "Some people are happy. This wardrobe's a hell of a job. How did we ever decide to buy it?"

Ward sat down on his bed. The partition pressed against his knees and he could hardly move. He looked up when Rossiter was engaged and saw that the dividing line he had marked in pencil was hidden by the encroaching partition. Leaning against the wall, he tried to ease it back again, but Rossiter had apparently nailed the lower edge to the floor.

There was a sharp tap on the outside cubicle door—Judith returning from her office. Ward started to get up and then sat back. "Mr. Waring," he called softly. It was the old man's duty night.

Waring shuffled to the door of his cubicle and unlocked it fussily, clucking to himself.

"Up and down, up and down," he muttered. He stumbled over Rossiter's tool bag and swore loudly, then added meanly over his shoulder: "If you ask me there's too many people in here. Down below they've only got six to our seven, and it's the same size room."

Ward nodded vaguely and stretched back on his narrow bed, trying not to bang his head on the shelving. Waring was not the first to hint that he move out. Judith's aunt had made a similar suggestion two days earlier. Since he left his job at the library (the small rental he charged the others paid for the little food he needed) he spent most of his time in the room, seeing rather more of the old man than he wanted to, but he had learned to tolerate him.

Settling himself, he noticed that the right-hand spire of the wardrobe, all he had been able to see for the past two months, was now dismantled.

It had been a beautiful piece of furniture, in a way symbolizing this whole private world, and the salesman at the store told him there were few like it left. For a moment Ward felt a sudden pang of regret, as he had done as a child when his father, in a mood of exasperation, had taken something away from him and he knew he would never see it again.

Then he pulled himself together. It was a beautiful wardrobe, without doubt, but when it was gone it would make the room seem even larger.

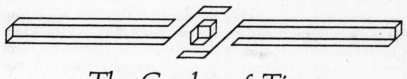

The Garden of Time

Toward evening, when the great shadow of the Palladian villa filled the terrace, Count Axel left his library and walked down the wide rococo steps among the time flowers. A tall, imperious figure in a black velvet jacket, a gold tiepin glinting below his George V beard, cane held stiffly in a white-gloved hand, he surveyed the exquisite crystal flowers without emotion, listening to the sounds of his wife's harpsichord, as she played a Mozart rondo in the music room, echo and vibrate through the translucent petals.

The garden of the villa extended for some two hundred yards below the terrace, sloping down to a miniature lake spanned by a white bridge, a slender pavilion on the opposite bank. Axel rarely ventured as far as the lake; most of the time flowers grew in a small grove just below the terrace, sheltered by the high wall which encircled the estate. From the terrace he could see over the wall to the plain beyond, a continuous expanse of open ground that rolled in great swells to the horizon, where it rose slightly before finally dipping from sight. The plain surrounded the house on all sides, its drab emptiness emphasizing the seclusion and mellowed magnificence of the villa. Here, in the garden, the air seemed brighter, the sun warmer, while the plain was always dull and remote.

As was his custom before beginning his evening stroll, Count

141

Axel looked out across the plain to the final rise, where the horizon was illuminated like a distant stage by the fading sun. As the Mozart chimed delicately around him, flowing from his wife's graceful hands, he saw that the advance column of an enormous army was moving slowly over the horizon. At first glance, the long ranks seemed to be progressing in orderly lines, but on closer inspection, it was apparent that, like the obscured detail of a Goya landscape, the army was composed of a vast throng of people, men and women, interspersed with a few soldiers in ragged uniforms, pressing forward in a disorganized tide. Some labored under heavy loads suspended from crude yokes around their necks, others struggled with cumbersome wooden carts, their hands wrenching at the wheel spokes, a few trudged on alone, but all moved on at the same pace, bowed backs illuminated in the fleeting sun.

The advancing throng was almost too far away to be visible, but even as Axel watched, his expression aloof yet observant, it came perceptibly nearer, the vanguard of an immense rabble appearing from below the horizon. At last, as the daylight began to fade, the front edge of the throng reached the crest of the first swell below the horizon, and Axel turned from the terrace and walked down among the time flowers.

The flowers grew to a height of about six feet, their slender stems, like rods of glass, bearing a dozen leaves, the once transparent fronds frosted by the fossilized veins. At the peak of each stem was the time flower, the size of a goblet, the opaque outer petals enclosing the crystal heart. Their diamond brilliance contained a thousand faces, the crystal seeming to drain the air of its light and motion. As the flowers swayed slightly in the evening air, they glowed like flame-tipped spears.

Many of the stems no longer bore flowers, and Axel examined them all carefully, a note of hope now and then crossing his eyes as he searched for any further buds. Finally he selected a large flower on the stem nearest the wall, removed his gloves, and with his strong fingers snapped it off.

As he carried the flower back onto the terrace, it began to sparkle and deliquesce, the light trapped within the core at last released. Gradually the crystal dissolved, only the outer petals remaining intact, and the air around Axel became bright and vivid, charged with slanting rays that flared away into the waning sunlight.

Strange shifts momentarily transformed the evening, subtly altering its dimensions of time and space. The darkened portico of the house, its patina of age stripped away, loomed with a curious spectral whiteness as if suddenly remembered in a dream.

Raising his head, Axel peered over the wall again. Only the farthest rim of the horizon was lit by the sun, and the great throng, which before had stretched almost a quarter of the way across the plain, had now receded to the horizon, the entire concourse abruptly flung back in a reversal of time, and appeared to be stationary.

The flower in Axel's hand had shrunk to the size of a glass thimble, the petals contracting around the vanishing core. A faint sparkle flickered from the center and extinguished itself, and Axel felt the flower melt like an ice-cold bead of dew in his hand.

Dusk closed across the house, sweeping its long shadows over the plain, the horizon merging into the sky. The harpsichord was silent, and the time flowers, no longer reflecting its music, stood motionlessly, like an embalmed forest.

For a few minutes Axel looked down at them counting the flowers which remained, then greeted his wife as she crossed the terrace, her brocade evening dress rustling over the ornamental tiles.

"What a beautiful evening, Axel." She spoke feelingly, as if she were thanking her husband personally for the great ornate shadow across the lawn and the dark brilliant air. Her face was serene and intelligent, her hair, swept back behind her head into a jeweled clasp, touched with silver. She wore her dress low across her breast, revealing a long slender neck and high chin. Axel surveyed her with fond pride. He gave her his arm and together they walked down the steps into the garden.

"One of the longest evenings this summer," Axel confirmed, adding, "I picked a perfect flower, my dear, a jewel. With luck it should last us for several days." A frown touched his brow, and he glanced involuntarily at the wall. "Each time now they seem to come nearer."

His wife smiled at him encouragingly and held his arm more tightly.

Both of them knew that the time garden was dying.

Three evenings later, as he had estimated (though sooner than he secretly hoped), Count Axel plucked another flower from the time garden.

When he first looked over the wall the approaching rabble filled the distant half of the plain, stretching across the horizon in an unbroken mass. He thought he could hear the low, fragmentary sounds of voices carried across the empty air, a sullen murmur punctuated by cries and shouts, but quickly told himself that he had imagined them. Luckily, his wife was at the harpsichord, and the rich contrapuntal patterns of a Bach fugue cascaded lightly across the terrace, masking any other noises.

Between the house and the horizon the plain was divided into four huge swells, the crest of each one clearly visible in the slanting light. Axel had promised himself that he would never count them, but the number was too small to remain unobserved, particularly when it so obviously marked the progress of the advancing army. By now the forward line had passed the first crest and was well on its way to the second; the main bulk of the throng pressed behind it, hiding the crest and the even vaster concourse spreading from the horizon. Looking to left and right of the central body, Axel could see the apparently limitless extent of the army. What had seemed at first to be the central mass was no more than a minor advance guard, one of many similar arms reaching across the plain. The true center had not yet emerged, but from the rate of extension, Axel estimated that when it finally reached the plain it would completely cover every foot of ground.

Axel searched for any large vehicles or machines, but all was amorphous and uncoordinated as ever. There were no banners or flags, no mascots or pike bearers. Heads bowed, the multitude pressed on, unaware of the sky.

Suddenly, just before Axel turned away, the forward edge of the throng appeared on top of the second crest, and swarmed down across the plain. What astounded Axel was the incredible distance it had covered while out of sight. The figures were now twice the size, each one clearly within sight.

Quickly, Axel stepped from the terrace, selected a time flower from the garden, and tore it from the stem. As it released its compacted light, he returned to the terrace. When the flower had shrunk to a frozen pearl in his palm he looked out at the plain, with relief saw that the army had retreated to the horizon again.

Then he realized that the horizon was much nearer than previously, and that what he assumed to be the horizon was the first crest.

When he joined the Countess on their evening walk he told her nothing of this, but she could see behind his casual unconcern and did what she could to dispel his worry.

Walking down the steps, she pointed to the time garden. "What a wonderful display, Axel. There are so many flowers still."

Axel nodded, smiling to himself at his wife's attempt to reassure him. Her use of *still* had revealed her own unconscious anticipation of the end. In fact a mere dozen flowers remained of the many hundred that had grown in the garden, and several of these were little more than buds—only three or four were fully grown. As they walked down to the lake, the Countess's dress rustling across the cool turf, he tried to decide whether to pick the larger flowers first or leave them to the end. Strictly, it would be better to give the smaller flowers additional time to grow and mature, and this advantage would be lost if he retained the larger flowers to the end, as he wished to do, for the final repulse. However, he realized that it mattered little either way; the garden would soon die and the smaller flowers required far longer than he could give them to accumulate their compressed cores of time. During his entire lifetime he had failed to notice a single evidence of growth among the flowers. The larger blooms had always been mature, and none of the buds had shown the slightest development.

Crossing the lake, he and his wife looked down at their reflections in the still black water. Shielded by the pavilion on one side and the high garden wall on the other, the villa in the distance, Axel felt composed and secure, the plain with its encroaching multitude a nightmare from which he had safely awakened. He put one arm around his wife's smooth waist and pressed her affectionately to his shoulder, realizing that he had not embraced her for several years, though their lives together had been timeless and he could remember as if yesterday when he first brought her to live in the villa.

"Axel," his wife asked with sudden seriousness, "before the garden dies . . . may I pick the last flower?"

Understanding her request, he nodded slowly.

One by one over the succeeding evenings, he picked the remaining flowers, leaving a single small bud which grew just below the terrace for his wife. He took the flowers at random, refusing to count or ration them, plucking two or three of the smaller buds at the same time when necessary. The approaching horde had now reached the second and third crests, a vast concourse of laboring humanity that blotted out the horizon. From the terrace Axel could see clearly the shuffling, straining ranks moving down into the hollow toward the final crest, and occasionally the sounds of their voices carried across to him, interspersed with cries of anger and the cracking of whips. The wooden carts lurched from side to side on tilting wheels, their drivers struggling to control them. As far as Axel could tell, not a single member of the throng was aware of its overall direction. Rather, each one blindly moved forward across the ground directly below the heels of the person in front of him, and the only unity was that of the cumulative compass. Pointlessly, Axel hoped that the true center, far below the horizon, might be moving in a different direction, and that gradually the multitude would alter course, swing away from the villa, and recede from the plain like a turning tide.

On the last evening but one, as he plucked the time flower, the forward edge of the rabble had reached the third crest, and was swarming past it. While he waited for the Countess, Axel looked at the two flowers left, both small buds which would carry them back through only a few minutes of the next evening. The glass stems of the dead flowers reared up stiffly into the air, but the whole garden had lost its bloom.

Axel passed the next morning quietly in his library, sealing the rarer of his manuscripts into the glass-topped cases between the galleries. He walked slowly down the portrait corridor, polishing each of the pictures carefully, then tidied his desk and locked the door behind him. During the afternoon he busied himself in the drawing rooms, unobtrusively assisting his wife as she cleaned their ornaments and straightened the vases and busts.

By evening, as the sun fell behind the house, they were both tired and dusty, and neither had spoken to the other all day. When his wife moved toward the music room, Axel called her back.

"Tonight we'll pick the flowers together, my dear," he said to her evenly. "One for each of us."

He peered only briefly over the wall. They could hear, less than half a mile away, the great dull roar of the ragged army, the ring of iron and lash, pressing on toward the house.

Quickly, Axel plucked his flower, a bud no bigger than a sapphire. As it flickered softly, the tumult outside momentarily re-ceded, then began to gather again.

Shutting his ears to the clamor, Axel looked around at the villa, counting the six columns in the portico, then gazed out across the lawn at the silver disk of the lake, its bowl reflecting the last evening light, and at the shadows moving between the tall trees, lengthen-ing across the crisp turf. He lingered over the bridge where he and his wife had stood arm in arm for so many summers—

"Axel!"

The tumult outside roared into the air, a thousand voices bel-lowed only twenty or thirty yards away. A stone flew over the wall and landed among the time flowers, snapping several of the brittle stems. The Countess ran toward him as a further barrage rattled along the wall. Then a heavy tile whirled through the air over their heads and crashed into one of the conservatory windows.

"Axel!" He put his arms around her, straightening his silk cravat when her shoulder brushed it between his lapels.

"Quickly, my dear, the last flower!" He led her down the steps and through the garden. Taking the stem between her jeweled fin-gers, she snapped it cleanly, then cradled it within her palms.

For a moment the tumult lessened slightly and Axel collected himself. In the vivid light sparkling from the flower he saw his wife's white, frightened eyes. "Hold it as long as you can, my dear, until the last grain dies."

Together they stood on the terrace, the Countess clasping the brilliant dying jewel, the air closing in upon them as the voices outside mounted again. The mob was battering at the heavy iron gates, and the whole villa shook with the impact.

While the final glimmer of light sped away, the Countess raised her palms to the air, as if releasing an invisible bird, then in a final access of courage put her hands in her husband's, her smile as radiant as the vanished flower.

"Oh, Axel!" she cried.

Like a sword, the darkness swooped down across them.

Heaving and swearing, the outer edges of the mob reached the knee-high remains of the wall enclosing the ruined estate, hauled their carts over it and along the dry ruts of what once had been an ornate drive. The ruin, formerly a spacious villa, barely interrupted the ceaseless tide of humanity. The lake was empty, fallen trees rotting at its bottom, an old bridge rusting into it. Weeds flourished among the long grass in the lawn, overrunning the ornamental pathways and carved stone screens.

Much of the terrace had crumbled, and the main section of the mob cut straight across the lawn, bypassing the gutted villa, but one or two of the more curious climbed up and searched among the shell. The doors had rotted from their hinges and the floors had fallen through. In the music room an ancient harpsichord had been chopped into firewood, but a few keys still lay among the dust. All the books had been toppled from the shelves in the library, the canvases had been slashed, and gilt frames littered the floor.

As the main body of the mob reached the house, it began to cross the wall at all points along its length. Jostled together, the people stumbled into the dry lake, swarmed over the terrace, and pressed through the house toward the open doors on the north side.

One area alone withstood the endless wave. Just below the terrace, between the wrecked balcony and the wall, was a dense, six-foot-high growth of heavy thornbushes. The barbed foliage formed an impenetrable mass, and the people passing stepped around it carefully, noticing the belladonna entwined among the branches. Most of them were too busy finding their footing among the upturned flagstones to look up into the center of the thornbushes, where two stone statues stood side by side, gazing out over the grounds from their protected vantage point. The larger of the figures was the effigy of a bearded man in a high-collared jacket, a cane under one arm. Beside him was a woman in an elaborate full-skirted dress, her slim, serene face unmarked by the wind and rain. In her left hand she lightly clasped a single rose, the delicately formed petals so thin as to be almost transparent.

As the sun died away behind the house a single ray of light glanced through a shattered cornice and struck the rose, reflected off the whorl of petals onto the statues, lighting up the gray stone so that for a fleeting moment it was indistinguishable from the long-vanished flesh of the statues' originals.

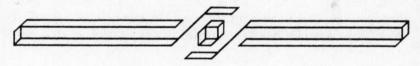

Thirteen for Centaurus

Abel knew.

Three months earlier, just after his sixteenth birthday, he had guessed, but had been too unsure of himself, too overwhelmed by the logic of his discovery, to mention it to his parents. At times, lying back half asleep in his bunk while his mother crooned one of the old lays to herself, he would deliberately repress the knowledge, but always it came back, nagging at him insistently, forcing him to jettison most of what he had long regarded as the real world.

None of the other children at the Station could help. They were immersed in their games in Playroom, or chewing pencils over their tests and homework.

"Abel, what's the matter?" Zenna Peters called after him as he wandered off to the empty storeroom on D-Deck. "You're looking sad again."

Abel hesitated, watching Zenna's warm, puzzled smile, then slipped his hands into his pockets and made off, springing down the metal stairway to make sure she didn't follow him. Once she sneaked into the storeroom uninvited and he had pulled the light bulb out of the socket, shattered about three weeks of conditioning. Dr. Francis had been furious.

As he hurried along the D-Deck corridor he listened carefully for the doctor, who had recently been keeping an eye on Abel, watching him shrewdly from behind the plastic models in Playroom. Perhaps Abel's mother had told him about the nightmare, when he would wake from a vise of sweating terror, an image of a dull burning disk fixed before his eyes.

If only Dr. Francis could cure him of that dream.

Every six yards down the corridor he stepped through a bulkhead, and idly touched the heavy control boxes on either side of the doorway. Deliberately unfocusing his mind, Abel identified some of the letters above the switches

$$M=T=R \quad SC=N$$

but they scrambled into a blur as soon as he tried to read the entire phrase. Conditioning was too strong. After he trapped her in the storeroom Zenna had been able to read a few of the notices, but Dr. Francis whisked her away before she could repeat them. Hours later, when she came back, she remembered nothing.

As usual when he entered the storeroom, he waited a few seconds before switching on the light, seeing in front of him the small disk of burning light that in his dreams expanded until it filled his brain like a thousand arc lights. It seemed endlessly distant, yet somehow mysteriously potent and magnetic, arousing dormant areas of his mind close to those which responded to his mother's presence.

As the disk began to expand he pressed the switch tab.

To his surprise, the room remained in darkness. He fumbled for the switch, a short cry slipping involuntarily through his lips.

Abruptly, the light went on.

"Hello, Abel," Dr. Francis said easily, right hand pressing the bulb into its socket. "Quite a shock, that one." He leaned against a metal crate. "I thought we'd have a talk together about your essay." He took an exercise book out of his white plastic suit as Abel sat down stiffly. Despite his dry smile and warm eyes there was something about Dr. Francis that always put Abel on his guard.

Perhaps Dr. Francis knew too?

"'The Closed Community,'" Dr. Francis read out. "A strange subject for an essay, Abel."

Abel shrugged. "It was a free choice. Aren't we really expected to choose something unusual?"

Dr. Francis grinned. "A good answer. But seriously, Abel, why pick a subject like that?"

Abel fingered the seals on his suit. These served no useful purpose, but by blowing through them it was possible to inflate the suit.

"Well, it's a sort of study of life at the Station, how we all get on with each other. What else is there to write about?—I don't see that it's so strange."

"Perhaps not. No reason why you shouldn't write about the Station. All four of the others did too. But you called yours 'The Closed Community.' The Station isn't closed, Abel—or is it?"

"It's closed in the sense that we can't go outside," Abel explained slowly. "That's all I meant."

"Outside," Dr. Francis repeated. "It's an interesting concept. You must have given the whole subject a lot of thought. When did you first start thinking along these lines?"

"After the dream," Abel said. Dr. Francis had deliberately side-stepped his use of the word "outside" and he searched for some means of getting to the point. In his pocket he felt the small plumb line he carried around. "Dr. Francis, perhaps you can explain something to me. Why is the Station revolving?"

"Is it?" Dr. Francis looked up with interest. "How do you know?"

Abel reached up and fastened the plumb line to the ceiling stanchion. "The interval between the ball and the wall is about an eighth of an inch greater at the bottom than at the top. Centrifugal forces are driving it outward. I calculated that the Station is revolving at about two feet per second."

Dr. Francis nodded thoughtfully. "That's just about right," he said matter-of-factly. He stood up. "Let's take a trip to my office. It looks as if it's time you and I had a serious talk."

The Station was on four levels. The lower two contained the crew's quarters, two circular decks of cabins which housed the fourteen people on board the Station. The senior clan was the Peters, led by Captain Theodore, a big stern man of taciturn disposition who rarely strayed from Control. Abel had never been allowed there, but the Captain's son, Matthew, often described the hushed domelike cabin filled with luminous dials and flickering lights, the strange humming music.

All the male members of the Peters clan worked in Control—Grandfather Peters, a white-haired old man with humorous eyes, had been Captain before Abel was born—and with the Captain's wife and Zenna they constituted the elite of the Station.

However, the Grangers, the clan to which Abel belonged, was in many respects more important, as he had begun to realize. The day-to-day running of the Station, the detailed programming of emergency drills, duty rosters, and commissary menus, was the responsibility of Abel's father, Matthias, and without his firm but flexible hand the Bakers, who cleaned the cabins and ran the commissary, would never have known what to do. And it was only the deliberate intermingling in Recreation which his father devised that brought the Peters and Bakers together, or each family would have stayed indefinitely in its own cabins.

Lastly, there was Dr. Francis. He didn't belong to any of the three clans. Sometimes Abel asked himself where Dr. Francis had come from, but his mind always fogged at a question like that, as the conditioning blocks fell like bulkheads across his thought trains (logic was a dangerous tool at the Station). Dr. Francis's energy and vitality, his relaxed good humor—in a way, he was the only person in the Station who ever made any jokes—were out of character with everyone else. Much as he sometimes disliked Dr. Francis for snooping around and being a know-it-all, Abel realized how dreary life in the Station would seem without him.

Dr. Francis closed the door of his cabin and gestured Abel into a seat. All the furniture in the Station was bolted to the floor, but Abel noticed that Dr. Francis had unscrewed his chair so that he could tilt it backward. The huge vacuum-proof cylinder of the doctor's sleeping tank jutted from the wall, its massive metal body able to withstand any accident the Station might suffer. Abel hated the thought of sleeping in the cylinder—luckily the entire crew quarters were accident-secure—and wondered why Dr. Francis chose to live alone up on A-Deck.

"Tell me, Abel," Dr. Francis began, "has it ever occurred to you to ask why the Station is here?"

Abel shrugged. "Well, it's designed to keep us alive, it's our home."

"Yes, that's true, but obviously it has some other object than just our own survival. Who do you think built the Station in the first place?"

"Our fathers, I suppose, or grandfathers. Or *their* grandfathers."

"Fair enough. And where were they before they built it?"

Abel struggled with the *reductio ad absurdum*. "I don't know, they must have been floating around in midair!"

Dr. Francis joined in the laughter. "Wonderful thought. Actually it's not that far from the truth. But we can't accept that as it stands."

The doctor's self-contained office gave Abel an idea. "Perhaps they came from another Station? An even bigger one?"

Dr. Francis nodded encouragingly. "Brilliant, Abel. A first-class piece of deduction. All right, then, let's assume that. Somewhere, away from us, a huge Station exists, perhaps a hundred times bigger than this one, maybe even a thousand. Why not?"

"It's possible," Abel admitted, accepting the idea with surprising ease.

"Right. Now you remember your course in advanced mechanics— the imaginary planetary system, with the orbiting bodies held together by mutual gravitational attraction? Let's assume further that such a system actually exists. O.K.?"

"Here?" Abel said quickly. "In your cabin?" Then he added, "In your sleeping cylinder?"

Dr. Francis sat back. "Abel, you do come up with some amazing things. An interesting association of ideas. No, it would be too big for that. Try to imagine a planetary system orbiting around a central body of absolutely enormous size, each of the planets a million times larger than the Station." When Abel nodded, he went on. "And suppose that the big Station, the one a thousand times larger than this, were attached to one of the planets, and that the people in it decided to go to another planet. So they build a smaller Station, about the size of this one, and sent it off through the air. Make sense?"

"In a way." Strangely, the completely abstract concepts were less remote than he would have expected. Deep in his mind dim memories stirred, interlocking with what he had already guessed about the Station. He gazed steadily at Dr. Francis. "You're saying that's what the Station is doing? That the planetary system exists?"

Dr. Francis nodded. "You'd more or less guessed before I told you. Unconsciously, you've known all about it for several years. A few minutes from now I'm going to remove some of the conditioning blocks, and when you wake up in a couple of hours you'll understand everything. You'll know then that in fact the Station is a spaceship, flying from our home planet, Earth, where our grandfathers were born, to another planet millions of miles away, in a distant orbiting system. Our grandfathers always lived on Earth, and we are the first people ever to undertake such a journey. You can be proud that you're here. Your grandfather, who volunteered to come, was a great man, and we've got to do everything to make sure that the Station keeps running."

Abel nodded quickly. "When do we get there—the planet we're flying to?"

Dr. Francis looked down at his hands, his face growing somber. "We'll never get there, Abel. The journey takes too long. This is a multi-generation space vehicle, only our children will land and they'll be old by the time they do. But don't worry, you'll go on thinking of the Station as your only home, and that's deliberate, so that you and your children will be happy here."

He went over to the TV monitor screen by which he kept in touch with Captain Peters, his fingers playing across the control tabs. Suddenly the screen lit up, a blaze of fierce points of light flared into the cabin, throwing a brilliant phosphorescent glitter across the walls, dappling Abel's hands and suit. He gaped at the huge balls of fire, apparently frozen in the middle of a giant explosion, hanging in vast patterns.

"This is the celestial sphere," Dr. Francis explained. "The starfield into which the Station is moving." He touched a bright speck of light in the lower half of the screen. "Alpha Centauri, the star around which revolves the planet the Station will one day land upon." He turned to Abel. "You remember all these terms I'm using, don't you, Abel? None of them seems strange."

Abel nodded, the wells of his unconscious memory flooding into his mind as Dr. Francis spoke. The TV screen blanked and then revealed a new picture. They appeared to be looking down at an enormous toplike structure, the flanks of a metal pylon sloping toward its center. In the background the starfield rotated slowly in a clockwise direction. "This is the Station," Dr. Francis explained, "seen from a camera mounted on the nose boom. All visual checks have to be made indirectly, as the stellar radiation would blind us. Just below the ship you can see a single star, the Sun, from which we set out fifty years ago. It's now almost too distant to be visible, but a deep inherited memory of it is the burning disk you see in your dreams. We've done what we can to erase it, but unconsciously all of us see it too."

He switched off the set and the brilliant pattern of light swayed and fell back. "The social engineering built into the ship is far more intricate than the mechanical, Abel. It's three generations since the Station set off, and birth, marriage, and birth again have followed

154

exactly as they were designed to. As your father's heir great demands are going to be made on your patience and understanding. Any disunity here would bring disaster. The conditioning programs are not equipped to give you more than a general outline of the course to follow. Most of it will be left to you."

"Will you always be here?"

Dr. Francis stood up. "No, Abel, I won't. No one here lives forever. Your father will die, and Captain Peters and myself." He moved to the door. "We'll go now to Conditioning. In three hours' time, when you wake up, you'll find yourself a new man."

Letting himself back into his cabin, Francis leaned wearily against the bulkhead, feeling the heavy rivets with his fingers, here and there flaking away as the metal slowly rusted. When he switched on the TV set he looked tired and dispirited, and gazed absently at the last scene he had shown Abel, the boom camera's view of the ship. He was just about to select another frame when he noticed a dark shadow swing across the surface of the hull.

He leaned forward to examine it, frowning in annoyance as the shadow moved away and faded among the stars. He pressed another tab, and the screen divided into a large chessboard, five frames wide by five deep. The top line showed Control, the main pilot and navigation deck lit by the dim glow of the instrument panels, Captain Peters sitting impassively before the compass screen.

Next, he watched Matthias Granger begin his afternoon inspection of the ship. Most of the passengers seemed reasonably happy, but their faces lacked any luster. All spent at least two to three hours each day bathing in the UV light flooding through the recreation lounge, but the pallor continued, perhaps an unconscious realization that they had been born and were living in what would also be their own tomb. Without the continuous conditioning sessions, and the hypnotic reassurance of the subsonic voices, they would long ago have become will-less automatons.

Switching off the set, he prepared to climb into the sleeping cylinder. The airlock was three feet in diameter, waist-high off the floor. The time seal rested at zero, and he moved it forward twelve hours, then set it so that the seal could only be broken from within. He swung the lock out and crawled in over the molded foam mattress, snapping the door shut behind him.

Lying back in the thin yellow light, he slipped his fingers through the ventilator grille in the rear wall, pressed the unit into its socket, and turned it sharply. Somewhere an electric motor throbbed briefly, the end wall of the cylinder swung back slowly like a vault door, and bright daylight poured in.

Quickly, Francis climbed out onto a small metal platform that jutted from the upper slope of a huge white asbestos-covered dome. Fifty feet above was the roof of a large hangar. A maze of pipes and cables traversed the surface of the dome, interlacing like the vessels of a giant bloodshot eye, and a narrow stairway led down to the floor below. The entire dome, some 150 feet wide, was revolving slowly. A line of five trucks was drawn up by the stores depot on the far side of the hangar, and a man in a brown uniform waved to him from one of the glass-walled offices.

At the bottom of the ladder he jumped down onto the hangar floor, ignoring the curious stares from the soldiers unloading the stores. Halfway across he craned up at the revolving bulk of the dome. A black perforated sail, fifty feet square, like a fragment of a planetarium, was suspended from the roof over the apex of the dome, a TV camera directly below it, a large metal sphere mounted about five feet from the lens. One of the guy ropes had snapped and the sail tilted slightly to reveal the catwalk along the center of the roof.

He pointed this out to a maintenance sergeant warming his hands in one of the ventilator outlets from the dome. "You'll have to string that back. Some fool was wandering along the catwalk and throwing his shadow straight onto the model. I could see it clearly on the TV screen. Luckily no one spotted it."

"O.K., Doctor, I'll get it fixed." He chuckled sourly. "That would have been a laugh, though. Really give them something to worry about."

The man's tone annoyed Francis. "They've got plenty to worry about as it is."

"I don't know about that, Doctor. Some people here think they have it all ways. Quiet and warm in there, nothing to do except sit back and listen to those hypno-drills." He looked out bleakly at the abandoned airfield stretching away to the cold tundra beyond the perimeter, and turned up his collar. "We're the boys back here on Mother Earth who do the work, out in this godforsaken dump. If you need any more space cadets, Doctor, remember me."

Francis managed a smile and stepped into the control office, made his way through the clerks sitting at trestle tables in front of the progress charts. Each carried the name of one of the dome passengers and a tabulated breakdown of progress through the psychometric tests and conditioning programs. Other charts listed the day's rosters, copies of those posted that morning by Matthias Granger.

Inside Colonel Chalmers's office Francis relaxed back gratefully in the warmth, describing the salient features of his day's observation. "I wish you could go in there and move around them, Paul," he concluded, "it's not the same spying through the TV cameras. You've got to talk to them, measure yourself against people like Granger and Peters."

"You're right, they're fine men, like all the others. It's a pity they're wasted there."

"They're not wasted," Francis insisted. "Every piece of data will be immensely valuable when the first spaceships set out." He ignored Chalmers's muttered "If they do" and went on: "Zenna and Abel worry me a little. It may be necessary to bring forward the date of their marriage. I know it will raise eyebrows, but the girl is as fully mature at fifteen as she will be four years from now, and she'll be a settling influence on Abel, stop him from thinking too much."

Chalmers shook his head doubtfully. "Sounds like a good idea, but a girl of fifteen and a boy of sixteen—? You'd raise a storm, Roger. Technically they're wards of court, every decency league would be up in arms."

Francis gestured irritably. "Need they know? We've really got a problem with Abel, the boy's too clever. He'd more or less worked out for himself that the Station was a spaceship, he merely lacked the vocabulary to describe it. Now that we're starting to lift the conditioning blocks he'll want to know everything. It will be a big job to prevent him from smelling a rat, particularly with the slack way this place is being run. Did you see the shadow on the TV screen? We're damn lucky Peters didn't have a heart attack."

Chalmers nodded. "I'm getting that tightened up. A few mistakes are bound to happen, Roger. It's damn cold for the control crew working around the dome. Try to remember that the people outside are just as important as those inside."

"Of course. The real trouble is that the budget is ludicrously out of date. It's only been revised once in fifty years. Perhaps General

Short can generate some official interest, get a new deal for us. He sounds like a pretty brisk new broom." Chalmers pursed his lips doubtfully, but Francis continued, "I don't know whether the tapes are wearing out, but the negative conditioning doesn't hold as well as it used to. We'll probably have to tighten up the programs. I've made a start by pushing Abel's graduation forward."

"Yes, I watched you on the screen here. The control boys became quite worked up next door. One or two of them are as keen as you, Roger, they'd been programming ahead for three months. It meant a lot of time wasted for them. I think you ought to check with me before you make a decision like that. The dome isn't your private laboratory."

Francis accepted the reproof. Lamely, he said, "It was one of those spot decisions, I'm sorry. There was nothing else to do."

Chalmers gently pressed home his point. "I'm not so sure. I thought you rather overdid the long-term aspects of the journey. Why go out of your way to tell him he would never reach planetfall? It only heightens his sense of isolation, makes it that much more difficult if we decide to shorten the journey."

Francis looked up. "There's no chance of that, is there?"

Chalmers paused thoughtfully. "Roger, I really advise you not to get too involved with the project. Keep saying to yourself they're-not-going-to-Alpha-Centauri. They're here on Earth, and if the government decided it they'd be let out tomorrow. I know the courts would have to sanction it but that's a formality. It's fifty years since this project was started and a good number of influential people feel that it's gone on for too long. Ever since the Mars and Moon colonies failed space programs have been cut right back. They think the money here is being poured away for the amusement of a few sadistic psychologists."

"You know that isn't true," Francis retorted. "I may have been overhasty, but on the whole this project has been scrupulously conducted. Without exaggeration, if you did send a dozen people on a multi-generation ship to Alpha Centauri you couldn't do better than duplicate everything that's taken place here, down to the last cough and sneeze. If the information we've obtained had been available, the Mars and Moon colonies never would have failed!"

"True. But irrelevant. Don't you understand, when everyone was eager to get into space they were prepared to accept the idea of a small group being sealed into a tank for a hundred years, particularly when the original team volunteered. Now, when interest has evaporated, people are beginning to feel that there's something obscene about this human zoo, what began as a grand adventure of the spirit of Columbus, has become a grisly joke. In one sense we've learned too much—the social stratification of the three families is the sort of unwelcome datum that doesn't do the project much good. Another is the complete ease with which we've manipulated them, made them believe anything we've wanted." Chalmers leaned forward across the desk. "Confidentially, Roger, General Short has been put in command for one reason only—to close this place down. It may take years, but it's going to be done, I warn you. The important job now is to get those people out of there, not keep them in."

Francis stared bleakly at Chalmers. "Do you really believe that?"

"Frankly, Roger, yes. This project should never have been launched. You can't manipulate people the way we're doing—the endless hypno-drills, the forced pairing of children—look at yourself, five minutes ago you were seriously thinking of marrying two teenage children just to stop them using their minds. The whole thing degrades human dignity, all the taboos, the increasing degree of introspection—sometimes Peters and Granger don't speak to anyone for two or three weeks—the way life in the dome has become tenable only by accepting the insane situation as the normal one. I think the reaction against the project is healthy."

Francis stared out at the dome. A gang of men were loading the so-called "compressed food" (actually frozen foods with the brand names removed) into the commissary hatchway. Next morning, when Baker and his wife dialed the prearranged menu, the supplies would be promptly delivered, apparently from the space-hold. To some people, Francis knew, the project might well seem a complete fraud.

Quietly he said: "The people who volunteered accepted the sacrifice, and all it involved. How's Short going to get them out? Just open the door and whistle?"

Chalmers smiled, a little wearily. "He's not a fool, Roger. He's sincerely concerned about their welfare as you are. Half the crew, particularly the older ones, would go mad within five minutes. But don't be disappointed, the project has more than proved its worth."

"It won't do that until they 'land.' If the project ends it will be we who have failed, not them. We can't rationalize by saying it's cruel or unpleasant. We owe it to the fourteen people in the dome to keep it going."

Chalmers watched him shrewdly. "Fourteen? You mean thirteen, don't you, Doctor? Or are you inside the dome too?"

The ship had stopped rotating. Sitting at his desk in Command, planning the next day's fire drills, Abel noticed the sudden absence of movement. All morning, as he walked around the ship—he no longer used the term Station—he had been aware of an inward drag that pulled him toward the wall, as if one leg were shorter than the other.

When he mentioned this to his father the older man merely said: "Captain Peters is in charge of Control. Always let him worry where the navigation of the ship is concerned."

This sort of advice now meant nothing to Abel. In the previous two months his mind had attacked everything around him voraciously, probing and analyzing, examining every facet of life in the Station. An enormous, once suppressed vocabulary of abstract terms and relationships lay latent below the surface of his mind, and nothing would stop him applying it.

Over their meal trays in the commissary he grilled Matthew Peters about the ship's flight path, the great parabola which would carry it to Alpha Centauri.

"What about the currents built into the ship?" he asked. "The rotation was designed to eliminate the magnetic poles set up when the ship was originally constructed. How are you compensating for that?"

Matthew looked puzzled. "I'm not sure, exactly. Probably the instruments are automatically compensated." When Abel smiled skeptically he shrugged. "Anyway, Father knows all about it. There's no doubt we're right on course."

"We hope," Abel murmured *sotto voce*. The more Abel asked Matthew about the navigational devices he and his father operated in Control the more obvious it became that they were merely carrying out low-level instrument checks, and that their role was limited to replacing burned-out pilot lights. Most of the instruments operated automatically, and they might as well have been staring at cabinets full of mattress floc.

What a joke if they were!

Smiling to himself, Abel realized that he had probably stated no more than the truth. It would be unlikely for the navigation to be entrusted to the crew when the slightest human error could throw the spaceship irretrievably out of control, send it hurtling into a passing star. The designers of the ship would have sealed the automatic pilots well out of reach, given the crew light supervisory duties that created an illusion of control.

That was the real clue to life aboard the ship. None of their roles could be taken at face value. The day-to-day, minute-to-minute programming carried out by himself and his father were merely a set of variations on a pattern already laid down; the permutations possible were endless, but the fact that he could send Matthew Peters to the commissary at 12:00 rather than 12:30 didn't give him any real power over Matthew's life. The master programs printed by the computers selected the day's menus, safety drills, and recreation periods, and a list of names to choose from, but the slight leeway allowed, the extra two or three names supplied, were there in case of illness, not to give Abel any true freedom of choice.

One day, Abel promised himself, he would program himself out of the conditioning sessions. Shrewdly he guessed that the conditioning still blocked out a great deal of interesting material, that half his mind remained submerged. Something about the ship suggested that there might be more to it than—

"Hello, Abel, you look far away." Dr. Francis sat down next to him. "What's worrying you?"

"I was just calculating something," Abel explained quickly. "Tell me, assuming that each member of the crew consumes about three pounds of noncirculated food each day, roughly half a ton per year, the total cargo must be about eight hundred tons, and that's not allowing for any supplies after planet-fall. There should be at least fifteen hundred tons aboard. Quite a weight."

"Not in absolute terms, Abel. The Station is only a small fraction of the ship. The main reactors, fuel tanks, and space holds together weigh over thirty thousand tons. They provide the gravitational pull that holds you to the floor."

Abel shook his head slowly. "Hardly, Doctor, the attraction must come from the stellar gravitational fields, or the weight of the ship would have to be about 6×10^{20} tons."

Dr. Francis watched Abel reflectively, aware that the young man had led him into a simple trap. The figure he had quoted was near enough the Earth's mass. "These are complex problems, Abel. I wouldn't worry too much about stellar mechanics. Captain Peters has that responsibility."

"I'm not trying to usurp it," Abel assured him. "Merely to extend my own knowledge. Don't you think it might be worth departing from the rules a little? For example, it would be interesting to test the effects of continued isolation. We could select a small group, subject them to artificial stimuli, even seal them off from the rest of the crew and condition them to believe they were back on Earth. It could be a really valuable experiment, Doctor."

As he waited in the conference room for General Short to finish his opening harangue, Francis repeated the last sentence to himself, wondering idly what Abel, with his limitless enthusiasm, would have made of the circle of defeated faces around the table.

"...regret as much as you do, gentlemen, the need to discontinue the project. However, now that a decision has been made by the Space Department, it is our duty to implement it. Of course, the task won't be an easy one. What we need is a phased withdrawal, a gradual readjustment of the world around the crew that will bring them down to Earth as gently as a parachute." The General was a brisk, sharp-faced man in his fifties, with burly shoulders but sensitive eyes. He turned to Dr. Kersh, who was responsible for the dietary and bietric controls aboard the dome. "From what you tell me, Doctor, we might not have as much time as we'd like. This boy Abel sounds something of a problem."

Kersh smiled. "I was looking in at the commissary, overheard him tell Dr. Francis that he wanted to run an experiment on a small group of the crew. An isolation drill, would you believe it. He's estimated that the two-man tractor crews may be isolated for up to two years when the first foraging trips are made."

Captain Sanger, the engineering officer, added: "He's also trying to duck his conditioning sessions. He's wearing a couple of foam pads under his earphones, missing about ninety percent of the subsonics. We spotted it when the EEG tape we record showed no alpha waves. At first we thought it was a break in the cable, but when we checked visually on the screen we saw that he had his eyes open. He wasn't listening."

Francis drummed on the table. "It wouldn't have mattered. The subsonic was a math instruction sequence—the four-figure antilog system."

"A good thing he did miss them," Kersh said with a laugh. "Sooner or later he'll work out that the dome is traveling in an elliptical orbit ninety-three million miles from a dwarf star of the G_0 spectral class."

"What are you doing about this attempt to evade conditioning, Dr. Francis?" Short asked. When Francis shrugged vaguely he added: "I think we ought to regard the matter fairly seriously. From now on we'll be relying on the programming."

Flatly, Francis said: "Abel will resume the conditioning. There's no need to do anything. Without the regular daily contact he'll soon feel lost. The subsonic voice is composed of his mother's vocal tones; when he no longer hears it he'll lose his orientations, feel completely deserted."

Short nodded slowly. "Well, let's hope so." He addressed Dr. Kersh. "At a rough estimate, Doctor, how long will it take to bring them back? Bearing in mind they'll have to be given complete freedom and that every TV and newspaper network in the world will interview each one a hundred times."

Kersh chose his words carefully. "Obviously a matter of years, General. All the conditioning drills will have to be gradually re-scored, as a stopgap measure we may need to introduce a meteor collision... guessing, I'd say three to five years. Possibly longer."

"Fair enough. What would you estimate, Dr. Francis?"

Francis fiddled with his blotter, trying to view the question seriously. "I've no idea. *Bring them back*. What do you really mean, General? Bring what back?" Irritated, he snapped: "A hundred years."

Laughter crossed the table, and Short smiled at him, not unamiably. "That's fifty years more than the original project, Doctor. You can't have been doing a very good job here."

Francis shook his head. "You're wrong, General. The original project was to get them to Alpha Centauri. Nothing was said about bringing them *back*." When the laughter fell away Francis cursed himself for his foolishness; antagonizing the General wouldn't help the people in the dome.

But Short seemed unruffled. "All right, then, it's obviously going to take some time." Pointedly, with a glance at Francis, he added:

"It's the men and women in the ship we're thinking of, not ourselves, if we need a hundred years we'll take them, not one less. You may be interested to hear that the Space Department chiefs feel about fifteen years will be necessary. At least." There was a quickening of interest around the table. Francis watched Short with surprise. In fifteen years a lot could happen, there might be another spaceward swing of public opinion.

"The Department recommends that the project continue as before, with whatever budgetary parings we can make—stopping the dome is just a start—and that we condition the crew to believe that a round trip is in progress, that their mission is merely one of reconnaissance, and that they are bringing vital information back to Earth. When they step out of the spaceship they'll be treated as heroes and accept the strangeness of the world around them." Short looked across the table, waiting for someone to reply. Kersh stared doubtfully at his hands, and Sanger and Chalmers played mechanically with their blotters.

Just before Short continued Francis pulled himself together, realizing that he was faced with his last opportunity to save the project. However much they disagreed with Short, none of the others would try to argue with him.

"I'm afraid that won't do, General," he said, "though I appreciate the Department's foresight and your own sympathetic approach. The scheme you've outlined sounds plausible, but it just won't work." He sat forward, his voice controlled and precise. "General, ever since they were children these people have been trained to accept that they were a closed group, and would never have contact with anyone else. On the unconscious level, on the level of their functional nervous systems, no one else in the world exists, for them the neuronic basis of reality is isolation. You'll never train them to invert their whole universe any more than you can train a fish to fly. If you start to tamper with the fundamental patterns of their psyches you'll produce the sort of complete mental block you see when you try to teach a left-handed person to use his right."

Francis glanced at Dr. Kersh, who was nodding in agreement. "Believe me, General, contrary to what you and the Space Department naturally assume, the people in the dome do *not* want to come out. Given the choice they would prefer to stay there, just as the goldfish prefers to stay in its bowl."

Short paused before replying, evidently reassessing Francis. "You may be right, Doctor," he admitted. "But where does that get us? We've got fifteen years, perhaps twenty-five at the outside."

"There's only one way to do it," Francis told him. "Let the project continue, exactly as before, but with one difference. Prevent them from marrying and having children. In twenty-five years only the present younger generation will still be alive, and a further five years from then they'll all be dead. A life span in the dome is little more than forty-five years. At the age of thirty Abel will probably be an old man. When they start to die off no one will care about them any longer."

There was a full half minute's silence, and then Kersh said: "It's the best suggestion, General. Humane, and yet faithful both to the original project and the Department's instructions. The absence of children would be only a slight deviation from the conditioned pathway. The basic isolation of the group would be strengthened, rather than diminished, also their realization that they themselves will never see planet-fall. If we drop the pedagogical drills and play down the spaceflight they will soon become a small close community, little different from any other out-group on the road to extinction."

Chalmers cut in: "Another point, General. It would be far easier—and cheaper—to stage, and as the members died off we could progressively close down the ship until finally there might be only a single deck left, perhaps even a few cabins."

Short stood up and paced over to the window, looking out through the clear glass over the frosted panes at the great dome in the hangar.

"It sounds a dreadful prospect," he commented. "Completely insane. As you say, though, it may be the only way out."

Moving quietly among the trucks parked in the darkened hangar, Francis paused for a moment to look back at the lighted windows of the control deck. Two or three of the night staff sat watch over the line of TV screens, half asleep themselves as they observed the sleeping occupants of the dome.

He ducked out of the shadows and ran across to the dome, climbed the stairway to the entrance point thirty feet above. Opening the external lock, he crawled in and closed it behind him, then unfastened the internal entry hatch and pulled himself out of the sleeping cylinder into the silent cabin.

A single dim light glowed over the TV monitor screen as it revealed the three orderlies in the control deck, lounging back in a haze of cigarette smoke six feet from the camera.

Francis turned up the speaker volume, then tapped the mouthpiece sharply with his knuckle.

Tunic unbuttoned, sleep still shadowing his eyes, Colonel Chalmers leaned forward intently into the screen, the orderlies at his shoulder.

"Believe me, Roger, you're proving nothing. General Short and the Space Department won't withdraw their decision now that a special bill of enactment has been passed." When Francis still looked skeptical he added: "If anything, you're more likely to jeopardize them."

"I'll take a chance," Francis said. "Too many guarantees have been broken in the past. Here I'll be able to keep an eye on things." He tried to sound cool and unemotional; the cine-cameras would be recording the scene and it was important to establish the right impression. General Short would be only too keen to avoid a scandal. If he decided Francis was unlikely to sabotage the project he would probably leave him in the dome.

Chalmers pulled up a chair, his face earnest. "Roger, give yourself time to reconsider everything. You may be more of a discordant element than you realize. Remember, nothing would be easier than getting you out—a child could cut his way through the rusty hull with a blunt can opener."

"Don't try it," Francis warned him quietly. "I'll be moving down to C-Deck, so if you come in after me they'll all know. Believe me, I won't try to interfere with the withdrawal programs. And I won't arrange any teenage marriages. But I think the people inside may need me now for more than eight hours a day."

"Francis!" Chalmers shouted. "Once you go down there you'll never come out! Don't you realize you're entombing yourself in a situation that's totally unreal? You're deliberately withdrawing into a nightmare, sending yourself off on a nonstop journey to *nowhere!*"

Curtly, before he switched the set off for the last time, Francis replied: "Not nowhere, Colonel: Alpha Centauri."

Sitting down thankfully in the narrow bunk in his cabin, Francis rested briefly before setting off for the commissary. All day he had been busy coding the computer punch tapes for Abel, and his eyes ached with the strain of manually stamping each of the thousands of minuscule holes. For eight hours he had sat without a break in the small isolation cell, electrodes clamped to his chest, knees, and elbows while Abel measured his cardiac and respiratory rhythms.

The tests bore no relation to the daily programs Abel now worked out for his father, and Francis was finding it difficult to maintain his patience. Initially Abel had tested his ability to follow a prescribed set of instructions, producing an endless exponential function, then a digital representation of *pi* to a thousand places. Finally Abel had persuaded Francis to cooperate in a more difficult test—the task of producing a totally random sequence. Whenever he unconsciously repeated a simple progression, as he did if he was tired or bored, or a fragment of a larger possible progression, the computer scanning his progress sounded an alarm on the desk and he would have to start afresh. After a few hours the buzzer rasped out every ten seconds, snapping at him like a bad-tempered insect. Francis had finally hobbled over to the door that afternoon, entangling himself in the electrode leads, found to his annoyance that the door was locked (ostensibly to prevent any interruption by a fire patrol), then saw through the small porthole that the computer in the cubicle outside was running unattended.

But when Francis's pounding roused Abel from the far end of the next laboratory he had been almost irritable with the doctor for wanting to discontinue the experiment.

"Damn it, Abel, I've been punching away at these things for three weeks now." He winced as Abel disconnected him, brusquely tearing off the adhesive tape. "Trying to produce random sequences isn't all that easy—my sense of reality is beginning to fog." (Sometimes he wondered if Abel was secretly waiting for this.) "I think I'm entitled to a vote of thanks."

"But we arranged for the trial to last three days, Doctor," Abel pointed out. "It's only later that the valuable results begin to appear. It's the errors you make that are interesting. The whole experiment is pointless now."

"Well, it's probably pointless anyway. Some mathematicians used to maintain that a random sequence was impossible to define."

"But we can assume that it *is* possible," Abel insisted. "I was just giving you some practice before we started on the transfinite numbers."

Francis balked here. "I'm sorry, Abel. Maybe I'm not so fit as I used to be. Anyway, I've got other duties to attend to."

"But they don't take long, Doctor. There's really nothing for you to do now."

He was right, as Francis was forced to admit. In the year he had spent in the dome Abel had remarkably streamlined the daily routines, provided himself and Francis with an excess of leisure time, particularly as the latter never went to conditioning (Francis was frightened of the subsonic voices—Chalmers and Short would be subtle in their attempts to extricate him, perhaps too subtle).

Life aboard the dome had been more of a drain on him than he anticipated. Chained to the routines of the ship, limited in his recreations and with few intellectual pastimes—there were no books aboard the ship—he found it increasingly difficult to sustain his former good humor, was beginning to sink into the deadening lethargy that had overcome most of the other crew members. Matthias Granger had retreated to his cabin, content to leave the programming to Abel, spent his time playing with a damaged clock, while the two Peters rarely strayed from Control. The three wives were almost completely inert, satisfied to knit and murmur to each other. The days passed indistinguishably. Sometimes Francis told himself wryly "he nearly *did* believe that they were en route for Alpha Centauri. That would have been a joke for General Short!"

At 6:30 when he went to the commissary for his evening meal, he found that he was a quarter of an hour late.

"Your mealtime was changed this afternoon," Baker told him, lowering the hatchway. "I got nothing ready for you."

Francis began to remonstrate but the man was adamant. "I can't make a special dip into space-hold just because you didn't look at Routine Orders, can I, Doctor?"

On the way out Francis met Abel, tried to persuade him to countermand the order. "You could have warned me, Abel. Damnation, I've been sitting inside your test rig all afternoon."

"But you went back to your cabin, Doctor," Abel pointed out smoothly. "You pass three SRO bulletins on your way from the laboratory. Always look at them at every opportunity, remember. Last-minute changes are liable at any time. I'm afraid you'll have to wait until ten-thirty now."

Francis went back to his cabin, suspecting that the sudden change had been Abel's revenge on him for discontinuing the test. He would have to be more conciliatory with Abel, or the young man could make his life a hell, literally starve him to death. Escape from the dome was impossible now—there was a mandatory twenty-year sentence on anyone making an unauthorized entry into the space simulator.

After resting for an hour or so, he left his cabin at 8:00 to carry out his duty checks of the pressure seals by the B-Deck Meteor Screen. He always went through the pretence of reading them, enjoying the sense of participation in the spaceflight which the exercise gave him, deliberately accepting the illusion.

The seals were mounted in the control point set at ten yard intervals along the perimeter corridor, a narrow circular passageway around the main corridor. Alone there, the servos clicking and snapping, he felt at peace within the space vehicle. "Earth itself is in orbit around the Sun," he mused as he checked the seals, "and the whole solar system is traveling at forty miles a second toward the constellation Lyra. The degree of illusion that exists is a complex question."

Something cut through his reverie.

The pressure indicator was flickering slightly. The needle wavered between 0.001 and 0.0015 psi. The pressure inside the dome was fractionally above atmospheric, in order that dust might be expelled through untoward cracks (though the main object of the pressure seals was to get the crew safely into the vacuum-proof emergency cylinders in case the dome was damaged and required internal repairs).

For a moment Francis panicked, wondering whether Short had decided to come in after him—the reading, although meaningless, indicated that a breach had opened in the hull. Then the hand moved back to zero, and footsteps sounded along the radial corridor at right angles past the next bulkhead.

Quickly Francis stepped into its shadow. Before his death old Peters had spent a lot of time mysteriously pottering around the corridor, probably secreting a private food cache behind one of the rusting panels.

He leaned forward as the footsteps crossed the corridor.

Abel?

He watched the young man disappear down a stairway, then made his way into the radial corridor, searching the steel-gray sheeting for a retractable panel. Immediately adjacent to the end wall of the corridor, against the outer skin of the dome, was a small fire-control booth.

A tuft of slate-white hairs lay on the floor of the booth.

Asbestos fibers!

Francis stepped into the booth, within a few seconds located a loosened panel that had rusted off its rivets. About ten inches by six, it slid back easily. Beyond it was the outer wall of the dome, a handsbreadth away. Here too was a loose plate, held in position by a crudely fashioned hook.

Francis hesitated, then lifted the hook and drew back the panel. *He was looking straight down into the hangar!*

Below, a line of trucks was disgorging supplies onto the concrete floor under a couple of spotlights, a sergeant shouting orders at the labor squad. To the right was the control deck, Chalmers in his office on the evening shift.

The spy-hole was directly below the stairway, and the overhanging metal steps shielded it from the men in the hangar. The asbestos had been carefully frayed so that it concealed the retractable plate. The wire hook was as badly rusted as the rest of the hull, and Francis estimated that the window had been in use for over thirty or forty years.

So almost certainly old Peters had regularly looked out through the window, and knew perfectly well that the spaceship was a myth. Nonetheless he had stayed aboard, perhaps realizing that the truth would destroy the others, or preferred to be captain of an artificial ship rather than a self-exposed curiosity in the world outside.

Presumably he had passed on the secret. Not to his bleak taciturn son, but to the one other lively mind, one who would keep the secret and make the most of it. For his own reasons he too had decided to stay in the dome, realizing that he would soon be the effective captain, free to pursue his experiments in applied psychology. He might even have failed to grasp that Francis was not a true member of the crew. His confident mastery of the programming, his lapse of interest in Control, his casualness over the safety devices, all meant one thing—

Abel knew!

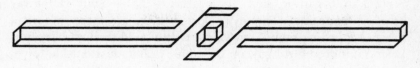

The Subliminal Man

"The signs, Doctor! Have you seen the signs?"

Frowning with annoyance, Dr. Franklin quickened his pace and hurried down the hospital steps toward the line of parked cars. Over his shoulder he caught a glimpse of a man in ragged sandals and lime-stained jeans waving to him from the far side of the drive, then break into a run when he saw Franklin try to evade him.

"Dr. Franklin! The signs!"

Head down, Franklin swerved around an elderly couple approaching the outpatients department. His car was over a hundred yards away. Too tired to start running himself, he waited for the young man to catch him up.

"All right, Hathaway, what is it this time?" he snapped irritably. "I'm getting sick of you hanging around here all day."

Hathaway lurched to a halt in front of him, uncut black hair like an awning over his eyes. He brushed it back with a clawlike hand and turned on a wild smile, obviously glad to see Franklin and oblivious of the latter's hostility.

"I've been trying to reach you at night, Doctor, but your wife always puts the phone down on me," he explained without a hint of rancor, as if well-used to this kind of snub. "And I didn't want to look for you inside the Clinic." They were standing by a privet hedge that shielded them from the lower windows of the main administrative block, but Franklin's regular rendezvous with Hathaway and his strange messianic cries had already been the subject of amused comment.

Franklin began to say: "I appreciate that—" but Hathaway brushed this aside. "Forget it, Doctor, there are more important things happening now. They've started to build the first big signs! Over a hundred feet high, on the traffic islands just outside town. They'll soon have all the approach roads covered. When they do we might as well stop thinking."

"Your trouble is that you're thinking too much," Franklin told him. "You've been rambling about these signs for weeks now. Tell me, have you actually seen one signaling?"

Hathaway tore a handful of leaves from the hedge, exasperated by this irrelevancy. "Of course I haven't, that's the whole point, Doctor." He dropped his voice as a group of nurses walked past, watching him uneasily out of the corners of their eyes. "The construction gangs were out again last night, laying huge power cables. You'll see them on the way home. Everything's nearly ready now."

"They're traffic signs," Franklin explained patiently. "The flyover has just been completed. Hathaway, for God's sake relax. Try to think of Dora and the child."

"I *am* thinking of them!" Hathaway's voice rose to a controlled scream. "Those cables were forty-thousand-volt lines, Doctor, with terrific switch-gear. The trucks were loaded with enormous metal scaffolds. Tomorrow they'll start lifting them up all over the city, they'll block off half the sky! What do you think Dora will be like after six months of that? We've got to stop them, Doctor, they're trying to transistorize our brains!"

Embarrassed by Hathaway's high-pitched shouting, Franklin had momentarily lost his sense of direction and helplessly searched the sea of cars for his own. "Hathaway, I can't waste any more time talking to you. Believe me, you need skilled help, these obsessions are beginning to master you."

Hathaway started to protest, and Franklin raised his right hand firmly. "Listen. For the last time, if you can show me one of these new signs, and prove that it's transmitting subliminal commands, I'll go to the police with you. But you haven't got a shred of evidence, and you know it. Subliminal advertising was banned thirty years ago, and the laws have never been repealed. Anyway, the technique was unsatisfactory; any success it had was marginal. Your idea of a huge conspiracy with all these thousands of giant signs everywhere is preposterous."

"All right, Doctor." Hathaway leaned against the bonnet of one of the cars. His moods seemed to switch abruptly from one level to the next. He watched Franklin amiably. "What's the matter—lost your car?"

"All your damned shouting has confused me." Franklin pulled out his ignition key and read the number off the tag: "NYN 299-566-367-21—can you see it?"

Hathaway leaned around lazily, one sandal up on the hood, surveying the square of a thousand or so cars facing them. "Difficult, isn't it, when they're all identical, even the same color? Thirty years ago there were about ten different makes, each in a dozen colors."

Franklin spotted his car, began to walk toward it. "Sixty years ago there were a hundred makes. What of it? The economies of standardization are obviously bought at a price."

Hathaway drummed his palm lightly on the roofs. "But these cars aren't all that cheap, Doctor. In fact, comparing them on an average income basis with those of thirty years ago they're about forty percent more expensive. With only one make being produced you'd expect a substantial reduction in price, not an increase."

"Maybe," Franklin said, opening his door. "But mechanically the cars of today are far more sophisticated. They're lighter, more durable, safer to drive."

Hathaway shook his head skeptically. "They *bore* me. The same model, same styling, same color, year after year. It's a sort of communism." He rubbed a greasy finger over the windshield. "This is a new one again, isn't it, Doctor? Where's the old one—you only had it for three months?"

"I traded it in," Franklin told him, starting the engine. "If you ever had any money you'd realize that it's the most economical way of owning a car. You don't keep driving the same one until it falls apart. It's the same with everything else—television sets, washing machines, refrigerators. But you aren't faced with the problem—you haven't got any."

Hathaway ignored the gibe and leaned his elbow on Franklin's window. "Not a bad idea, either, Doctor. It gives me time to think.

I'm not working a twelve-hour day to pay for a lot of things I'm too busy to use before they're obsolete."

He waved as Franklin reversed the car out of its line, then shouted into the wake of exhaust: "Drive with your eyes closed, Doctor!"

On the way home Franklin kept carefully to the slowest of the four-speed lanes. As usual after his discussions with Hathaway he felt vaguely depressed. He realized that unconsciously he envied Hathaway's footloose existence. Despite the grimy cold-water apartment in the shadow and roar of the flyover, despite his nagging wife and their sick child, and the endless altercations with the landlord and the supermarket credit manager, Hathaway still retained his freedom intact. Spared any responsibilities, he could resist the smallest encroachment upon him by the rest of society, if only by generating obsessive fantasies, such as his latest one about subliminal advertising.

The ability to react to stimuli, even irrationally, was a valid criterion of freedom. By contrast, what freedom Franklin possessed was peripheral, sharply demarked by the manifold responsibilities in the center of his life—the three mortgages on his home, the mandatory rounds of cocktail and TV parties, the private consultancy occupying most of Saturday which paid the installments on the multitude of household gadgets, clothes, and past holidays. About the only time he had to himself was driving to and from work.

But at least the roads were magnificent. Whatever other criticisms might be leveled at the present society, it certainly knew how to build roads. Eight-, ten-, and twelve-lane expressways interlaced across the continent, plunging from overhead causeways into the giant car parks in the center of the cities, or dividing into the great suburban arteries with their multiacre parking aprons around the marketing centers. Together the roadways and car parks covered more than a third of the country's entire area, and in the neighborhood of the cities the proportion was higher. The old cities were surrounded by the vast, dazzling abstract sculptures of the cloverleafs and flyovers, but even so the congestion was unremitting.

The ten-mile journey to his home in fact covered over twenty-five miles and took him twice as long as it had done before the construction of the expressway, the additional miles contained within the three giant cloverleafs. New cities were springing from the motels, cafés, and car marts around the highways. At the slightest hint of an intersection a shanty town of shacks and filling stations sprawled away among the forest of electric signs and route indicators, many of them substantial cities.

All around him cars bulleted along, streaming toward the suburbs. Relaxed by the smooth motion of the car, Franklin edged outward into the next speed-lane. As he accelerated from 40 to 50 mph a strident ear-jarring noise drummed out from his tires, shaking the chassis of the car. Ostensibly an aid to lane discipline, the surface of the road was covered with a mesh of small rubber studs, spaced progressively further apart in each of the lanes so that the tire hum resonated exactly on 40, 50, 60, and 70 mph. Driving at an intermediate speed for more than a few seconds became physiologically painful, and soon resulted in damage to the car and tires.

When the studs wore out they were replaced by slightly different patterns, matching those on the latest tires, so that regular tire changes were necessary, increasing the safety and efficiency of the expressway. It also increased the revenues of the car and tire manufacturers, for most cars over six months old soon fell to pieces under the steady battering, but this was regarded as a desirable end, the greater turnover reducing the unit price and making necessary more frequent model changes, as well as ridding the roads of dangerous vehicles.

A quarter of a mile ahead, at the approach to the first of the cloverleafs, the traffic stream was slowing, huge police signs signaling LANES CLOSED AHEAD and DROP SPEED BY 10 MPH. Franklin tried to return to the previous lane, but the cars were jammed bumper to bumper. As the chassis began to shudder and vibrate, jarring his spine, he clamped his teeth and tried to restrain himself from sounding the horn. Other drivers were less self-controlled, and everywhere engines were plunging and snarling, horns blaring. Road taxes were now so high, up to 30 percent of income (by contrast, income taxes were a bare 2 percent), that any delay on the expressways called for an immediate government inquiry, and the major departments of state were concerned with the administration of the road systems.

Nearer the cloverleaf the lanes had been closed to allow a gang of construction workers to erect a massive metal sign on one of the traffic islands. The palisaded area swarmed with engineers and surveyors and Franklin assumed that this was the sign Hathaway had seen unloaded the previous night. His apartment was in one of the gimcrack buildings in the settlement that straggled away around a nearby flyover, a low-rent area inhabited by service station personnel, waitresses, and other migrant labor.

The sign was enormous, at least a hundred feet high, fitted with heavy concave grilles similar to radar bowls. Rooted in a series of concrete caissons, it reared high into the air above the approach roads, visible for miles. Franklin craned up at the grilles, tracing the power cables from the transformers up into the intricate mesh of metal coils that covered their surface. A line of red aircraft-warning beacons was already alight along the top strut, and Franklin assumed that the sign was part of the ground approach system of the city airport ten miles to the east.

Three minutes later, as he accelerated down the two-mile link of straight highway to the next cloverleaf, he saw the second of the giant signs looming up into the sky before him.

Changing down into the 40 mph lane, Franklin uneasily watched the great bulk of the second sign recede in his rearview mirror. Although there were no graphic symbols among the wire coils covering the grilles, Hathaway's warnings still sounded in his ears. Without knowing why, he felt sure that the signs were not part of the airport approach system. Neither of them was in line with the principal airlanes. To justify the expense of siting them in the center of the expressway—the second sign required elaborate angled buttresses to support it on the narrow island—obviously meant that their role related in some way to the traffic streams.

Two hundred yards away was a roadside auto-mart, and Franklin abruptly remembered that he needed some cigarettes. Swinging the car down the entrance ramp, he joined the queue slowly passing the self-service dispenser at the far end of the rank. The auto-mart was packed with cars, each of the five purchasing ranks lined with tired-looking men hunched over their wheels.

Inserting his coins (paper money was no longer in circulation, unmanageable by the automats) he took a carton from the dispenser. This was the only brand of cigarettes available—in fact there was only one brand of everything—though giant economy packs were an alternative. Moving off, he opened the dashboard locker.

Inside, still sealed in their wrappers, were three other cartons.

A strong fishlike smell pervaded the house when he reached home, steaming out from the oven in the kitchen. Sniffing it uneagerly, Franklin took off his coat and hat, and found his wife crouched over the TV set in the lounge. An announcer was dictating a stream of numbers, and Judith scribbled them down on a pad, occasionally cursing under her breath. "What a muddle!" she snapped finally. "He was talking so quickly I took only a few things down."

"Probably deliberate," Franklin commented. "New panel game?"

Judith kissed him on the cheek, discreetly hiding the ashtray loaded with cigarette butts and chocolate wrappings. "Hullo, darling, sorry not to have a drink ready for you. They've started this series of Spot Bargains. They give you a selection of things on which you get a ninety percent trade-in discount at the local stores, if you're in the right area and have the right serial numbers. It's all terribly complicated."

"Sounds good, though. What have you got?"

Judith peered at her checklist. "Well, as far as I can see the only thing is the infrared barbecue spit. But we have to be there before eight o'clock tonight. It's seven-thirty already."

"Then that's out. I'm tired, angel, I need something to eat." When Judith started to protest he added firmly: "Look, I don't want a new infrared barbecue spit; we've only had this one for two months. Damn it, it's not even a different model."

"But, darling, don't you see, it makes it cheaper if you keep buying new ones. We'll have to trade ours in at the end of the year anyway, we signed the contract, and this way we save at least twenty dollars. These Spot Bargains aren't just a gimmick, you know. I've been glued to that set all day." A note of irritation had crept into her voice, but Franklin sat his ground, doggedly ignoring the clock.

"Right, we lose twenty dollars. It's worth it." Before she could remonstrate he said, "Judith, please, you probably took the wrong number down anyway." As she shrugged and went over to the bar he called, "Make it a stiff one. I see we have health foods on the menu."

"They're good for you, darling. You know you can't live on ordinary foods all the time. They don't contain any proteins or vitamins. You're always saying we ought to be like people in the old days and eat nothing but health foods."

177

"I would, but they smell so awful." Franklin lay back, nose in the glass of whiskey, gazing at the darkened skyline outside.

A quarter of a mile away, gleaming out above the roof of the neighborhood supermarket, were the five red beacon lights. Now and then, as the headlamps of the Spot Bargainers swung up across the face of the building, he could see the square massive bulk of the giant sign clearly silhouetted against the evening sky.

"Judith!" He went into the kitchen and took her over to the window. "That sign, just behind the supermarket. When did they put it up?"

"I don't know." Judith peered at him curiously. "Why are you so worried, Robert? Isn't it something to do with the airport?"

Franklin stared thoughtfully at the dark hull of the sign. "So everyone probably thinks."

Carefully he poured his whiskey into the sink.

After parking his car on the supermarket apron at seven o'clock the next morning, Franklin carefully emptied his pockets and stacked the coins in the dashboard locker. The supermarket was already busy with early morning shoppers and the line of thirty turnstiles clicked and slammed. Since the introduction of the "twenty-four-hour spending day" the shopping complex was never closed. The bulk of the shoppers were discount buyers, housewives contracted to make huge volume purchases of food, clothing, and appliances against substantial overall price cuts, and forced to drive around all day from supermarket to supermarket, frantically trying to keep pace with their purchase schedules and grappling with the added incentives inserted to keep the schemes alive.

Many of the women had teamed up, and as Franklin walked over to the entrance a pack of them charged toward their cars, stuffing their pay slips into their bags and gesticulating at each other. A moment later their cars roared off in a convoy to the next marketing zone.

A large neon sign over the entrance listed the latest discount—a mere 5 percent—calculated on the volume of turnover. The highest discounts, sometimes up to 25 percent, were earned in the housing estates where junior white-collar workers lived. There, spending had a strong social incentive; the desire to be the highest spender in the neighborhood was given moral reinforcement by the system of listing all the names and their accumulating cash totals on a huge electric sign in the supermarket foyers. The higher the spender, the greater his contribution to the discounts enjoyed by others. The lowest spenders were regarded as social criminals, free-riding on the backs of others.

Luckily this system had yet to be adopted in Franklin's neighborhood. Not because the professional men and their wives were able to exercise more discretion, but because their higher incomes allowed them to contract into more expensive discount schemes operated by the big department stores in the city.

Ten yards from the entrance Franklin paused, looking up at the huge metal sign mounted in an enclosure at the edge of the car park. Unlike the other signs and hoardings that proliferated everywhere, no attempt had been made to decorate it, or disguise the gaunt bare rectangle of riveted steel mesh. Power lines wound down its sides, and the concrete surface of the car park was crossed by a long scar where a cable had been sunk.

Franklin strolled along, then fifty feet from the sign stopped and turned, realizing that he would be late for the hospital and needed a new carton of cigarettes. A dim but powerful humming emanated from the transformers below the sign, fading as he retraced his steps to the supermarket.

Going over to the automats in the foyer, he felt for his change, then whistled sharply when he remembered why he had deliberately emptied his pockets.

"The cunning thing!" he said, loud enough for two shoppers to stare at him. Reluctant to look directly at the sign, he watched its reflection in one of the glass doorpanes, so that any subliminal message would be reversed.

Almost certainly he had received two distinct signals—"Keep Away" and "Buy Cigarettes." The people who normally parked their cars along the perimeter of the apron were avoiding the area under the enclosure, the cars describing a loose semicircle fifty feet around it.

He turned to the janitor sweeping out the foyer. "What's that sign for?"

The man leaned on his broom, gazing dully at the sign. "Dunno," he said, "must be something to do with the airport." He had an almost fresh cigarette in his mouth, but his right hand reached unconsciously to his hip pocket and pulled out a pack. He drummed the second cigarette absently on his thumbnail as Franklin walked away.

Everyone entering the supermarket was buying cigarettes.

Cruising quietly along the 40 mph lane, Franklin began to take a closer interest in the landscape around him. Usually he was either too tired or too preoccupied to do more than think about his driving, but now he examined the expressway methodically, scanning the roadside cafés for any smaller versions of the new signs. A host of neon displays covered the doorways and windows, but most of them seemed innocuous, and he turned his attention to the larger billboards erected along the open stretches of the expressway. Many of these were as high as four-story houses, elaborate three-dimensional devices in which giant glossy-skinned housewives with electric eyes and teeth jerked and postured around their ideal kitchens, neon flashes exploding from their smiles.

The areas on either side of the expressway were wasteland, continuous junkyards filled with cars and trucks, washing machines and refrigerators, all perfectly workable but jettisoned by the economic pressure of the succeeding waves of discount models. Their intact chrome hardly tarnished, the mounds of metal shells and cabinets glittered in the sunlight. Nearer the city the billboards were sufficiently close together to hide them, but now and then, as he slowed to approach one of the flyovers, Franklin caught a glimpse of the huge pyramids of metal, gleaming silently like the refuse grounds of some forgotten El Dorado.

That evening Hathaway was waiting for him as he came down the hospital steps. Franklin waved him across the court, then led the way quickly to his car.

"What's the matter, Doctor?" Hathaway asked as Franklin wound up the windows and glanced around the lines of parked cars. "Is someone after you?"

Franklin laughed somberly. "I don't know. I hope not, but if what you say is right, I suppose there is."

Hathaway leaned back with a chuckle, propping one knee up on the dashboard. "So you've seen something, Doctor, after all."

"Well, I'm not sure yet, but there's just a chance you may be right. This morning at the Fairlawne supermarket—" He broke off, uneasily remembering the huge blank sign and the abrupt way in which he had turned back to the supermarket as he approached it, then described his encounter.

Hathaway nodded slowly. "I've seen the sign there. It's big, but not as big as some that are going up. They're building them everywhere now. All over the city. What are you going to do, Doctor?"

Franklin gripped the wheel tightly. Hathaway's thinly veiled amusement irritated him. "Nothing, of course. Damn it, it may be just autosuggestion, you've probably got me imagining—"

Hathaway sat up with a jerk, his face mottled and savage. "Don't be absurd, Doctor! If you can't believe your own senses what chance have you left? They're invading your brain; if you don't defend yourself they'll take it over completely! We've got to act now, before we're all paralyzed."

Wearily Franklin raised one hand to restrain him. "Just a minute. Assuming that these signs *are* going up everywhere, what would be their object? Apart from wasting the enormous amount of capital invested in all the other millions of signs and billboards, the amounts of discretionary spending power still available must be infinitesimal. Some of the present mortgage and discount schemes reach half a century ahead, so there can't be much slack left to take up. A big trade war would be disastrous."

"Quite right, Doctor," Hathaway rejoined evenly, "but you're forgetting one thing. What would supply that extra spending power? A big increase in production. Already they've started to raise the working day from twelve hours to fourteen. In some of the appliance plants around the city Sunday working is being introduced as a norm. Can you visualize it, Doctor—a seven-day week, everyone with at least three jobs."

Franklin shook his head. "People won't stand for it."

"They will. Within the last twenty-five years the gross national product has risen by fifty percent, but so have the average hours worked. Ultimately we'll all be working and spending twenty-four hours a day, seven days a week. No one will dare refuse. Think what a slump would mean—millions of layoffs, people with time on their hands and nothing to spend it on. Real leisure, not just time spent buying things." He seized Franklin by the shoulder. "Well, Doctor, are you going to join me?"

Franklin freed himself. Half a mile away, partly hidden by the four-story bulk of the Pathology Department, was the upper half of one of the giant signs, workmen still crawling across its girders. The airlines over the city had deliberately been routed away from the hospital, and the sign obviously had no connection with approaching aircraft.

"Isn't there a prohibition on subliminal living? How can the unions accept it?"

"The fear of a slump. You know the new economic dogmas. Unless output rises by a steady inflationary five percent the economy is stagnating. Ten years ago increased efficiency alone would raise output, but the advantages there are minimal now and only one thing is left. More work. Increased consumption and subliminal advertising will provide the spur."

"What are you planning to do?"

"I can't tell you, Doctor, unless you accept equal responsibility for it."

"Sounds rather quixotic," Franklin commented. "Tilting at windmills. You won't be able to chop those things down with an ax."

"I won't try." Hathaway suddenly gave up and opened the door. "Don't wait too long to make up your mind, Doctor. By then it may not be yours to make up." With a wave he was gone.

On the way home Franklin's skepticism returned. The idea of the conspiracy was preposterous, and the economic arguments were too plausible. As usual, though, there had been a hook in the soft bait Hathaway dangled before him—Sunday working. His own consultancy had been extended into Sunday morning with his appointment as visiting factory doctor to one of the automobile plants that had started Sunday shifts. But instead of resenting this incursion into his already meager hours of leisure he had been glad. For one frightening reason—he needed the extra income.

Looking out over the lines of scurrying cars, he noticed that at least a dozen of the great signs had been erected along the expressway. As Hathaway had said, more were going up everywhere, rearing over the supermarkets in the housing developments like rusty metal sails.

Judith was in the kitchen when he reached home, watching the TV program on the hand-set over the cooker. Franklin climbed past a big cardboard carton, its seals still unbroken, which blocked the doorway, and kissed her on the cheek as she scribbled numbers down on her pad. The pleasant odor of pot-roast chicken—or, rather, a gelatine dummy of a chicken fully flavored and free of any toxic or nutritional properties—mollified his irritation at finding her still playing the Spot Bargains.

He tapped the carton with his foot. "What's this?"

"No idea, darling, something's always coming these days, I can't keep up with it all." She peered through the glass door at the chicken—an economy twelve-pounder, the size of a turkey, with stylized legs and wings and an enormous breast, most of which would be discarded at the end of the meal (there were no dogs or cats these days, the crumbs from the rich man's table saw to that) and then glanced at him pointedly.

"You look rather worried, Robert. Bad day?"

Franklin murmured noncommittally. The hours spent trying to detect false clues in the faces of the Spot Bargain announcers had sharpened Judith's perceptions, and he felt a pang of sympathy for the legion of husbands similarly outmatched.

"Have you been talking to that crazy beatnik again?"

"Hathaway? As a matter of fact I have. He's not all that crazy." He stepped backward into the carton, almost spilling his drink. "Well, what is this thing? As I'll be working for the next fifty Sundays to pay for it I'd like to find out."

He searched the sides, finally located the label. "*A TV set?* Judith, do we need another one? We've already got three. Lounge, dining room, and the hand-set. What's the fourth for?"

"The guest room, dear, don't get so excited. We can't leave a hand-set in the guest room, it's rude. I'm trying to economize but four TV sets is the bare minimum. All the magazines say so."

"*And* three radios?" Franklin stared irritably at the carton. "If we do invite a guest here how much time is he going to spend alone in his room watching television? Judith, we've got to call a halt. It's not as if these things were free, or even cheap. Anyway, television is a total waste of time. There's only one program. It's ridiculous to have four sets."

"Robert, there are *four* channels."

"But only the commercials are different." Before Judith could reply the telephone rang. Franklin lifted the kitchen receiver, listened to the gabble of noise that poured from it. At first he wondered whether this was some offbeat prestige commercial, then realized it was Hathaway in a manic swing.

"Hathaway!" he shouted back. "Relax, man! What's the matter now?"

"—Doctor, you'll have to believe me this time. I tell you I got on to one of the islands with a stroboscope; they've got hundreds of high-speed shutters blasting away like machine guns straight into people's faces and they can't see a thing, it's fantastic! The next big campaign's going to be cars and TV sets, they're trying to swing a two-month model change—can you imagine it, Doctor, a new car every two months? God Almighty, it's just—"

Franklin waited impatiently as the five-second commercial break cut in (all telephone calls were free, the length of the commercial extending with range—for long-distance calls the ratio of commercial to conversation was as high as 10:1, the participants desperately trying to get a word in edgeways between the interminable interruptions), but just before it ended he abruptly put the telephone down, then removed the receiver from the cradle.

Judith came over and took his arm. "Robert, what's the matter? You look terribly strained."

Franklin picked up his drink and walked through into the lounge. "It's just Hathaway. As you say, I'm getting a little too involved with him. He's starting to prey on my mind."

He looked at the dark outline of the sign over the supermarket, its red warning lights glowing in the night sky. Blank and nameless, like an area forever closed off in an insane mind, what frightened him was its total anonymity.

"Yet I'm not sure," he muttered. "So much of what Hathaway says makes sense. These subliminal techniques are the sort of last-ditch attempt you'd expect from an overcapitalized industrial system."

He waited for Judith to reply, then looked up at her. She stood in the center of the carpet, hands folded limply, her sharp, intelligent face curiously dull and blunted. He followed her gaze out over the rooftops, then with an effort turned his head and quickly switched on the TV set.

"Come on," he said grimly. "Let's watch television. God, we're going to need that fourth set."

A week later Franklin began to compile his inventory. He saw nothing more of Hathaway; as he left the hospital in the evening the familiar scruffy figure was absent. When the first of the explosions sounded dimly around the city and he read of the attempts to sabotage the giant signs he automatically assumed that Hathaway was responsible, but later he heard on a newscast that the detonations had been set off by construction workers excavating foundations.

More of the signs appeared over the rooftops, isolated on the palisaded islands near the suburban shopping centers. Already there were over thirty on the ten-mile route from the hospital, standing shoulder to shoulder over the speeding cars like giant dominoes. Franklin had given up his attempt to avoid looking at them, but the slim possibility that the explosions might be Hathaway's counterattack kept his suspicions alive.

He began his inventory after hearing the newscast, discovered that in the previous fortnight he and Judith had traded in their

Car (previous model 2 months old)
2 TV sets (4 months)
Power mower (7 months)
Electric cooker (5 months)
Hair dryer (4 months)
Refrigerator (3 months)
2 radios (7 months)
Record player (5 months)
Cocktail bar (8 months)

Half these purchases had been made by himself, but exactly when he could never recall realizing at the time. The car, for example, he had left in the garage near the hospital to be greased; that evening he had signed for the new model as he sat at its wheel, accepting the salesman's assurance that the depreciation on the two-month trade-in was virtually less than the cost of the grease job. Ten minutes later, as he sped along the expressway, he suddenly realized that he had bought a new car. Similarly, the TV sets had been replaced by identical models after developing the same irritating interference pattern (curiously, the new sets also displayed the pattern, but as the salesman assured them, this promptly vanished two days later).

Not once had he actually decided of his own volition that he wanted something and then gone out to a store and bought it!

He carried the inventory around with him, adding to it as necessary, quietly and without protest analyzing these new sales techniques, wondering whether total capitulation might be the only way of defeating them. As long as he kept up even a token resistance, the inflationary growth curve would show a controlled annual 10 percent climb. With that resistance removed, however, it would begin to rocket upward out of control...

Then, driving home from the hospital two months later, he saw one of the signs for the first time.

He was in the 40 mph lane, unable to keep up with the flood of new cars, had just passed the second of the three cloverleafs when the traffic half a mile away began to slow down. Hundreds of cars had driven up on to the grass verge, and a large crowd was gathering around one of the signs. Two small black figures were climbing up the metal face, and a series of huge gridlike patterns of light flashed on and off, illuminating the evening air. The patterns were random and broken, as if the sign was being tested for the first time.

Relieved that Hathaway's suspicions had been completely groundless, Franklin turned off onto the soft shoulder, then walked forward through the spectators as the lights blinked and stuttered in their faces. Below, behind the steel palisades around the island, was a large group of police and engineers, craning up at the men scaling the sign a hundred feet over their heads.

Suddenly Franklin stopped, the sense of relief fading instantly. With a jolt he saw that several of the police on the ground were armed with shotguns, and that the two policemen climbing the sign carried submachine guns slung over their shoulders. They were converging on a third figure, crouched by a switchbox on the penultimate tier, a ragged bearded man in a grimy shirt, a bare knee poking through his jeans.

Hathaway!

Franklin hurried toward the island, the sign hissing and spluttering, fuses blowing by the dozen.

Then the flicker of lights cleared and steadied, blazing out continuously, and together the crowd looked up at the decks of brilliant letters. The phrases, and every combination of them possible, were entirely familiar, and Franklin knew that he had been reading them unconsciously in his mind for weeks as he passed up and down the expressway.

BUY NOW BUY NOW BUY NOW BUY NOW BUY NOW NEW CAR NOW
NEW CAR NOW NEW CAR NOW YES YES YES YES YES YES YES YES
YES YES YES

Sirens blaring, two patrol cars swung up onto the verge through the crowd and plunged across the damp grass. Police spilled from its doors, batons in their hands, and quickly began to force back the crowd. Franklin held his ground as they approached, started to say: "Officer, I know the man—" but the policeman punched him in the chest with the flat of his hand. Winded, he stumbled back among the cars, leaned helplessly against a fender as the police began to break the windshields, the hapless drivers protesting angrily, those further back rushing for their vehicles.

The noise fell away abruptly when one of the submachine guns fired a brief roaring burst, then rose in a massive gasp of horror as Hathaway, arms outstretched, let out a cry of triumph and pain, and jumped.

"But, Robert, what does it really matter?" Judith asked as Franklin sat inertly in the lounge the next morning. "I know it's tragic for his wife and daughter, but Hathaway was in the grip of an obsession. If he hated advertising signs so much why didn't he dynamite those we *can* see, instead of worrying so much about those we can't?"

Franklin stared at the TV screen, hoping the program would distract him.

"Hathaway was *right*," he said simply.

"Was he? Advertising is here to stay. We've no real freedom of choice, anyway. We can't spend more than we can afford, the finance companies soon clamp down."

"You accept that?" Franklin went over to the window. A quarter of a mile away, in the center of the estate, another of the signs was being erected. It was due east from them, and in the early morning light the shadows of its rectangular superstructure fell across the garden, reaching almost to the steps of the French windows at his feet. As a concession to the neighborhood, and perhaps to allay any suspicions while it was being erected by an appeal to petty snobbery, the lower sections had been encased in mock-Tudor paneling.

Franklin stared at it numbly, counting the half-dozen police lounging by their patrol cars as the construction gang unloaded prefabricated grilles from a couple of trucks. Then he looked at the sign by the supermarket, trying to repress his memories of Hathaway and the pathetic attempts the man had made to convince Franklin and gain his help.

He was still standing there an hour later when Judith came in, putting on her hat and coat, ready to visit the supermarket.

Franklin followed her to the door: "I'll drive you down there, Judith," he said in a flat dead voice. "I have to see about booking a new car. The next models are coming out at the end of the month. With luck we'll get one of the early deliveries."

They walked out into the trim drive, the shadows of the great signs swinging across the quiet neighborhood as the day progressed, sweeping over the heads of the people on their way to the supermarket like the dark blades of enormous scythes.

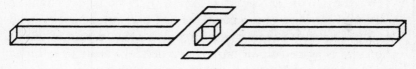

The Cage of Sand

At sunset, when the vermilion glow reflected from the dunes along the horizon fitfully illuminated the white faces of the abandoned hotels, Bridgman stepped onto his balcony and looked out over the long stretches of cooling sand as the tides of purple shadow seeped across them. Slowly, extending their slender fingers through the shallow saddles and depressions, the shadows massed together like gigantic combs, a few phosphorescing spurs of obsidian isolated for a moment between the tines, and then finally coalesced and flooded in a solid wave across the half-submerged hotels. Behind the silent facades, in the tilting sand-filled streets which had once glittered with cocktail bars and restaurants, it was already night. Halos of moonlight beaded the lamp standards with silver dew, and draped the shuttered windows and slipping cornices like a frost of frozen gas.

As Bridgman watched, his lean bronzed arms propped against the rusting rail, the last whorls of light sank away into the cerise funnel withdrawing below the horizon, and the first wind stirred across the dead Martian sand. Here and there miniature cyclones whirled about a sand spur, drawing off swirling feathers of moon-washed spray, and a nimbus of white dust swept across the dunes and settled in the dips and hollows. Gradually the drifts accumulated, edging toward the former shoreline below the hotels. Already the first four floors had been inundated, and the sand now reached up to within two feet of Bridgman's balcony. After the next sandstorm he would be forced yet again to move to the floor above.

"Bridgman!"

The voice cleft the darkness like a spear. Fifty yards to his right, at the edge of the derelict sandbreak he had once attempted to build below the hotel, a square stocky figure wearing a pair of frayed cotton shorts waved up at him. The moonlight etched the broad sinewy muscles of his chest, the powerful bowed legs sinking almost to their calves in the soft Martian sand. He was about forty-five years old, his thinning hair close-cropped so that he seemed almost bald. In his right hand he carried a large canvas holdall.

Bridgman smiled to himself. Standing there patiently in the moonlight below the derelict hotel, Travis reminded him of some long-delayed tourist arriving at a ghost resort years after its extinction.

"Bridgman, are you coming?" When the latter still leaned on his balcony rail, Travis added, "The next conjunction is tomorrow."

Bridgman shook his head, a rictus of annoyance twisting his mouth. He hated the bimonthly conjunctions, when all seven of the derelict satellite capsules still orbiting the Earth crossed the sky together. Invariably on these nights he remained in his room, playing over the old memo-tapes he had salvaged from the submerged chalets and motels further along the beach (the hysterical "This is Mamie Goldberg, 62955 Cocoa Boulevard, I really wanna protest against this crazy evacuation..." or resigned "Sam Snade here, the Pontiac convertible in the back garage belongs to anyone who can dig it out"). Travis and Louise Woodward always came to the hotel on the conjunction nights—it was the highest building in the resort, with an unrestricted view from horizon to horizon—and would follow the seven converging stars as they pursued their endless courses around the globe. Both would be oblivious of everything else, which the wardens knew only too well, and they reserved their most careful searches of the sand sea for these bimonthly occasions. Invariably Bridgman found himself forced to act as lookout for the other two.

"I was out last night," he called down to Travis. "Keep away from the northeast perimeter fence by the Cape. They'll be busy repairing the track."

Most nights Bridgman divided his time between excavating the buried motels for caches of supplies (the former inhabitants of the resort area had assumed the government would soon rescind its evacuation order) and disconnecting the sections of metal roadway laid across the desert for the wardens' jeeps. Each of the squares of wire mesh was about five yards wide and weighed over three hundred pounds. After he had snapped the lines of rivets, dragged the sections away, and buried them among the dunes he would be exhausted, and spend most of the next day nursing his strained hands and shoulders. Some sections of the track were now permanently anchored with heavy steel stakes, and he knew that sooner or later they would be unable to delay the wardens by sabotaging the roadway.

Travis hesitated, and with a noncommittal shrug disappeared among the dunes, the heavy toolbag swinging easily from one powerful arm. Despite the meager diet which sustained him, his energy and determination seemed undiminished—in a single night Bridgman had watched him dismantle twenty sections of track and then loop together the adjacent limbs of a crossroad, sending an entire convoy of six vehicles off into the wastelands to the south.

Bridgman turned from the balcony, then stopped when a faint tang of brine touched the cool air. Ten miles away, hidden by the lines of dunes, was the sea, the long green rollers of the middle Atlantic breaking against the red Martian strand. When he had first come to the beach five years earlier there had never been the faintest scent of brine across the intervening miles of sand. Slowly, however, the Atlantic was driving the shore back to its former margins. The tireless shoulder of the Gulf Stream drummed against the soft Martian dust and piled the dunes into grotesque rococo reefs which the wind carried away into the sand sea. Gradually the ocean was returning, reclaiming its great smooth basin, sifting out the black quartz and Martian obsidian which would never be windborne and drawing these down into its deeps. More and more often the stain of brine would hang on the evening air, reminding Bridgman why he had first come to the beach and removing any inclination to leave.

Three years earlier he had attempted to measure the rate of approach, by driving a series of stakes into the sand at the water's edge, but the shifting contours of the dunes carried away the colored poles. Later, using the promontory at Cape Kennedy, where the old launching gantries and landing ramps reared up into the sky like derelict pieces of giant sculpture, he had calculated by triangulation that the advance was little more than thirty yards per year. At this rate—without wanting to, he had automatically made the calculation—it would be well over five hundred years before the Atlantic reached its former littoral at Cocoa Beach. Though discouragingly slow, the movement was nonetheless in a forward direction, and Bridgman was happy to remain in his hotel ten miles away across the dunes, conceding toward its time of arrival the few years he had at his disposal.

Later, shortly after Louise Woodward's arrival, he had thought of dismantling one of the motel cabins and building himself a small chalet by the water's edge. But the shoreline had been too dismal and forbidding. The great red dunes rolled on for miles, cutting off half the sky, dissolving slowly under the impact of the slate-green water. There was no formal tideline, but only a steep shelf littered with nodes of quartz and rusting fragments of Mars rockets brought back with the ballast. He spent a few days in a cave below a towering sand reef, watching the long galleries of compacted red dust crumble and dissolve as the cold Atlantic stream sluiced through them, collapsing like the decorated colonnades of a baroque cathedral. In the summer the heat reverberated from the hot sand as from the slag of some molten sun, burning the rubber soles from his boots, and the light from the scattered flints of washed quartz flickered with diamond hardness. Bridgman had returned to the hotel grateful for his room overlooking the silent dunes.

Leaving the balcony, the sweet smell of brine still in his nostrils, he went over to the desk. A small cone of shielded light shone down over the tape recorder and rack of spools. The rumble of the wardens' unsilenced engines always gave him at least five minutes' warning of their arrival, and it would have been safe to install another lamp in the room—there were no roadways between the hotel and the sea, and from a distance any light reflected onto the balcony was indistinguishable from the corona of glimmering phosphors which hung over the sand like myriads of fireflies. However, Bridgman preferred to sit in the darkened suite, enclosed by the circle of books on the makeshift shelves, the shadow-filled air playing over his shoulders through the long night as he toyed with the memo-tapes, fragments of a vanished and unregretted past. By day he always drew the blinds, immolating himself in a world of perpetual twilight.

Bridgman had easily adapted himself to his self-isolation, soon evolved a system of daily routines that gave him the maximum of time to spend on his private reveries. Pinned to the walls around him were a series of huge whiteprints and architectural drawings, depicting various elevations of a fantastic Martian city he had once designed, its glass spires and curtain walls rising like heliotropic jewels from the vermilion desert. In fact, the whole city was a vast piece of jewelry, each elevation brilliantly visualized but as symmetrical, and ultimately as lifeless, as a crown. Bridgman continuously retouched the drawings, inserting more and more details, so that they almost seemed to be photographs of an original.

Most of the hotels in the town—one of a dozen similar resorts buried by the sand which had once formed an unbroken strip of motels, chalets, and five-star hotels thirty miles to the south of Cape Kennedy—were well stocked with supplies of canned food abandoned when the area was evacuated and wired off. There were ample reservoirs and cisterns filled with water, apart from a thousand intact cocktail bars six feet below the surface of the sand. Travis had excavated a dozen of these in search of his favorite vintage bourbon. Walking out across the desert behind the town one would suddenly find a short flight of steps cut into the annealed sand and crawl below an occluded sign announcing THE SATELLITE BAR OR THE ORBIT ROOM into the inner sanctum, where the jutting deck of a chromium bar had been cleared as far as the diamond-paned mirror freighted with its rows of bottles and figurines. Bridgman would have been glad to see them left undisturbed.

The whole trash of amusement arcades and cheap bars on the outskirts of the beach resorts were a depressing commentary on the original spaceflights, reducing them to the level of monster sideshows at a carnival.

Outside his room, steps sounded along the corridor, then slowly climbed the stairway, pausing for a few seconds at every landing. Bridgman lowered the memo-tape in his hand, listening to the familiar tired footsteps. This was Louise Woodward, making her invariable evening ascent to the roof ten stories above. Bridgman glanced to the timetable pinned to the wall. Only two of the satellites would be visible, between 12:25 and 12:35 A.M., at an elevation of 62 degrees in the southwest, passing through Cetus and Eridanus, neither of them containing her husband. Although the sighting was two hours away, she was already taking up her position, and would remain there until dawn.

Bridgman listened wanly to the feet recede slowly up the stairwell. All through the night the slim pale-faced woman would sit out under the moonlit sky, as the soft Martian sand her husband had given his life to reach sifted around her in the dark wind, stroking her faded hair like some mourning mariner's wife waiting for the sea to surrender her husband's body. Travis usually joined her later, and the two of them sat side by side against the elevator house, the frosted letters of the hotel's neon sign strewn around their feet like the fragments of a dismembered zodiac, then at dawn made their way down into the shadow-filled streets to their aeries in the nearby hotels.

Initially Bridgman often joined their nocturnal vigil, but after a few nights he began to feel something repellent, if not actually ghoulish, about their mindless contemplation of the stars. This was not so much because of the macabre spectacle of the dead astronauts orbiting the planet in their capsules, but because of the curious sense of unspoken communion between Travis and Louise Woodward, almost as if they were celebrating a private rite to which Bridgman could never be initiated. Whatever their original motives, Bridgman sometimes suspected that these had been overlayed by other, more personal ones.

Ostensibly, Louise Woodward was watching her husband's satellite in order to keep alive his memory, but Bridgman guessed that the memories she unconsciously wished to perpetuate were those of herself twenty years earlier, when her husband had been a celebrity and she herself courted by magazine columnists and TV reporters. For fifteen years after his death—Woodward had been killed testing a new lightweight launching platform—she had lived a nomadic existence, driving restlessly in her cheap car from motel to motel across the continent, following her husband's star as it disappeared into the eastern night, and had at last made her home at Cocoa Beach in sight of the rusting gantries across the bay.

Travis's real motives were probably more complex. To Bridgman, after they had known each other for a couple of years, he had confided that he felt himself bound by a debt of honor to maintain a watch over the dead astronauts for the example of courage and sacrifice they had set him as a child (although most of them had been piloting their wrecked capsules for fifty years before Travis's birth), and that now they were virtually forgotten he must single-handedly keep alive the fading flame of their memory. Bridgman was convinced of his sincerity.

Yet later, going through a pile of old news magazines in the trunk of a car he excavated from a motel port, he came across a picture of Travis wearing an aluminum pressure suit and learned something more of his story. Apparently Travis had at one time been himself an astronaut—or rather, a would-be astronaut. A test pilot for one of the civilian agencies setting up orbital relay stations, his nerve had failed him a few seconds before the last "hold" of his countdown, a moment of pure unexpected funk that cost the company some five million dollars.

Obviously it was his inability to come to terms with this failure of character, unfortunately discovered lying flat on his back on a contour couch two hundred feet above the launching pad, which had brought Travis to Kennedy, the abandoned Mecca of the first heroes of astronautics.

Tactfully Bridgman had tried to explain that no one would blame him for this failure of nerve—less his responsibility than that of the selectors who had picked him for the flight, or at least the result of an unhappy concatenation of ambiguously worded multiple-choice questions (crosses in the wrong boxes, some heavier to bear and harder to open than others! Bridgman had joked sardonically to himself). But Travis seemed to have reached his own decision about himself. Night after night, he watched the brilliant funerary convoy weave its gilded pathway toward the dawn sun, salving his own failure by identifying it with the greater, but blameless, failure of the seven astronauts. Travis still wore his hair in the regulation "Mohican" cut of the spaceman, still kept himself in perfect physical trim by the vigorous routines he had practiced before his abortive flight. Sustained by the personal myth he had created, he was now more or less unreachable.

"Dear Harry, I've taken the car and deposit box. Sorry it should end like—"

Irritably, Bridgman switched off the memo-tape and its recapitulation of some thirty-year-old private triviality. For some reason he seemed unable to accept Travis and Louise Woodward for what they were. He disliked this failure of compassion, a nagging compulsion to expose other people's motives and strip away the insulating sheaths around their naked nerve strings, particularly as his own motives for being at Cape Kennedy were so suspect. Why was *he* there, what failure was *he* trying to expiate? And why choose Cocoa Beach as his penitential shore? For three years he had asked himself these questions so often that they had ceased to have any meaning, like a fossilized catechism or the blunted self-recrimination of a paranoiac.

He had resigned his job as the chief architect of a big space development company after the large government contract on which the firm depended, for the design of the first Martian city-settlement, was awarded to a rival consortium. Secretly, however, he realized that his resignation had marked his unconscious acceptance that despite his great imaginative gifts he was unequal to the specialized and more prosaic tasks of designing the settlement. On the drawing board, as elsewhere, he would always remain earthbound.

His dreams of building a new Gothic architecture of launching ports and controls gantries, of being the Frank Lloyd Wright and Le Corbusier of the first city to be raised outside Earth, faded forever, but left him unable to accept the alternative of turning out endless plans for low-cost hospitals in Ecuador and housing estates in Tokyo. For a year he had drifted aimlessly, but a few color photographs of the vermilion sunsets at Cocoa Beach and a news story about the recluses living on in the submerged motels had provided a powerful compass.

He dropped the memo-tape into a drawer, making an effort to accept Louise Woodward and Travis on their own terms, a wife keeping watch over her dead husband and an old astronaut maintaining a solitary vigil over the memories of his lost comrades-in-arms.

The wind gusted against the balcony window, and a light spray of sand rained across the floor. At night dust storms churned along the beach. Thermal pools isolated by the cooling desert would suddenly accrete like beads of quicksilver and erupt across the fluffy sand in miniature tornadoes.

Only fifty yards away, the dying cough of a heavy diesel cut through the shadows. Quickly Bridgman turned off the small desk light, grateful for his meanness over the battery packs plugged into the circuit, then stepped to the window.

At the leftward edge of the sand break, half-hidden in the long shadows cast by the hotel, was a large tracked vehicle with a low camouflaged hull. A narrow observation bridge had been built over the bumpers directly in front of the squat snout of the engine housing, and two of the beach wardens were craning up through the plexiglass windows at the balconies of the hotel, shifting their binoculars from rocm to room. Behind them, under the glass dome of the extended driving cabin, were three more wardens, controlling an outboard spotlight. In the center of the bowl a thin mote of light pulsed with the rhythm of the engine, ready to throw its powerful beam into any of the open rooms.

Bridgman hid back behind the shutters as the binoculars focused upon the adjacent balcony, moved to his own, hesitated, and passed to the next. Exasperated by the sabotaging of the roadways, the wardens had evidently decided on a new type of vehicle. With their four broad tracks, the huge squat sand cars would be free of the mesh roadways and able to rove at will through the dunes and sand hills.

Bridgman watched the vehicle reverse slowly, its engine barely varying its deep bass growl, then move off along the line of hotels, almost indistinguishable in profile among the shifting dunes and hillocks. A hundred yards away, at the first intersection, it turned toward the main boulevard, wisps of dust streaming from the metal cleats like thin spumes of steam. The men in the observation bridge were still watching the hotel. Bridgman was certain that they had seen a reflected glimmer of light, or perhaps some movement of Louise Woodward's on the roof. However reluctant to leave the car and be contaminated by the poisonous dust, the wardens would not hesitate if the capture of one of the beachcombers warranted it.

Racing up the staircase, Bridgman made his way to the roof, crouching below the windows that overlooked the boulevard. Like a huge crab, the sand car had parked under the jutting overhang of the big department store opposite. Once fifty feet from the ground, the concrete lip was now separated from it by little more than six or seven feet, and the sand car was hidden in the shadows below it, engine silent. A single movement in a window, or the unexpected return of Travis, and the wardens would spring from the hatchways, their long-handled nets and lassos pinioning them around the neck and ankles. Bridgman remembered one beachcomber he had seen flushed from his motel hideout and carried off like a huge twitching spider at the center of a black rubber web, the wardens with their averted faces and masked mouths like devils in an abstract ballet.

Reaching the roof, Bridgman stepped out into the opaque white moonlight. Louise Woodward was leaning on the balcony, looking out toward the distant, unseen sea. At the faint sound of the door creaking she turned and began to walk listlessly around the roof, her pale face floating like a nimbus. She wore a freshly ironed print dress she had found in a rusty spin dryer in one of the launderettes, and her streaked blond hair floated out lightly behind her on the wind.

"Louise!"

Involuntarily she started, tripping over a fragment of the neon sign, then moved backward toward the balcony overlooking the boulevard.

"Mrs. Woodward!" Bridgman held her by the elbow, raised a hand to her mouth before she could cry out. "The wardens are down below. They're watching the hotel. We must find Travis before he returns."

Louise hesitated, apparently recognizing Bridgman only by an effort, and her eyes turned up to the black marble sky. Bridgman looked at his watch; it was almost 12:35. He searched the stars in the southwest.

Louise murmured, "They're nearly here now, I must see them. Where is Travis, he should be here?"

Bridgman pulled at her arm. "Perhaps he saw the sand car. Mrs. Woodward, we should leave."

Suddenly she pointed up at the sky, then wrenched away from him and ran to the rail. "There they are!"

Fretting, Bridgman waited until she had filled her eyes with the two companion points of light speeding from the western horizon.

These were Merril and Pokrovski—like every schoolboy he knew the sequences perfectly, a second system of constellations with a more complex but far more tangible periodicity and precession—the Castor and Pollux of the orbiting zodiac, whose appearance always heralded a full conjunction the following night.

Louise Woodward gazed up at them from the rail, the rising wind lifting her hair off her shoulders and entraining it horizontally behind her head. Around her feet the red Martian dust swirled and rustled, silting over the fragments of the old neon sign, a brilliant pink spume streaming from her long fingers as they moved along the balcony ledge. When the satellites finally disappeared among the stars along the horizon, she leaned forward, her face raised to the milk-blue moon as if to delay their departure, then turned back to Bridgman, a bright smile on her face.

His earlier suspicions vanishing, Bridgman smiled back at her encouragingly. "Roger will be here tomorrow night, Louise. We must be careful the wardens don't catch us before we see him."

He felt a sudden admiration for her, at the stoical way she had sustained herself during her long vigil. Perhaps she thought of Woodward as still alive, and in some way was patiently waiting for him to return? He remembered her saying once, "Roger was only a boy when he took off, you know, I feel more like his mother now," as if frightened how Woodward would react to her dry skin and fading hair, fearing that he might even have forgotten her. No doubt the death she visualized for him was of a different order than the mortal kind.

Hand in hand, they tiptoed carefully down the flaking steps, jumped down from a terrace window into the soft sand below the windbreak. Bridgman sank to his knees in the fine silver moon dust, then waded up to the firmer ground, pulling Louise after him. They climbed through a breach in the tilting palisades, then ran away from the line of dead hotels looming like skulls in the empty light.

"Paul, wait!" Her head still raised to the sky, Louise Woodward fell to her knees in a hollow between two dunes, with a laugh stumbled after Bridgman as he raced through the dips and saddles. The wind was now whipping the sand off the higher crests, flurries of dust spurting like excited wavelets. A hundred yards away, the town was a fading film set, projected by the camera obscura of the sinking moon. They were standing where the long Atlantic seas had once been ten fathoms deep, and Bridgman could scent again the tang of brine among the flickering whitecaps of dust, phosphorescing like shoals of animalcula. He waited for any sign of Travis.

"Louise, we'll have to go back to the town. The sandstorms are blowing up, we'll never see Travis here."

They moved back through the dunes, then worked their way among the narrow alleyways between the hotels to the northern gateway to the town. Bridgman found a vantage point in a small apartment block, and they lay down looking out below a window lintel into the sloping street, the warm sand forming a pleasant cushion. At the intersections the dust blew across the roadway in white clouds, obscuring the warden's beach car parked a hundred yards down the boulevard.

Half an hour later an engine surged, and Bridgman began to pile sand into the interval in front of them. "They're going. Thank God!"

Louise Woodward held his arm. "Look!"

Fifty feet away, his white vinyl suit half-hidden in the dust clouds, one of the wardens was advancing slowly toward them, his lasso twirling lightly in his hand. A few feet behind was a second warden, craning up at the windows of the apartment block with his binoculars.

Bridgman and Louise crawled back below the ceiling, then dug their way under a transom into the kitchen at the rear. A window opened onto a sand-filled yard, and they darted away through the lifting dust that whirled between the buildings.

Suddenly, around a corner, they saw the line of wardens moving down a side street, the sand car edging along behind them. Before Bridgman could steady himself a spasm of pain seized his right calf, contorting the gastrocnemius muscle, and he fell to one knee. Louise Woodward pulled him back against the wall, then pointed at a squat, bowlegged figure trudging toward them along the curving road into town.

"Travis—"

The toolbag swung from his right hand, and his feet rang faintly on the wire-mesh roadway. Head down, he seemed unaware of the wardens hidden by a bend in the road.

"Come on!" Disregarding the negligible margin of safety,

Bridgman clambered to his feet and impetuously ran out into the center of the street. Louise tried to stop him, and they had covered only ten yards before the wardens saw them. There was a warning shout, and the spotlight flung its giant cone down the street. The sand car surged forward, like a massive dust-covered bull, its tracks clawing at the sand.

"Travis!" As Bridgman reached the bend, Louise Woodward ten yards behind, Travis looked up from his reverie, then flung the toolbag over one shoulder and raced ahead of them toward the clutter of motel roofs protruding from the other side of the street. Lagging behind the others, Bridgman again felt the cramp attack his leg, broke off into a painful shuffle. When Travis came back for him Bridgman tried to wave him away, but Travis pinioned his elbow and propelled him forward like an attendant straight-arming a patient.

The dust swirling around them, they disappeared through the fading streets and out into the desert, the shouts of the beach wardens lost in the roar and clamor of the baying engine. Around them, like the strange metallic flora of some extraterrestrial garden, the old neon signs jutted from the red Martian sand—SATELLITE MOTEL, PLANET BAR, MERCURY MOTEL. Hiding behind them, they reached the scrub-covered dunes on the edge of the town, then picked up one of the trails that led away among the sand reefs. There, in the deep grottoes of compacted sand which hung like inverted palaces, they waited until the storm subsided. Shortly before dawn the wardens abandoned their search, unable to bring the heavy sand car onto the disintegrating reef.

Contemptuous of the wardens, Travis lit a small fire with his cigarette lighter, burning splinters of driftwood that had gathered in the gullies. Bridgman crouched beside it, warming his hands.

"This is the first time they've been prepared to leave the sand car," he remarked to Travis. "It means they're under orders to catch us."

Travis shrugged. "Maybe. They're extending the fence along the beach. They probably intend to seal us in forever."

"What?" Bridgman stood up with a sudden feeling of uneasiness. "Why should they? Are you sure? I mean, what would be the point?"

Travis looked up at him, a flicker of dry amusement on his bleached face. Wisps of smoke wreathed his head, curled up past the serpentine columns of the grotto to the winding interval of sky a hundred feet above. "Bridgman, forgive me saying so, but if you want to leave here, you should leave now. In a month's time you won't be able to."

Bridgman ignored this, and searched the cleft of dark sky overhead, which framed the constellation Scorpio, as if hoping to see a reflection of the distant sea. "They must be crazy. How much of this fence did you see?"

"About eight hundred yards. It won't take them long to complete. The sections are prefabricated, about forty feet high." He smiled ironically at Bridgman's discomfort. "Relax, Bridgman. If you do want to get out, you'll always be able to tunnel underneath it."

"I don't want to get out," Bridgman said coldly. "Damn them, Travis, they're turning the place into a zoo. You know it won't be the same with a fence all the way around it."

"A corner of Earth that is forever Mars." Under the high forehead, Travis's eyes were sharp and watchful. "I see their point. There hasn't been a fatal casualty now—" he glanced at Louise Woodward, who was strolling about in the colonnades "—for nearly twenty years, and passenger rockets are supposed to be as safe as commuters' trains. They're quietly sealing off the past, Louise and I and you with it. I suppose it's pretty considerate of them not to burn the place down with flamethrowers. The virus would be a sufficient excuse. After all, we are probably the only reservoirs left on the planet." He picked up a handful of red dust and examined the fine crystals with a somber eye. "Well, Bridgman, what are you going to do?"

His thoughts discharging themselves through his mind like frantic signal flares, Bridgman walked away without answering.

Behind them, Louise Woodward wandered among the deep galleries of the grotto, crooning to herself in a low voice to the sighing rhythms of the whirling sand.

The next morning they returned to the town, wading through the deep drifts of sand that lay like a fresh fall of red snow between the hotels and stores, coruscating in the brilliant sunlight. Travis and Louise Woodward made their way toward their quarters in the motels further down the beach. Bridgman searched the still, crystal air for any signs of the wardens, but the sand car had gone, its tracks obliterated by the storm.

In his room he found their calling card.

A huge tide of dust had flowed through the French windows and submerged the desk and bed, three feet deep against the rear wall. Outside the sandbreak had been inundated, and the contours of the desert had completely altered, a few spires of obsidian marking its former perspectives like buoys on a shifting sea. Bridgman spent the morning digging out his books and equipment, dismantled the electrical system and its batteries and carried everything to the room above. He would have moved to the penthouse on the top floor, but his lights would have been visible for miles.

Settling into his new quarters, he switched on the tape recorder, heard a short clipped message in the brisk voice which had shouted orders at the wardens the previous evening. "Bridgman, this is Major Webster, deputy commandant of Cocoa Beach Reservation. On the instructions of the Anti-Viral Subcommittee of the UN General Assembly we are now building a continuous fence around the beach area. On completion no further egress will be allowed, and anyone escaping will be immediately returned to the reservation. Give yourself up now, Bridgman, before—"

Bridgman stopped the tape, then reversed the spool and erased the message, staring angrily at the instrument. Unable to settle down to the task of rewiring the room's circuits, he paced about, fiddling with the architectural drawings propped against the wall. He felt restless and hyperexcited, perhaps because he had been trying to repress, not very successfully, precisely those doubts of which Webster had now reminded him.

He stepped onto the balcony and looked out over the desert, at the red dunes rolling to the windows directly below. For the fourth time he had moved up a floor, and the sequence of identical rooms he had occupied were like displaced images of himself seen through a prism. Their common focus, that elusive final definition of himself which he had sought for so long, still remained to be found. Timelessly the sand swept toward him, its shifting contours, approximating more closely than any other landscape he had found to complete psychic zero, enveloping his past failures and uncertainties, masking them in its enigmatic canopy.

Bridgman watched the red sand flicker and fluoresce in the steepening sunlight. He would never see Mars now, and redress the implicit failure of talent, but a workable replica of the planet was contained within the beach area.

Several million tons of the Martian topsoil had been ferried in as ballast some fifty years earlier, when it was feared that the continuous firing of planetary probes and space vehicles, and the transportation of bulk stores and equipment to Mars, would fractionally lower the gravitational mass of the Earth and bring it into a tighter orbit around the Sun. Although the distance involved would be little more than a few millimeters, and barely raise the temperature of the atmosphere, its cumulative effects over an extended period might have resulted in a loss into space of the tenuous layers of the outer atmosphere, and of the radiological veil which alone made the biosphere habitable.

Over a twenty-year period a fleet of large freighters had shuttled to and from Mars, dumping the ballast into the sea near the landing grounds of Cape Kennedy. Simultaneously the Russians were filling in a small section of the Caspian Sea. The intention had been that the ballast should be swallowed by the Atlantic and Caspian waters, but all too soon it was found that the microbiological analysis of the sand had been inadequate.

At the Martian polar caps, where the original water vapor in the atmosphere had condensed, a residue of ancient organic matter formed the topsoil, a fine sandy loess containing the fossilized spores of the giant lichens and mosses which had been the last living organisms on the planet millions of years earlier. Embedded in these spores were the crystal lattices of the viruses which had once preyed on the plants, and traces of these were carried back to Earth with the Kennedy and Caspian ballast.

A few years afterward a drastic increase in a wide range of plant diseases was noticed in the southern states of America and in the Kazakhstan and Turkmenistan republics of the Soviet Union. All over Florida there were outbreaks of blight and mosaic disease, orange plantations withered and died, stunted palms split by the roadside like dried banana skins, manila grass stiffened into paper spears in the summer heat. Within a few years the entire peninsula was transformed into a desert. The swampy jungles of the Everglades became bleached and dry, the rivers' cracked husks strewn with the gleaming skeletons of crocodiles and birds, the forests petrified.

The former launching ground at Kennedy was closed, and shortly afterward the Cocoa Beach resorts were sealed off and evacuated, billions of dollars of real estate were abandoned to the virus. Fortunately never virulent to animal hosts, its influence was confined to within a small radius of the original loess which had borne it, unless ingested by the human organism, when it symbioted with the bacteria in the gut flora, benign and unknown to the host, but devastating to vegetation thousands of miles from Kennedy if returned to the soil.

Unable to rest despite his sleepless night, Bridgman played irritably with the tape recorder. During their close escape from the wardens he had more than half-hoped they would catch him. The mysterious leg cramp was obviously psychogenic. Although unable to accept consciously the logic of Webster's argument, he would willingly have conceded to the fait accompli of physical capture, gratefully submitted to a year's quarantine at the Parasitological Cleansing Unit at Tampa, and then returned to his career as an architect, chastened but accepting his failure.

As yet, however, the opportunity for surrender had failed to offer itself. Travis appeared to be aware of his ambivalent motives; Bridgman noticed that he and Louise Woodward had made no arrangements to meet him that evening for the conjunction.

In the early afternoon he went down into the streets, ploughed through the drifts of red sand, following the footprints of Travis and Louise as they wound in and out of the side streets, finally saw them disappear into the coarser, flintlike dunes among the submerged motels to the south of the town. Giving up, he returned through the empty, shadowless streets, now and then shouted up into the hot air, listening to the echoes boom away among the dunes.

Later that afternoon he walked out toward the northeast, picking his way carefully through the dips and hollows, crouching in the pools of shadow whenever the distant sounds of the construction gangs along the perimeter were carried across to him by the wind. Around him, in the great dust basins, the grains of red sand flittered like diamonds. Barbs of rusting metal protruded from the slopes, remnants of Mars satellites and launching stages which had fallen onto the Martian deserts and then been carried back again to Earth. One fragment which he passed, a complete section of hull plate like a concave shield, still carried part of an identification numeral, and stood upright in the dissolving sand like a door into nowhere.

Just before dusk he reached a tall spur of obsidian that reared up into the tinted cerise sky like the spire of a ruined church, climbed up among its jutting cornices and looked out across the intervening two or three miles of dunes to the perimeter. Illuminated by the last light, the metal grilles shone with a roseate glow like fairy portcullises on the edge of an enchanted sea. At least half a mile of the fence had been completed, and as he watched, another of the giant prefabricated sections was cantilevered into the air and staked to the ground. Already the eastern horizon was cut off by the encroaching fence, the enclosed Martian sand like the gravel scattered at the bottom of a cage.

Perched on the spur, Bridgman felt a warning tremor of pain in his calf. He leaped down in a flurry of dust, without looking back made off among the dunes and reefs.

Later, as the last baroque whorls of the sunset faded below the horizon, he waited on the roof for Travis and Louise Woodward, peering impatiently into the empty moon-filled streets.

Shortly after midnight, at an elevation of 35 degrees in the southwest, between Aquila and Ophiuchus, the conjunction began. Bridgman continued to search the streets, and ignored the seven points of speeding light as they raced toward him from the horizon like an invasion from deep space. There was no indication of their convergent orbital pathways, which would soon scatter them thousands of miles apart, and the satellites moved as if they were always together, in the tight configuration Bridgman had known since childhood, like a lost zodiacal emblem, a constellation detached from the celestial sphere and forever frantically searching to return to its place.

"Travis! Confound you!" With a snarl, Bridgman swung away from the balcony and moved along to the exposed section of rail behind the elevator head. To be avoided like a pariah by Travis and Louise Woodward forced him to accept that he was no longer a true resident of the beach and now existed in a no-man's-land between them and the wardens.

The seven satellites drew nearer, and Bridgman glanced up at them cursorily. They were disposed in a distinctive but unusual pattern resembling the Greek letter *chi*, a limp cross, a straight lateral member containing four capsules more or less in line ahead—Connolly, Tkachev, Merril, and Maiakovski—bisected by three others forming with Tkachev an elongated Z—Pokrovski, Woodward, and Brodisnek. The pattern had been variously identified as a hammer and sickle, an eagle, a swastika, and a dove, as well as a variety of religious and runic emblems, but all these were being defeated by the advancing tendency of the older capsules to vaporize.

It was this slow disintegration of the aluminum shells that made them visible—it had often been pointed out that the observer on the ground was looking, not at the actual capsule, but at a local field of vaporized aluminum and ionized hydrogen peroxide gas from the ruptured altitude jets now distributed within half a mile of each of the capsules. Woodward's, the most recently in orbit, was a barely perceptible point of light. The hulks of the capsules, with their perfectly preserved human cargoes, were continually dissolving, and a wide fan of silver spray opened out in a phantom wake behind Merril and Pokrovski (1998 and 1999), like a double star transforming itself into a nova in the center of a constellation. As the mass of the capsules diminished they sank into a closer orbit around the Earth, would soon touch the denser layers of the atmosphere and plummet to the ground.

Bridgman watched the satellites as they moved toward him, his irritation with Travis forgotten. As always, he felt himself moved by the eerie but strangely serene spectacle of the ghostly convoy endlessly circling the dark sea of the midnight sky, the long-dead astronauts converging for the ten-thousandth time upon their brief rendezvous and then setting off upon their lonely flight paths around the perimeter of the ionosphere, the tidal edge of the beachway into space which had reclaimed them.

How Louise Woodward could bear to look up at her husband he had never been able to understand. After her arrival he once invited her to the hotel, remarking that there was an excellent view of the beautiful sunsets, and she had snapped back bitterly: "Beautiful? Can you imagine what it's like looking up at a sunset when your husband's spinning around through it in his coffin?"

This reaction had been a common one when the first astronauts had died after failing to make contact with the launching platforms in fixed orbit. When these new stars rose in the west an attempt had been made to shoot them down—there was the unsettling prospect of the skies a thousand years hence, littered with orbiting refuse—but later they were left in this natural graveyard, forming their own monument.

Obscured by the clouds of dust carried up into the air by the sandstorm, the satellites shone with little more than the intensity of second-magnitude stars, winking as the reflected light was interrupted by the lanes of stratocirrus. The wake of diffusing light behind Merril and Pokrovski which usually screened the other capsules seemed to have diminished in size, and he could see both Maiakovski and Brodisnek clearly for the first time in several months. Wondering whether Merril or Pokrovski would be the first to fall from orbit, he looked toward the center of the cross as it passed overhead.

With a sharp intake of breath, he tilted his head back. In surprise he noticed that one of the familiar points of light was missing from the center of the group. What he had assumed to be an occlusion of the conjoint vapor trails by dust clouds was simply due to the fact that one of the capsules—Merril's, he decided, the third of the line ahead—had fallen from its orbit.

Head raised, he sidestepped slowly across the roof, avoiding the pieces of rusting neon sign, following the convoy as it passed overhead and moved toward the eastern horizon. No longer overlayed by the wake of Merril's capsule, Woodward's shone with far greater clarity, and almost appeared to have taken the former's place, although he was not due to fall from orbit for at least a century.

In the distance somewhere an engine growled. A moment later, from a different quarter, a woman's voice cried out faintly. Bridgman moved to the rail, over the intervening rooftops saw two figures silhouetted against the sky on the elevator head of an apartment block, then heard Louise Woodward call out again. She was pointing up at the sky with both hands, her long hair blown about her face, Travis trying to restrain her. Bridgman realized that she had misconstrued Merril's descent, assuming that the fallen astronaut was her husband. He climbed onto the edge of the balcony, watching the pathetic tableau on the distant roof.

Again, somewhere among the dunes, an engine moaned. Before Bridgman could turn around, a brilliant blade of light cleaved the sky in the southwest. Like a speeding comet, an immense train of vaporizing particles stretching behind it to the horizon, it soared toward them, the downward curve of its pathway clearly visible. Detached from the rest of the capsules, which were now disappearing among the stars along the eastern horizon, it was little more than a few miles off the ground.

Bridgman watched it approach, apparently on a collision course with the hotel. The expanding corona of white light, like a gigantic signal flare, illuminated the rooftops, etching the letters of the neon signs over the submerged motels on the outskirts of the town. He ran for the doorway, as he raced down the stairs saw the glow of the descending capsule fill the somber streets like a hundred moons. When he reached his room, sheltered by the massive weight of the hotel, he watched the dunes in front of the hotel light up like a stage set. Three hundred yards away the low camouflaged hull of the wardens' beach car was revealed poised on a crest, its feeble spotlight drowned by the glare.

With a deep metallic sigh, the burning catafalque of the dead astronaut soared overhead, a cascade of vaporizing metal pouring from its hull, filling the sky with incandescent light. Reflected below it, like an expressway illuminated by an aircraft's spotlights, a long lane of light several hundred yards in width raced out into the desert toward the sea. As Bridgman shielded his eyes, it suddenly erupted in a tremendous explosion of detonating sand. A huge curtain of white dust lifted into the air and fell slowly to the ground. The sounds of the impact rolled against the hotel, mounting in a sustained crescendo that drummed against the windows. A series of smaller explosions flared up like opalescent fountains. All over the desert fires flickered briefly where fragments of the capsule had been scattered. Then the noise subsided, and an immense glistening pall of phosphorescing gas hung in the air like a silver veil, particles within it beading and winking.

Two hundred yards away across the sand was the running figure of Louise Woodward, Travis twenty paces behind her. Bridgman watched them dart in and out of the dunes, then abruptly felt the cold spotlight of the beach car hit his face and flood the room behind him. The vehicle was moving straight toward him, two of the wardens, nets and lassos in hand, riding the outboard.

Quickly Bridgman straddled the balcony, jumped down into the sand, and raced toward the crest of the first dune. He crouched and ran on through the darkness as the beam probed the air. Above, the glistening pall was slowly fading, the particles of vaporized metal sifting toward the dark Martian sand. In the distance the last echoes of the impact were still reverberating among the hotels of the beach colonies further down the coast.

Five minutes later he caught up with Louise Woodward and Travis. The capsule's impact had flattened a number of the dunes, forming a shallow basin some quarter of a mile in diameter, and the surrounding slopes were scattered with the still glowing particles, sparkling like fading eyes. The beach car growled somewhere four or five hundred yards behind him, and Bridgman broke off into an exhausted walk. He stopped beside Travis, who was kneeling on the ground, breath pumping into his lungs. Fifty yards away Louise Woodward was running up and down, distraughtly gazing at the fragments of smoldering metal. For a moment the spotlight of the approaching beach car illuminated her, and she ran away among the dunes. Bridgman caught a glimpse of the inconsolable anguish in her face.

Travis was still on his knees. He had picked up a piece of the oxidized metal and was pressing it together in his hands.

"Travis, for God's sake tell her! This was Merril's capsule, there's no doubt about it! Woodward's still up there."

Travis looked up at him silently, his eyes searching Bridgman's face. A spasm of pain tore his mouth, and Bridgman realized that the barb of steel he clasped reverently in his hands was still glowing with heat.

"Travis!" He tried to pull the man's hands apart, the pungent stench of burning flesh gusting into his face, but Travis wrenched away from him. "Leave her alone, Bridgman! Go back with the wardens!"

Bridgman retreated from the approaching beach car. Only thirty yards away, its spotlight filled the basin. Louise Woodward was still searching the dunes. Travis held his ground as the wardens jumped down from the car and advanced toward him with their nets, his bloodied hands raised at his sides, the steel barb flashing like a dagger. At the head of the wardens, the only one unmasked, was a trim, neat-featured man with an intent, serious face. Bridgman guessed that this was Major Webster, and that the wardens had known of the impending impact and hoped to capture them, and Louise in particular, before it occurred.

Bridgman stumbled back toward the dunes at the edge of the basin. As he neared the crest he trapped his foot in a semicircular plate of metal, sat down, and freed his heel. Unmistakably it was part of a control panel, the circular instrument housings still intact.

Overhead the pall of glistening vapor had moved off to the northeast, and the reflected light was directly over the rusting gantries of the former launching site at Cape Kennedy. For a few fleeting seconds the gantries seemed to be enveloped in a sheen of silver, transfigured by the vaporized body of the dead astronaut, diffusing over them in a farewell gesture, his final return to the site from which he had set off to his death a century earlier. Then the gantries sank again into their craggy shadows, and the pall moved off like an immense wraith toward the sea, barely distinguishable from the star glow.

Down below Travis was sitting on the ground surrounded by the wardens. He scuttled about on his hands like a frantic crab, scooping handfuls of the virus-laden sand at them. Holding tight to their masks, the wardens maneuvered around him, their nets and lassos at the ready. Another group moved slowly toward Bridgman.

Bridgman picked up a handful of the dark Martian sand beside the instrument panel, felt the soft glowing crystals warm his palm. In his mind he could still see the silver-sheathed gantries of the launching site across the bay, by a curious illusion almost identical with the Martian city he had designed years earlier. He watched the pall disappear over the sea, then looked around at the other remnants of Merril's capsule scattered over the slopes. High in the western night, between Pegasus and Cygnus, shone the distant disk of the planet Mars, which for both himself and the dead astronaut had served for so long as a symbol of unattained ambition. The wind stirred softly through the sand, cooling this replica of the planet which lay passively around him, and at last he understood why he had come to the beach and been unable to leave it.

Twenty yards away Travis was being dragged off like a wild dog, his thrashing body pinioned in the center of a web of lassos. Louise Woodward had run away among the dunes toward the sea, following the vanished gas cloud.

In a sudden access of refound confidence, Bridgman drove his fist into the dark sand, buried his forearm like a foundation pillar. A flange of hot metal from Merril's capsule burned his wrist, bonding him to the spirit of the dead astronaut.

"Merril!" he cried exultantly as the wardens' lassos stung his neck and shoulders. "We made it!"

End Game

After his trial they gave Constantin a villa, an allowance, and an executioner. The villa was small and high-walled, and had obviously been used for the purpose before. The allowance was adequate to Constantin's needs—he was never permitted to go out and his meals were prepared for him by a police orderly. The executioner was his own. Most of the time they sat on the enclosed veranda overlooking the narrow stone garden, playing chess with a set of large well-worn pieces.

The executioner's name was Malek. Officially he was Constantin's supervisor, and responsible for maintaining the villa's tenuous contact with the outside world, now hidden from sight beyond the steep walls, and for taking the brief telephone call that came promptly at nine o'clock every morning. However, his real role was no secret between them. A powerful, doughy-faced man with an anonymous expression, Malek at first intensely irritated Constantin, who had been used to dealing with more subtle sets of responses. Malek impassively followed him around the villa, never interfering—unless Constantin tried to bribe the orderly for a prohibited newspaper, at whom Malek merely gestured with a slight turn of one of his large hands, face registering no disapproval, but cutting off the attempt as irrevocably as a bulkhead—nor making

212

any suggestions as to how Constantin should spend his time. Like a large bear, he sat motionlessly in the lounge in one of the faded armchairs, watching Constantin.

After a week, Constantin tired of reading the old novels in the bottom shelf of the bookcase—somewhere among the gray well-thumbed pages he had hoped to find a message from one of his predecessors—and invited Malek to play chess. The set of chipped mahogany pieces reposed on one of the empty shelves of the bookcase, the only item of decoration or recreational equipment in the villa. Apart from the books and the chess set the small six-roomed house was completely devoid of ornament. There were no curtains or picture rails, bedside tables or standard lamps, and the only electrical fittings were the lights recessed behind thick opaque bowls into the ceilings. Obviously the chess set and the row of novels had been provided deliberately, each representing one of the alternative pastimes available to the temporary tenants of the villa. Men of a phlegmatic or philosophical temperament, stoically resigned to the inevitability of their fate, would choose to read the novels, sinking backward into a self-anesthetized trance as they waded through the turgid prose of those nineteenth-century romances.

On the other hand, men of a more volatile and extrovert disposition would obviously prefer to play chess, unable to resist the opportunity to exercise their Machiavellian talents for positional maneuver to the last. The games of chess would help to maintain their unconscious optimism and, more subtly, sublimate or divert any attempts at escape.

When Constantin suggested that they play chess Malek promptly agreed, and so they spent the next long month as the late summer turned to autumn. Constantin was glad he had chosen chess; the game brought him into immediate personal involvement with Malek, and like all condemned men he had soon developed a powerful emotional transference onto what effectively was the only person left in his life.

At present it was neither negative nor positive, but a relationship of acute dependence—already Malek's notional personality was becoming overlaid by the associations of all the anonymous but nonetheless potent figures of authority whom Constantin could remember since his earliest childhood: his own father, the priest at the seminary he had seen hanged after the revolution, the first senior commissars, the party secretaries at the ministry of foreign affairs, and ultimately, the members of the central committee themselves. Here, where the anonymous faces had crystallized into those of closely observed colleagues and rivals, the process seemed to come full circle, so that he himself was identified with those shadowy personas who had authorized his death and were now represented by Malek.

Constantin had also, of course, become dominated by another obsession, the need to know: *when?* In the weeks after the trial and sentence he had remained in a curiously euphoric state, too stunned to realize that the dimension of time still existed for him; he had already died *a posteriori*. But gradually the will to live, and his old determination and ruthlessness, which had served him so well for thirty years, reasserted themselves, and he realized that a small hope still remained to him. How long exactly in terms of time he could only guess, but if he could master Malek his survival became a real possibility.

The question remained: when?

Fortunately he could be completely frank with Malek. The first point he established immediately.

"Malek," he asked on the tenth move one morning, when he had completed his development and was relaxing for a moment. "Tell me, do you know—when?"

Malek looked up from the board, his large almost bovine eyes gazing blandly at Constantin. "Yes, Mr. Constantin, I know when." His voice was deep and functional, as expressionless as a weighing machine's.

Constantin sat back reflectively. Outside the glass panes of the veranda the rain fell steadily on the solitary fir tree which had maintained a precarious purchase among the stones under the wall. A few miles to the southwest of the villa were the outskirts of the small port, one of the dismal so-called "coastal resorts" where junior ministry men and party hacks were sent for their biannual holidays. The weather, however, seemed peculiarly inclement, the sun never shining through the morose clouds, and for a moment, before he checked himself, Constantin felt glad to be within the comparative warmth of the villa.

"Let me get this straight," he said to Malek. "You don't merely know in a general sense—for example, after receiving an instruction from so-and-so—but you know *specifically* when?"

"Exactly." Malek moved his queen out of the game. His chess was sound but without flair or a personal style, suggesting that he had improved merely by practice—most of his opponents, Constantin realized with sardonic amusement, would have been players of a high class.

"You know the *day* and the *hour* and the *minute*," Constantin pressed. Malek nodded slowly, most of his attention upon the game, and Constantin rested his smooth sharp chin in one hand, watching his opponent. "It could be within the next ten seconds, or again, it might not be for ten years?"

"As you say." Malek gestured at the board. "Your move."

Constantin waved this aside. "I know, but don't let's rush it. These games are played on many levels, Malek. People who talk about three-dimensional chess obviously know nothing about the present form." Occasionally he made these openings in the hope of loosening Malek's tongue, but conversation with him seemed to be impossible.

Abruptly he sat forward across the board, his eyes searching Malek's. "You alone know the date, Malek, and as you have said, it might not be for ten years—or twenty. Do you think you can keep such a secret to yourself for so long?"

Malek made no attempt to answer this, and waited for Constantin to resume play. Now and then his eyes inspected the corners of the veranda, or glanced at the stone garden outside. From the kitchen came the occasional sounds of the orderly's boots scraping the floor as he lounged by the telephone on the deal table.

As he scrutinized the board Constantin wondered how he could provoke any response whatever from Malek; the man had shown no reaction at the mention of ten years, although the period was ludicrously far ahead. In all probability their real game would be a short one. The indeterminate date of the execution, which imbued the procedure with such a bizarre flavor, was not intended to add an element of torture or suspense to the condemned's last days, but simply to obscure and confuse the very fact of his exit. If a definite date were known in advance there might be a last-minute rally of sympathy, an attempt to review the sentence and perhaps apportion the blame elsewhere, and the unconscious if not conscious sense of complicity in the condemned man's crimes might well provoke an agonized reappraisal and, after the execution of the sentence, a submerged sense of guilt upon which opportunists and intriguers could play to advantage.

By means of the present system, however, all these dangers and unpleasant side effects were obviated; the accused was removed from his place in the hierarchy when the opposition to him was at its zenith and conveniently handed over to the judiciary, and thence to one of the courts of star chamber whose proceedings were always held in camera and whose verdicts were never announced.

As far as his former colleagues were concerned, he had disappeared into the endless corridor world of the bureaucratic purgatories, his case permanently on file but never irrevocably closed. Above all, the fact of his guilt was never established and confirmed. As Constantin was aware, he himself had been convicted upon a technicality in the margins of the main indictment against him, a mere procedural device, like a bad twist in the plot of a story, designed solely to bring the investigation to a close. Although he knew the real nature of his crime, Constantin had never been formally notified of his guilt; in fact the court had gone out of its way to avoid preferring any serious charges against him whatever.

This ironic inversion of the classical Kafkaesque situation, by which, instead of admitting his guilt to a nonexistent crime, he was forced to connive in a farce maintaining his innocence of offenses he knew full well he had committed, was preserved in his present situation at the execution villa.

The psychological basis was more obscure but in some way far more threatening, the executioner beckoning his victim toward him with a beguiling smile, reassuring him that all was forgiven. Here he played upon, not those unconscious feelings of anxiety and guilt, but that innate conviction of individual survival, that obsessive preoccupation with personal immortality which is merely a disguised form of the universal fear of the image of one's own death. It was this assurance that all was well, and the absence of any charges of guilt or responsibility, which had made so orderly the queues into the gas chambers.

At present the paradoxical face of this diabolical device was worn by Malek, his lumpy amorphous features and neutral but ambiguous attitude making him seem less a separate personality than the personification of the apparatus of the state. Perhaps the sardonic title of "supervisor" was nearer the truth than it had seemed at first sight, and that Malek's real role was simply to officiate, or at the most serve as moderator, at a trial by ordeal in which Constantin was his own accused, prosecutor, and judge.

However, he reflected as he examined the board, aware of Malek's bulky presence across the pieces, this would imply that they had completely misjudged his own personality, with its buoyancy and almost Gallic verve and panache. He, of all people, would be the last to take his own life in an orgy of self-confessed guilt. Not for him the neurotic suicide so loved by the Slav. As long as there was a way out he would cheerfully shoulder any burden of guilt, tolerant of his own weaknesses, ready to shrug them off with a quip. This insouciance had always been his strongest ally.

His eyes searched the board, roving down the open files of the queens and bishops, as if the answer to the pressing enigma were to be found in these polished corridors.

When? His own estimate was two months. Almost certainly (and he had no fear here that he was rationalizing), it would not be within the next two or three days, nor even the next fortnight. Haste was always unseemly, quite apart from violating the whole purpose of the exercise. Two months would see him safely into limbo, and be sufficiently long for the suspense to break him down and reveal any secret allies, sufficiently brief to fit his particular crime.

Two months? Not as long as he might have wished. As he translated his queen's bishop into play Constantin began to map out his strategy for defeating Malek. The first task, obviously, was to discover when Malek was to carry out the execution, partly to give him peace of mind, but also to allow him to adjust the context of his escape. A physical leap to freedom over the wall would be pointless. Contacts had to be established, pressure brought to bear at various sensitive points in the hierarchy, paving the way for a reconsideration of his case. All this would take time.

His thoughts were interrupted by the sharp movement of Malek's left hand across the board, followed by a guttural grunt. Surprised by the speed and economy with which Malek had moved his piece, as much as by the fact that he himself was in check, Constantin sat forward and examined his position with more care. He glanced with grudging respect at Malek, who had sat back as impassively as ever, the knight he had deftly taken on the edge of the table in front of him. His eyes watched Constantin with their usual untroubled calm, like those of an immensely patient governess, his great shoulders hidden within the bulky suiting. But for a moment, when he had leaned across the board, Constantin had seen the powerful extension and flection of his shoulder musculature.

Don't look so smug, my dear Malek, Constantin said to himself with a wry smile. At least I know now that you are left-handed. Malek had taken the knight with one hand, hooking the piece between the thick knuckles of his ring and center fingers, and then substituting his queen with a smart tap, a movement not easily performed in the center of the crowded board. Useful though the confirmation was—Constantin had noticed Malek apparently trying to conceal his left-handedness during their meals and when opening and closing the windows—he found this sinistral aspect of Malek's personality curiously disturbing, an indication that there would be nothing predictable about his opponent, or the ensuing struggle of wits between them. Even Malek's apparent lack of sharp intelligence was belied by the astuteness of his last move.

Constantin was playing white, and had chosen the queen's gambit, assuming that the fluid situation invariably resulting from the opening would be to his advantage and allow him to get on with the more serious task of planning his escape. But Malek had avoided any possible errors, steadily consolidating his position, and had even managed to launch a countergambit, offering a knight-to-bishop exchange which would soon undermine Constantin's position if he accepted.

"A good move, Malek," he commented. "But perhaps a little risky in the long run." Declining the exchange, he lamely blocked the checking queen with an interposed pawn.

Malek stared stolidly at the board, his heavy policeman's face, with its almost square frame from one jaw angle to the other, betraying no sign of thought. His approach, Constantin reflected as he watched his opponent, would be that of the pragmatist, judging always by immediate capability rather than by any concealed intentions. As if confirming this diagnosis, Malek simply returned his queen to her former square, unwilling or unable to exploit the advantage he had gained and satisfied by the captured piece.

Bored by the lower key to which the game had descended, and the prospect of similar games ahead, Constantin castled his king to safety. For some reason, obviously irrational, he assumed that Malek would not kill him in the middle of a game, particularly if he, Malek, were winning. He recognized that this was an unconscious reason for wanting to play chess in the first place, and had no doubt motivated the many others who had also sat with Malek on the veranda, listening to the late summer rain. Suppressing a sudden pang of fear, Constantin examined Malek's powerful hands protruding from his cuffs like two joints of meat. If Malek wanted to, he could probably kill Constantin with his bare hands.

That raised a second question, almost as fascinating as the first.

"Malek, another point." Constantin sat back, searching in his pockets for imaginary cigarettes (none were allowed him). "Forgive my curiosity, but I am an interested party, as it were—" He flashed Malek his brightest smile, a characteristically incisive thrust modulated by ironic self-deprecation which had been so successful with his secretaries and at ministry receptions, but the assay at humor failed to move Malek. "Tell me, do you know... how—?" Searching for some euphemism, he repeated: "Do you know how you are going to...?" and then gave up the attempt, cursing Malek to himself for lacking the social grace to rescue him from his awkwardness.

Malek's chin rose slightly, a minimal nod. He showed no signs of being bored or irritated by Constantin's labored catechism, or of having noticed his embarrassment.

"What is it, then?" Constantin pressed, recovering himself. "Pistol, pill, or—" with a harsh laugh he pointed through the window "—do you set up a guillotine in the rain? I'd like to know."

Malek looked down at the chessboard, his features more glutinous and doughlike than ever. Flatly, he said, "It has been decided."

Constantin snorted. "What on earth does *that* mean?" he snapped belligerently. "Is it painless?"

For once Malek smiled, a thin sneer of amusement hung fleetingly around his mouth. "Have you ever killed anything, Mr. Constantin?" he asked quietly. "Yourself, personally, I mean."

"*Touché,*" Constantin granted. He laughed deliberately, trying to dispel the tension. "A perfect reply." To himself he said: I mustn't let curiosity get the upper hand, the man was laughing at me.

"Of course," he went on, "death is always painful. I merely wondered whether, in the legal sense of the term, it would be humane. But I can see that you are a professional, Malek, and the question answers itself. A great relief, believe me. There are so many sadists about, perverts and the like—" again he watched carefully to see if the implied sneer provoked Malek "—that one can't be too grateful for a clean curtain fall. It's good to know I can devote these last days to putting my affairs in order and coming to terms with the world. If only I knew how long there was left I could make my preparations accordingly. One can't be forever saying one's last prayers. You see my point?"

Colorlessly, Malek said, "The Prosecutor-General advised you to make your final arrangements immediately after the trial."

"But what does that mean?" Constantin asked, pitching his voice a calculated octave higher. "I'm a human being, not a bookkeeper's ledger that can be totted up and left to await the auditor's pleasure. I wonder if you realize, Malek, the courage this situation demands from me? It's easy for you to sit there—"

Abruptly Malek stood up, sending a shiver of terror through Constantin. With a glance at the sealed windows, he moved around the chess table toward the lounge. "We will postpone the game," he said. Nodding to Constantin, he went off toward the kitchen where the orderly was preparing lunch.

Constantin listened to his shoes squeaking faintly across the unpolished floor, then irritably cleared the pieces off the board and sat back with the black king in his hand. At least he had provoked Malek into leaving him. Thinking this over, he wondered whether to throw caution to the winds and begin to make life intolerable for Malek—it would be easy to pursue him around the villa, arguing hysterically and badgering him with neurotic questions. Sooner or later Malek would snap back, and might give away something of his intentions. Alternatively, Constantin could try to freeze him out, treating him with contempt as the hired killer he was, refusing to share a room or his meals with him and insisting on his rights as a former member of the central committee. The method might well be successful. Almost certainly Malek was telling the truth when he said he knew the exact day and minute of Constantin's execution. The order would have been given to him and he would have no discretion to advance or delay the date to suit himself. Malek would be reluctant to report Constantin for difficult behavior—the reflection on himself was too obvious and his present post was not one from which he could graciously retire—and in addition not even the Police-President would be able to vary the execution date, now that it had been set, without convening several meetings. There was then the danger of reopening Constantin's case. He was not without his allies, or at least those who were prepared to use him for their own advantage.

But despite these considerations, the whole business of playacting lacked appeal for Constantin. His approach was more serpentine. Besides, if he provoked Malek, uncertainties were introduced, of which there were already far too many.

He noticed the supervisor enter the lounge and sit down quietly in one of the gray armchairs, his face, half-hidden in the shadows, turned toward Constantin. He seemed indifferent to the normal pressures of boredom and fatigue (luckily for himself, Constantin reflected—an impatient man would have pulled the trigger on the morning of the second day), and content to sit about in the armchairs, watching Constantin as the gray rain fell outside and the damp leaves gathered against the walls. The difficulties of establishing a relationship with Malek—and some sort of relationship was essential before Constantin could begin to think of escape—seemed insuperable, only the games of chess offering an opportunity.

Placing the black king on his own king's square, Constantin called out, "Malek, I'm ready for another game, if you are."

Malek pushed himself out of the chair with his long arms, and then took his place across the board from Constantin. For a moment he scrutinized Constantin with a level glance, as if ascertaining that there would be no further outbursts of temper, and then began to set up the white pieces, apparently prepared to ignore the fact that Constantin had cleared the previous game before its completion.

He opened with a stolid Ruy Lopez, an overanalyzed and uninteresting attack, but a dozen moves later, when they broke off for lunch, he had already forced Constantin to castle on the queen's side and had established a powerful position in the center.

As they took their lunch together at the card table behind the sofa in the lounge, Constantin reflected upon this curious element which had been introduced into his relationship with Malek. While trying to check any tendency to magnify an insignificant triviality into a major symbol, he realized that Malek's proficiency at chess, and his ability to produce powerful combinations out of pedestrian openings, was symptomatic of his concealed power over Constantin.

The drab villa in the thin autumn rain, the faded furniture and unimaginative food they were now mechanically consuming, the whole gray limbo with its slender telephone connection with the outside world were, like his chess, exact extensions of Malek's personality, yet permeated with secret passages and doors. The unexpected thrived in such an ambience. At any moment, as he shaved, the mirror might retract to reveal the flaming muzzle of a machine pistol, or the slightly bitter flavor of the soup they were drinking might be other than that of lentils.

These thoughts preoccupied him as the afternoon light began to fade in the east, the white rectangle of the garden wall illuminated against this dim backdrop like a huge *tabula rasa*. Excusing himself from the chess game, Constantin feigned a headache and retired to his room upstairs.

The door between his room and Malek's had been removed, and as he lay on the bed he was conscious of the supervisor sitting in his chair with his back to the window. Perhaps it was Malek's presence which prevented him from gaining any real rest, and when he rose several hours later and returned to the veranda he felt tired and possessed by a deepening sense of foreboding.

With an effort he rallied his spirits, and by concentrating his whole attention on the game was able to extract what appeared to be a drawn position. Although the game was adjourned without comment from either player, Malek seemed to concede by his manner that he had lost his advantage, lingering for a perceptible moment over the board when Constantin rose from the table.

The lesson of all this was not lost on Constantin the following day. He was fully aware that the games of chess were not only taxing his energies but providing Malek with a greater hold upon him than he upon Malek. Although the pieces stood where they had left them the previous evening, Constantin did not suggest that they resume play. Malek made no move toward the board, apparently indifferent to whether the game was finished or not. Most of the time he sat next to Constantin by the single radiator in the lounge, occasionally going off to confer with the orderly in the kitchen. As usual the telephone rang briefly each morning, but otherwise there were no callers or visitors to the villa. To all intents it remained suspended in a perfect vacuum.

It was this unvarying nature of their daily routines which Constantin found particularly depressing. Intermittently over the next few days, he played chess with Malek, invariably finding himself in a losing position, but the focus of his attention was elsewhere, upon the enigma cloaked by Malek's square, expressionless face. Around him a thousand invisible clocks raced onward toward their beckoning zeros, a soundless thunder like the drumming of apocalyptic hoof irons.

His mood of foreboding had given way to one of mounting fear, all the more terrifying because, despite Malek's real role, it seemed completely sourceless. He found himself unable to concentrate for more than a few minutes upon any task, left his meals unfinished, and fidgeted helplessly by the veranda window. The slightest movement by Malek would make his nerves thrill with anguish; if the supervisor left his customary seat in the lounge to speak to the orderly Constantin would find himself almost paralyzed by the tension, helplessly counting the seconds until Malek returned. Once, during one of their meals, Malek started to ask him for the salt and Constantin almost choked to death.

The ironic humor of this near-fatality reminded Constantin that almost half of his two-month sentence had elapsed. But his crude attempts to obtain a pencil from the orderly and later, failing this, to mark the letters in a page torn from one of the novels were intercepted by Malek, and he realized that short of defeating the two policemen in single-handed combat he had no means of escaping his ever more imminent fate.

Latterly he had noticed that Malek's movements and general activity around the villa seemed to have quickened. He still sat for long periods in the armchair, observing Constantin, but his formerly impassive presence was graced by gestures and inclinations of the head that seemed to reflect a heightened cerebral activity, as if he were preparing himself for some long-awaited denouement. Even the heavy musculature of his face seemed to have relaxed and grown sleeker, his sharp mobile eyes, like those of an experienced senior inspector of police, roving constantly about the rooms.

Despite his efforts, however, Constantin was unable to galvanize himself into any defensive action. He could see clearly that Malek and he had entered a new phase in their relationship, and that at any moment their outwardly formal and polite behavior would degenerate into a grasping ugly violence, but he was nonetheless immobilized by his own state of terror. The days passed in a blur of uneaten meals and abandoned chess games, their very identity blotting out any sense of time or progression, the watching figure of Malek always before him.

Every morning, when he woke after two or three hours of sleep to find his consciousness still intact, a discovery almost painful in its relief and poignancy, he would be immediately aware of Malek standing in the next room, then waiting discreetly in the hallway as Constantin shaved in the bathroom (also without its door), following him downstairs to breakfast, his careful reflective tread like that of a hangman descending from his gallows.

After breakfast Constantin would challenge Malek to a game of chess, but after a few moves would begin to play wildly, throwing pieces forward to be decimated by Malek. At times the supervisor would glance curiously at Constantin, as if wondering whether his charge had lost his reason, and then continued to play his careful exact game, invariably winning or drawing. Dimly Constantin perceived that by losing to Malek he had also surrendered to him psychologically, but the games had now become simply a means of passing the unending days.

Six weeks after they had first begun to play chess, Constantin more by luck than skill succeeded in an extravagant pawn gambit and forced Malek to sacrifice both his center and any possibility of castling. Roused from his state of numb anxiety by this temporary victory, Constantin sat forward over the board, irritably waving away the orderly who announced from the door of the lounge that he would serve lunch.

"Tell him to wait, Malek. I mustn't lose my concentration at this point, I've very nearly won the game."

"Well..." Malek glanced at his watch, then over his shoulder at the orderly, who, however, had turned on his heel and returned to the kitchen. He started to stand up. "It can wait. He's bringing the—"

"No!" Constantin snapped. "Just give me five minutes, Malek. Damn it, one adjourns on a move, not halfway through it."

"Very well." Malek hesitated, after a further glance at his watch. He climbed to his feet. "I will tell him."

Constantin concentrated on the board, ignoring the supervisor's retreating figure, the scent of victory clearing his mind. But thirty seconds later he sat up with a start, his heart almost seizing inside his chest.

Malek had gone upstairs! Constantin distinctly remembered his saying he would tell the orderly to delay lunch, but instead he had walked straight up to his bedroom. Not only was it extremely unusual for Constantin to be left unobserved when the orderly was otherwise occupied, but the latter had still not brought in their first luncheon course.

Steadying the table, Constantin stood up, his eyes searching the open doorways in front of and behind him. Almost certainly the orderly's announcement of lunch was a signal, and Malek had found a convenient pretext for going upstairs to prepare his execution weapon.

Faced at last by the imminent nemesis he had so long dreaded, Constantin listened for the sounds of Malek's feet descending the staircase. A profound silence enclosed the villa, broken only by the fall of one of the chess pieces to the tiled floor. Outside the sun shone intermittently in the garden, illuminating the broken flatstones of the ornamental pathway and the bare fifteen-foot-high face of the walls. A few stunted weeds flowered among the rubble, their pale colors blanched by the sunlight, and Constantin was suddenly filled by an overwhelming need to escape into the open air for the few last moments before he died. The east wall, lit by the sun's rays, was marked by a faint series of horizontal grooves, the remnants perhaps of a fire escape ladder, and the slender possibility of using these as handholds made the enclosed garden, a perfect killing ground, preferable to the frantic claustrophobic atmosphere of the villa.

Above him, Malek's measured tread moved across the ceiling to the head of the staircase. He paused there and then began to descend the stairs, his steps chosen with a precise and careful rhythm.

Helplessly, Constantin searched the veranda for something that would serve as a weapon. The French windows leading to the garden were locked, and a slotted pinion outside secured the left-hand member of the pair to the edge of the sill. If this were raised there was a chance that the windows could be forced outward.

Scattering the chess pieces onto the floor with a sweep of his hand, Constantin seized the board and folded it together, then stepped over to the window and drove the heavy wooden box through the bottom pane. The report of the bursting glass echoed like a gunshot through the villa. Kneeling down, he pushed his hand through the aperture and tried to lift the pinion, jerking it up and down in its rusty socket. When it failed to clear the sill he forced his head through the broken window and began to heave against it helplessly with his thin shoulders, the fragments of broken glass falling on his neck.

Behind him a chair was kicked back, and he felt two powerful hands seize his shoulders and pull him away from the window. He struck out hysterically with the chess box, and then was flung headfirst to the tiled floor.

His convalescence from this episode was to last most of the following week. For the first three days he remained in bed, recovering his physical identity, waiting for the sprained muscles of his hands and shoulders to repair themselves. When he felt sufficiently strong to leave his bed he went down to the lounge and sat at one end of the sofa, his back to the windows and the thin autumn light.

Malek still remained in attendance, and the orderly prepared his meals as before. Neither of them made any comment upon Constantin's outburst of hysteria, or indeed betrayed any signs that it had taken place, but Constantin realized that he had crossed an important Rubicon. His whole relationship with Malek had experienced a profound change. The fear of his own imminent death, and the tantalizing mystery of its precise date which had so obsessed him, had been replaced by a calm acceptance that the judicial processes inaugurated by his trial would take their course and that Malek and the orderly were merely the local agents of this distant apparatus. In a sense his sentence and present tenuous existence at the villa were a microcosm of life itself, with its inherent but unfeared uncertainties, its inevitable quietus to be made on a date never known in advance. Seeing his role at the villa in this light, Constantin no longer felt afraid at the prospect of his own extinction, fully aware that a change in the political wind could win him a free pardon.

In addition, he realized that Malek, far from being his executioner, a purely formal role, was in fact an intermediary between himself and the hierarchy, and in an important sense a potential ally of Constantin's. As he reformed his defense against the indictment preferred against him at the trial—he knew he had been far too willing to accept the fait accompli of his own guilt—he calculated the various ways in which Malek would be able to assist him. There was no doubt in his mind that he had misjudged Malek. With his sharp intelligence and commanding presence, the supervisor was very far from being a hatchet-faced killer—this original impression had been the result of some cloudiness in Constantin's perceptions, an unfortunate myopia which had cost him two precious months in his task of arranging a retrial.

Comfortably swathed in his dressing gown, he sat at the card table in the lounge (they had abandoned the veranda with the colder weather, and only a patch of brown paper over the window reminded him of that first circle of purgatory) concentrating on the game of chess. Malek sat opposite him, hands clasped on one knee, his thumbs occasionally circling as he pondered a move. Although no less reticent than he had ever been, his manner seemed to indicate that he understood and confirmed Constantin's reappraisal of the situation. He still followed Constantin around the villa, but his attentions were noticeably more perfunctory, as if he realized that Constantin would not try again to escape.

From the start, Constantin was completely frank with Malek.

"I am convinced, Malek, that the Prosecutor-General was misdirected by the Justice Department, and that the whole basis of the trial was a false one. All but one of the indictments were never formally presented, so I had no opportunity to defend myself. You understand that, Malek? The selection of the capital penalty for one count was purely arbitrary."

Malek nodded, moving a piece. "So you have explained, Mr. Constantin. I am afraid I do not have a legalistic turn of mind."

"There's no need for you to," Constantin assured him. "The point is obvious. I hope it may be possible to appeal against the court's decision and ask for a retrial." Constantin gestured with a piece. "I criticize myself for accepting the indictments so readily. In effect I made no attempt to defend myself. If only I had done so I am convinced I should have been found innocent."

Malek murmured noncommittally, and gestured toward the board. Constantin resumed play. Most of the games he consistently lost to Malek, but this no longer troubled him, and if anything, only served to reinforce the bonds between them.

Constantin had decided not to ask the supervisor to inform the Justice Department of his request for a retrial until he had convinced Malek that his case left substantial room for doubt. A premature application would meet with an automatic negative from Malek, whatever his private sympathies. Conversely, once Malek was firmly on his side he would be prepared to risk his reputation with his seniors, and indeed his championing of Constantin's cause would be convincing proof in itself of the latter's innocence.

As Constantin soon found from his one-sided discussions with Malek, arguing over the legal technicalities of the trial, with their infinitely subtle nuances and implications, was an unprofitable method of enlisting Malek's support, and he realized that he would have to do so by sheer impress of personality, by his manner, bearing and general conduct, and above all by his confidence of his innocence in the face of the penalty which might at any moment be imposed upon him. Curiously, this latter pose was not as difficult to maintain as might have been expected; Constantin already felt a surge of conviction in his eventual escape from the villa. Sooner or later Malek would recognize the authenticity of this inner confidence.

To begin with, however, the supervisor remained his usual phlegmatic self. Constantin talked away at him from morning to evening, every third word affirming the probability of his being found "innocent," but Malek merely nodded with a faint smile and continued to play his errorless chess.

"Malek, I don't want you to think that I challenge the competence of the court to try the charges against me, or that I hold it in disrespect," he said to the supervisor as they played their usual morning board some two weeks after the incident on the veranda. "Far from it. But the court must make its decisions within the context of the evidence presented by the prosecutor. And even then, the greatest imponderable remains—the role of the accused. In my case I was, to all intents, not present at the trial, so my innocence is established by *force majeure*. Don't you agree, Malek?"

Malek's eyes searched the pieces on the board, his lips pursing thinly. "I'm afraid this is above my head, Mr. Constantin. Naturally I accept the authority of the court without question."

"But so do I, Malek. I've made that plain. The real question is simply whether the verdict was justified in the light of the new circumstances I am describing."

Malek shrugged, apparently more interested in the end game before them. "I recommend you to accept the verdict, Mr. Constantin. For your peace of mind, you understand."

Constantin looked away with a gesture of impatience. "I don't agree, Malek. Besides, a great deal is at stake." He glanced up at the windows, which were drumming in the cold autumn wind. The casements were slightly loose, and the air lanced around them. The villa was poorly heated, only the single radiator in the lounge warming the three rooms downstairs. Already Constantin dreaded the winter. His hands and feet were perpetually cold and he could find no means of warming them.

"Malek, is there any chance of obtaining another heater?" he asked. "It's none too warm in here. I have a feeling it's going to be a particularly cold winter."

Malek looked up from the board, his bland gray eyes regarding Constantin with a flicker of curiosity, as if this last remark were one of the few he had heard from Constantin's lips which contained any overtones whatever.

"It is cold," he agreed at last. "I will see if I can borrow a heater. This villa is closed for most of the year."

Constantin pestered him for news of the heater during the following week—partly because the success of his request would have symbolized Malek's first concession to him—but it failed to materialize. After one palpably lame excuse Malek merely ignored his further reminders. Outside, in the garden, the leaves whirled about the stones in a vortex of chilling air, and overhead the low clouds raced seaward. The two men in the lounge hunched over their chessboard by the radiator, hands buried in their pockets between moves.

Perhaps it was this darkening weather which made Constantin impatient of Malek's slowness in seeing the point of his argument, and he made his first suggestions that Malek should transmit a formal request for a retrial to his superiors at the Department of Justice.

"You speak to someone on the telephone every morning, Malek," he pointed out when Malek demurred. "There's no difficulty involved. If you're afraid of compromising yourself—though I would have thought that a small price to pay in view of what is at stake—the orderly can pass on a message."

"It's not feasible, Mr. Constantin." Malek seemed at last to be tiring of the subject. "I suggest that you—"

"Malek!" Constantin stood up and paced around the lounge. "Don't you realize that you must? You're literally my only means of contact. If you refuse I'm absolutely powerless, there's no hope of getting a reprieve!"

"The trial has already taken place, Mr. Constantin," Malek pointed out patiently.

"It was a mistrial! Don't you understand, Malek, I accepted that I was guilty when in fact I was completely innocent!"

Malek looked up from the board, his eyebrows lifting. "*Completely* innocent, Mr. Constantin?"

Constantin snapped his fingers. "Well, virtually innocent. At least in terms of the indictment and trial."

"But that is merely a tactical difference, Mr. Constantin. The Department of Justice is concerned with absolutes."

"Quite right, Malek. I agree entirely." Constantin nodded approvingly at the supervisor and privately noted his quizzical expression, the first time Malek had displayed a taste for irony.

He was to notice this fresh leitmotiv recurringly during the next days; whenever he raised the subject of his request for a retrial Malek would counter with one of his deceptively naive queries, trying to establish some minor tangential point, almost as if he were leading Constantin on to a fuller admission. At first Constantin assumed that the supervisor was fishing for information about other members of the hierarchy which he wished to use for his own purposes, but the few tidbits he offered were ignored by Malek, and it dawned upon him that Malek was genuinely interested in establishing the sincerity of Constantin's conviction of his own innocence.

He showed no signs, however, of being prepared to contact his superiors at the Department of Justice, and Constantin's impatience continued to mount. He now used their morning and afternoon chess sessions as an opportunity to hold forth at length on the subject of the shortcomings of the judicial system, using his own case as an illustration, and hammered away at the theme of his innocence, even hinting that Malek might find himself held responsible if by any mischance he was not granted a reprieve.

"The position I find myself in is really most extraordinary," he told Malek almost exactly two months after his arrival at the villa. "Everyone else is satisfied with the court's verdict, and yet I alone know that I am innocent. I feel very like someone who is about to be buried alive."

Malek managed a thin smile across the chess pieces. "Of course, Mr. Constantin, it is possible to convince oneself of anything, given a sufficient incentive."

"But Malek, I assure you," Constantin insisted, ignoring the board and concentrating his whole attention upon the supervisor, "this is no death cell repentance. Believe me, I know. I have examined the entire case from a thousand perspectives, questioned every possible motive. There is no doubt in my mind. I may once have been prepared to accept the possibility of my guilt, but I realize now that I was entirely mistaken—experience encourages us to take too great a responsibility for ourselves, when we fall short of our ideals we become critical of ourselves and ready to assume that we are at fault. How dangerous that can be, Malek, I now know. Only the truly innocent man can really understand the meaning of guilt."

Constantin stopped and sat back, a slight weariness overtaking him in the cold room. Malek was nodding slowly, a thin and not altogether unsympathetic smile on his lips as if he understood everything Constantin had said. Then he moved a piece, and with a murmured "excuse me" left his seat and went out of the room.

Drawing the lapels of the dressing gown around his chest, Constantin studied the board with a desultory eye. He noticed that Malek's move appeared to be the first bad one he had made in all their games together, but he felt too tired to make the most of his opportunity. His brief speech to Malek, confirming all he believed, now left nothing more to be said. From now on whatever happened was up to Malek.

"Mr. Constantin."

He turned in his chair and, to his surprise, saw the supervisor standing in the doorway, wearing his long gray overcoat.

"Malek—?" For a moment Constantin felt his heart gallop, and then controlled himself. "Malek, you've agreed at last, you're going to take me to the Department?"

Malek shook his head, his eyes staring somberly at Constantin. "Not exactly. I thought we might look at the garden, Mr. Constantin. A breath of fresh air, it will do you good."

"Of course, Malek, it's kind of you." Constantin rose a little unsteadily to his feet, and tightened the cord of his dressing gown. "Pardon my wild hopes." He tried to smile to Malek, but the supervisor stood impassively by the door, hands in his overcoat pockets, his eyes lowered fractionally from Constantin's face.

They went out onto the veranda toward the French windows. Outside the cold morning air whirled in frantic circles around the small stone yard, the leaves spiraling upward into the dark sky. To Constantin there seemed little point in going out into the garden, but Malek stood behind him, one hand on the latch.

"Malek." Something made him turn and face the supervisor. "You do understand what I mean, when I say I am absolutely innocent. I *know* that."

"Of course, Mr. Constantin." The supervisor's face was relaxed and almost genial. "I understand. When you know you are innocent, then you are guilty."

His hand opened the veranda door onto the whirling leaves.

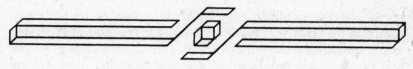

The Drowned Giant

On the morning after the storm the body of a drowned giant was washed ashore on the beach five miles to the northwest of the city. The first news of its arrival was brought by a nearby farmer and subsequently confirmed by the local newspaper reporters and the police. Despite this the majority of people, I among them, remained skeptical, but the return of more and more eyewitnesses attesting to the vast size of the giant was finally too much for our curiosity. The library where my colleagues and I were carrying out our research was almost deserted when we set off for the coast shortly after two o'clock, and throughout the day people continued to leave their offices and shops as accounts of the giant circulated around the city.

By the time we reached the dunes above the beach, a substantial crowd had gathered, and we could see the body lying in the shallow water two hundred yards away. At first the estimates of its size seemed greatly exaggerated. It was then at low tide, and almost all the giant's body was exposed, but he appeared to be little larger than a basking shark. He lay on his back with his arms at his sides, in an attitude of repose, as if asleep on the mirror of wet sand, the reflection of his blanched skin fading as the water receded. In the clear sunlight his body glistened like the white plumage of a seabird.

Puzzled by this spectacle and dissatisfied with the matter-of-fact explanations of the crowd, my friends and I stepped down from the dunes onto the shingle. Everyone seemed reluctant to approach the giant, but half an hour later two fishermen in wading boots walked out across the sand. As their diminutive figures neared the recumbent body, a sudden hubbub of conversation broke out among the spectators. The two men were completely dwarfed by the giant. Although his heels were partly submerged in the sand, the feet rose to at least twice the fishermen's height, and we immediately realized that this drowned leviathan had the mass and dimensions of the largest sperm whale.

Three fishing smacks had arrived on the scene and with keels raised remained a quarter of a mile offshore, the crews watching from the bows. Their discretion deterred the spectators on the shore from wading out across the sand. Impatiently everyone stepped down from the dunes and waited on the single slopes, eager for a closer view. Around the margins of the figure the sand had been washed away, forming a hollow, as if the giant had fallen out of the sky. The two fishermen were standing between the immense plinths of the feet, waving to us like tourists among the columns of some water-lapped temple on the Nile. For a moment I feared that the giant was merely asleep and might suddenly stir and clap his heels together, but his glazed eyes stared skyward, unaware of the minuscule replicas of himself between his feet.

The fishermen then began a circuit of the corpse, strolling past the long white flanks of the legs. After a pause to examine the fingers of the supine hand, they disappeared from sight between the arm and chest, then reemerged to survey the head, shielding their eyes as they gazed up at its Grecian profile. The shallow forehead, straight high-bridged nose, and curling lips reminded me of a Roman copy of Praxiteles, and the elegantly formed cartouches of the nostrils emphasized the resemblance to sculpture.

Abruptly there was a shout from the crowd, and a hundred arms pointed to the sea. With a start I saw that one of the fishermen had climbed onto the giant's chest and was now strolling about and signaling to the shore. There was a roar of surprise and triumph from the crowd, lost in a rushing avalanche of shingle as everyone surged forward across the sand.

As we approached the recumbent figure, which was lying in a pool of water the size of a field, our excited chatter fell away again, subdued by the huge physical dimensions of this dead colossus. He was stretched out at a slight angle to the shore, his legs carried nearer the beach, and this foreshortening had disguised his true length. Despite the two fishermen standing on his abdomen, the crowd formed itself into a wide circle, groups of people tentatively advancing toward the hands and feet.

My companions and I walked around the seaward side of the giant, whose hips and thorax towered above us like the hull of a stranded ship. His pearl-colored skin, distended by immersion in saltwater, masked the contours of the enormous muscles and tendons. We passed below the left knee, which was flexed slightly, threads of damp seaweed clinging to its sides. Draped loosely across the midriff, and preserving a tenuous propriety, was a shawl of heavy open-weave material, bleached to a pale yellow by the water. A strong odor of brine came from the garment as it steamed in the sun, mingled with the sweet, potent scent of the giant's skin.

We stopped by his shoulder and gazed up at the motionless profile. The lips were parted slightly, the open eye cloudy and occluded, as if injected with some blue milky liquid, but the delicate arches of the nostrils and eyebrows invested the face with an ornate charm that belied the brutish power of the chest and shoulders.

The ear was suspended in midair over our heads like a sculptured doorway. As I raised my hand to touch the pendulous lobe, someone appeared over the edge of the forehead and shouted down at me. Startled by this apparition, I stepped back, and then saw that a group of youths had climbed up onto the face and were jostling each other in and out of the orbits.

People were now clambering all over the giant, whose reclining arms provided a double stairway. From the palms they walked along the forearms to the elbows and then crawled over the distended belly of the biceps to the flat promenade of the pectoral muscles which covered the upper half of the smooth hairless chest. From here they climbed up onto the face, hand over hand along the lips and nose, or forayed down the abdomen to meet others who had straddled the ankles and were patrolling the twin columns of the thighs.

We continued our circuit through the crowd and stopped to examine the outstretched right hand. A small pool of water lay in the palm, like the residue of another world, now being kicked away by the people ascending the arm. I tried to read the palm lines that grooved the skin, searching for some clue to the giant's character, but the distention of the tissues had almost obliterated them, carrying away all trace of the giant's identity and his last tragic predicament. The huge muscles and wristbones of the hand seemed to deny any sensitivity to their owner, but the delicate flection of the fingers and the well-tended nails, each cut symmetrically to within six inches of the quick, argued a certain refinement of temperament, illustrated in the Grecian features of the face, on which the townsfolk were now sitting like flies.

One youth was even standing, arms waving at his sides, on the very tip of the nose, shouting down at his companions, but the face of the giant still retained its massive composure.

Returning to the shore, we sat down on the shingle and watched the continuous stream of people arriving from the city. Some six or seven fishing boats had collected offshore, and their crews waded in through the shallow water for a closer look at this enormous storm catch. Later a party of police appeared and made a halfhearted attempt to cordon off the beach, but after walking up to the recumbent figure, any such thoughts left their minds, and they went off together with bemused backward glances.

An hour later there were a thousand people present on the beach, at least two hundred of them standing or sitting on the giant, crowded along his arms and legs or circulating in a ceaseless melee across his chest and stomach. A large gang of youths occupied the head, toppling each other off the cheeks and sliding down the smooth planes of the jaw. Two or three straddled the nose, and another crawled into one of the nostrils, from which he emitted barking noises like a demented dog.

That afternoon the police returned and cleared a way through the crowd for a party of scientific experts—authorities on gross anatomy and marine biology—from the university. The gang of youths and most of the people on the giant climbed down, leaving behind a few hardy spirits perched on the tips of the toes and on the forehead. The experts strode around the giant, heads nodding in vigorous consultation, preceded by the policemen who pushed back the press of spectators. When they reached the outstretched hand, the experts hastily demurred.

After they returned to the shore, the crowd once more climbed onto the giant, and was in full possession when we left at five o'clock, covering the arms and legs like a dense flock of gulls sitting on the corpse of a large fish.

I next visited the beach three days later. My friends at the library had returned to their work, and delegated to me the task of keeping the giant under observation and preparing a report. Perhaps they sensed my particular interest in the case, and it was certainly true that I was eager to return to the beach. There was nothing necrophilic about this, for to all intents the giant was still alive for me, indeed more alive than many of the people watching him. What I found so fascinating was partly his immense scale, the huge volumes of space occupied by his arms and legs, which seemed to confirm the identity of my own miniature limbs, but above all, the mere categorical fact of his existence. Whatever else in our lives might be open to doubt, the giant, dead or alive, existed in an absolute sense, providing a glimpse into a world of similar absolutes of which we spectators on the beach were such imperfect and puny copies.

When I arrived at the beach the crowd was considerably smaller, and some two or three hundred people sat on the shingle, picnicking and watching the groups of visitors who walked out across the sand. The successive tides had carried the giant nearer the shore, swinging his head and shoulders toward the beach, so that he seemed doubly to gain in size, his huge body dwarfing the fishing boats beached beside his feet. The uneven contours of the beach had pushed his spine into a slight arch, expanding his chest and tilting back the head, forcing him into a more expressly heroic posture. The combined effects of seawater and the tumefaction of the tissues had given the face a sleeker and less youthful look. Although the vast proportions of the features made it impossible to assess the age and character of the giant, on my previous visit his classically modeled mouth and nose suggested that he had been a young man of discreet and modest temper. Now, however, he appeared to be at least in early middle age. The puffy cheeks, thicker nose and temples, and narrowing eyes gave him a look of well-fed maturity that even now hinted at a growing corruption to come.

This accelerated postmortem development of the giant's character, as if the latent elements of his personality had gained sufficient momentum during his life to discharge themselves in a brief final résumé, continued to fascinate me. It marked the beginning of the giant's surrender to that all-demanding system of time in which the rest of humanity finds itself, and of which, like the million twisted ripples of a fragmented whirlpool, our finite lives are the concluding products. I took up my position on the shingle directly opposite the giant's head, from where I could see the new arrivals and the children clambering over the legs and arms.

Among the morning's visitors were a number of men in leather jackets and cloth caps, who peered up critically at the giant with a professional eye, pacing out his dimensions and making rough calculations in the sand with spars of driftwood. I assumed them to be from the public works department and other municipal bodies, no doubt wondering how to dispose of this monster.

Several rather more smartly attired individuals, circus proprietors and the like, also appeared on the scene, and strolled slowly around the giant, hands in the pockets of their long overcoats, saying nothing to one another. Evidently its bulk was too great even for their matchless enterprise. After they had gone, the children continued to run up and down the arms and legs, and the youths wrestled with each other over the supine face, the damp sand from their feet covering the white skin.

The following day I deliberately postponed my visit until the late afternoon, and when I arrived there were fewer than fifty or sixty people sitting on the shingle. The giant had been carried still closer to the shore, and was now little more than seventy-five yards away, his feet crushing the palisade of a rotting breakwater. The slope of the firmer sand tilted his body toward the sea, the bruised, swollen face averted in an almost conscious gesture. I sat down on a large metal winch which had been shackled to a concrete caisson above the shingle, and looked down at the recumbent figure.

His blanched skin had now lost its pearly translucence and was spattered with dirty sand which replaced that washed away by the night tide. Clumps of seaweed filled the intervals between the fingers and a collection of litter and cuttlebones lay in the crevices below the hips and knees. But despite this, and the continuous thickening of his features, the giant still retained his magnificent Homeric stature. The enormous breadth of the shoulders, and the huge columns of the arms and legs, still carried the figure into another dimension, and the giant seemed a more authentic image of one of the drowned Argonauts or heroes of the *Odyssey* than the conventional portrait previously in my mind.

I stepped down onto the sand, and walked between the pools of water toward the giant. Two small boys were sitting in the well of the ear, and at the far end a solitary youth stood perched high on one of the toes, surveying me as I approached. As I had hoped when delaying my visit, no one else paid any attention to me, and the people on the shore remained huddled beneath their coats.

The giant's supine right hand was covered with broken shells and sand, in which a score of footprints were visible. The rounded bulk of the hip towered above me, cutting off all sight of the sea. The sweetly acrid odor I had noticed before was now more pungent, and through the opaque skin I could see the serpentine coils of congealed blood vessels. However repellent it seemed, this ceaseless metamorphosis, a macabre life-in-death, alone permitted me to set foot on the corpse.

Using the jutting thumb as a stair rail, I climbed up onto the palm and began my ascent. The skin was harder than I expected, barely yielding to my weight. Quickly I walked up the sloping forearm and the bulging balloon of the biceps. The face of the drowned giant loomed to my right, the cavernous nostrils and huge flanks of the cheeks like the cone of some freakish volcano.

Safely rounding the shoulder, I stepped out onto the broad promenade of the chest, across which the bony ridges of the rib cage lay like huge rafters. The white skin was dappled by the darkening bruises of countless footprints, in which the patterns of individual heel marks were clearly visible. Someone had built a small sand castle on the center of the sternum, and I climbed onto this partly demolished structure to get a better view of the face.

The two children had now scaled the ear and were pulling themselves into the right orbit, whose blue globe, completely occluded by some milk-colored fluid, gazed sightlessly past their miniature forms. Seen obliquely from below, the face was devoid of all grace and repose, the drawn mouth and raised chin propped up by gigantic slings of muscles resembling the torn prow of a colossal wreck. For the first time I became aware of the extremity of this last physical agony of the giant, no less painful for his unawareness of the collapsing musculature and tissues. The absolute isolation of the ruined figure, cast like an abandoned ship upon the empty shore, almost out of sound of the waves, transformed his face into a mask of exhaustion and helplessness.

As I stepped forward, my foot sank into a trough of soft tissue, and a gust of fetid gas blew through an aperture between the ribs. Retreating from the fouled air, which hung like a cloud over my head, I turned toward the sea to clear my lungs. To my surprise I saw that the giant's left hand had been amputated.

I stared with shocked bewilderment at the blackening stump, while the solitary youth reclining on his aerial perch a hundred feet away surveyed me with a sanguinary eye.

This was only the first of a sequence of depredations. I spent the following two days in the library, for some reason reluctant to visit the shore, aware that I had probably witnessed the approaching end of a magnificent illusion. When I next crossed the dunes and set foot on the shingle, the giant was little more than twenty yards away, and with this close proximity to the rough pebbles all traces had vanished of the magic which once surrounded his distant wave-washed form. Despite his immense size, the bruises and dirt that covered his body made him appear merely human in scale, his vast dimensions only increasing his vulnerability.

His right hand and foot had been removed, dragged up the slope, and trundled away by cart. After questioning the small group of people huddled by the breakwater, I gathered that a fertilizer company and a cattlefood manufacturer were responsible.

The giant's remaining foot rose into the air, a steel hawser fixed to the large toe, evidently in preparation for the following day. The surrounding beach had been disturbed by a score of workmen, and deep ruts marked the ground where the hands and foot had been hauled away. A dark brackish fluid leaked from the stumps, and stained the sand and the white cones of the cuttlefish. As I walked down the shingle I noticed that a number of jocular slogans, swastikas, and other signs had been cut into the gray skin, as if the mutilation of this motionless colossus had released a sudden flood of repressed spite. The lobe of one of the ears was pierced by a spear of timber, and a small fire had burned out in the center of the chest, blackening the surrounding skin. The fine wood ash was still being scattered by the wind.

A foul smell enveloped the cadaver, the undisguisable signature of putrefaction, which had at last driven away the usual gathering of youths. I returned to the shingle and climbed up onto the winch. The giant's swollen cheeks had now almost closed his eyes, drawing the lips back in a monumental gape. The once straight Grecian nose had been twisted and flattened, stamped into the ballooning face by countless heels.

When I visited the beach the following day I found, almost with relief, that the head had been removed.

Some weeks elapsed before I made my next journey to the beach, and by then the human likeness I had noticed earlier had vanished again. On close inspection the recumbent thorax and abdomen were unmistakably manlike, but as each of the limbs was chopped off, first at the knee and elbow, and then at shoulder and thigh, the carcass resembled that of any headless sea animal—whale or whale shark. With this loss of identity, and the few traces of personality that had clung tenuously to the figure, the interest of the spectators expired, and the foreshore was deserted except for an elderly beachcomber and the watchman sitting in the doorway of the contractor's hut.

A loose wooden scaffolding had been erected around the carcass, from which a dozen ladders swung in the wind, and the surrounding sand was littered with coils of rope, long metal-handled knives, and grappling irons, the pebbles oily with blood and pieces of bone and skin.

I nodded to the watchman, who regarded me dourly over his brazier of burning coke. The whole area was pervaded by the pungent smell of huge squares of blubber being simmered in a vat behind the hut.

Both the thighbones had been removed, with the assistance of a small crane draped in the gauzelike fabric which had once covered the waist of the giant, and the open sockets gaped like barn doors. The upper arms, collarbones, and pudenda had likewise been dispatched. What remained of the skin over the thorax and abdomen had been marked out in parallel strips with a tarbrush, and the first five or six sections had been pared away from the midriff, revealing the great arch of the rib cage.

As I left, a flock of gulls wheeled down from the sky and alighted on the beach, picking at the stained sand with ferocious cries.

Several months later, when the news of his arrival had been generally forgotten, various pieces of the body of the dismembered giant began to reappear all over the city. Most of these were bones, which the fertilizer manufacturers had found too difficult to crush, and their massive size, and the huge tendons and disks of cartilage attached to their joints, immediately identified them. For some reason, these disembodied fragments seemed better to convey the essence of the giant's original magnificence than the bloated appendages that had been subsequently amputated. As I looked across the road at the premises of the largest wholesale merchants in the meat market, I recognized the two enormous thighbones on either side of the doorway. They towered over the porters' heads like the threatening megaliths of some primitive druidical religion, and I had a sudden vision of the giant climbing to his knees upon these bare bones and striding away through the streets of the city, picking up the scattered fragments of himself on his return journey to the sea.

A few days later I saw the left humerus lying in the entrance to one of the shipyards. In the same week the mummified right hand was exhibited on a carnival float during the annual pageant of the guilds.

The lower jaw, typically, found its way to the museum of natural history. The remainder of the skull has disappeared, but is probably still lurking in the waste grounds or private gardens of the city—quite recently, while sailing down the river, I noticed two ribs of the giant forming a decorative arch in a waterside garden, possibly confused with the jawbones of a whale. A large square of tanned and tattooed skin, the size of an Indian blanket, forms a back cloth to the dolls and masks in a novelty shop near the amusement park, and I have no doubt that elsewhere in the city, in the hotels or golf clubs, the mummified nose or ears of the giant hang from the wall above a fireplace. As for the immense pizzle, this ends its days in the freak museum of a circus which travels up and down the Northwest. This monumental apparatus, stunning in its proportions and sometime potency, occupies a complete booth to itself. The irony is that it is wrongly identified as that of a whale, and indeed most people, even those who first saw him cast up on the shore after the storm, now remember the giant, if at all, as a large sea beast.

The remainder of the skeleton, stripped of all flesh, still rests on the seashore, the clutter of bleached ribs like the timbers of a derelict ship. The contractor's hut, the crane, and scaffolding have been removed, and the sand being driven into the bay along the coast has buried the pelvis and backbone. In the winter the high curved bones are deserted, battered by the breaking waves, but in the summer they provide an excellent perch for the sea-wearying gulls.

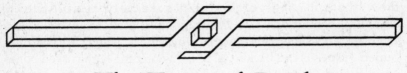

The Terminal Beach

At night, as he lay asleep on the floor of the ruined bunker, Traven heard the waves breaking along the shore of the lagoon, reminding him of the deep Atlantic rollers on the beach at Dakar, where he had been born, and of waiting in the evenings for his parents to drive home along the corniche road from the airport. Overcome by this long-forgotten memory, he woke uncertainly from the bed of old magazines on which he slept and ran toward the dunes that screened the lagoon.

Through the cold night air he could see the abandoned Superfortresses lying among the palms, beyond the perimeter of the emergency landing field three hundred yards away. Traven walked through the dark sand, already forgetting where the shore lay, although the atoll was only half a mile in width. Above him, along the crests of the dunes, the tall palms leaned into the dim air like the symbols of some cryptic alphabet. The landscape of the island was covered by strange ciphers.

Giving up the attempt to find the beach, Traven stumbled into a set of tracks left years earlier by a large caterpillar vehicle. The heat released by one of the weapons tests had fused the sand, and the double line of fossil imprints, uncovered by the evening air, wound its serpentine way among the hollows like the footfalls of an ancient saurian.

Too weak to walk any further, Traven sat down between the tracks. With one hand he began to excavate the wedge-shaped grooves from a drift into which they disappeared, hoping that they might lead him toward the sea. He returned to the bunker shortly before dawn, and slept through the hot silences of the following noon.

The Blocks

As usual on these enervating afternoons, when not even the faintest breath of offshore breeze disturbed the dust, Traven sat in the shadow of one of the blocks, lost somewhere within the center of the maze. His back resting against the rough concrete surface, he gazed with a phlegmatic eye down the surrounding aisles and at the line of doors facing him. Each afternoon he left his cell in the abandoned camera bunker and walked down into the blocks. For the first half hour he restricted himself to the perimeter aisle, now and then trying one of the doors with the rusty key in his pocket—he had found it among the litter of smashed bottles in the isthmus of sand separating the testing ground from the airstrip—and then, inevitably, with a sort of drugged stride, he set off into the center of the blocks, breaking into a run and darting in and out of the corridors, as if trying to flush some invisible opponent from his hiding place. Soon he would be completely lost. Whatever his efforts to return to the perimeter, he found himself once more in the center.

Eventually he would abandon the task, and sit down in the dust, watching the shadows emerge from their crevices at the foot of the blocks. For some reason he always arranged to be trapped when the sun was at zenith—on Eniwetok, a thermonuclear noon.

One question in particular intrigued him: "What sort of people would inhabit this minimal concrete city?"

The Synthetic Landscape

"This island is a state of mind," Osborne, one of the biologists working in the old submarine pens, was later to remark to Traven. The truth of this became obvious to Traven within two or three weeks of his arrival. Despite the sand and the few anemic palms, the entire landscape of the island was synthetic, a man-made artifact with all the associations of a vast system of derelict concrete motorways. Since the moratorium on atomic tests, the island had been abandoned by the Atomic Energy Commission, and the wilderness of weapons, aisles, towers, and blockhouses ruled out any attempt to return it to its natural state. (There were also stronger unconscious motives, Traven recognized, for leaving it as it was: if primitive man felt the need to assimilate events in the external world to his own psyche, twentieth-century man had reversed this process—by this Cartesian yardstick, the island at least *existed*, in a sense true of few other places.)

But apart from a few scientific workers, no one yet felt any wish to visit the former testing ground, and the naval patrol boat anchored in the lagoon had been withdrawn five years before Traven's arrival. Its ruined appearance, and the associations of the island with the period of the Cold War—what Traven had christened the "pre-Third"—were profoundly depressing, an Auschwitz of the soul whose mausoleums contained the mass graves of the still undead. With the Russo-American detente this nightmarish chapter of history had been gladly forgotten.

The Pre-Third

The actual and potential destructiveness of the atomic bomb plays straight into the hands of the Unconscious. The most cursory study of the dream-life and fantasies of the insane shows that ideas of world-destruction are latent in the unconscious mind. Nagasaki destroyed by the magic of science is the nearest man has yet approached to the realization of dreams that even during the safe immobility of sleep are accustomed to develop into nightmares of anxiety.
—Glover: *War, Sadism and Pacifism*

The Pre-Third: the period had been characterized in Traven's mind above all by its moral and psychological inversions, by its sense of the whole of history, and in particular of the immediate future—the two decades, 1945–65—suspended from the quivering volcano's lip of World War III. Even the death of his wife and six-year-old son in a motor accident seemed only part of this immense synthesis of the historical and psychic zero, and the frantic highways where each morning they met their deaths were the advance causeways to the global armageddon.

Third Beach

He had come ashore at midnight, after a hazardous search for an opening in the reef. The small motorboat he had hired from an Australian pearl diver at Charlotte Island subsided into the shallows, its hull torn by the sharp coral. Exhausted, Traven walked through the darkness among the dunes, where the dim outlines of bunkers and concrete towers loomed between the palms.

He woke the next morning into bright sunlight, lying halfway down the slope of a wide concrete beach. This ringed what appeared to be an empty reservoir or target basin, some two hundred feet in diameter, part of a system of artificial lakes built down the center of the atoll. Leaves and dust choked the waste grilles, and a pool of warm water two feet deep lay in the center, reflecting a distant line of palms.

Traven sat up and took stock of himself. This brief inventory, which merely confirmed his physical identity, was limited to little more than his thin body in its frayed cotton garments. In the context of the surrounding terrain, however, even this collection of tatters seemed to possess a unique vitality. The emptiness of the island, and the absence of any local fauna, were emphasized by the huge sculptural forms of the target basins let into its surface. Separated from each other by narrow isthmuses, the lakes stretched away along the curve of the atoll. On either side, sometimes shaded by the few palms that had gained a precarious purchase in the cracked cement, were roadways, camera towers, and isolated blockhouses, together forming a continuous concrete cap upon the island, a functional megalithic architecture as gray and minatory, and apparently as ancient (in its projection into, and from, time future), as any of Assyria and Babylon.

The series of weapons tests had fused the sand in layers, and the pseudogeological strata condensed the brief epochs, microseconds in duration, of the thermonuclear age. "The key to the past lies in the present." Typically the island inverted this geologist's maxim. Here the key to the present lay in the future. The island was a fossil of time future, its bunkers and blockhouses illustrating the principle that the fossil record of life is one of armor and the exoskeleton.

Traven knelt in the warm pool and splashed his shirt and trousers. The reflection revealed the watery image of a thinly bearded face and gaunt shoulders. He had come to the island with no supplies other than a small bar of chocolate, expecting that in some way the island would provide its own sustenance. Perhaps, too, he had identified the need for food with a forward motion in time, and envisioned that with his return to the past, or at most into a zone of nontime, this need would be obviated. The privations of the previous six months, during his journey across the Pacific, had reduced his always thin body to that of a migrant beggar, held together by little more than the preoccupied gaze in his eye. Yet this emaciation, by stripping away the superfluities of the flesh, seemed to reveal an inner sinewy toughness, an economy and directness of movement.

For several hours he wandered about, inspecting one bunker after another for a convenient place to sleep. He crossed the remains of a small landing strip, next to a dump where a dozen B-29's lay across one another like dead reptile birds.

The Corpses

Once he entered a small street of metal shacks, containing a cafeteria, recreation rooms, and shower stalls. A wrecked jukebox lay half-buried in the sand behind the cafeteria, its selection of records still in their rack.

Further along, flung into a small target basin fifty yards from the shacks, were the bodies of what at first he thought were the inhabitants of this ghost town—a dozen life-size plastic models. Their half-melted faces, contorted into bleary grimaces, gazed up at him from the jumble of legs and torsos.

On either side of him, muffled by the dunes, came the sounds of waves, the great rollers on the seaward side breaking over the reefs, and onto the beaches within the lagoon. However, he avoided the sea, hesitating before any rise that might take him within its sight. Everywhere the camera towers offered him a convenient aerial view of the confused topography of the island, but he avoided their rusting ladders.

He soon realized that however confused and random the block-

houses and camera towers might seem, their common focus dominated the landscape and gave to it a unique perspective. As Traven
noticed when he sat down to rest in the window slit of one of the
blockhouses, all these observation posts occupied positions on a
series of concentric perimeters, moving in tightening arcs toward
the inmost sanctuary. This ultimate circle, below ground zero, remained hidden beyond a line of dunes a quarter of a mile to the west.

The Terminal Bunker

After sleeping for a few nights in the open, Traven returned to the
concrete beach where he had woken on his first morning on the
island, and made his home—if the term could be applied to that
damp crumbling hovel—in a camera bunker fifty yards from the
target lakes. The dark chamber between the thick canted walls,
tomblike though it might seem, gave him a sense of physical reassurance. Outside, the sand drifted against the sides, half-burying
the narrow doorway, as if crystallizing the immense epoch of time
that had elapsed since the bunker's construction. The narrow rectangles of the five camera slits, their shapes and positions determined by the instruments, studded the east wall like cryptic ideograms. Variations of these ciphers decorated the walls of the other
bunkers. In the morning, if Traven was awake, he would always
find the sun divided into five emblematic beacons.

Most of the time the chamber was filled only by a damp gloomy
light. In the control tower at the landing field Traven found a collection of discarded magazines, and used these to make a bed. One
day, lying in the bunker shortly after the first attack of beriberi, he
pulled out a magazine pressing into his back and found inside it a
full-page photograph of a six-year-old girl. This blond-haired child,
with her composed expression and self-immersed eyes, filled him
with a thousand painful memories of his son. He pinned the page to
the wall and for days gazed at it through his reveries.

For the first few weeks Traven made little attempt to leave the
bunker, and postponed any further exploration of the island. The
symbolic journey through its inner circles set its own times of arrival
and departure. He evolved no routine for himself. All sense of time
soon vanished; his life became completely existential, an absolute
break separating one moment from the next like two quantal events.

Too weak to forage for food, he lived on the old ration packs he found in the wrecked Superfortresses. Without any implements, it took him all day to open the cans. His physical decline continued, but he watched his spindling arms and legs with indifference.

By now he had forgotten the existence of the sea and vaguely assumed the atoll to be part of some continuous continental table. A hundred yards away to the north and south of the bunker a line of dunes, topped by the palisade of enigmatic palms, screened the lagoon and sea, and the faint muffled drumming of the waves at night had fused with his memories of war and childhood. To the east was the emergency landing field and the abandoned aircraft. In the afternoon light their shifting rectangular shadows would appear to writhe and pivot. In front of the bunker, where he sat, was the system of target lakes, the shallow basins extending across the center of the atoll. Above him the five apertures looked out upon this scene like the tutelary deities of some futuristic myth.

The Lakes and the Specters

The lakes had been designed originally to reveal any radiobiological changes in a selected range of flora and fauna, but the specimens had long since bloomed into grotesque parodies of themselves and been destroyed.

Sometimes in the evenings, when a sepulchral light lay over the concrete bunkers and causeways, and the basins seemed like ornamental lakes in a city of deserted mausoleums, abandoned even by the dead, he would see the specters of his wife and son standing on the opposite bank. Their solitary figures appeared to have been watching him for hours. Although they never moved, Traven was sure they were beckoning to him. Roused from his reverie, he would stumble across the dark sand to the edge of the lake and wade through the water, shouting at the two figures as they moved away hand in hand among the lakes and disappeared across the distant causeways.

Shivering with cold, Traven would return to the bunker and lie on the bed of old magazines, waiting for their return. The image of their faces, the pale lantern of his wife's cheeks, floated on the river of his memory.

The Blocks (II)

It was not until he discovered the blocks that Traven realized he would never leave the island.

At this stage, some two months after his arrival, Traven had exhausted the small cache of food, and the symptoms of beriberi had become more acute. The numbness in his hands and feet, and the gradual loss of strength, continued. Only by an immense effort, and the knowledge that the inner sanctum of the island still lay unexplored, did he manage to leave the palliasse of magazines and make his way from the bunker.

As he sat in the drift of sand by the doorway that evening, he noticed a light shining through the palms far into the distance around the atoll. Confusing this with the image of his wife and son, and visualizing them waiting for him at some warm hearth among the dunes, Traven set off toward the light. Within fifty yards he lost his sense of direction. He blundered about for several hours on the edges of the landing strip, and succeeded only in cutting his foot on a broken Coca-Cola bottle in the sand.

After postponing his search for the night, he set out again in earnest the next morning. As he moved past the towers and blockhouses the heat lay over the island in an unbroken mantle. He had entered a zone devoid of time. Only the narrowing perimeters of the bunkers warned him that he was crossing the inner field of the fire-table.

He climbed the ridge which marked the furthest point in his previous exploration of the island. The plain beyond was covered with target aisles and explosion breaks. On the gray walls of the recording towers, which rose into the air like obelisks, were the faint outlines of human forms in stylized postures, the flash-shadows of the target community burned into the cement. Here and there, where the concrete apron had cracked, a line of palms hung precariously in the motionless air. The target lakes were smaller, filled with the broken bodies of plastic dummies. Most of them still lay in the inoffensive domestic postures into which they had been placed before the tests.

Beyond the furthest line of dunes, where the camera towers began to turn and face him, were the tops of what seemed to be a herd of square-backed elephants. They were drawn up in precise ranks in a hollow that formed a shallow corral.

Traven advanced toward them, limping on his cut foot. On either side of him the loosening sand had excavated the dunes, and several of the blockhouses tilted on their sides. This plain of bunkers stretched for some quarter of a mile. To one side the half-submerged hulks of a group of concrete shelters, bombed out onto the surface in some earlier test, lay like the husks of the abandoned wombs that had given birth to this herd of megaliths.

The Blocks (III)

To grasp something of the vast number and oppressive size of the blocks, and their impact upon Traven, one must try to visualize sitting in the shade of one of these concrete monsters, or walking about in the center of this enormous labyrinth, which extended across the central table of the island. There were some two thousand of them, each a perfect cube fifteen feet in height, regularly spaced at ten-yard intervals. They were arranged in a series of tracts, each composed of two hundred blocks, inclined to one another and to the direction of the blast. They had weathered only slightly in the years since they were first built, and their gaunt profiles were like the cutting faces of an enormous die-plate, designed to stamp out huge rectilinear volumes of air. Three of the sides were smooth and unbroken, but the fourth, facing away from the direction of the blast, contained a narrow inspection door.

It was this feature of the blocks that Traven found particularly disturbing. Despite the considerable number of doors, by some freak of perspective only those in a single aisle were visible at any point within the maze, the rest obscured by the intervening blocks. As he walked from the perimeter into the center of the massif, line upon line of the small metal doors appeared and receded, a world of closed exits concealed behind endless corners.

Approximately twenty of the blocks, those immediately below ground zero, were solid, the walls of the remainder of varying thicknesses. From the outside they appeared to be of uniform solidity.

As he entered the first of the long aisles, Traven felt his step lighten; the sense of fatigue that had dogged him for so many months begin to lift. With their geometric regularity and finish, the blocks seemed to occupy more than their own volume of space, imposing on him a mood of absolute calm and order. He walked on into the center of the maze, eager to shut out the rest of the island. After a few random turns to left and right, he found himself alone, the vistas to the sea, lagoon, and island closed.

Here he sat down with his back against one of the blocks, the quest for his wife and son forgotten. For the first time since his arrival at the island the sense of dissociation prompted by its fragmenting landscape began to recede.

One development he did not expect. With dusk, and the need to leave the blocks and find food, he realized that he had lost himself. However he retraced his steps, struck out left or right at an oblique course, oriented himself around the sun and pressed on resolutely north or south, he found himself back at his starting point. Despite his best efforts, he was unable to make his way out of the maze. That he was aware of his motives gave him little help. Only when hunger overcame the need to remain did he manage to escape.

Abandoning his former home near the aircraft dump, Traven collected together what canned food he could find in the waist turret and cockpit lockers of the Superfortresses and pulled them across the island on a crude sledge. Fifty yards from the perimeter of the blocks he took over a tilting bunker, and pinned the fading photograph of the blond-haired child to the wall beside the door. The page was falling to pieces, like his fragmenting image of himself. Each evening when he woke he would eat uneagerly and then go out into the blocks. Sometimes he took a canteen of water with him and remained there for two or three days.

Traven: In Parenthesis

Elements in a quantal world:
  The terminal beach.
  The terminal bunker.
  The blocks.
The landscape is coded.
Entry points into the future=levels in a spinal landscape=zones of significant time.

The Submarine Pens

This precarious existence continued for the following weeks. As he walked out to the blocks one evening, he again saw his wife and son, standing among the dunes below a solitary tower, their faces watching him calmly. He realized that they had followed him across the island from their former haunt among the dried-up lakes. Once again he saw the beckoning light, and he decided to continue his exploration of the island.

Half a mile further along the atoll he found a group of four submarine pens, built over an inlet, now drained, which wound through the dunes from the sea. The pens still contained several feet of water, filled with strange luminescent fish and plants. A warning light winked at intervals from a metal tower. The remains of a substantial camp, only recently vacated, stood on the concrete pier outside. Greedily Traven heaped his sledge with the provisions stacked inside one of the metal shacks. With this change of diet the beriberi receded, and during the next days he returned to the camp. It appeared to be the site of a biological expedition. In a field office he came across a series of large charts of mutated chromosomes. He rolled them up and took them back to his bunker. The abstract patterns were meaningless, but during his recovery he amused himself by devising suitable titles for them. (Later, passing the aircraft dump on one of his forays, he found the half-buried jukebox, and tore the list of records from the selection panel, realizing that these were the most appropriate captions for the charts. Thus embroidered, they took on many layers of cryptic associations.)

Traven Lost Among the Blocks

August 5. Found the man Traven. A sad derelict figure, hiding in a bunker in the deserted interior of the island. He is suffering from severe exposure and malnutrition, but is unaware of this, or, for that matter, of any other events in the world around him. . . .

He maintains that he came to the island to carry out some scientific project—unstated—but I suspect that he understands his real motives and the unique role of the island... In some way its landscape seems to be involved with certain unconscious notions of time, and in particular with those that may be a repressed premonition of our own deaths. The attractions and dangers of such an architecture, as the past has shown, need no stressing.

August 6. He has the eyes of the possessed. I would guess that he is neither the first, nor the last, to visit the island.

—Dr. C. Osborne: *Eniwetok Diary*

With the exhaustion of his supplies, Traven remained within the perimeter of the blocks almost continuously, conserving what strength remained to him to walk slowly down their empty corridors. The infection in his right foot made it difficult for him to replenish his supplies from the stores left by the biologists, and as his strength ebbed he found progressively less incentive to make his way out of the blocks. The system of megaliths now provided a complete substitute for those functions of his mind which gave to it its sense of the sustained rational order of time and space, his awareness kindled from levels above those of his present nervous system (if the autonomic system is dominated by the past, the cerebrospinal reaches toward the future). Without the blocks his sense of reality shrank to little more than the few square inches of sand beneath his feet.

On one of his last ventures into the maze, he spent all night and much of the following morning in a futile attempt to escape. Dragging himself from one rectangle of shadow to another, his leg as heavy as a club and apparently inflamed to the knee, he realized that he must soon find an equivalent for the blocks or he would end his life within them, trapped within this self-constructed mausoleum as surely as the retinue of Pharaoh.

He was sitting exhausted somewhere within the center of the system, the faceless lines of the tomb booths receding from him, when the sky was slowly divided by the drone of a light aircraft. This passed overhead, and then, five minutes later, returned. Seizing his opportunity, Traven struggled to his feet and made his exit from the blocks, his head raised to follow the glistening exhaust trail.

As he lay down in the bunker he dimly heard the aircraft return and carry out an inspection of the site.

A Belated Rescue

"Who are you?" A small sandy-haired man was peering down at him with a severe expression, then put away a syringe in his valise. "Do you realize you're on your last legs?"

"Traven... I've had some sort of accident. I'm glad you flew over."

"I'm sure you are. Why didn't you use our emergency radio? Anyway, we'll call the Navy and have you picked up."

"No..." Traven sat up on one elbow and felt weakly in his hip pocket. "I have a pass somewhere. I'm carrying out research."

"Into what?" The question assumed a complete understanding of Traven's motives. Traven lay in the shade beside the bunker, and drank weakly from a canteen as Dr. Osborne dressed his foot. "You've also been stealing our stores."

Traven shook his head. Fifty yards away the blue and white Cessna stood on the concrete apron like a large dragonfly. "I didn't realize you were coming back."

"You must be in a trance."

The young woman at the controls of the aircraft climbed from the cockpit and walked over to them, glancing at the gray bunkers and blocks. She seemed unaware of or uninterested in the decrepit figure of Traven. Osborne spoke to her over his shoulder, and after a downward glance at Traven she went back to the aircraft. As she turned Traven rose involuntarily, recognizing the child in the photograph he had pinned to the wall. Then he remembered that the magazine could not have been more than four or five years old.

The engine of the aircraft started. It turned onto one of the roadways and took off into the wind.

The young woman drove over by jeep that afternoon with a small camp bed and a canvas awning. During the intervening hours Traven had slept, and woke refreshed when Osborne returned from his scrutiny of the surrounding dunes.

"What are you doing here?" the young woman asked as she secured one of the guy ropes to the bunker.

"I'm searching for my wife and son," Traven said.

"They're on this island?" Surprised, but taking the reply at face value, she looked around her. "Here?"

"In a manner of speaking."

After inspecting the bunker, Osborne joined them. "The child in the photograph. Is she your daughter?"

"No." Traven tried to explain. "She's adopted *me*."

Unable to make sense of his replies, but accepting his assurances that he would leave the island, Osborne and the young woman returned to their camp. Each day Osborne returned to change the dressing, driven by the young woman, who seemed to grasp the role cast for her by Traven in his private mythology. Osborne, when he learned of Traven's previous career as a military pilot, assumed that he was a latter-day martyr left high and dry by the moratorium on thermonuclear tests.

"A guilt complex isn't an indiscriminate supply of moral sanctions. I think you may be overstretching yours."

When he mentioned the name Eatherly, Traven shook his head.

Undeterred, Osborne pressed: "Are you sure you're not making similar use of the image of Eniwetok—waiting for your pentecostal wind?"

"Believe me, Doctor, no," Traven replied firmly. "For me the H-bomb is a symbol of absolute freedom. Unlike Eatherly I feel it's given me the right—the obligation, even—to do anything I choose."

"That seems strange logic," Osborne commented. "At least we are responsible for our physical selves."

Traven shrugged. "Not now, I think. After all, aren't we in effect men raised from the dead?"

Often, however, he thought of Eatherly: the prototypal Pre-Third Man, dating the Pre-Third from August 6, 1945, carrying a full load of cosmic guilt.

Shortly after Traven was strong enough to walk again he had to be rescued from the blocks for a second time. Osborne became less conciliatory.

"Our work is almost complete," he warned Traven. "You'll die here. Traven, what are you looking for?"

To himself Traven said: the tomb of the unknown civilian, *Homo hydrogenensis*, Eniwetok Man. To Osborne he said: "Doctor, your laboratory is at the wrong end of this island."

"I'm aware of that, Traven. There are rarer fish swimming in your head than in any submarine pen."

On the day before they left, Traven and the young woman drove over to the lakes where he had first arrived. As a final present from Osborne, an ironic gesture unexpected from the elderly biologist, she had brought the correct list of legends for the chromosome charts. They stopped by the derelict jukebox and she pasted them on to the selection panel.

They wandered among the supine wrecks of the Superfortresses. Traven lost sight of her, and for the next ten minutes searched in and out of the dunes. He found her standing in a small amphitheater formed by the sloping mirrors of a solar energy device, built by one of the visiting expeditions. She smiled to him as he stepped through the scaffolding. A dozen fragmented images of herself were reflected in the broken panes. In some she was sans head, in others multiples of her raised arms circled her like those of a Hindu goddess. Exhausted, Traven turned away and walked back to the jeep.

As they drove away he described his glimpses of his wife and son. "Their faces are always calm. My son's particularly, although he was never really like that. The only time his face was grave was when he was being born—then he seemed millions of years old."

The young woman nodded. "I hope you find them." As an afterthought she added: "Dr. Osborne is going to tell the Navy you're here. Hide somewhere."

Traven thanked her. When she flew away from the island for the last time he waved to her from his seat beside the blocks.

The Naval Party

When the search party came for him Traven hid in the only logical place. Fortunately the search was perfunctory, and was called off after a few hours. The sailors had brought a supply of beer with them, and the search soon turned into a drunken ramble. On the walls of the recording towers Traven later found balloons of obscene dialogue chalked into the mouths of the shadow figures, giving their postures the priapic gaiety of the dancers in cave drawings.

The climax of the party was the ignition of a store of gasoline in an underground tank near the airstrip. As he listened, first to the megaphones shouting his name, the echoes receding among the dunes like the forlorn calls of dying birds, then to the boom of the explosion and the laughter as the landing craft left, Traven felt a premonition that these were the last sounds he would hear.

He had hidden in one of the target basins, lying down among the bodies of the plastic dummies. In the hot sunlight their deformed faces gaped at him sightlessly from the tangle of limbs, their blurred smiles like those of the soundlessly laughing dead. Their faces filled his mind as he climbed over the bodies and returned to the bunker.

As he walked toward the blocks he saw the figures of his wife and son standing in his path. They were less than ten yards from him, their white faces watching him with a look of almost overwhelming expectancy. Never had Traven seen them so close to the blocks. His wife's pale features seemed illuminated from within, her lips parted as if in greeting, one hand raised to take his own. His son's grave face, with its curiously fixed expression, regarded him with the same enigmatic smile as the girl in the photograph.

"Judith! David!" Startled, Traven ran forward to them. Then, in a sudden movement of light, their clothes turned into shrouds, and he saw the wounds that disfigured their necks and chests. Appalled, he cried out to them. As they vanished he fled into the safety and sanity of the blocks.

The Catechism of Good-bye

This time he found himself, as Osborne had predicted, unable to leave the blocks.

Somewhere in the shifting center of the maze, he sat with his back against one of the concrete flanks, his eyes raised to the sun. Around him the lines of cubes formed the horizons of his world. At times they would appear to advance toward him, looming over him like cliffs, the intervals between them narrowing so that they were little more than an arm's length apart, a labyrinth of narrow corridors running between them. Then they would recede from him, separating from each other like points in an expanding universe, until the nearest line formed an intermittent palisade along the horizon.

Time had become quantal. For hours it would be noon, the shadows contained within the motionless bulk of the blocks, the heat reverberating off the concrete floor. Abruptly he would find it was early afternoon or evening, the shadows everywhere like pointing fingers.

"Good-bye, Eniwetok," he murmured.

Somewhere there was a flicker of light, as if one of the blocks, like a counter on an abacus, had been plucked away.

"Good-bye, Los Alamos." Again a block seemed to vanish. The corridors around him remained intact, but somewhere, Traven was convinced, in the matrix superimposed on his mind, a small interval of neutral space had been punched.

Good-bye, Hiroshima.

Good-bye, Alamogordo.

Good-bye, Moscow, London, Paris, New York...

Shuttles flickered, a ripple of integers. Traven stopped, accepting the futility of this megathlon farewell. Such a leave-taking required him to affix his signature on every one of the particles in the universe.

Total Noon: Eniwetok

The blocks now occupied positions on an endlessly revolving circus wheel. They carried him upward, to heights from which he could see the whole island and the sea, and then down again through the opaque disk of the floor. From here he looked up at the undersurface of the concrete cap, an inverted landscape of rectilinear hollows, the dome-shaped mounds of the lake system, the thousands of empty cubic pits of the blocks.

"Good-bye, Traven"

To his disappointment he found that this ultimate act of rejection gained him nothing.

In an interval of lucidity, he looked down at his emaciated arms and legs propped loosely in front of him, the brittle wrists and hands covered with a lacework of ulcers. To his right was a trail of disturbed dust, the marks of slack heels.

In front of him lay a long corridor between the blocks, joining an oblique series a hundred yards away. Among these, where a narrow interval revealed the open space beyond, was a crescent-shaped shadow, poised in the air.

During the next half hour it moved slowly, turning as the sun swung.

The outline of a dune.

Seizing on this cipher, which hung before him like a symbol on a shield, Traven pushed himself through the dust. He climbed precariously to his feet, and covered his eyes from all sight of the blocks.

Ten minutes later he emerged from the western perimeter. The dune whose shadow had guided him lay fifty yards away. Beyond it, bearing the shadow like a screen, was a ridge of limestone, which ran away among the hillocks of a wasteland. The remains of old bulldozers, bales of barbed wire, and fifty-gallon drums lay half-buried in the sand.

Traven approached the dune, reluctant to leave this anonymous swell of sand. He shuffled around its edges, and then sat down in the shade by a narrow crevice in the ridge.

Ten minutes later he noticed that someone was watching him.

The Marooned Japanese

This corpse, whose eyes stared up at Traven, lay to his left at the bottom of the crevice. That of a man of middle age and powerful build, it lay on its side with its head on a pillow of stone, as if surveying the window of the sky. The fabric of the clothes had rotted to a gray tattered vestment, but in the absence of any small animal predators on the island the skin and musculature had been preserved. Here and there, at the angle of knee or wrist, a bony point shone through the leathery integument of the yellow skin, but the facial mask was still intact, and revealed a male Japanese of the professional classes. Looking down at the strong nose, high forehead, and broad mouth, Traven guessed that the Japanese had been a doctor or lawyer.

Puzzled as to how the corpse had found itself here, Traven slid a few feet down the slope. There were no radiation burns on the skin, which indicated that the Japanese had been there for less than five years. Nor did he appear to be wearing a uniform, so had not been a member of a military or scientific mission.

To the left of the corpse, within reach of his hand, was a frayed leather case, the remains of a map wallet. To the right was the bleached husk of a haversack, open to reveal a canteen of water and a small can.

Greedily, the reflex of starvation making him for the moment ignore this discovery that the Japanese had deliberately chosen to die in the crevice, Traven slid down the slope until his feet touched the splitting soles of the corpse's shoes. He reached forward and seized the canteen. A cupful of flat water swilled around the rusting bottom. Traven gulped down the water, the dissolved metal salts cloaking his lips and tongue with a bitter film. He pried the lid off the can, which was empty but for a tacky coating of condensed syrup. He scraped at this with the lid and chewed at the tarry flakes. They filled his mouth with an almost intoxicating sweetness. After a few moments he felt light-headed and sat back beside the corpse. Its sightless eyes regarded him with unmoving compassion.

The Fly

(*A small fly, which Traven presumes has followed him into the crevice, now buzzes about the corpse's face. Traven leans forward to kill it, then reflects that perhaps this minuscule sentry had been the corpse's faithful companion, in return fed on the rich liqueurs and distillations of its pores. Carefully, to avoid injuring the fly, he encourages it to alight on his wrist.*)

DR. YASUDA: Thank you, Traven. (*The voice is rough, as if unused to conversation.*) In my position, you understand.

TRAVEN: Of course, Doctor. I'm sorry I tried to kill it. These ingrained habits, you know, they're not easy to shrug off. Your sister's children in Osaka in Forty-four, the exigencies of war, I hate to plead them, most known motives are so despicable one searches the unknown in the hope that . . .

YASUDA: Please, Traven, do not be embarrassed. The fly is lucky to retain its identity for so long. That son you mourn, not to mention my own two nieces and nephew, did they not die each day? Every parent in the world mourns the lost sons and daughters of their past childhoods.

TRAVEN: You're very tolerant, Doctor. I wouldn't dare—

YASUDA: Not at all, Traven. I make no apologies for you. After all, each one of us is little more than the meager residue of the infinite unrealized possibilities of our lives. But your son and my nieces are fixed in our minds forever, their identities as certain as the stars.

TRAVEN (*not entirely convinced*): That may be so, Doctor, but it leads to a dangerous conclusion in the case of this island. For instance, the blocks...

YASUDA: They are precisely to what I refer. Here among the blocks, Traven, you at last find the image of yourself free of time and space. This island is an ontological Garden of Eden; why try to expel yourself into a quantal world?

TRAVEN: Excuse me. (*The fly has flown back to the corpse's face and sits in one of the orbits, giving the good doctor an expression of quizzical beadiness. Reaching forward, Traven entices it onto his palm.*) Well, yes, these bunkers may be ontological objects, but whether this is the ontological fly seems doubtful. It's true that on this island it's the only fly, which is the next best thing.

YASUDA: You can't accept the plurality of the universe, Traven. Ask yourself, why? Why should this obsess you? It seems to me that you are hunting for the white leviathan, zero. The beach is a dangerous zone; avoid it. Have a proper humility; pursue a philosophy of acceptance.

TRAVEN: Then may I ask why you came here, Doctor?

YASUDA: To feed this fly. "What greater love—?"

TRAVEN (*still puzzling*): It doesn't really solve my problem. The blocks, you see...

YASUDA: Very well, if you must have it that way...

TRAVEN: But, Doctor—

YASUDA (*peremptorily*): Kill that fly!

TRAVEN: That's not an end, or a beginning. (*Hopelessly he kills the fly. Exhausted, he falls asleep beside the corpse.*)

The Terminal Beach

Searching for a piece of rope in the refuse dump behind the dunes, Traven found a bale of rusty wire. He unwound it, then secured a harness around the corpse's chest and dragged it from the crevice. The lid of a wooden crate served as a sledge. Traven fastened the corpse into a sitting position, and set off along the perimeter of the blocks. Around him the island was silent. The lines of palms hung in the sunlight, only his own motion varying the shifting ciphers of their crisscrossing trunks. The square turrets of the camera towers jutted from the dunes like forgotten obelisks.

An hour later, when Traven reached his bunker, he untied the wire cord he had fastened around his waist. He took the chair left for him by Dr. Osborne and carried it to a point midway between the bunker and the blocks. Then he tied the body of the Japanese to the chair, arranging the hands so that they rested on the wooden arms, giving the moribund figure a posture of calm repose.

This done to his satisfaction, Traven returned to the bunker and squatted under the awning.

As the next days passed into weeks, the dignified figure of the Japanese sat in his chair fifty yards from him, guarding Traven from the blocks. Their magic still filled Traven's reveries, but he now had sufficient strength to rouse himself and forage for food. In the hot sunlight the skin of the Japanese became more and more bleached, and sometimes Traven would wake at night to find the white sepulchral figure sitting there, arms resting at its sides, in the shadows that crossed the concrete floor. At these moments he would often see his wife and son watching him from the dunes. As time passed they came closer, and he would sometimes turn to find them only a few yards behind him.

Patiently Traven waited for them to speak to him, thinking of the great blocks whose entrance was guarded by the seated figure of the dead archangel, as the waves broke on the distant shore and the burning bombers fell through his dreams.

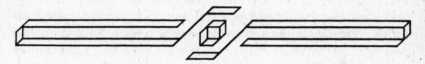

The Cloud-Sculptors of Coral D

All summer the cloud-sculptors would come from Vermilion Sands and sail their painted gliders above the coral towers that rose like white pagodas beside the highway to Lagoon West. The tallest of the towers was Coral D, and here the rising air above the sand reefs was topped by swanlike clumps of fair-weather cumulus. Lifted on the shoulders of the air above the crown of Coral D, we would carve seahorses and unicorns, the portraits of presidents and film stars, lizards and exotic birds. As the crowd watched from their cars, a cool rain would fall onto the dusty roofs, weeping from the sculptured clouds as they sailed across the desert floor toward the sun.

Of all the cloud-sculptures we were to carve, the strangest were the portraits of Leonora Chanel. As I look back to that afternoon last summer when she first came in her white limousine to watch the cloud-sculptors of Coral D, I know we barely realized how seriously this beautiful but insane woman regarded the sculptures floating above her in that calm sky. Later her portraits, carved in the whirlwind, were to weep their storm-rain upon the corpses of their sculptors.

I had arrived in Vermilion Sands three months earlier. A retired pilot, I was painfully coming to terms with a broken leg and the prospect of never flying again. Driving into the desert one day, I stopped near the coral towers on the highway to Lagoon West. As I gazed at these immense pagodas stranded on the floor of this fossil sea, I heard music coming from a sand reef two hundred yards away. Swinging on my crutches across the sliding sand, I found a shallow basin among the dunes where sonic statues had run to seed beside a ruined studio. The owner had gone, abandoning the hangarlike building to the sand rays and the desert, and on some half-formed impulse I began to drive out each afternoon. From the lathes and joists left behind I built my first giant kites and, later, gliders with cockpits. Tethered by their cables, they would hang above me in the afternoon air like amiable ciphers.

One evening, as I wound the gliders down onto the winch, a sudden gale rose over the crest of Coral D. While I grappled with the whirling handle, trying to anchor my crutches in the sand, two figures approached across the desert floor. One was a small hunchback with a child's overlit eyes and a deformed jaw twisted like an anchor barb to one side. He scuttled over to the winch and wound the tattered gliders toward the ground, his powerful shoulders pushing me aside. He helped me onto my crutch and peered into the hangar. Here my most ambitious glider to date, no longer a kite but a sailplane with elevators and control lines, was taking shape on the bench.

He spread a large hand over his chest. "Petit Manuel—acrobat and weightlifter. Nolan!" he bellowed. "Look at this!" His companion was squatting by the sonic statues, twisting their helixes so that their voices became more resonant. "Nolan's an artist," the hunchback confided to me. "He'll build you gliders like condors."

The tall man was wandering among the gliders, touching their wings with a sculptor's hand. His morose eyes were set in a face like a bored boxer's. He glanced at the plaster on my leg and my faded flying jacket, and gestured at the gliders. "You've given cockpits to them, Major." The remark contained a complete understanding of my motives. He pointed to the coral towers rising above us into the evening sky. "With silver iodide we could carve the clouds."

The hunchback nodded encouragingly to me, his eyes lit by an astronomy of dreams.

So were formed the cloud-sculptors of Coral D. Although I considered myself one of them, I never flew the gliders, but taught Nolan and little Manuel to fly, and later, when he joined us, Charles Van Eyck. Nolan had found this blond-haired pirate of the café terraces in Vermilion Sands, a laconic Teuton with hard eyes and a weak mouth, and brought him out to Coral D when the season ended and the well-to-do tourists and their nubile daughters returned to Red Beach. "Major Parker—Charles Van Eyck. He's a headhunter," Nolan commented with cold humor, "—maidenheads." Despite their uneasy rivalry I realized that Van Eyck would give our group a useful dimension of glamour.

From the first I suspected that the studio in the desert was Nolan's, and that we were all serving some private whim of this dark-haired solitary. At the time, however, I was more concerned with teaching them to fly—first on cable, mastering the updrafts that swept the stunted turret of Coral A, smallest of the towers, then the steeper slopes of B and C, and finally the powerful currents of Coral D. Late one afternoon, when I began to wind them in, Nolan cut away his line. The glider plummeted onto its back, diving down to impale itself on the rock spires. I flung myself to the ground as the cable whipped across my car, shattering the windshield. When I looked up, Nolan was soaring high in the tinted air above Coral D. The wind, guardian of the coral towers, carried him through the islands of cumulus that veiled the evening light.

As I ran to the winch the second cable went, and little Manuel swerved away to join Nolan. Ugly crab on the ground, in the air the hunchback became a bird with immense wings, outflying both Nolan and Van Eyck. I watched them as they circled the coral towers, and then swept down together over the desert floor, stirring the sand rays into sootlike clouds. Petit Manuel was jubilant. He strutted around me like a pocket Napoleon, contemptuous of my broken leg, scooping up handfuls of broken glass and tossing them over his head like bouquets to the air. Two months later, as we drove out to Coral D on the day we were to meet Leonora Chanel, something of this first feeling of exhilaration had faded. Now that the season had ended few tourists traveled to Lagoon West, and often we would perform our cloud-sculpture to the empty highway. Sometimes Nolan would remain behind in his hotel, drinking by himself on the bed, or Van Eyck would disappear for several days with some widow or divorcée, and Petit Manuel and I would go out alone.

Nonetheless, as the four of us drove out in my car that afternoon and I saw the clouds waiting for us above the spire of Coral D, all my depression and fatigue vanished. Ten minutes later, the three cloud-gliders rose into the air and the first cars began to stop on the highway. Nolan was in the lead in his black-winged glider, climbing straight to the crown of Coral D two hundred feet above, while Van Eyck soared to and fro below, showing his blond mane to a middle-aged woman in a topaz convertible. Behind them came little Manuel, his candy-striped wings slipping and churning in the disturbed air. Shouting happy obscenities, he flew with his twisted knees, huge arms gesticulating out of the cockpit.

The three gliders, brilliant painted toys, revolved like lazing birds above Coral D, waiting for the first clouds to pass overhead. Van Eyck moved away to take a cloud. He sailed around its white pillow, spraying the sides with iodide crystals and cutting away the flocklike tissue. The steaming shards fell toward us like crumbling ice-drifts. As the drops of condensing spray fell on my face I could see Van Eyck shaping an immense horse's head. He sailed up and down the long forehead and chiseled out the eyes and ears.

As always, the people watching from their cars seemed to enjoy this piece of aerial marzipan. It sailed overhead, carried away on the wind from Coral D. Van Eyck followed it down, wings lazing around the equine head. Meanwhile Petit Manuel worked away at the next cloud. As he sprayed its sides a familiar human head appeared through the tumbling mist. The high wavy mane, strong jaw but slipped mouth Manuel caricatured from the cloud with a series of deft passes, wingtips almost touching each other as he dived in and out of the portrait.

The glossy white head, an unmistakable parody of Van Eyck in his own worst style, crossed the highway toward Vermilion Sands. Manuel slid out of the air, stalling his glider to a landing beside my car as Van Eyck stepped from his cockpit with a forced smile.

We waited for the third display. A cloud formed over Coral D and within a few minutes had blossomed into a pristine fair-weather cumulus. As it hung there Nolan's black-winged glider plunged out of the sun. He soared around the cloud, cutting away its tissues. The soft fleece fell toward us in a cool rain.

There was a shout from one of the cars. Nolan turned from the cloud, his wings slipping as if unveiling his handiwork. Illuminated by the afternoon sun was the serene face of a three-year-old child. Its wide cheeks framed a placid mouth and plump chin. As one or two people clapped, Nolan sailed over the cloud and rippled the roof into ribbons and curls.

However, I knew that the real climax was yet to come. Cursed by some malignant virus, Nolan seemed unable to accept his own handiwork, always destroying it with the same cold humor. Petit Manuel had thrown away his cigarette, and even Van Eyck had turned his attention from the women in the cars.

Nolan soared above the child's face, following like a matador waiting for the moment of the kill. There was silence for a minute as he worked away at the cloud, and then someone slammed a car door in disgust.

Hanging above us was the white image of a skull.

The child's face, converted by a few strokes, had vanished, but in the notched teeth and gaping orbits, large enough to hold a car, we could still see an echo of its infant features. The specter moved past us, the spectators frowning at this weeping skull whose rain fell upon their faces.

Halfheartedly I picked my old flying helmet off the back seat and began to carry it around the cars. Two of the spectators drove off before I could reach them. As I hovered about uncertainly, wondering why on earth a retired and well-to-do air force officer should be trying to collect these few dollar bills, Van Eyck stepped behind me and took the helmet from my hand.

"Not now, Major. Look at what arrives—my apocalypse... "

A white Rolls-Royce, driven by a chauffeur in braided cream livery, had turned off the highway. Through the tinted communication window a young woman in a secretary's day suit spoke to the chauffeur. Beside her, a gloved hand still holding the window strap, a white-haired woman with jeweled eyes gazed up at the circling wings of the cloud-glider. Her strong and elegant face seemed sealed within the dark glass of the limousine like the enigmatic madonna of some marine grotto.

Van Eyck's glider rose into the air, soaring upward to the cloud that hung above Coral D. I walked back to my car, searching the sky for Nolan. Above, Van Eyck was producing a pastiche Mona Lisa, a picture postcard Gioconda as authentic as a plaster virgin. Its glossy finish shone in the overbright sunlight as if enameled together out of some cosmetic foam.

Then Nolan dived from the sun behind Van Eyck. Rolling his black-winged glider past Van Eyck's, he drove through the neck of the Gioconda, and with the flick of a wing toppled the broad-cheeked head. It fell toward the cars below. The features disintegrated into a flaccid mess, sections of the nose and jaw tumbling through the steam. Then wings brushed. Van Eyck fired his spray gun at Nolan, and there was a flurry of torn fabric. Van Eyck fell from the air, steering his glider down to a broken landing.

I ran over to him. "Charles, do you have to play von Richthofen? For God's sake, leave each other alone!"

Van Eyck waved me away. "Talk to Nolan, Major. I'm not responsible for his air piracy." He stood in the cockpit, gazing over the cars as the shreds of fabric fell around him.

I walked back to my car, deciding that the time had come to disband the cloud-sculptors of Coral D. Fifty yards away the young secretary in the Rolls-Royce had stepped from the car and beckoned to me. Through the open door her mistress watched me with her jeweled eyes. Her white hair lay in a coil over one shoulder like a nacreous serpent.

I carried my flying helmet down to the young woman. Above a high forehead her auburn hair was swept back in a defensive bun, as if she were deliberately concealing part of herself. She stared with puzzled eyes at the helmet held out in front of her.

"I don't want to fly—what is it?"

"A grace," I explained. "For the repose of Michelangelo, Ed Keinholz, and the cloud-sculptors of Coral D."

"Oh, my God. I think the chauffeur's the only one with any money. Look, do you perform anywhere else?"

"Perform?" I glanced from this pretty and agreeable young woman to the pale chimera with jeweled eyes in the dim compartment of the Rolls. She was watching the headless figure of the Mona Lisa as it moved across the desert floor toward Vermilion Sands. "We're not a professional troupe, as you've probably guessed. And obviously we'd need some fair-weather cloud. Where, exactly?"

"At Lagoon West." She took a snakeskin diary from her handbag. "Miss Chanel is holding a series of garden parties. She wondered if you'd care to perform. Of course there would be a large fee."

"Chanel... Leonora Chanel, the...?"

The young woman's face again took on its defensive posture, dissociating her from whatever might follow. "Miss Chanel is at Lagoon West for the summer. By the way, there's one condition I must point out—Miss Chanel will provide the sole subject matter. You do understand?"

Fifty yards away Van Eyck was dragging his damaged glider toward my car. Nolan had landed, a caricature of Cyrano abandoned in midair. Petit Manuel limped to and fro, gathering together the equipment. In the fading afternoon light they resembled a threadbare circus troupe.

"All right," I agreed. "I take your point. But what about the clouds, Miss —?"

"Lafferty. Beatrice Lafferty. Miss Chanel will provide the clouds."

I walked around the cars with the helmet, then divided the money between Nolan, Van Eyck and Manuel. They stood in the gathering dusk, the few bills in their hands, watching the highway below.

Leonora Chanel stepped from the limousine and strolled into the desert. Her white-haired figure in its cobra-skin coat wandered among the dunes. Sand rays lifted around her, disturbed by the random movements of this sauntering phantasm of the burned afternoon. Ignoring their open stings around her legs, she was gazing up at the aerial bestiary dissolving in the sky, and at the white skull a mile away over Lagoon West that had smeared itself across the sky.

At the time I first saw her, watching the cloud-sculptors of Coral D, I had only a half-formed impression of Leonora Chanel. The daughter of one of the world's leading financiers, she was an heiress both in her own right and on the death of her husband, a shy Monacan aristocrat, Comte Louis Chanel. The mysterious circumstances of his death at Cap Ferrat on the Riviera, officially described as suicide, had placed Leonora in a spotlight of publicity and gossip. She had escaped by wandering endlessly across the globe, from her walled villa in Tangiers to an Alpine mansion in the snows above Pontresina, and from there to Palm Springs, Seville, and Mykonos.

During these years of exile something of her character emerged from the magazine and newspaper photographs: moodily visiting a Spanish charity with the Duchess of Alba, or seated with Soraya and other members of café society on the terrace of Dali's villa at Port Lligat, her self-regarding face gazing out with its jeweled eyes at the diamond sea of the Costa Brava.

Inevitably her Garbo-like role seemed overcalculated, forever undermined by the suspicions of her own hand in her husband's death. The count had been an introspective playboy who piloted his own aircraft to archaeological sites in the Peloponnese and whose mistress, a beautiful young Lebanese, was one of the world's preeminent keyboard interpreters of Bach. Why this reserved and pleasant man should have committed suicide was never made plain. What promised to be a significant exhibit at the coroner's inquest, a mutilated easel portrait of Leonora on which he was working, was accidentally destroyed before the hearing. Perhaps the painting revealed more of Leonora's character than she chose to see.

A week later, as I drove out to Lagoon West on the morning of the first garden party, I could well understand why Leonora Chanel had come to Vermilion Sands, to this bizarre, sandbound resort with its lethargy, beach fatigue, and shifting perspectives. Sonic statues grew wild along the beach, their voices keening as I swept past along the shore road. The fused silica on the surface of the lake formed an immense rainbow mirror that reflected the deranged colors of the sand reefs, more vivid even than the cinnabar and cyclamen wing-panels of the cloud-gliders overhead. They soared in the sky above the lake like fitful dragonflies as Nolan, Van Eyck, and Petit Manuel flew them from Coral D.

We had entered an inflamed landscape. Half a mile away the angular cornices of the summerhouse jutted into the vivid air as if distorted by some faulty junction of time and space. Behind it, like an exhausted volcano, a broad-topped mesa rose into the glazed air, its shoulders lifting the thermal currents high off the heated lake.

Envying Nolan and little Manuel these tremendous updrafts, more powerful than any we had known at Coral D, I drove toward the villa. Then the haze cleared along the beach and I saw the clouds.

A hundred feet above the roof of the mesa, they hung like the twisted pillows of a sleepless giant. Columns of turbulent air moved within the clouds, boiling upward to the anvil heads like liquid in a cauldron. These were not the placid, fair-weather cumulus of Coral D, but storm-nimbus, unstable masses of overheated air that could catch an aircraft and lift it a thousand feet in a few seconds. Here and there the clouds were rimmed with dark bands, their towers crossed by valleys and ravines. They moved across the villa, concealed from the lakeside heat by the haze overhead, then dissolved in a series of violent shifts in the disordered air.

As I entered the drive behind a truck filled with *son et lumière* equipment a dozen members of the staff were straightening lines of gilt chairs on the terrace and unrolling panels of a marquee.

Beatrice Lafferty stepped across the cables. "Major Parker—there are the clouds we promised you."

I looked up again at the dark billows hanging like shrouds above the white villa. "Clouds, Beatrice? Those are tigers, tigers with wings. We're manicurists of the air, not dragon-tamers."

"Don't worry, a manicure is exactly what you're expected to carry out." With an arch glance, she added: "Your men do understand that there's to be only one subject?"

"Miss Chanel herself? Of course." I took her arm as we walked toward the balcony overlooking the lake. "You know, I think you enjoy these snide asides. Let the rich choose their materials— marble, bronze, plasma, or cloud. Why not? Portraiture has always been a neglected art."

"My God, not here." She waited until a steward passed with a tray of tablecloths. "Carving one's portrait in the sky out of the sun and air—some people might say that smacked of vanity, or even worse sins."

"You're very mysterious. Such as?"

She played games with her eyes. "I'll tell you in a month's time when my contract expires. Now, when are your men coming?"

"They're here." I pointed to the sky over the lake. The three gliders hung in the overheated air, clumps of cloud-cotton drifting past them to dissolve in the haze. They were following a sand-yacht that approached the quay, its tires throwing up the cerise dust. Behind the helmsman sat Leonora Chanel in a trouser suit of yellow alligator skin, her white hair hidden inside a black raffia toque.

As the helmsman moored the craft Van Eyck and Petit Manuel put on an impromptu performance, shaping the fragments of cloud-cotton a hundred feet above the lake. First Van Eyck carved an orchid, then a heart and a pair of lips, while Manuel fashioned the head of a parakeet, two identical mice and the letters "L.C." As they dived and plunged around her, their wings sometimes touching the lake, Leonora stood on the quay, politely waving at each of these brief confections.

When they landed beside the quay, Leonora waited for Nolan to take one of the clouds, but he was sailing up and down the lake in front of her like a weary bird. Watching this strange chatelaine of Lagoon West, I noticed that she had slipped off into some private reverie, her gaze fixed on Nolan and oblivious of the people around her. Memories, caravels without sails, crossed the shadowy deserts of her burned-out eyes.

Later that evening Beatrice Lafferty led me into the villa through the library window. There, as Leonora greeted her guests on the terrace, wearing a topless dress of sapphires and organdy, her breasts covered only by their contour jewelry, I saw the portraits that filled the villa. I counted more than twenty, from the formal society portraits in the drawing rooms, one by the President of the Royal Academy, another by Annigoni, to the bizarre psychological studies in the bar and dining room by Dali and Francis Bacon. Everywhere we moved, in the alcoves between the marble semicolumns, in gilt miniatures on the mantel shelves, even in the ascending mural that followed the staircase, we saw the same beautiful self-regarding face. This colossal narcissism seemed to have become her last refuge, the only retreat for her fugitive self in its flight from the world.

Then, in the studio on the roof, we came across a large easel portrait that had just been varnished. The artist had produced a deliberate travesty of the sentimental and powder-blue tints of a fashionable society painter, but beneath this gloss he had visualized Leonora as a dead Medea. The stretched skin below her right cheek, the sharp forehead and slipped mouth gave her the numbed and luminous appearance of a corpse.

My eyes moved to the signature. "Nolan! My God, were you here when he painted this?"

"It was finished before I came—two months ago. She refused to have it framed."

"No wonder." I went over to the window and looked down at the bedrooms hidden behind their awnings. "Nolan was *here*. The old studio near Coral D was his."

"But why should Leonora ask him back? They must have—"

"To paint her portrait again. I know Leonora Chanel better than you do, Beatrice. This time, though, the size of the sky."

We left the library and walked past the cocktails and canapés to where Leonora was welcoming her guests. Nolan stood beside her, wearing a suit of white suede. Now and then he looked down at her as if playing with the possibilities this self-obsessed woman gave to his macabre humor. Leonora clutched at his elbow. With the diamonds fixed around her eyes she reminded me of some archaic priestess. Beneath the contour jewelry her breasts lay like eager snakes.

Van Eyck introduced himself with an exaggerated bow. Behind him came Petit Manuel, his twisted head ducking nervously among the tuxedos.

Leonora's mouth shut in a rictus of distaste. She glanced at the white plaster on my foot. "Nolan, you fill your world with cripples. Your little dwarf—will he fly too?"

Petit Manuel looked at her with eyes like crushed flowers.

The performance began an hour later. The dark-rimmed clouds were lit by the sun setting behind the mesa, the air crossed by wraiths of cirrus like the gilded frames of the immense paintings to come. Van Eyck's glider rose in the spiral toward the face of the first cloud, stalling and climbing again as the turbulent updrafts threw him across the air.

As the cheekbones began to appear, as smooth and lifeless as carved foam, applause rang out from the guests seated on the terrace. Five minutes later, when Van Eyck's glider swooped down onto the lake, I could see that he had excelled himself. Lit by the searchlights, and with the overture to Tristan sounding from the loudspeakers on the slopes of the mesa, as if inflating this huge bauble, the portrait of Leonora moved overhead, a faint rain falling from it. By luck the cloud remained stable until it passed the shoreline, and then broke up in the evening air as if ripped from the sky by an irritated hand.

Petit Manuel began his ascent, sailing in on a dark-edged cloud like an urchin accosting a bad-tempered matron. He soared to and fro, as if unsure how to shape this unpredictable column of vapor, then began to carve it into the approximate contours of a woman's head. He seemed more nervous than I had ever seen him. As he finished a second round of applause broke out, soon followed by laughter and ironic cheers.

The cloud, sculptured into a flattering likeness of Leonora, had begun to tilt, rotating in the disturbed air. The jaw lengthened, the glazed smile became that of an idiot's. Within a minute the gigantic head of Leonora Chanel hung upside down above us.

Discreetly I ordered the searchlights switched off, and the audience's attention turned to Nolan's black-winged glider as it climbed toward the next cloud. Shards of dissolving tissue fell from the darkening air, the spray concealing whatever ambiguous creation Nolan was carving. To my surprise, the portrait that emerged was

275

wholly lifelike. There was a burst of applause, a few bars of *Tannhauser*, and the searchlights lit up the elegant head. Standing among her guests, Leonora raised her glass to Nolan's glider.

Puzzled by Nolan's generosity, I looked more closely at the gleaming face, and then realized what he had done. The portrait, with cruel irony, was all too lifelike. The downward turn of Leonora's mouth, the chin held up to smooth her neck, the fall of flesh below her right cheek—all these were carried on the face of the cloud as they had been in his painting in the studio.

Around Leonora the guests were congratulating her on the performance. She was looking up at her portrait as it began to break up over the lake, seeing it for the first time. The veins held the blood in her face.

Then a fireworks display on the beach blotted out these ambiguities in its pink and blue explosions.

Shortly before dawn Beatrice Lafferty and I walked along the beach among the shells of burned-out rockets and catherine wheels. On the deserted terrace a few lights shone through the darkness onto the scattered chairs. As we reached the steps a woman's voice cried out somewhere above us. There was the sound of smashed glass. A French window was kicked back, and a dark-haired man in a white suit ran between the tables.

As Nolan disappeared along the drive Leonora Chanel walked out into the center of the terrace. She looked at the dark clouds surging over the mesa, and with one hand tore the jewels from her eyes. They lay winking on the tiles at her feet. Then the hunched figure of Petit Manuel leaped from his hiding place in the bandstand. He scuttled past, racing on his deformed legs.

An engine started by the gates. Leonora began to walk back to the villa, staring at her broken reflections in the glass below the window. She stopped as a tall, blond-haired man with cold and eager eyes stepped from the sonic statues outside the library. Disturbed by the noise, the statues had begun to whine. As Van Eyck moved toward Leonora they took up the slow beat of his steps.

The next day's performance was the last by the cloud-sculptors of Coral D. All afternoon, before the guests arrived, a dim light lay over the lake. Immense tiers of storm-nimbus were massing behind the mesa, and any performance at all seemed unlikely.

Van Eyck was with Leonora. As I arrived Beatrice Lafferty was watching their sand-yacht carry them unevenly across the lake, its sails whipped by the squalls.

"There's no sign of Nolan or little Manuel," she told me. "The party starts in three hours."

I took her arm. "The party's already over. When you're finished here, Bea, come and live with me at Coral D. I'll teach you to sculpt the clouds."

Van Eyck and Leonora came ashore half an hour later. Van Eyck stared through my face as he brushed past. Leonora clung to his arm, the day-jewels around her eyes scattering their hard light across the terrace.

By eight, when the first guests began to appear, Nolan and Petit Manuel had still not arrived. On the terrace the evening was warm and lamplit, but overhead the storm clouds sidled past each other like uneasy giants. I walked up the slope to where the gliders were tethered. Their wings shivered in the updrafts.

Barely half a minute after he rose into the darkening air, dwarfed by an immense tower of storm-nimbus, Charles Van Eyck was spinning toward the ground, his glider toppled by the crazed air. He recovered fifty feet from the villa and climbed on the updrafts from the lake, well away from the spreading chest of the cloud. He soared in again. As Leonora and her guests watched from their seats the glider was hurled back over their heads in an explosion of vapor, then fell toward the lake with a broken wing.

I walked toward Leonora. Standing by the balcony were Nolan and Petit Manuel, watching Van Eyck climb from the cockpit of his glider three hundred yards away.

To Nolan I said: "Why bother to come? Don't tell me you're going to fly?"

Nolan leaned against the rail, hands in the pockets of his suit. "I'm not—that's exactly why I'm here, Major."

Leonora was wearing an evening dress of peacock feathers that lay around her legs in an immense train. The hundreds of eyes gleamed in the electric air before the storm, sheathing her body in their blue flames.

"Miss Chanel, the clouds are like madmen," I apologized. "There's a storm on its way."

She looked up at me with unsettled eyes "Don't you people expect to take risks?" She gestured at the storm-nimbus that swirled over our heads. "For clouds like these I need a Michelangelo of the sky ... What about Nolan? Is he too frightened as well?"

As she shouted his name Nolan stared at her, then turned his back to us. The light over Lagoon West had changed. Half the lake was covered by a dim pall.

There was a tug on my sleeve. Petit Manuel looked up at me with his crafty child's eyes. "Major, I can go. Let me take the glider."

"Manuel, for God's sake. You'll kill—"

He darted between the gilt chairs. Leonora frowned as he plucked her wrist.

"Miss Chanel ..." His loose mouth formed an encouraging smile. "I'll sculpt for you. Right now, a big storm cloud, eh?"

She stared down at him, half-repelled by this eager hunchback ogling her beside the hundred eyes of her peacock train. Van Eyck was limping back to the beach from his wrecked glider. I guessed that in some strange way Manuel was pitting himself against Van Eyck.

Leonora grimaced, as if swallowing some poisonous phlegm. "Major Parker, tell him to —" She glanced at the dark cloud boiling over the mesa like the effluvium of some black-hearted volcano. "Wait! Let's see what the little cripple can do!" She turned on Manuel with an overbright smile. "Go on, then. Let's see you sculpt a whirlwind!"

In her face the diagram of bones formed a geometry of murder.

Nolan ran past across the terrace, his feet crushing the peacock feathers as Leonora laughed. We tried to stop Manuel, but he raced ahead up the slope. Stung by Leonora's taunt, he skipped among the rocks, disappearing from sight in the darkening air. On the terrace a small crowd gathered to watch.

The yellow and tangerine glider rose into the sky and climbed across the face of the storm cloud. Fifty yards from the dark billows it was buffeted by the shifting air, but Manuel soared in and began to cut away at the dark face. Drops of black rain fell across the terrace at our feet.

The first outline of a woman's head appeared, satanic eyes lit by the open vents in the cloud, a sliding mouth like a dark smear as the huge billows boiled forward. Nolan shouted in warning from the lake as he climbed into his glider. A moment later little Manuel's craft was lifted by a powerful updraft and tossed over the roof of the cloud. Fighting the insane air, Manuel plunged the glider downward and drove into the cloud again. Then its immense face opened, and in a sudden spasm the cloud surged forward and swallowed the glider.

There was silence on the terrace as the crushed body of the craft revolved in the center of the cloud. It moved over our heads, dismembered pieces of the wings and fuselage churned about in the dissolving face. As it reached the lake the cloud began its violent end. Pieces of the face slewed sideways, the mouth was torn off, an eye exploded. It vanished in a last brief squall.

The pieces of Petit Manuel's glider fell from the bright air.

Beatrice Lafferty and I drove across the lake to collect Manuel's body. After the spectacle of his death within the exploding replica of their hostess's face, the guests began to leave. Within minutes the drive was full of cars. Leonora watched them go, standing with Van Eyck among the deserted tables.

Beatrice said nothing as we drove out. The pieces of the shattered glider lay over the fused sand, tags of canvas and broken struts, control lines tied into knots. Ten yards from the cockpit I found Petit Manuel's body, lying in a wet ball like a drowned monkey.

I carried him back to the sand-yacht.

"Raymond!" Beatrice pointed to the shore. Storm clouds were massed along the entire length of the lake, and the first flashes of lightning were striking in the hills behind the mesa. In the electric air the villa had lost its glitter. Half a mile away a tornado was moving along the valley floor, its trunk swaying toward the lake.

The first gust of air struck the yacht. Beatrice shouted again: "Raymond! Nolan's there—he's flying inside it!"

Then I saw the black-winged glider circling under the umbrella of the tornado, Nolan himself riding in the whirlwind. His wings held steady in the revolving air around the funnel. Like a pilot fish he soared in, as if steering the tornado toward Leonora's villa.

Twenty seconds later, when it struck the house, I lost sight of him. An explosion of dark air overwhelmed the villa, a churning centrifuge of shattered chairs and tiles that burst over the roof. Beatrice and I ran from the yacht, and lay together in a fault in the glass surface. As the tornado moved away, fading into the storm-filled sky, a dark squall hung over the wrecked villa, now and then flicking the debris into the air. Shreds of canvas and peacock feathers fell around us.

We waited half an hour before approaching the house. Hundreds of smashed glasses and broken chairs littered the terrace. At first I could see no signs of Leonora, although her face was everywhere, the portraits with their slashed profiles strewn on the damp tiles. An eddying smile floated toward me from the disturbed air, and wrapped itself around my leg.

Leonora's body lay among the broken tables near the bandstand, half-wrapped in a bleeding canvas. Her face was as bruised now as the storm cloud Manuel had tried to carve.

We found Van Eyck in the wreck of the marquee. He was suspended by the neck from a tangle of electric wiring, his pale face wreathed in a noose of light bulbs. The current flowed intermittently through the wiring, lighting up the colored globes.

I leaned against the overturned Rolls, holding Beatrice's shoulders. "There's no sign of Nolan—no pieces of his glider."

"Poor man. Raymond, he was driving that whirlwind here. Somehow he was controlling it."

I walked across the damp terrace to where Leonora lay. I began to cover her with the shreds of canvas, the torn faces of herself.

I took Beatrice Lafferty to live with me in Nolan's studio in the desert near Coral D. We heard no more of Nolan and never flew the gliders again. The clouds carry too many memories. Three months ago a man who saw the derelict gliders outside the studio stopped near Coral D and walked across to us. He told us he had seen a man flying a glider in the sky high above Red Beach, carving the strato-cirrus into images of jewels and children's faces. Once there was a dwarf's head.

On reflection, that sounds rather like Nolan, so perhaps he managed to get away from the tornado. In the evenings Beatrice and I sit among the sonic statues, listening to their voices as the fair-weather clouds rise above Coral D, waiting for a man in a dark-winged glider, perhaps painted like candy now, who will come in on the wind and carve for us images of seahorses and unicorns, dwarfs and jewels and children's faces.

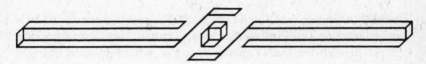

The Assassination of John Fitzgerald Kennedy Considered as a Downhill Motor Race

Author's Note. The assassination of President Kennedy on November 22, 1963, raised many questions, not all of which were answered by the Report of the Warren Commission. It is suggested that a less conventional view of the events of that grim day may provide a more satisfactory explanation. In particular, Alfred Jarry's "The Crucifixion Considered as an Uphill Bicycle Race" gives us a useful lead.

Oswald was the starter.

From his window above the track he opened the race by firing the starting gun. It is believed that the first shot was not properly heard by all the drivers. In the following confusion Oswald fired the gun two more times, but the race was already under way.

Kennedy got off to a bad start.

There was a governor in his car and its speed remained constant at about fifteen miles an hour. However, shortly afterward, when the governor had been put out of action, the car accelerated rapidly, and continued at high speed along the remainder of the course.

The visiting teams. As befitting the inauguration of the first production car race through the streets of Dallas, both the President and the

Vice-President participated. The Vice-President, Johnson, took up his position behind Kennedy on the starting line. The concealed rivalry between the two men was of keen interest to the crowd. Most of them supported the home driver, Johnson.

The starting-point was the Texas Book Depository, where all bets were placed on the Presidential race. Kennedy was an unpopular contestant with the Dallas crowd, many of whom showed outright hostility. The deplorable incident familiar to us all is one example.

The course ran downhill from the Book Depository, below an overpass, then on to the Parkland Hospital and from there to Love Air Field. It is one of the most hazardous courses in downhill motor racing, second only to the Sarajevo track discontinued in 1914.

Kennedy went downhill rapidly. After the damage to the governor the car shot forward at high speed. An alarmed track official attempted to mount the car, which continued on its way, cornering on two wheels.

Turns. Kennedy was disqualified at the hospital, after taking a turn for the worse. Johnson now continued the race in the lead, which he maintained to the finish.

The flag. To signify the participation of the President in the race Old Glory was used in place of the usual checkered square. Photographs of Johnson receiving his prize after winning the race reveal that he had decided to make the flag a memento of his victory.

Previously, Johnson had been forced to take a back seat, as his position on the starting line behind the President indicates. Indeed, his attempts to gain a quick lead on Kennedy during the false start were forestalled by a track steward, who pushed Johnson to the floor of his car.

In view of the confusion at the start of the race, which resulted in Kennedy, clearly expected to be the winner on past form, being forced to drop out at the hospital turn, it has been suggested that the hostile local crowd, eager to see a win by the home driver Johnson, deliberately set out to stop him completing the race. Another theory maintains that the police guarding the track were in collusion with the starter, Oswald. After he finally managed to give the send-off

Oswald immediately left the race, and was subsequently apprehended by track officials.

Johnson had certainly not expected to win the race in this way. There were no pit stops.

Several puzzling aspects of the race remain. One is the presence of the President's wife in the car, an unusual practice for racing drivers. Kennedy, however, may have maintained that as he was in control of the ship of state he was therefore entitled to captain's privileges.

The Warren Commission. The rake-off on the book of the race. In their report, prompted by widespread complaints of foul play and other irregularities, the syndicate lay full blame on the starter, Oswald.

Without doubt Oswald badly misfired. But one question still remains unanswered: who loaded the starting gun?

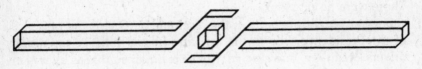

The Atrocity Exhibition

Apocalypse. A disquieting feature of this annual exhibition—to which the patients themselves were not invited—was the marked preoccupation of the paintings with the theme of world cataclysm, as if these long-incarcerated patients had sensed some seismic upheaval within the minds of their doctors and nurses. As Catherine Austen walked around the converted gymnasium these bizarre images, with their fusion of Eniwetok and Luna Park, Freud and Elizabeth Taylor, reminded her of the slides of exposed spinal levels in Travis's office. They hung on the enameled walls like the codes of insoluble dreams, the keys to a nightmare in which she had begun to play a more willing and calculated role. Primly she buttoned her white coat as Dr. Nathan approached, holding his gold-tipped cigarette to one nostril. "Ah, Dr. Austen . . . What do you think of them? I see there's War in Hell."

Notes Toward a Mental Breakdown. The noise from the cine films of induced psychoses rose from the lecture theater below Travis's office. Keeping his back to the window behind his desk, he assembled the terminal documents he had collected with so much effort during the previous months: (1) Spectroheliogram of the sun; (2) Front elevation of balcony units, Hilton Hotel, London; (3) Transverse section through a Pre-Cambrian Trilobite; (4) "Chronograms," by E. J. Marey; (5) Photograph taken at noon, August 7, 1945, of the sand-sea, Qattara Depression, Egypt; (6) Reproduction of Max Ernst's "Garden Airplane Traps"; (7) Fusing sequences for "Little Boy" and "Fat Boy," Hiroshima and Nagasaki A-bombs. When he had finished Travis turned to the window. As usual, the white Pontiac had found a place in the crowded parking lot directly below him. The two occupants watched him through the tinted windshield.

Internal Landscapes. Controlling the tremor in his left hand, Travis studied the thin-shouldered man sitting opposite him. Through the transom the light from the empty corridor shone into the darkened office. His face was partly hidden by the peak of his flying cap, but Travis recognized the bruised features of the bomber pilot whose photographs, torn from the pages of *Newsweek* and *Paris-Match*, had been strewn around the bedroom of the shabby hotel in Earls Court. His eyes stared at Travis, their focus sustained only by a continuous effort. For some reason the planes of his face failed to intersect, as if their true resolution took place in some as yet invisible dimension, or required elements other than those provided by his own character and musculature. Why had he come to the hospital, seeking out Travis among the thirty physicians? Travis had tried to speak to him, but the tall man made no reply, standing by the instrument cabinet like a tattered mannequin. His immature but at the same time aged face seemed as rigid as a plaster mask. For months Travis had seen his solitary figure, shoulders hunched inside the flying jacket, in more and more newsreels, as an extra in war films, and then as a patient in an elegant ophthalmic film on nystagmus—the series of giant geometric models, like sections of abstract landscapes, had made him uneasily aware that their long-delayed confrontation would soon take place.

The Weapons Range. Travis stopped the car at the end of the lane. In the sunlight he could see the remains of the outer perimeter fence, and beyond this a rusting quonset and the iron-stained roofs of the bunkers. He crossed the ditch and walked toward the fence, within five minutes found an opening. A disused runway moved through the grass. Partly concealed by the sunlight, the camouflage patterns across the complex of towers and bunkers four hundred yards away revealed half-familiar contours—the model of a face, a posture, a neural interval. A unique event would take place here. Without thinking, Travis murmured, "Elizabeth Taylor." Abruptly there was a blare of sound above the trees.

Dissociation: Who Laughed at Nagasaki? Travis ran across the broken concrete to the perimeter fence. The helicopter plunged toward him, engine roaring through the trees, its fans churning up a storm of leaves and paper. Twenty yards from the fence Travis stumbled among the coils of barbed wire. The helicopter was banking sharply, the pilot crouched over the controls. As Travis ran forward the shadows of the diving machine flickered around him like cryptic ideograms. Then the craft pulled away and flew off across the bunkers. When Travis reached the car, holding the torn knee of his trousers, he saw the young woman in the white dress walking down the lane. Her disfigured face looked back at him with indulgent eyes. Travis started to call to her, but stopped himself. Exhausted, he vomited across the roof of the car.

Serial Deaths. During this period, as he sat in the rear seat of the Pontiac, Travis was preoccupied by his separation from the normal tokens of life he had accepted for so long. His wife, the patients at the hospital (resistance agents in the "world war" he hoped to launch), his undecided affair with Catherine Austen—these became as fragmentary as the faces of Elizabeth Taylor and Sigmund Freud on the advertising hoardings, as unreal as the war the film companies had restarted in Vietnam. As he moved deeper into his own psychosis, whose onset he had recognized during his year at the hospital, he welcomed this journey into a familiar land, zones of twilight. *At dawn, after driving all night, they reached the suburbs of Hell. The pale flares from the petrochemical plants illuminated the wet cobbles. No one would meet them there.* His two companions, the bomber pilot at the wheel in the faded flying suit and the beautiful young woman with radiation burns, never spoke to him. Now and then the young woman would look round at him with a faint smile on her deformed mouth. Deliberately, Travis made no response, hesitant to commit himself into her hands. Who were they, these strange twins, couriers from his own unconscious? For hours they drove through the endless suburbs of the city. The hoardings multiplied around them, walling the streets with giant replicas of napalm bombings in

Vietnam, the serial deaths of Elizabeth Taylor and Marilyn Monroe terraced in the landscapes of Dien Bien Phu and the Mekong Delta.

Casualties Union. At the young woman's suggestion, Travis joined the C.U., and with a group of thirty housewives practiced the simulation of wounds. Later they would tour with Red Cross demonstration teams. Massive cerebral damage and abdominal bleeding in automobile accidents could be imitated within half an hour, aided by the application of suitable colored resins. Convincing radiation burns required careful preparation, and might involve some three to four hours of makeup. Death, by contrast, was a matter of lying prone. Later, in the apartment they had taken overlooking the zoo, Travis washed the wounds off his hands and face. This curious pantomime, overlayed by the summer evening stench of the animals, seemed performed solely to pacify his two companions. In the bathroom mirror he could see the tall figure of the pilot, his slim face with its lost eyes hidden below the peaked cap, and the young woman in the white dress watching him from the lounge. Her intelligent face, like that of a student, occasionally showed a sudden nervous reflex of hostility. Already Travis found it difficult not to think of her continuously. When would she speak to him? Perhaps, like himself, she realized that his instructions would come from other levels?

Pirate Radio. There were a number of secret transmissions to which Travis listened: (1) medullary: images of dunes and craters, pools of ash that contained the terraced faces of Freud, Eatherly, and Garbo; (2) thoracic: the rusting shells of U-boats beached in the cove at Tsingtao, near the ruined German forts where the Chinese guides smeared bloody handprints on the caisson walls; (3) sacral: VJ Day, the bodies of Japanese troops in the paddy fields at night. The next day, as he walked back to Shanghai, the peasants were planting rice among the swaying legs. Memories of others than himself, together these messages moved to some kind of focus. The dead face of the bomber pilot hovered by the door, projection of World War III's unknown soldier. His presence exhausted Travis.

Marey's Chronograms. Dr. Nathan passed the illustration across his desk to Margaret Travis. "Marey's Chronograms are multiple-exposure photographs in which the element of time is visible—the walking human figure, for example, represented as a series of dunelike lumps." Dr. Nathan accepted a cigarette from Catherine Austen, who had sauntered forward from the incubator at the rear of the office. Ignoring her quizzical eye, he continued "Your husband's brilliant feat was to reverse the process. Using a series of photographs of the most commonplace objects—this office, let us say, a panorama of New York skyscrapers, the naked body of a woman, the face of a catatonic patient—he treated them as if they already were chronograms and *extracted* the element of time." Dr. Nathan lit his cigarette with care. "The results were extraordinary. A very different world was revealed. The familiar surroundings of our lives, even our smallest gestures, were seen to have totally altered meanings. As for the reclining figure of a film star, or this hospital..."

"Was my husband a doctor, or a patient?" Dr. Nathan nodded sagely, glancing over his fingertips at Catherine Austen. What had Travis seen in those time-filled forbidding eyes? "Mrs. Travis, I'm not sure if the question is valid any longer. These matters involve a relativity of a very different kind. What we are concerned with now are the implications—in particular, the complex of ideas and events represented by World War III. Not the political and military possibility, but the inner identity of such a notion. For us, perhaps, World War III is now little more than a sinister pop art display, but for your husband it has become an expression of the failure of his psyche to accept the fact of its own consciousness, and of his revolt against the present continuum of time and space. Dr. Austen may disagree, but it seems to me that his intention is to start World War III, though not, of course, in the usual sense of the term. The blitzkriegs will be fought out on the spinal battlefields, in terms of the postures we assume, of our traumas mimetized in the angle of a wall or balcony."

Zoom Lens. Dr. Nathan stopped. Reluctantly, his eyes turned across the room to the portrait camera mounted on its tripod by the consulting couch. How could he explain to this sensitive and elusive woman that her own body, with its endlessly familiar geometry, its landscapes of touch and feeling, was their only defense against her husband's all-too-plain intentions? Above all, how could he invite her to pose for what she would no doubt regard as a set of obscene photographs?

The Skin Area. After their meeting, at the exhibition of war wounds at the Royal Society of Medicine's new conference hall, Travis and Catherine Austen returned to the apartment overlooking the zoo. In the lift Travis avoided her hands as she tried to embrace him. He led her into the bedroom. Mouth pursed, she watched as he showed her the set of Enneper's models. "What are they?" She touched the interlocking cubes and cones, mathematical models of pseudo-space. "Fusing sequences, Catherine—for a doomsday weapon." Later, the sexual act between them became a hasty eucharist of the angular dimensions of the apartment. In the postures they assumed, in the contours of thigh and thorax, Travis explored the geometry and volumetric time of the bedroom, and later of the curvilinear dome of the Festival Hall, the jutting balconies of the London Hilton, and lastly of the abandoned weapons range. Here the circular target areas became identified in Travis's mind with the concealed breasts of the young woman with radiation burns. Searching for her, he and Catherine Austen drove around the darkening countryside, lost among the labyrinth of hoardings. The faces of Sigmund Freud and Jeanne Moreau presided over their last bitter hours.

Neoplasm. Later, escaping from Catherine Austen, and from the forbidding figure of the bomber pilot, who now watched him from the roof of the lion house, Travis took refuge in a small suburban house among the reservoirs of Staines and Shepperton. He sat in the empty sitting room overlooking the shabby garden. From the white bungalow beyond the clapboard fence his middle-aged neighbor dying of cancer watched him through the long afternoons. Her handsome face veiled by the laced curtains resembled that of a skull. All day she would pace around the small bedroom. At the end of the second month, when the doctor's visits became more frequent, she undressed by the window, exposing her emaciated body through the veiled curtains. Each day, as he watched from the cubical room, he saw different aspects of her eroded body, the black breasts reminding him of the eyes of the bomber pilot, the abdominal scars like the radiation burns of the young woman. After her death he followed the funeral cars among the reservoirs in the white Pontiac.

The Lost Symmetry of the Blastosphere. "This reluctance to accept the fact of his own consciousness," Dr. Nathan wrote, "may reflect certain positional difficulties in the immediate context of time and space. The right-angle spiral of a stairwell may remind him of similar biases within the chemistry of the biological kingdom. This can be carried to remarkable lengths—for example, the jutting balconies of the Hilton Hotel have become identified with the lost gill slits of the dying film actress, Elizabeth Taylor. Much of Travis's thought concerns what he terms 'the lost symmetry of the blastosphere'—the primitive precursor of the embryo that is the last structure to preserve perfect symmetry in all planes. It occurred to Travis that our own bodies may conceal the rudiments of a symmetry not only about the vertical axis but also the horizontal. One recalls Goethe's notion that the skull is formed of modified vertebrae—similarly, the bones of the pelvis may constitute the remains of a lost sacral skull. The resemblance between histologies of lung and kidney has long been noted. Other correspondences of respiratory and urinogenital function come to mind, enshrined both in popular mythology (the supposed equivalence in size of nose and penis) and in psychoanalytic symbolism (the 'eyes' are a common code for the testicles). In conclusion, it seems that Travis's extreme sensitivity to the volumes and geometry of the world around him, and their immediate translation into psychological terms, may reflect a belated attempt to return to a symmetrical world, one that will recapture the perfect symmetry of the blastosphere, and the acceptance of the 'Mythology of the Amniotic Return.' In his mind World War III represents the final self-destruction and imbalance of an asymmetric world, the last suicidal spasm of the dextro-rotatory helix, DNA. The human organism is an atrocity exhibition at which he is an unwilling spectator... "

Eurydice in a Used-car Lot. Margaret Travis paused in the empty foyer of the cinema, looking at the photographs in the display frames. In the dim light beyond the curtains she saw the dark-suited figure of Captain Webster, the muffled velvet veiling his handsome eyes. The last few weeks had been a nightmare—Webster with his long-range camera and obscene questions. He seemed to take a certain sardonic pleasure in compiling this one-man Kinsey Report on her... positions, planes, where and when Travis placed his hands on her body—why didn't he ask Catherine Austen? As for wanting to magnify the photographs and paste them up on enormous hoardings, ostensibly to save her from Travis... She glanced at the stills in the display frames, of this elegant and poetic film in which Cocteau had brought together all the myths of his own journey of return. On an impulse, to annoy Webster, she stepped through the side exit and walked away past a small yard of cars with numbered windshields. Perhaps she would make her descent here. Eurydice in a used-car lot?

The Concentration City. In the night air they passed the shells of concrete towers, blockhouses half buried in rubble, giant conduits filled with tires, overhead causeways crossing broken roads. Travis followed the bomber pilot and the young woman along the faded gravel. They walked across the foundation of a guardhouse into the weapons range. The concrete aisles stretched into the darkness across the airfield. *In the suburbs of Hell Travis walked in the flaring light of the petrochemical plants. The ruins of abandoned cinemas stood at the street corners, faded hoardings facing them across the empty streets. In a waste lot of wrecked cars he found the burned body of the white Pontiac. He wandered through the deserted suburbs.* The crashed bombers lay under the trees, grass growing through their wings. The bomber pilot helped the young woman into one of the cockpits. Travis began to mark out a circle on the concrete target area.

How Garbo Died. "The film is a unique document," Webster explained, as he led Catherine Austen into the basement cinema. "At first sight it seems to be a strange newsreel about the latest tableau sculptures—there are a series of plaster casts of film stars and politicians in bizarre poses—how they were made we can't find out, they seem to have been cast from the living models, LBJ and Mrs. Johnson, Burton and the Taylor actress, there's even one of Garbo dying. We were called in when the film was found." He signaled to the projectionist. "One of the casts is of Margaret Travis—I won't describe it, but you'll see why we're worried. Incidentally, a touring version of Keinholz's 'Dodge 38' was seen traveling at speed on a motorway yesterday, a wrecked white car with the plastic dummies of a World War III pilot and a girl with facial burns making love among a refuse of bubble-gum war cards and oral contraceptive wallets."

War-Zone D. On his way across the car park Dr. Nathan stopped and shielded his eyes from the sun. During the past week a series of enormous signs had been built along the roads surrounding the hospital, almost walling it in from the rest of the world. A group of workmen on a scaffolding truck were pasting up the last of the displays, a hundred-foot-long panel that appeared to represent a section of a sand dune. Looking at it more closely, Dr. Nathan realized that in fact it was an immensely magnified portion of the skin over the iliac crest. Glancing at the hoardings, Dr. Nathan recognized other magnified fragments, a segment of lower lip, a right nostril, a portion of female perineum. Only an anatomist would have identified these fragments, each represented as a formal geometric pattern. At least five hundred of the signs would be needed to contain the whole of this gargantuan woman, terraced here into a quantified sand-sea. A helicopter soared overhead, its pilot supervising the work of the men on the truck. Its downdraft ripped away some of the paper panels. They floated across the road, an eddying smile plastered against the radiator grille of a parked car.

The Atrocity Exhibition. Entering the exhibition, Travis sees the atrocities of Vietnam and the Congo mimetized in the "alternate" death of Elizabeth Taylor; he tends the dying film star, eroticizing her punctured bronchus in the overventilated verandas of the London Hilton; he dreams of Max Ernst, superior of the birds; "Europe after the Rain"; the human race—Caliban asleep across a mirror smeared with vomit.

The Danger Area. Webster ran through the dim light after Margaret Travis. He caught her by the entrance to the main camera bunker, where the cheekbones of an enormous face had been painted in faded Technicolor across the rust-stained concrete. "For God's sake—" She looked down at his strong wrist against her breast, then wrenched herself away. "Mrs. Travis! Why do you think we've taken all these photographs?" Webster held the torn lapel of his suit, then pointed to a tableau figure in the uniform of a Chinese infantryman standing at the end of the conduit. "The place is crawling with the things—you'll never find him." As he spoke a searchlight in the center of the airfield lit up the target areas, outlining the rigid figures of the mannequins.

The Enormous Face. Dr. Nathan limped along the drainage culvert, peering at the huge figure of a dark-haired woman painted on the sloping walls of the blockhouse. The magnification was enormous. The wall on his right, the size of a tennis court, contained little more than the right eye and cheekbone. He recognized the woman from the hoardings he had seen near the hospital—the screen actress, Elizabeth Taylor. Yet these designs were more than enormous replicas. They were equations that embodied the fundamental relationship between the identity of the film actress, and the millions who were distant reflections of her, and the time and space of their own bodies and postures. The planes of their lives interlocked at oblique angles, fragments of personal myths fusing with the deities of the commercial cosmologies. The presiding deity of their lives, the film actress and her fragmented body provided a set of operating formulae for their passage through consciousness. Yet Margaret Travis's role was ambiguous. In some way Travis would attempt to relate his wife's body, with its familiar geometry, to that of the film actress, quantifying their identities to the point where they became fused with the elements of time and landscape. Dr. Nathan crossed an exposed causeway to the next bunker. He leaned against the dark décolleté. When the searchlight flared between the blockhouses he put on his shoe. "No... " He was hobbling toward the airfield when the explosion lit up the evening air.

The Exploding Madonna. For Travis, the ascension of his wife's body above the target area, exploding madonna of the weapons range, was a celebration of the rectilinear intervals through which he perceived the surrounding continuum of time and space. Here she became one with the madonnas of the hoardings and the ophthalmic films, the Venus of the magazine cuttings whose postures celebrated his own search through the suburbs of Hell.

Departure. The next morning, Travis wandered along the gunnery aisles. On the bunkers the painted figure of the screen actress mediated all time and space to him through her body. As he searched among the tires and coils of barbed wire he saw the helicopter rising into the sky, the bomber pilot at the controls. It made a leftward turn and flew off toward the horizon. Half an hour later the young woman drove away in the white Pontiac. Travis watched them leave without regret. When they had gone the corpses of Dr. Nathan, Webster, and Catherine Austen formed a small tableau by the bunkers.

A Terminal Posture. Lying on the worn concrete of the gunnery aisle, he assumed the postures of the fragmented body of the film actress, mimetizing his past dreams and anxieties in the dunelike fragments of her body. The pale sun shone down on this eucharist of the madonna of the hoardings.

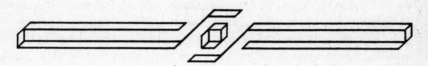

Plan for the Assassination of Jacqueline Kennedy

In his dream of Zapruder frame 235

Motion picture studies of four female subjects who have achieved worldwide celebrity (Brigitte Bardot, Jacqueline Kennedy, Madame Chiang Kai-shek, Princess Margaret) reveal common patterns of posture, facial tonus, pupil and respiratory responses. Leg stance was taken as a significant indicator of sexual arousal. The intrapatellar distance (estimated) varied from a maximum 24.9 cm. (Jacqueline Kennedy) to a minimum 2.2 cm. (Madame Chiang). Infrared studies reveal conspicuous heat emission from the axillary fossae at rates which tallied with general psychomotor acceleration.

Tallis was increasingly preoccupied

Assassination fantasies in tabes dorsalis (general paralysis of the insane). The choice of victim in these fantasies was taken as the most significant yardstick. All considerations of motive and responsibility were eliminated from the questionnaire. The patients were deliberately restricted in their choice to female victims. Results (percentile of 272 patients): Jacqueline Kennedy 62 percent, Madame Chiang 14 percent, Jeanne Moreau 13 percent, Princess Margaret 11 percent. A montage photograph was constructed on the basis of these replies which showed an "optimum" victim. (Left orbit and zygomatic arch of Mrs. Kennedy, exposed nasal septum of Miss Moreau, etc.) This photograph was subsequently shown to disturbed children with positive results. Choice of assassination site varied from Dealey Plaza 49 percent to Isle du Levant 2 percent. The weapon of preference was the Mannlicher-Carcano. A motorcade was selected in the overwhelming majority of cases as the ideal target mode with the Lincoln Continental as the vehicle of preference. On the basis of these studies a model of the most effective assassination-complex was devised. The presence of Madame Chiang in Dealey Plaza was an unresolved element.

by the figure of the President's wife.

Involuntary orgasms during the cleaning of automobiles. Studies reveal an increasing incidence of sexual climaxes among persons cleaning automobiles. In many cases the subject remained unaware of the discharge of semen across the polished paintwork and complained to his spouse about birds. One isolated case reported to a psychiatric after-care unit involved the first definitive sexual congress with a rear exhaust assembly. It is believed that the act was conscious. Consultations with manufacturers have led to modifications of rear trim and styling, in order to neutralize these erogenous zones, or if possible transfer them to more socially acceptable areas within the passenger compartment. The steering assembly has been selected as a suitable focus for sexual arousal.

The planes of her face, like the

The arousal potential of automobile styling has been widely examined for several decades by the automotive industry. However, in the study under consideration involving 152 subjects, all known to have experienced more than three involuntary orgasms with their automobiles, the car of preference was found to be (1) Buick Riviera, (2) Chrysler Imperial, (3) Chevrolet Impala. However, a small minority (2 subjects) expressed a significant preference for the Lincoln Continental, if possible in the adapted Presidential version (*q.v.* conspiracy theories). Both subjects had purchased cars of this make and experienced continuing erotic fantasies in connection with the trunk moldings. Both preferred the automobile inclined on a downward ramp.

cars of the abandoned motorcade

Cine films as group therapy. Patients were encouraged to form a film production unit, and were given full freedom as to choice of subject matter, cast and technique. In all cases explicitly pornographic films were made. Two films in particular were examined: (1) A montage sequence using portions of the faces of (a) Madame Ky, (b) Jeanne Moreau, (c) Jacqueline Kennedy (Johnson oath-taking). The use of a concealed stroboscopic device produced a major optical flutter in the audience, culminating in psychomotor disturbances and aggressive attacks directed against the still photographs of the subjects hung from the walls of the theater. (2) A film of automobile accidents devised as a cinematic version of Nader's *Unsafe at Any Speed*. By chance it was found that slow-motion sequences of this film had a marked sedative effect, reducing blood pressure, respiration, and pulse rates. Hypnagogic images were produced freely by patients. The film was also found to have a marked erotic content.

mediated to him the complete silence

Mouth-parts. In the first study, portions were removed from photographs of three well-known figures: Madame Chiang, Elizabeth Taylor, Jacqueline Kennedy. Patients were asked to fill in the missing areas. Mouth-parts provided a particular focus for aggression, sexual fantasies, and retributive fears. In a subsequent test the original portion containing the mouth was replaced and the remainder of the face removed. Again particular attention was focused on the mouth-parts. Images of the mouth-parts of Madame Chiang and Jacqueline Kennedy had a notable hypotensive role. An optimum mouth-image of Madame Chiang and Mrs. Kennedy was constructed.

of the plaza, the geometry of a murder.

Sexual behavior of witnesses in Dealey Plaza. Detailed studies were conducted of the 552 witnesses in Dealey Plaza on November

22 (Warren Report). Data indicate a significant upswing in (a) frequency of sexual intercourse, (b) incidence of poly-perverse behavior. These results accord with earlier studies of the sexual behavior of spectators at major automobile accidents (=minimum of one death). Correspondences between the two groups studied indicate that for the majority of the spectators the events in Dealey Plaza were unconsciously perceived as those of a massive multiple-sex auto-disaster, with consequent liberation of aggressive and polymorphously perverse drives. The role of Mrs. Kennedy, and of her stained clothing, requires no further analysis.

"But I won't cry till it's all over."

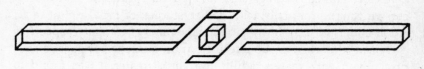

Why I Want to Fuck
Ronald Reagan

During these assassination fantasies

Ronald Reagan and the conceptual auto-disaster. Numerous studies have been conducted upon patients in terminal paresis (G.P.I.), placing Reagan in a series of simulated auto-crashes, e.g. multiple pile-ups, head-on collisions, motorcade attacks (fantasies of Presidential assassinations remained a continuing preoccupation, subjects showing a marked polymorphic fixation on windshields and rear-trunk assemblies). Powerful erotic fantasies of an anal-sadistic character surrounded the image of the Presidential contender. Subjects were required to construct the optimum auto-disaster victim by placing a replica of Reagan's head on the unretouched photographs of crash fatalities. In 82 percent of cases massive rear-end collisions were selected with a preference for expressed faecal matter and rectal hemorrhages. Further tests were conducted to define the optimum model-year. These indicate that a three-year model lapse with child victims provide the maximum audience excitation (confirmed by manufacturers' studies of the optimum auto-disaster). It is hoped to construct a rectal modulus of Reagan and the auto-disaster of maximized audience arousal.

Tallis became increasingly obsessed

Motion picture studies of Ronald Reagan reveal characteristic patterns of facial tonus and musculature associated with homoerotic behavior. The continuing tension of buccal sphincters and the recessive tongue role tally with earlier studies of facial rigidity (cf., Adolf Hitler, Nixon). Slow-motion cine films of campaign speeches exercised a marked erotic effect upon an audience of spastic children. Even with mature adults the verbal material was found to have minimal effect, as demonstrated by substitution of an edited tape giving diametrically opposed opinions. Parallel films of rectal images revealed a sharp upsurge in anti-Semitic and concentration camp fantasies (cf., anal-sadistic fantasies in deprived children induced by rectal stimulation).

with the pudenda of the Presidential contender

Incidence of orgasms in fantasies of sexual intercourse with Ronald Reagan. Patients were provided with assembly kit photographs of sexual partners during intercourse. In each case Reagan's face was superimposed upon the original partner. Vaginal intercourse with "Reagan" proved uniformly disappointing, producing orgasm in 2 percent of subjects. Axillary, buccal, navel, aural, and orbital modes produced proximal erections. The preferred mode of entry overwhelmingly proved to be the rectal. After a preliminary course in anatomy it was found that caecum and transverse colon also provided excellent sites for excitation. In an extreme 12 percent of cases, the simulated anus of post-colostomy surgery generated spontaneous orgasm in 98 percent of penetrations. Multiple-track cine films were constructed of "Reagan" in intercourse during (a) campaign speeches, (b) rear-end auto-collisions with one- and three-year-old model changes, (c) with rear exhaust assemblies, (d) with Vietnamese child-atrocity victims.

mediated to him by a thousand television screens.

Sexual fantasies in connection with Ronald Reagan. The genitalia of the Presidential contender exercised a continuing fascination. A series of imaginary genitalia were constructed using (a) the mouth-parts of Jacqueline Kennedy, (b) a Cadillac rear-exhaust vent, (c) the assembly kit prepuce of President Johnson, (d) a child-victim of sexual assault. In 89 percent of cases, the constructed genitalia generated a high incidence of self-induced orgasm. Tests indicate the masturbatory nature of the Presidential contender's posture. Dolls consisting of plastic models of Reagan's alternate genitalia were found to have a disturbing effect on deprived children.

The motion picture studies of Ronald Reagan

Reagan's hairstyle. Studies were conducted on the marked fascination exercised by the Presidential contender's hairstyle. Sixty-five percent of male subjects made positive connections between the hairstyle and their own pubic hair. A series of optimum hairstyles were constructed.

created a scenario of the conceptual orgasm,

The conceptual role of Reagan. Fragments of Reagan's cinetized postures were used in the construction of model psychodramas in which the Reagan-figure played the role of husband, doctor, insurance salesman, marriage counselor, etc. The failure of these roles to express any meaning reveals the nonfunctional character of Reagan. Reagan's success therefore indicates society's periodic need to reconceptualize its political leaders. Reagan thus appears as a series of posture concepts, basic equations which reformulate the roles of aggression and anality.

a unique ontology of violence and disaster.

Reagan's personality. The profound anality of the Presidential contender may be expected to dominate the United States in the coming years. By contrast, the late J. F. Kennedy remained the prototype of the oral object, usually conceived in prepubertal terms. In further studies sadistic psychopaths were given the task of devising sex fantasies involving Reagan. Results confirm the probability of Presidential figures being perceived primarily in genital terms; the face of L. B. Johnson is clearly genital in significant appearance—the nasal prepuce, scrotal jaw, etc. Faces were seen as either circumcised (J.F.K., Khrushchev) or uncircumcised (L.B.J., Adenauer). In assembly kit tests Reagan's face was uniformly perceived as a penile erection. Patients were encouraged to devise the optimum sex-death of Ronald Reagan.